EDEN HILL

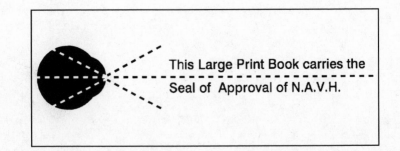

This Large Print Book carries the
Seal of Approval of N.A.V.H.

EDEN HILL

BILL HIGGS

THORNDIKE PRESS
A part of Gale, Cengage Learning

GALE
CENGAGE Learning·

Farmington Hills, Mich • San Francisco • New York • Waterville, Maine
Meriden, Conn • Mason, Ohio • Chicago

11-18

GALE
CENGAGE Learning®

LIBRARY OF CONGRESS CATALOGING-IN-PUBLICATION DATA

Names: Higgs, Bill (Christian writer), author.
Title: Eden Hill / by Bill Higgs.
Description: Large print edition. | Waterville, Maine : Thorndike Press, 2016. |
    Series: Thorndike Press large print clean reads
Identifiers: LCCN 2016027742 | ISBN 9781410493170 (hardcover) | ISBN 1410493172
    (hardcover)
Subjects: LCSH: Service stations—Fiction. | Large type books. | Domestic fiction. |
    GSAFD: Christian fiction.
Classification: LCC PS3608.I3675 E34 2016b | DDC 813/.6—dc23
LC record available at https://lccn.loc.gov/2016027742

Published in 2016 by arrangement with Tyndale House Publishers, Inc.

Printed in Mexico
3 4 5 6 7 8 20 19 18 17 16

Eden Hill *is dedicated to the sweet memory of my beloved grandparents.*

Robert Taylor Higgs (1898-1971) contentedly pumped gas and checked oil for much of his working life — and always with a smile. He taught me the value of fishing, took me for long rides in the country on Sunday afternoons, and knew everyone in town.

Jimmie T. Higgs (1904-2009 — yes, she lived to 105!) loved her homemakers' club, pulled khaki work pants onto clangy metal stretchers, and cooked hamburgers in a seasoned iron skillet.

Together, they modeled love and faith to their only grandson and showed me beyond a shadow of a doubt that grace and Eden Hill are real.

1

Eden Hill, Kentucky, November 1962

Something was wrong. Definitely wrong. Even he knew it.

Virgil T. Osgood had just poured his coffee from the familiar speckled enamel percolator and said good morning to his wife, Mavine. Rather than a broad smile and her usual "Good morning, Virgil," he got nothing. Instead, she sat quietly at their little Formica dinette wrapped in her blue chenille housecoat, her reading glasses perched on her nose, perusing a small magazine. Very odd. Mavine was usually hovering over the stove, banging pots and pans around, and was generally eager to engage in some lively conversation.

And even beyond Mavine's silence, the kitchen was far too quiet. The radio on the counter was usually tuned in to WNTC for the 4-H report, which came on just after "The Star-Spangled Banner" and the early morning farm news. This morning, the old Philco sat dark and silent, sandwiched between the flour and the cornflakes.

The only sounds were the ticking of the red apple clock over the stove, along with an occasional noise from Vee Junior's room upstairs.

"Morning, Mavine?" Maybe she was engrossed in her reading and hadn't heard him. "Okay, what is it?"

She peered at him over the top of her eyeglasses, unsmiling. "Why don't you feed the hens and bring in some eggs." A command, not a question. And certainly not an answer.

"Good idea." Was she sad? Angry? Upset with him? Mavine, gentle woman that she was, would occasionally become frustrated and flustered, but quiet?

"And Virgil. The chicken coop needs painting."

"Yes, Mavine. I'll paint it."

So it was going to be a guessing game. Virgil pulled on his poplin jacket against the chilly morning, scooped out a tin bucket of chicken feed from the bag on the back porch, and stepped outside. Clearly he'd gotten himself into some kind of trouble, and he could use chore time to think it through.

Forgotten her birthday? No, that wasn't until February. Couldn't be their anniversary. They'd married on the second of May — he wasn't about to miss that one again. Last year he'd overlooked it somehow, and it had cost him a new washing machine to get back into her good graces. The poker game at Grover's hadn't run *that* late, and had been over a week ago, so he'd have heard about it long before now. For all his pondering, he had few answers. Well, he'd find out soon enough. Whenever Mavine was ready, she'd tell him. He'd just have to wait it out.

He tossed handfuls of meal into the trough until the pail was empty, and then collected several nice fresh eggs. Quickly. The brisk air cut right through his flannel pajamas, sending shivers down both legs.

A full plate of buttermilk biscuits and a jar of Mavine's strawberry preserves sat on the table when he returned, and the radio had warmed up and the sports report was on. Bacon sizzled and crackled in Mavine's cast-iron skillet, its smoky scent seasoning the room. Without a word, she took the bucket from his hands and cracked the eggs into a clear glass mixing bowl. Vee Junior had finally found his way downstairs and was reading a *Fantastic Four* comic book as he waited for his breakfast.

Maybe Mavine was just in a quiet mood. He could hope, anyway.

"Morning, Vee." He studied his son, a younger and smaller version of himself. Their son did not return his gaze. "Where's your Sunday school quarterly? You promised Mrs. Prewitt you'd read your lesson before school."

"Dunno. Maybe left it in the car."

Virgil leaned across the table. "Vee, you're ten years old now. It's time you showed some responsibility and took on a few chores of your own." Like feeding the hens and fetching the eggs. He hung his jacket back on the hook and took his own chair. "I'll think of a few things you can get started on this Saturday."

"But I've got homework to do."

"On the weekend?"

"Maybe." The boy turned back to his questionable reading — hunting down Dr. Doom, from the looks of the cover. At least Vee seemed his usual self this morning.

"Vee, put that thing down. You know how your mother is about those comic books. We'll talk about this later."

Nothing on the radio gave Virgil a clue to Mavine's unusual demeanor, just a news report about something going on in Cuba

— wherever that was — and a weather report about the current cold snap. *Community Calendar* included a story about the university, as well as something about the new interstate highway being planned.

Monday morning blues, maybe? He hoped so.

Mavine selected clean dishes from the drainer and served them each their breakfast. She waited while Virgil said grace and then filled a plate for herself. They ate quickly with little in the way of conversation. The radio was still playing when he finished the last biscuit, and the announcer gave the time at the station break.

"Six thirty, Vee. Isn't it time for you to catch the school bus?" Virgil nodded toward the road.

"Yeah." The boy did not move.

"So?"

He mumbled something before stuffing the comic into his book satchel and starting for the door.

"Vee! Your lunch!" Mavine handed him a small tin box adorned with a picture of Zorro, his sword pointed high in the air. "And don't you dare trade your cheese sandwich for Twinkies again!" Vee grabbed his forgotten meal, muttered something else, and started out.

"And leave that comic book here!"

"Aw, Mom." Vee sighed, tossed the comic onto the couch, and left.

Mavine collected the plates and glasses from the table and refilled Virgil's mug with the last of the coffee. With a deliberate twist, she silenced the radio and returned to her seat across from her husband.

Then Mavine, his beloved wife, looked straight at him. She'd been crying. How had he missed that?

"Virgil, do you still love me?"

"Do I . . . what?" This had nothing to do with Cuba, Vee's lunch, Dr. Doom, or anything else from the morning's conversation. Whatever he'd been expecting, this wasn't it. He was mulling this over when she repeated herself.

"Virgil, do you still love me? We've been married fourteen years now, and . . ." She leaned forward and looked deep into his eyes. "Well, do you?"

Virgil T. Osgood, husband and father, raised an eyebrow and scratched at his chin. The question — was it a question? — was baffling, and he was about to say so when some deep wisdom stopped him, and he considered things for a moment. He needed time, and he needed clues. Anything. He knew the answer, but he wasn't sure that it was the one she needed to hear.

"Why in the world would you ask such a thing as that?" Certainly not the right response, he realized immediately.

She hesitated a moment. "Because I need to know. When I was at the beauty shop last week . . ."

The pieces of the puzzle fell into place like the letters in the Sunday crossword. Every other Friday was Mavine's beauty parlor day, when she would visit Gladys's Glamour Nook on Front Street. She would return with a restyled hairdo and fresh gossip, especially if Gladys had learned a new and juicy tidbit. And these tidbits usually had a romantic angle to them one way or another.

Come to think of it, she'd been acting strangely all weekend, especially during Reverend Caudill's sermon yesterday. The pastor was in the middle of a sermon series called "Godly Marriage" — straight out of the book of Ephesians — and all the married folk in the congregation were a bundle of nerves. " 'Wives, submit yourselves unto your own husbands,' " the preacher had intoned, and all the women looked at the ceiling. " 'Husbands, love your wives,' " he'd continued. Women were nodding — including Mavine — and most of the men were looking at their shoelaces. He should have seen something coming.

She pulled the magazine from the pocket of her housecoat and placed it in the spot where her plate had been. "I was reading an article in *Pageant* about married men losing their love for their wives after they — the married men, that is — turn forty. Some even look —" she blushed and hesitated — "elsewhere." She slid the small periodical across the table. "Gladys let me bring it home. I took the quiz on page forty-six."

So that was it. Virgil felt a chill, the memory of his fortieth birthday two months ago still fresh in his mind. A paper clip pointed to an article called, "Has Your Husband's Boiler Run Out of Steam?" by Betty LaMour, PhD. A small but fetching photograph of Dr. LaMour was featured with a caption describing her as a famous marriage counselor in New York City. Virgil stared at the photo and turned the page, holding his place with his thumb. He flipped through the rest of the issue, which included full-page ads for Glamour Stretchers and Swedish bust developers. It didn't take long to figure it out: more was better, according to *Pageant*. But more *what*? None of this made any sense.

"This is foolishness." He closed the magazine and pushed it across the table. "You're getting all worked up for no good reason, Mavine. They write this stuff just so they can sell magazines. Besides, don't I take good care of you and Vee?"

"Yes, you do, Virgil, but women want more than that. We need our husbands to be heroic." She placed the *Pageant* right back in his hands. "Dr. LaMour says that a good husband is romantic, and —" she squirmed — "he also pays, how shall I say it, closer attention to his wife."

Something welled up within Virgil that he didn't quite understand, a mixture of sorrow, regret, and anger. Clearly he'd disappointed his wife, and he was sorry for that, but what could he do that he wasn't doing? Had he failed as a husband, or had this sensational magazine misled his wife?

He'd done all he knew to do in life. His schooling ended after the eighth grade because he needed to help support his family, but he'd served his country during the war. With honor, and he had the discharge to prove it. With a veteran's loan and his father's help, he'd built Osgood's, the service station that proudly bore his name. He and his father had built it by hand, one concrete block at a time. His business was stable and secure as well, for the most part.

And while it wasn't going to make them rich, he'd never ended a month in the red. He was married to his childhood sweetheart, and they had a wonderful son, Virgil T. Osgood Jr. And a good marriage, as far as he could tell. Even Reverend Caudill couldn't fault him that.

All that ought to make him a hero. Vee Junior thought so, anyway. But it looked like Mavine didn't see it quite the same way.

"Mavine, you shouldn't be looking at this kind of thing. Not a word of truth in it." He started to return the *Pageant* again, but she held up her hand.

"How do you know? You haven't even read it." She crossed her arms and gave him a look that suggested he'd better keep it this time. He did.

Dr. Betty LaMour, with her feather boa and low-cut blouse, was hard for Virgil to take seriously. A PhD was a kind of doctor thing, and a woman who had one ought to look like Eleanor Roosevelt or Margaret Mead. Dr. LaMour looked more like Marilyn Monroe. The ads in the back for basketball-size radishes were outrageous, and the photo of the couple on a sailboat looking dreamily at each other while the sun went down behind them made little sense to him. Try as he might, he couldn't see where any of this applied to Virgil and Mavine Osgood.

He also couldn't see any way that he was going to win this argument, so he went for a draw.

"Okay, Mavine. I have to get ready for work, but I'll read it. I promise."

Ticky wagged her tail and brushed up against Virgil's khakis. Insightful pondering wasn't part of Virgil's toolbox, but he was doing his best as he and his bluetick coonhound walked the short path toward Osgood's. As promised, he paused to read the *Pageant* article. The light was still dim, so he regretted not having his reading glasses. The task was made more difficult by the chilly breeze, and by the big words he didn't recognize. Terms like *interlude* didn't turn up often in *Popular Mechanics,* and *amorous* wasn't one that Mrs. Wardlow taught in the eighth grade. After a couple of pages, he had the gist of it. Somehow, he didn't measure up.

Fourteen years. It had been a good marriage, hadn't it? He tried hard, but he was beginning to understand that Mavine might want more. Ticky nudged his leg, just as he came to the questions on page forty-six.

Question One: Has your husband been

working long hours at a boring career? Ma-vine had placed a check mark by this one. Boring career? He ran a simple but good service station. Of course the hours were long — Mrs. Crutcher's Buick had needed a full ring job and seals to boot. Welby, his mechanic, had worked with him on the engine, but he'd not made it home until after nine several nights running. Virgil let his finger fall to the line at the bottom where she had kept score. The question was a big one, worth twenty-five points for the right answer. Mavine's answer scored a mere five.

Question Two: How long has it been since you and your husband have had an intimate romantic dinner together? She had checked (c), "six months or more." This didn't make sense at all, because Mavine had cooked a full meal almost every night of their entire married life. Not counting last night's chicken meat loaf disaster, it couldn't have been more than two days. Three at the most. Five points.

Question Three: How long has it been since you and your husband have had marital relations? This was really puzzling. She'd checked (b), "two weeks or more" and then erased it and changed it to (c), "one month or more." Her mother had spent most of last Sunday afternoon at their house —

perhaps Mavine had forgotten. Besides, her other relations visited way too often. Or could the question be asking about . . . *that*?

The rest of the questions all had something to do with romantic encounters or expensive restaurants or the like, and Dr. LaMour's reasoning became harder to follow. A trip to somewhere exotic? Zero. Celebrating an anniversary? Another zero. Mavine had checked off several more questions and come up with a score of thirty-five, which, according to Dr. LaMour, meant "better stir the coals and check the pilot light." Whatever that meant. Pilot lights weren't for coal fires, anyhow. Besides, this whole article came down to Dr. LaMour's opinion, which said Mavine ought to be unhappy with him and who he was. He backed up a step and almost tripped over Ticky. *Who does this Betty LaMour think she is, anyway? And what gives her the right to give my wife these kinds of ideas?*

Virgil scratched his chin again. He and Mavine had both worked hard at making a life and a family, only to be told by some sleazy woman in a cheap magazine that it wasn't enough. They had a solid marriage, a fine son, and a comfortable life, didn't they? In Eden Hill, that meant far more than caviar and sailboats.

By now, his emotions had all boiled down to one: anger. Not at Mavine, but at Betty LaMour. Let this marriage counselor come here from New York City for a day or two, eat supper at their house, stay the night, and smell the wood smoke and country ham the next morning. Maybe even enjoy some of Mavine's biscuits and bacon. Though she'd have to skip any of Mavine's attempts at new recipes. Betty LaMour would see what life together was all about.

He was a good man, and this was a good place. He and Osgood's took care of decent people, the salt of the earth. The grocery on the corner did the same, with Grover Stacy and his wife, Anna Belle, offering ample provisions to the folks of the community, together with ample supplies of cold-cut sandwiches, ice cream, overalls, and flypaper. There was Willett's Dry Goods with clothing and fabric, and three churches. Three *fine* churches. Filled every Sunday with wonderful country people who'd give a person the high-bibs right off their backs. Farms and stores, tradesmen and everyday folks. Eden Hill may not be much, but it was everything that New York City could only dream about.

With that thought and another nudge from Ticky, Virgil tucked the *Pageant* into his coat pocket and returned to reality. He'd ask his mechanic, Welby, about it later. Welby and Alma had been married upwards of thirty years; surely he'd have some insight.

Virgil's coffee mug was empty again, so he must have paused and pondered for longer than he thought. No matter, Welby would certainly have a fresh pot brewing when he arrived.

"Let's go, Ticky." He bent down to scratch the dog's ears. "Folks'll be coming by to see us soon." The mid-November sun had now risen above the horizon, bathing the fields with twilight. Somewhere a tractor started with a rumble, and a truck stopped on Front Street, its brakes squeaking. Sounds of life — good life. He and Ticky walked the rest of the way down the hill to Osgood's, and Virgil opened the side door just as the sun cleared the clouds and touched the porch of the old house behind him. Another day had begun in little Eden Hill. Farms needed tending, stock had to be fed, and cars and trucks would soon show up to purchase gasoline and service.

He'd get back to the *Pageant* tomorrow, or the day after that. He had work to do.

"Hello, Virgil!" A man in faded khaki

21

coveralls stood up awkwardly from the front tire of a little two-tone Nash Metropolitan, having put the last squeaky twist on a lug nut. "How's the boss today?" A small but sturdy man of fifty-five, Welby, limping slightly, the result of a childhood bout with polio, crossed to greet Virgil.

"Just fine!" Virgil grinned. At least Welby, fifteen years his senior, seemed to be on his side this morning. The work may be hard, but here at the service station, Virgil always knew what to expect.

Virgil worked his way through the smells of motor oil and Monkey Grip until he located the aroma of fresh coffee drifting from a large pot on the workbench. His thinking was still hazy, and his mug was empty. At least one of these situations could be easily remedied; Welby brewed ten cups at a time. "Is Mr. Willett's car about ready to go?"

"Yep. Just need to check the brakes. He'll be coming by at lunchtime to pick it up."

"That'll be fine." Perhaps he and the world were indeed just fine. By now, Welby's joyful demeanor and a full mug of steaming black java had lifted his spirits.

"Welby, I've got a question for you." He'd just reached for the *Pageant* when a decrepit truck coughed into the front lot, rattling and squeaking its brakes.

"Arlie?" The sound of the ancient vehicle was distinctive and unmistakable.

"Mornin', folks." A disheveled but cheerful Arlie Prewitt met them at the front door. He wore a denim jacket over his union-made bib overalls, which looked as though they served as work pants, sportswear, and probably pajamas. "No gas today, just some Nabs." Arlie selected a cellophane package from the Tom's rack and dropped his quarter into the small can alongside with a noisy clang.

"Where are you going, Arlie?" Welby wiped his hands on a shop rag. He needn't have asked. There was only one place the farmer would be going this early in the morning without a hog in the back of his truck: the lake.

"Fishin'. Wanna go?" Arlie had often said he'd rather fish than eat, and he enjoyed eating very much. "Last good day of the year, probably. I got my boy Frank up early to feed the sows so I could go. Sure hope he doesn't hit anything with the old John Deere."

"Sorry, Arlie, but we've got too much work to do today." Virgil truly was sorry; he enjoyed fishing almost as much as his friend. "Let us know what you catch."

"I'll bring it by and show you! By the way, did you fellows see the sign?"

"Sign?" Virgil looked at Welby, who shook his head.

"Across the road. Sun's up, so you can see for yourself. Gotta go now, 'cause they won't be bitin' all day."

"Well, have fun. And tell Lula Mae that Vee will definitely read his Sunday school lesson tonight."

"I'll do it. See ya." Without further explanation, Arlie stuffed the package into one of his many pockets and climbed into the truck, which spat forth dark black fumes, ground its gears, and rumbled into the already-smoky morning.

The two stared in silence for a long time as Arlie's truck growled into the distance. Welby spoke first. "I'll be. What do you make of that?"

The sign, new and freshly painted, stood in the vacant lot across the road from Osgood's.

FOR SALE: 1.32 ACRE(S) —
COMMERCIAL POTENTIAL —
150 FOOT FRONTAGE —
WELL WATER —
IDEAL FOR SERVICE STATION OR
STORE

24

Underneath were the name and telephone number of a real estate firm in nearby Quincy.

Virgil's shaking hand lost what was left of its steadiness, sloshing coffee onto his shoes. Stable and secure had just flown out the window and headed for the treetops.

2

Mavine sat at the dinette for a long time, staring at the soiled dishes and silverware scattered about the counter. The morning hadn't gone at all the way she'd hoped. Was Virgil right, and was the *Pageant* article just a lot of foolishness? Her husband had seemed bewildered by her question. After all, the man was nothing if not practical. Could the question be important to her, but wrong to ask Virgil?

Out of habit, she turned the radio back on. *Town Talk* had already started, with the county extension specialist giving tips on choosing the freshest turkey and someone from the Rotary Club talking about their rummage sale. Poultry and used clothing were the furthest things from her mind this morning. With a twist of a knob the Philco fell silent again, leaving the clock as her only distraction. She opened the hot water tap, found a clean dishrag, and shoved all the tableware into the sink with a clatter.

Dr. LaMour's article had seemed to her both good and timely. The questions about romantic dinners and special evenings were a bit silly, she had to admit, but the part about working long hours had captured her interest. Virgil had been spending a lot of time down at Osgood's lately. Sometimes he'd leave the house right after breakfast and not return until after supper. He'd always call, but working through lunch? And a few evenings last week, he'd gone back out after a quick TV dinner and not come home until nearly nine o'clock.

Of course she trusted him. They'd met in grade school, when Virgil was ten and she was eight. Because he had started school late and had repeated a year, they found themselves in the same class. He was handsome and kind, and by the time they were in the eighth grade, she was smitten. When war came and he'd joined the Army, he'd promised to write every week and return to Eden Hill and marry her. Promises he'd kept.

They had a fine son — the spitting image of his father — and they had never wanted for a place to live or food on the table.

But she also respected her friend Gladys. They'd been in the same class all through school, and while Gladys might exaggerate now and then, she knew a lot about marriage — make that *marriages* — and how wedded bliss could become wedded bust. Her kidding was good-natured, of course, but she'd sent the *Pageant* home with Mavine and mentioned she ought to show it to Virgil.

Things had definitely gone wrong for Gladys. Her first husband divorced her some years ago. All she would say was that things didn't work out. "Don't let it happen to you," Gladys had said.

No, whatever might be going on, Virgil would never do anything like that. Mavine knew her husband. He'd never had a secret, and wouldn't be able to keep one anyway.

She dried the last item, her blue Fiesta biscuit plate, and glanced again at the clock. The hands on the dial had moved much more than she had expected, and the sun was now pouring in the window over the sink. Monday was laundry day, and Vee's blue jeans and Virgil's work khakis were piled in the basket on the back porch. Clothes needed to be cleaned, and housework couldn't wait any longer.

She started the water to fill the tub on the Maytag and picked up a pair of tan pants from the pile. As Virgil could be absent-

28

minded, she felt all the pockets for ballpoint pens and loose change. The texture was warm and familiar, gentle and well-worn. Yes, she could trust the man she'd married.

But Virgil *did* seem caught off his guard, defensive and irritated. Like a fox caught in the chicken coop.

Reverend Eugene Caudill sat on the edge of his bed, still dressed in his pajamas and slippers. He'd slept in until almost seven and was getting a late start. Last night's sermon on repentance had taken almost an hour, and followed the half-hour Sunday night hymn time that his song leader, Toler, had managed to drag out to forty-five minutes. After covering up the baptistery and turning down the furnace, he'd made it to bed sometime after eleven. Much later than he liked.

The framed photo next to the alarm clock drew his gaze, as it did every morning. Their framed wedding picture, hand-colored like they did in those days. Louise had been so beautiful in her long gown, and he looked confident and hopeful in his dark suit. His hair had been the coal black of his Scottish ancestors then, and her smile showed no hint of the weakened artery that would suddenly burst just four years later. The church had been very supportive, of course, and had helped him through the loss, though he'd nearly given up his pastorate to pursue something else. So his recent sermon series on marriage had been somewhat uninformed; even he recognized that. How should he know enough to preach on marriage when he had been widowed for twelve years? He still missed her dearly, and some days he wished he had resigned.

But he was a pastor, called to preach and to shepherd this flock. With effort, he struggled to his feet and made his way to the kitchen to start breakfast. The teakettle had just begun its low whistle when the phone rang. He turned off the gas flame as the telephone jangled a second time. The caller could wait.

He took a cup and saucer from the cupboard, arranged them on the counter, and answered the phone on the fifth ring. "Good morning, Madeline." The day would be a total waste unless Mrs. Madeline Crutcher called to raise Cain about something, and she rarely disappointed. Behind schedule, too; his phone usually rang at six in the morning.

The old woman was already in midsentence: ". . . selling the church's property! Where is the vision? Why was I not consulted?" The elderly widow was red in the face, something he could tell even over the telephone.

"And," she continued after a deep breath, "where will I park my Buick?"

He poured the boiling water into the cup with his free hand. "Madeline, the church didn't, doesn't, and won't need the vacant lot. What it *does* need is a new roof, and offerings are down. My vision's fine, thank you very much. You weren't consulted because you didn't need to be. You'll probably park your car in my space at the church like you do now. And furthermore, Madeline, how well are you keeping up on your stewardship pledge for this year?"

Mrs. Crutcher said something about her elite heritage and then questioned his own and hung up. Reverend Caudill shook his head and reached into the cabinet for a tin of Tetley and a Goody's headache powder. The week was not off to a good start.

He swirled his tea bag in the steaming water and then added the contents of the little foil pouch. As his cup began to turn cloudy, an alarming thought occurred to him. Could the woman possibly be right, and he and the board wrong? The First Evangelical Baptist Church had bought the adjacent property for a possible parking lot after Canter's feed store burned to the ground back in fifty-eight. He'd turned out to watch the fire along with the rest of Eden Hill's residents. Evangelist Lewis Pritchett, whom he'd brought to town for the church's spring revival meeting, was never one to miss a divine opportunity. Standing on the roof of his Cadillac, he'd preached to the whole community on the terrors of hellfire, using a bullhorn he kept in his trunk for just such occasions. More than forty people had come forward, including Madeline Crutcher. She'd convinced the board that Divine Providence had made the land available, and the church needed to purchase the property. Very persistent. So they did just that, against his recommendation.

Eventually everyone realized they'd been had. Most people in Eden Hill walked to services, and those who didn't parked on the grass or across the street at Osgood's, which was closed on Sundays. The congregation had voted again last week and decided to sell the lot and use the proceeds toward repairs to the building's aging roof. Reverend Caudill had called the real estate agency in Quincy and signed the papers. The agent had brought his sign late Sunday afternoon and set it up just back from the road.

Yes, it was the right thing to do. Absolutely. The aspirin in the medicine had begun to take effect, and the caffeine was helping to clear his foggy head. If — when — she called again, he'd tell her so.

The apostle Paul had a thorn in his flesh. Reverend Caudill had Mrs. Madeline Crutcher.

3

"Neil, will you please look at the map? We're just plain lost, and that's all there is to it. You've no idea how we got here."

Cornelius Alexander slowed the Chevy to a crawl as they crossed a narrow bridge, and turned toward his wife. "I am *not* lost, JoAnn. I know exactly where we are, and we can always go right back out the same road we came in on. We were on the state highway just a couple of minutes ago." He loved the woman dearly, especially when she called him Neil, her pet name for him, but there were days when she could be a challenge.

"More like ten minutes and three turns ago. Now stop at that service station and ask for directions." It seemed this would be one of those days.

Grumbling, he gave the steering wheel spinner a disgusted twist and slid into the gravel and up to the pump. A bell announced his appearance, and a short, white-haired man with a broad grin and a slight limp ambled to the side of the car. "Can I help you good folks?"

"I don't need gasoline, just directions back . . ." The hood of the Chevy was already open, and a somewhat younger and taller man with a rumpled khaki cap was deep into the engine compartment. "Wait! I really don't need —"

"Don't worry, Virgil is just checking your oil. Don't need to buy anything for that." The older man had produced a squeegee and a squirt bottle and was cleaning the windshield. "Now, just where are you trying to get back to?"

"Back to the state highway, I guess."

"You two work it out. I'm going to find a snack." JoAnn was already out of the car and walking toward the white concrete block building. Pregnancy had made her fickle and hungry all the time, it seemed. Eating for two, she said. No point staying in the car, so he opened his door as well. He could also use a stretch, and besides, he'd spotted something interesting across the street. He looked around. Not much to see here: a creek, a few houses, a couple of stores and churches, and as best he could tell, one pitiful service station. And a large empty lot with a very conspicuous sign.

"Bear to your left at the fork just past the bridge." The older man was pointing back down the road. "Don't turn right. That'll take you over by the lake. Good fishing, but maybe not what you'd want to do this afternoon. If you turn left again, you'll go straight to the state highway and from there into Quincy. You say that's where you're heading?"

"We're just out for a drive." Cornelius pointed across the street. "Property for sale. Yours?"

"No." The taller man had closed the hood and come over to where they were standing. "It belongs to the church there, but I guess they decided they didn't need it. By the way, your oil's just fine — right on the mark."

"Thank you. We'll be going now." JoAnn had returned with a cellophane package of Cheese Nibbles and was gobbling them like she hadn't eaten all day. Which, he had to admit, she hadn't. She slid carefully back into the car and closed the door.

Cornelius handed over a few coins for the snack and mumbled his appreciation as well, then climbed in. With a twist of the key, the well-tuned Chevrolet Bel Air roared to life, scattering dust and gravel as they pulled out. A few seconds later, he eased onto the shoulder.

"Neil, what are you doing now?" she asked, brushing away dusty crumbs from her maternity pedal pushers.

"Didn't you see that vacant lot for sale just across from those guys? I'm writing down the phone number before I forget it." He found a ballpoint pen and an old matchbook in the glove compartment. "It's the perfect location!"

"Perfect for what?"

"For our new Zipco Super Service station, JoAnn. I don't know which one of those two geezers owns that station, but it's hopelessly out of date. That little place wouldn't stand a chance against major competition. No premium gasoline. No lighted sign. Gravel lot. Made of cheap concrete blocks and needs a coat of paint. And was there even one restroom? 'Give the customer what he desires and he will patronize your establishment,' remember?" Cornelius knew the Zipco business manual like the back of his hand.

"I suppose so." JoAnn dabbed at her face with a Kleenex from the glove compartment, removing lipstick, crumbs, and sweat. "But just maybe people around here like that service station and those men. This might be one of those places where everyone knows or is kin to everyone else, and they may not take well to outsiders. Did you think of that? And did that wide place in the road even have a name?"

"We have to look ahead, JoAnn. That dinky service station is behind the times." The pen wouldn't write, so he licked at the end. "Remember, 'The future is in clean, bright, full-service fueling centers offering quality Zipco products. Uniformed attendants will assure that every customer's needs are met with confidence and competence.' " Straight out of the second chapter of the business manual, the section with the jet-powered cars on the title page. "Zipco is the future, JoAnn. That town, Eden . . . something, is absolutely the right place for our business. The sign said so!"

The pen finally started working, and he scrawled the number down as JoAnn continued to scowl. "What's the matter now?"

"I guess your mind's made up. Can we drive back to Quincy now?"

He tucked the matchbook into his shirt pocket and pulled onto the highway. More gravel went flying as he popped the clutch.

Soon JoAnn had fallen asleep. Not only did pregnancy make her hungry, but she also tired easily. Frankly, he was relieved. The highway was lightly traveled, and he needed time to think.

Cornelius Alexander III was determined not to be an embarrassment to his father, Cornelius Alexander Jr., nor especially to his grandfather, *the* Cornelius Alexander of Alexander Motors.

He hadn't started well. His parents had sent him to a fine college where he'd majored in frat parties and pool — and one particular coed — and flunked out after his first year. "No direction," the dean had said. He'd tried to enlist to serve his country, but he even failed the physical. "Flat feet," the doctor had said.

While sweeping floors at Alexander Motors, with fallen arches and uncertain goals, he'd accepted the eldest Mr. Alexander's offer of tuition to the Bluegrass College of Business. It turned out to be a perfect fit. Accounting and Bookkeeping had been challenging courses, but he'd sailed through Entrepreneurship I and II, and had aced Competitive Strategies without ever cracking a book. When he graduated at the end of the summer term, he married his girlfriend, JoAnn, and began to explore business opportunities. When he met the representative from the Zanesville International Petroleum Company at the school's job fair, it was a match made in heaven — or at least in a poolroom.

"Cornelius, a Zipco franchise has a lot to offer an outstanding young man like you." How well he remembered the meeting in the college recreation room. The rep had steadied his aim at the white ball, paused, and chalked the tip of his cue. "We have an outstanding growth strategy, and I'm going to give you an opportunity to get in on the ground floor." The cue ball took a solid hit, and in turn sent the red number three wobbling slowly down the rail.

"Just what's it going to cost?" Cornelius had asked, as he caromed the five into the corner, just missing the pocket. "And what's in it for me?"

"Excellent profits the first year. You have some debts to pay off, I suspect?" The rep grazed the eight ball, sending it dangerously near the side pocket.

"Maybe." Cornelius chalked his own cue and chuckled; the game — the more important one — was going nicely. A muted click and another ball dropped. One well-placed shot would leave him in perfect position. Unfortunately, his bank off the rail was wide to the right.

"Zipco can finance you — all you have to do is find a promising location. And with the money you make, you and the little lady will soon be in the house of your dreams." The rep took a shot at the number ten ball at the other end, grazing the eight ball again and gently nudging it into the side pocket. "Aw, shoot. Well, you won fair and square." The rep handed Cornelius a crisp five-dollar bill, and edged him toward a table where the preliminary papers were ready to sign.

Cornelius had pocketed the fiver. The house of their dreams? Wasn't that exactly what JoAnn wanted in life, especially with a little one on the way? "May I use your pen?"

The deal was all over in two minutes. JoAnn had cried when he told her, like he had done something very wrong. Even though he'd done it for her.

No, he would not be an embarrassment to JoAnn either. He would *not*.

"Now where do you suppose that young couple was from?" Virgil finished tightening the oil filter under the hood and wiped his hands on a rag only a bit cleaner than his palms.

"A couple of counties over, judging from his license plate." Welby and his mechanic's creeper had disappeared under the trunk of the tiny Nash, where clattering noises could be heard. "Young couple out for a drive, and got turned around somewhere along the way. Sure did seem interested in the old feed store property, though."

"Yeah. I've got a feeling that sign will lead to no good. What would you like to see go in over there?"

Welby stopped his clanking. "Cows! Or at least another feed store." He chuckled from somewhere behind the rear axle. "Would you make sure that jack's solid? Can't be too careful."

"Solid as a rock, Welby. That sign is *trouble*. Mark my words."

"Neil, I don't feel good about this. Any of it." JoAnn tipped her head forward and peered beneath her long Maybelline eyelashes.

"Trust me, JoAnn. We found the perfect spot quite by serendipity. I think it must be a sign."

"A sign. Did you see how the real estate agent was smiling? The banker was grinning like the Cheshire cat, and the man from Zipco was practically dancing on the tables."

"So?"

"Why am I the only one who isn't happy?"

"Because you're expecting?"

She turned away and paused for a long time. "No, because I should have expected something like this."

Virgil stood up and stepped to the doorway, where he could look across the road, scratching at his chin. A new sign was nailed over the old one.

COMING SOON —
ZIPCO SUPER SERVICE STATION

Virgil was a practical man, not given to worry, and especially not prone to excitement. He did note, however, that his coffee cup was upside down and empty. He'd poured the contents down the front of his trousers. Again.

Virgil refilled his mug, then entered his small office off the storage room and took a seat. He had run Osgood's since he and Mavine married back in '48. A simple but sturdy concrete block building, the business featured a single gasoline pump in the front. Osgood's sold only regular gasoline, a sensible motor fuel. Anyone fool enough to own a car that needed premium would just have to buy his gasoline somewhere else.

He'd never bothered with a name brand. The gasoline he sold was just fine, and as far as he was concerned it was Osgood's. Old crazy Sam Wright used to say that Virgil made the fuel himself in a copper still, just like moonshine. The old men who played pinochle on the porch at Stacy's Grocery claimed Virgil bought it second-hand from someplace in Louisville. Always good for a laugh. At any rate, he pumped it with a smile and checked every customer's oil. Over time he'd added Reddy-Start batteries, Safe-T-Made tires, and most importantly his mechanic, Welby. But it was still a *service* station, without frills and without apology. After all, it was Osgood's.

He stood up and stepped to the doorway, where he could look across the road. What was he so worried about? Whatever was going to be built in the vacant lot across the street, he could handle it.

Probably.

For the first time in a week, Mavine felt like her life was under control. The first load of clothes was clean, wrung out, and hanging to dry on the porch. The smell of bleach, while distasteful, meant that Virgil's white undershirts and socks would be clean and presentable. Vee's jeans and plaid shirts were still grinding away in the Maytag, waiting for rinsing and a trip through the wringer. She'd turned the radio on, with the volume up loud enough to drown out the chugging of the washing machine.

She had begun working in the kitchen and listening to *Swap 'n' Shop* on WNTC when Virgil came home for lunch. He slammed the door hard, which made the plates in the dish drainer rattle while she was trying to hear the phone number for the woman with the *Encyclopedia Americana* for sale. It was ". . . missing volume 1, A–Annuals, used very little." Fortunately, the announcer repeated it, since the seller also had ". . . a crystal punch bowl and a wedding gown, size twelve." The caller had choked up a little when describing the last item. Even twelve years old, the encyclopedia would be a good buy for Vee's school reports, and as long as he stayed away from papers on aardvarks and John Adams, he'd be just fine. She made a note on the small memo pad she kept next to the telephone.

"Your hamburger will be ready in a minute." She sniffed the smoke rising from the cast-iron skillet. Almost done. "Mayonnaise is in the refrigerator."

"Mavine, we've got ourselves a problem." Virgil had parked himself in his usual seat at the end of the dinette. He hadn't stopped for the mayo.

She froze as last Monday's conversation once again filled her mind. A problem?

Gladys had said much the same thing when she and George were getting ready to separate. Had Virgil actually read the article as he said he would? Maybe he'd talked to Welby about it. And might he have the wandering eye that Dr. LaMour said all men get? Surely not.

"What . . . what is it?"

"Somebody bought the lot across the street to put in a new service station!" He took off his khaki cap and slapped it on the table. "Welby says it's nothing to worry about, but how can another service station be anything but bad for Osgood's?"

This caught her completely by surprise. She couldn't recall any articles in *Pageant* or *Photoplay* about business competition, and had no idea how to respond to her husband, who was clearly concerned. "So, what will you do?"

"Don't know. I suppose we should clean the place up a bit."

"Maybe a new sign with your name on it would help." She sighed and snatched up the cap, hanging it on the hook next to his jacket.

"I don't think so. People know who we are and where to find us. Besides, a sign caused all this trouble to begin with."

"Well, let's not worry about it at lunch."

Mavine lifted the smoking patty from the pan and placed it on a bun with onions and pickles. "Meals ought to be calm and peaceful."

"I'll try." Virgil leaned over his plate and took a bite. He stopped chewing. "What," he asked, "is in this hamburger?"

"Oatmeal!" She brightened. "I found the recipe on the back of a cereal box."

Virgil lifted the top of the bun and stared at her creation. Without a word, he retrieved the mayonnaise jar from the refrigerator and slathered most of its contents onto his sandwich.

4

Virgil wandered down the hill after dinner, carefully picking his way along in the diminishing light. Not to work; this was a social visit — and a haircut. Opening the door, he could hear laughter and conversation from inside.

"A little longer on the top, Welby." Grover Stacy laughed at his own joke, his balding pate sparkling under the flickering and dusty fluorescent bulbs.

"I'll try." Welby chuckled through the whir of his clippers. "But I'll have to take it from the bottom."

Virgil smiled, in spite of himself. He and the others in the makeshift barbershop had heard this conversation again and again. Every time the local grocer climbed into Welby's chair, in fact. This was familiar and well-traveled ground.

Only two vehicles in the gravel lot: Arlie's truck and the telltale ancient red Farmall tractor that meant it was Sam Wright's week for a trim. The retired crop duster and local eccentric had been stripped of his driver's license a couple of years before, after driving his Oldsmobile into the front of Stacy's Grocery. He failed the ordered vision test, as expected, and his driving privileges were revoked. Somewhere, though, Sam learned that a license was not required for agricultural vehicles, so he bought the used Farmall from Arlie.

Virgil let his mechanic set up a barber chair in the storage room of his service station, since the men and boys of Eden Hill needed maintenance just as their cars and trucks did. Welby would trade his rumpled coveralls for a starched white coat, and exchange his box wrenches for electric clippers. He might cut hair the same way he cut engine gaskets, but the vehicles he repaired ran very well, and the menfolk of Eden Hill usually looked quite presentable. The little shop helped Welby with extra income and provided a place for the men to talk about the women, who would all get together at Gladys's on Fridays and talk about the men.

Virgil owed Welby this much and more. When his father, H. C. Osgood, had needed an assistant for his little machine shop, twenty-year-old Welby had joined the operation. When H. C. had spent eighteen months in the sanatorium with tuberculosis, Welby ran the business and made sure that the Osgood family had food on the table, even working part-time as a night watchman at a bank in Quincy. H. C. never forgot his kindness. Virgil hadn't either.

Welby and his wife, Alma, enjoyed being "uncle" and "aunt" to Vee. They had no children, nor any nearby nieces or nephews. Besides, they had all been like family for nearly as long as any of them could remember. It was a good arrangement.

Virgil always looked forward to Thursday nights, but this week he especially welcomed the diversion. The new Zipco station going in across the street had him rattled, he had to admit. At least Mavine seemed herself again, though he hadn't quite figured out that magazine incident. As with many things beyond his ken, he'd just let it rest, and thankfully the storm had blown over. For now, at least.

He was tired too. Much of the day had been spent ordering snow tires and antifreeze for the coming winter, and getting answers to some questions. He nodded to each familiar face before finding a seat on an old office chair.

The room went silent, and everyone's gaze fell on him. He felt like a smallmouth bass, snagged by Arlie's fishhook.

"So, Virgil. What's this about a new service station going in where the old feed store used to be?" Grover was still perched in Welby's chair, receiving his usual trim.

"Looks like the church sold it to somebody to build a Zipco Super Service station. Sounds like some kind of a big company like Texaco or Standard Oil."

"I've seen some of those fancy service stations, and they have all kinds of things going on. Road maps, free coffee cups with a fill-up." Grover twisted in his seat. "Some of those places are open late into the night, just like the truck stop. Think you can compete with this Zipco thing? I know when the A&P in Quincy has a sale going on, we lose some customers."

Compete? That's what he'd done in junior varsity football and what he'd seen on *Wide World of Sports* on TV. He never dreamed he'd have to *compete* for Osgood's. Was he supposed to tackle the Zipco operator and keep him away from the goal line?

Welby answered for him. "Oh, we'll be just fine. You and all the good folks in Eden Hill bring us your cars and trucks now, and we'll still be seeing them when this new Zipco

51

comes in. Isn't that right, Virgil?"

Virgil nodded. He was grateful for Welby's answer, as he was trying to come up with one of his own. "Yes, you've always done right well by us."

"Well, I'm seventy-five years old this year, and I've seen them come, and I've seen them go. The Depression got a lot of us." The croaky voice had come from Sam Wright, his silver hair freshly trimmed.

Grover leaned forward as Welby pumped up the chair. "Sam, just where did the Depression get you? Somewhere in the head?"

Sam stiffened. "Mr. Stacy, it cost two of my friends their crop-dusting business. Couldn't afford the gasoline to keep the planes in the air. I took a chance and bought my Waco from one of them. Got it for a song."

Grover rolled his eyes. "Sam, it's not 1935 and the New Deal anymore. We got John Kennedy, not FDR, in the White House. I think you want to forget that sometimes."

The elderly man's voice became louder and croakier, bordering on a cackle. "Kennedy? I voted for Nixon, of course, as any sensible person —"

"Gentlemen, an argument isn't helpful." Welby clipped both Sam's tirade and the scruff on Grover's neck.

"That's easy for you to say." Grover turned, almost losing an ear. "You voted for both Kennedy *and* Nixon in the last election."

"They're both such nice men." Welby was not easily dissuaded.

Virgil began to relax — the subject had changed, and the evening's entertainment had begun. Sam would liven up any conversation, whether here or playing pinochle on the porch in front of Stacy's Grocery. Reliable or not, he was at least amusing. Gladys said he was half blind and whole nuts and had spent time in a lunatic asylum in Ohio, but then again she couldn't always be trusted either.

He had to admit to some of the same doubts. H. C.'s shop had almost gone under in '35, and Virgil remembered many a night with thin soup and dry bread for dinner. Some said the stress of it all had put his father in the sanatorium. But the Osgoods had made it through, hadn't they?

"So, what about it, Reverend?" Welby changed the attachment on his clippers. "In for a trim?"

Virgil turned toward the door, where Reverend Caudill had appeared, unnoticed by almost everyone. The minister would come by about once a month for a haircut, but sometimes just to chat.

"No thanks, Welby, just stopped in to say hello."

Grover pointed his chin toward the sign across the street. "I expect you've seen the latest, Reverend?"

"Oh yes. Quite a stir in town about the new service station. I really am sorry, Virgil, if selling our land has put you in a bad situation, but whatever happens, I hope our whole town can welcome the new business and its owner with open arms. 'Love thy neighbour as thyself,' as the Good Book says. We ought to wish them every success."

"Well, I hope the Zipco does well too." Welby emphasized his point with a dash of Wildroot on Grover's scalp.

"As long as he doesn't sell produce and cold cuts, I guess a new business is always a good thing." Grover squirmed as Welby dusted off his collar with a small whisk broom.

Sam scratched his head again and topped it with an old baseball cap. "Gentlemen, I'm out past curfew. A pleasant evening to all." With that, he left, and the old Farmall could be heard rumbling off somewhere into the cool night.

"Sadly, I too must depart." Reverend Caudill still held his hat. "Might I expect each of you in church on Sunday?"

Everyone nodded as the minister took his leave.

Grover relaxed. "So, who's putting this new Zipco place in?"

"If it's the kid I met at the lake a few days ago, there's not much for Virgil to worry about." Arlie, who had been unusually quiet, paused to stuff another plug of tobacco in his ample jaw. "Boy's not too bright, if you ask me. Got himself lost trying to get back to the state highway. You gotta work at it to do that." He reached for the empty Quaker State can that served as his spittoon.

"That may be the same young fellow who came by here," said Welby. He exchanged his scissors for a hand mirror. "There you are, Grover — a little longer on the top."

Everyone enjoyed another good laugh. Grover paid Welby and took his place on a brake fluid crate as Virgil mounted the chair for a trim of his own. "Okay, Grover, what's all this about being able to compete? And if it is the young man we met, what do we need to do?"

"Stand up to it, Virgil. To be successful, you'll have to step up to your opponent. Go blow-by-blow with him." Grover had watched too many Saturday afternoon boxing matches. "Get him on the ropes. If he's going to do things the big-city way, you'll have to do the same."

Big city? This was Eden Hill, with maybe two hundred on Sunday afternoon when everyone was in church or at home. "Grover, what if it was a grocery instead of a service station?"

"Same thing. Read a book on that once. I'd need to cut prices, work harder. Probably spruce the place up. Might have to give up our vacation in Florida every year. Have a sale on something every now and then. Let the guy — and everybody else — know that you can do it better."

"What about what Reverend Caudill said about open arms?"

Grover looked out the door, where the preacher was nowhere to be seen. "Then I'd say that you're giving in to let the other guy win. Might as well take a fall. Oh, Arlie. Before you leave, what's the almanac say about this winter?"

The farmer had donned his cap and his barn jacket, and carefully set his oilcan upright on the floor. "Warmer'n last year. Four inches of snow for New Year's Day, freezin' rain on January eleventh, and another three inches of snow on Groundhog

Day. The critter's gonna see his shadow and put off spring 'til late March. By then," Arlie said, "it'll be time to get corn in the ground, snow or no snow." The most he'd said all evening.

The weather was always the closing topic, particularly if Sam had already gone and taken his woolly-worm stories with him. Grover picked up his own floppy hat and twisted it onto his freshly shorn head. "Good to know," he said to Arlie, who had already stepped toward the door. "At least I can put Anna Belle's decorations up on the roof and get them off again before the worst of it gets here. You know how she is about her Christmas lights!"

"Take care, gentlemen," said Welby, gathering his razors and scissors for his final customer. The door swung shut, and Grover and Arlie walked out through the garage toward Arlie's truck. After much grinding, the pitiful machine sprang to life, backfiring as he drove away.

"Okay, Virgil, you're all done." Welby was cleaning his implements with alcohol and tidying up. "What do you *really* know about this young fellow?"

Virgil sat up straight so Welby could lower the chair. "His name is Cornelius Alexander. Comes from a couple of counties over. Papa knew his granddad from back when he had the machine shop. The old man went into the car business right before the Depression hit. Cornelius's father is a pretty good mechanic, too, I hear. The boy's been to some business school, and has a wife and a baby on the way. You want to know any more than that?"

"Nope." Welby smiled, placing his tonsorial tools in a drawer. "Virgil, you're more like Mr. Osgood every day. How'd you find out all that?"

"Friends, and a few phone calls this afternoon." Virgil was pushing his long arms through the sleeves of his tattered jacket. "Papa always said that it pays to know something about people."

"Mr. Osgood was right," said Welby, as he stepped out the side door. "But I suppose it depends whether you know what's worth knowing. See you tomorrow."

Homer Cicero Osgood had been right about a lot of things. About being a good father, about how to run a good business, about life. After he got out of the sanatorium, H. C. had become a bricklayer, a trade that brought him through the war. He'd also learned how to lay concrete block, and had helped build Osgood's not long before a heart attack took him before his time.

Yes, indeed, his father had been a good man. Virgil put Arlie's Quaker State spittoon and his own office chair back in their places, picked up what he needed off his desk, turned out the lights, and closed the door.

The night air proved much cooler than he expected, so he put his left hand into his pocket to keep it warm. His right hand held the *Pageant* magazine. Mavine hadn't said any more about it, but while the storm had blown over, he was sure she hadn't forgotten. Mavine forgot nothing.

As he fingered the folded paper and the metal clip, the conversation with his wife came to mind. Life at home was almost back to normal. Mavine had been quite talkative at breakfast yesterday, had asked him at lunch how his day was going, and had made his favorite supper: spaghetti and meatballs. She'd even worn a new dress she bought on sale at Willett's Dry Goods. And he'd barely remembered to pay her a compliment.

Maybe he was the one who had been acting strangely.

He ought to just let it go, but he hadn't been able to get past the coming of the

Zipco service station. Activity had picked up across the road. A red pickup truck with out-of-state plates had been by at least twice. Folks had spotted a younger man with a ducktail haircut, presumably Mr. Alexander, going over what appeared to be blueprints. A lineman from the Rural Electric Cooperative had installed a pole and run some wire, and someone else had driven wooden stakes topped with bright-orange flags. Clearly something was about to happen.

Compete? Yes, he could do that. He wasn't on the mat, and he wouldn't need to be saved by the bell. Whatever roundhouse Zipco might swing, he was up to it. When all was said and done, he would be the one with his arm lifted and his chin held high. Winner and still champion.

But the *Pageant* magazine hadn't gone away either. Tomorrow was Friday, and Mavine was having her hair done early because of Thanksgiving. He'd be sure to compliment her on *that.* Hopefully Gladys wouldn't send anything else home with Mavine.

He opened the service station door, flipped the lights on, tossed the magazine facedown onto his cluttered desk, turned the lights back off, and locked the door behind him. One problem at a time.

5

Reverend Caudill was trying to write a timely Sunday morning message on a well-worn typewriter, but the words, verses, and illustrations he'd planned to use were all piling up in a mental train wreck. The chilly weather earlier in the day had turned stormy as well, soaking him to the skin as he'd hurriedly changed the letters on the sign in front of the church. It was still pouring, and rainwater from the leaky roof was dripping into a metal bucket in front of his desk. Each drop echoed like the tick of a clock, reminding him that Friday night was upon him and Sunday was one second nearer. It was annoying, and his joints and disposition were both deteriorating.

Well. He'd finished his series on marriage last Sunday, and this *was* Thanksgiving weekend, with Christmas coming on its heels. He'd put off his sermon preparation all week long, trying to decide on a topic he could live with. Certainly thankfulness would have to be somewhere in his homily, and God's providence needed to be a part of it as well. He'd known that all along, of course, so a few ideas had already been rolling around in his head. If he could toss in some Pilgrims and a feast, even better. But somehow with this very busy week, he'd found himself late to this part of his ministry. Again. Not somewhere he liked to be.

Giving thanks was hard.

He'd left the sermon title out of the bulletin, typed up on the same old Underwood earlier this morning. The Scripture passage was unspecified as well, but he'd chosen a couple of hymns that he thought even his song leader couldn't butcher, including "We Gather Together" and "Come, Ye Thankful People, Come."

Why was he having such a difficult time with this? Perhaps the estimates for the church roof repairs had gotten to him, with numbers in five figures that made his head spin. He'd spent all morning on the phone with contractors, and the revenue from the property sale wasn't going to cover even half of it. The couple in today's counseling session had gotten nowhere, and spent all afternoon getting there. Then there was Wednesday night's prayer meeting where

Madeline Crutcher prayed for the *next* pastor whenever the current pastor left, and that it might be soon. Another week like this, and he might do just that.

The thought gave him pause. Maybe he *had* overstayed his welcome. He shivered; the idea that Madeline Crutcher might be prophetic sent chills up and down his spine. Clearly the old woman had gotten under his skin. And what about Eden Hill? After sixteen years as pastor, was the church or the town better for his having been here?

He hoped so. The First Evangelical Baptist Church had called him as pastor straight out of Bible college in '46, still wet behind the ears but with a fire in his heart. The first few years hadn't been easy. The former pastor had retired after thirty years, having seen the little congregation through two world wars and the Great Depression. A fine leader, with a good legacy.

Still, since he and Louise arrived he'd watched the church grow, and there had been some glorious moments. He'd married Arlie and Lula Mae Prewitt as his first official wedding, and had recently baptized their daughter, Darlene. Virgil and Mavine tied the knot a couple of years later, and they remained involved in the church, as was their son, Vee Junior. Grover and Anna

Belle had become active members, close friends, and strong supporters. And Madeline Crutcher? Well.

He and Louise had hoped to raise a family here, to put down long tender roots in the rocky soil. He'd loved his work back in the early days, even the hard parts. Young and energetic, he found the days exciting and full of hope. The church was growing, with young families, veterans returning home, and babies booming.

Louise. Even after twelve years, the pain of her sudden passing was a weight he couldn't shake. Her death had left him insecure, broken, and unsure of his call. God was always good, but the unanswered questions were never far from his mind. Was he angry with God? Probably. Had he been knocked off his ministerial path? Certainly he'd wobbled a bit. Not a day went by without him wondering if he and Eden Hill wouldn't both be better off if he were selling life insurance or aluminum siding. But then something always reminded him that his calling hadn't changed yet. Still, it was hard to be thankful.

Louise had died on Thanksgiving Day.

Grover and Anna Belle had invited him over for the holiday yesterday, as they had for years, and offered strong encouragement along with good food. His church was solid, but little challenges kept coming along. All the things that weren't taught in Bible college, and he'd had to learn the hard way. Would a little bit of grace from the Almighty be too much to ask?

The machine still held a blank sheet of paper, and a full thirty minutes had gone by without a single hunt or peck at the keyboard. Something had to be done, and soon. All of his papers from Bible college were organized on the shelf behind him, and he pulled out two binders: one on the Psalms, and the other on Paul's letters to the Corinthians. He considered the thickness of the material on the Psalter, looked at the clock, and chose the shorter New Testament books instead. Dog-eared and well-worn, some of the pages had little tabs with subjects written on them. One had two topics: thanksgiving and grace.

Memories returned in a rush, especially those of a class on sermon preparation and delivery he'd taken his first year. His professor had been a gentle soul whose soft-spoken preaching style never shook the rafters, but whose words were penetrating and powerful. The man had said that grace and thanksgiving went hand in hand, and that everything given was given in grace.

Everything.

He opened his Bible to the text from 2 Corinthians and found himself in the fourth chapter, one of his favorites. The first verse immediately caught his eye, the one on which he'd initially centered his vocation: "Therefore seeing we have this ministry, as we have received mercy, we faint not." Easy to find; he'd underlined it years before. But what was that a bit below it? "For all things are for your sakes, that the abundant grace might through the thanksgiving of many redound to the glory of God." Grace?

And thanksgiving.

Had he been given a chance to begin anew, and not even realized it? Had he been so jaded by the loss of Louise that he couldn't even see the opportunity he'd been given? And wasn't God's grace wide enough to cover his own discouragement?

Yes, yes, and yes.

The men gathered at Welby's last week had seemed concerned about the change the new Zipco might make in Eden Hill; he'd seen it in their eyes. And he had a few worries of his own. But might not change be a good thing, an opportunity even? Should he be the first to say so?

And believe it?

Well. His sermon would be on thanksgiving and grace, and things made new! Using his two forefingers, he began typing. He tipped his head back so his bifocals could do their job; he could never remember which key went with which letter. Soon an opening line appeared at the top of the page, and he gave the carriage return lever a resounding shove. Another line, and then another.

It was well after eleven o'clock when he finished. Late again. The rain had finally ended, but the bucket was still announcing every drip with a softer plop, slower than before. The reverend twisted the knobs on the carriage and took out the last sheet. Done at last! It wasn't as elegant as he would like, and there were a few smudges where he'd used the little round eraser and the brush, but it *was* a sermon, and he was pleased.

He'd called it "Turning Points." Yes, change was good.

6

"Neil, you've barely touched your break-fast."

JoAnn was right. He'd eaten only a single piece of toast, and hadn't even bothered with butter. She'd eaten several slices as well as an apple and a bowl of Cheerios.

"I'll finish it." He scribbled a couple of notes on the yellow legal pad between his plate of fried Spam and his glass of Tang before looking up. "Breakfast is tasty, thank you."

Cornelius Alexander rearranged the papers and writing tablet, wishing he had a real desk instead of a cluttered folding table. Their tiny quarters at the Sleepy Head Tourist Court in Quincy were sparse, but would do for now. The little apartment featured a saggy bed, a kitchenette with a small but noisy refrigerator, and a single light bulb, which dimmed and brightened along with the blink of the aging neon sign in front. The bathroom walls were missing a few of their plastic tiles, but the water was hot and it was only fifteen dollars a week.

"Look at this, JoAnn. We have over an acre to work with, and the lot slopes off to one side. Good drainage. With the station here where it's already been leveled —" he pointed to a rough rectangle scribbled in blue pencil on the lined paper — "our home will fit nicely right back here. There's already a well for our water."

"Neil, right now the whole thing is nothing but a vacant lot. Just when do you expect to build this new home?"

"Soon, JoAnn, soon. Once the station gets up and running and the profits start accruing. Why don't you see if *Queen for a Day* is on TV?"

"What TV? It quit this morning. Right during the *Today* show."

"Our dream house will have a good television. Maybe even color!"

JoAnn bit her lip, then reached across the table to snag Cornelius's uneaten Spam.

He'd rented the little efficiency cabin a couple of weeks before. Far from ideal, it was still the closest thing they could find to Eden Hill, some twenty minutes away. Since the site of his new business was currently a small plot of bare land that had once been a feed store, much needed to be done. With so many things to arrange, he'd worked out a deal with the motel's owner to use the telephone in the office. Few wanted to stay here anymore, so it was little used anyway. The eight other units were temporary homes to traveling salesmen and farm workers passing through. By late November, the place housed one Fuller Brush distributor and the Alexanders.

Over the last week, he'd contracted for a concrete slab to be poured for the service station building, scheduled excavation for the two gasoline tanks, and lined up the electrical work. His bulldozer man agreed to level off another spot for their home, for only a few extra dollars. Deeds had been executed, permits secured, promissory notes signed, and the first shipment of building materials for the Zipco Super Service was on its way.

The figures were scary. Two pages of proposals for the concrete work, and a frightening dollar amount. A handwritten estimate from the backhoe operator, with another jaw-dropping number. The blacktop company had provided yet another. Of course, there were all the franchise costs from Zipco to consider. He added up the sums on a second sheet of yellow paper, comparing it against his line of credit with the company. It could be done, but barely.

Yesterday had been a holiday, so the Zipco offices were closed all day. It was just as well — his wife had insisted he put his paperwork away and celebrate Thanksgiving. She'd made something called a turkey loaf, and heated up a can of cranberry sauce. When she'd asked what he was thankful for, he'd drawn a blank. Certainly he was grateful for her, he'd said, which made her smile. He'd also mentioned Zipco and his business education. Maybe even his family; he couldn't remember. Their little broken-down home at the tourist court, such as it was . . .

Home?

"JoAnn, get your coat. We're going house hunting!"

"Not until we've had lunch. We've got leftovers in the refrigerator, and I'm eating for two now. Remember?"

"But we just had breakfast!"

"Neil, that was three hours ago. You've spent the entire morning going over all those papers and haven't spoken a word — at least not to me."

He sighed. Perhaps he had lost himself in this project. How could he have known how much it would cost to build a Zipco Super

Service station? "I'm sorry, JoAnn. Lunch, then we go for a drive."

JoAnn ate two platefuls, and he ate more than he expected, given the morning's discouraging progress. Afterward, they bundled up and climbed in the Chevy, drove across the railroad tracks, and pulled into a small lot behind the cold storage plant. He smiled. "Well, here we are."

"Neil, this is a trailer park."

"It's a manufactured housing dealership. I talked with the manager a couple of days ago, and he's got a fabulous deal on a slightly used unit."

"Then it's where trailer parks come from. Surely you're not thinking . . ."

"Come take a look. It's in great shape, and we could be in our own home within days instead of weeks or months! And we would only live there until we build your dream house."

She simply glared at him.

"JoAnn, we'll soon have a growing family and will need somewhere larger than a room at the Sleepy Head Tourist Court."

"You keep swinging for these pitches, Neil. Someday you're going to strike out."

The manager, a likable fellow, was indeed offering for sale a slightly used mobile home. "Only four years old, traded in for a new model. The furniture store repossessed the couch, but the dinette and curtains go with it."

JoAnn sighed, and agreed to look at the pink-and-white house on wheels. "It's ugly. But it does have the necessities and comes with a screen door and two bedrooms, which is twice the number we have now."

"So?"

"Well, I suppose it'll have to do." Without a further word, she turned on her heels and walked deliberately to the car.

Within five minutes, Cornelius had signed the papers and returned to the Chevy, doing his best to keep smiling. "Great news, JoAnn. He'll be able to deliver it as soon as the excavator can level a spot and we have the electrical and plumbing ready. With luck, we'll be in our new home in Eden Hill by Christmas."

She brightened a bit and dabbed at her red eyes with a tissue. "By Christmas?"

"Well, that's only four weeks away. But I think it might be possible."

Nervous or excited, which was it? Reverend Caudill climbed the steps to his pulpit on Sunday morning. His sermon was well prepared — and honestly, one of the best he'd ever written — but instead of the thunder and lightning his congregation was used to, it was more like a light and nourishing spring rain. He'd opted for the gentler approach that his Bible college professor had modeled for him, thought-provoking rather than incendiary. But would it keep his people's attention? More importantly, would he bring honor to his calling and the gospel? Still, amid his prayers for this message, he was somehow assured that these were the words they needed to hear. After all, these were the words he needed to hear himself.

After Toler led a dirgelike rendition of "Come, Ye Thankful People, Come," and one of the deacons gave a rather anemic reading of the text, he stepped behind the pulpit and faced a flock sagging in their seats. Not a good way to begin a sermon. But Reverend Caudill took a deep breath and began.

"Through the apostle Paul, the Lord has promised that all things are for your sakes. Are you worried about tomorrow? All things are for your sakes."

His voice was calm and steady. Talking, not shouting. "Are you staggering under financial burdens? All things are for your sakes. Are you grieving over a flagging relationship with a spouse, a friend, a child?

All things are for your sakes."

The reverend hardly dared to look up, but when he did, he saw curious and interested faces. Certainly there were scattered glassy-eyed stares and some looks of surprise, but more than a few were, if not hanging on his every word, at least attentive and engaged. Listening. Leaning forward in anticipation, not shrinking back in fear.

Reverend Eugene Caudill suddenly realized the difference. He wasn't angry anymore. At God or for God. It may not be fiery rhetoric, but it was hitting home, and God was showing himself faithful yet again.

7

On December 24, in spite of the snow and mud, a large truck carefully backed the pastel mobile home into its new location in Eden Hill. The electrician hooked up the wiring and turned on the lights, the propane man tied in the gas and lit the pilot, and the water and septic were connected. The driver had fitted a metal stairway up to the front door, and JoAnn hung a small wreath under the little round window.

"Well, JoAnn, we're here by Christmas. Just as I promised." Cornelius stuck the small evergreen he'd cut from the back fencerow into an abandoned flowerpot, and draped a single string of colored lights around its branches.

She threw her arms around him and gave him the closest thing to a bear hug that an expectant mother could manage, and a grin sprang across his face. Moments like this made him want to promise her the world.

"Neil, it's Christmas Eve. Let's go to the Christmas pageant at the church next door? The sign out front said it starts at seven thirty."

He broke their embrace and looked at the aging building next door with its sagging roof and crumbling front steps. Christmas pageant? Something inside balked at the idea. The only pageant he knew about was Miss America, and he certainly wasn't up for Bert Parks. Or maybe it was his father's distaste of anything religious, or his own stubbornness. Whatever the case, one look at his wife's earnest eyes filled with longing, and all his aversion melted away.

"Yes, JoAnn, I think we can."

"Hurry up, Vee," Mavine called up the steps, wrapped in her coat and scarf. "We can't be late for the Christmas pageant, and we want to see the Stacys' decorations first."

Virgil shook his head, hoping she wouldn't see. He never quite saw the point of the outrageous display. For most folks in Eden Hill, Christmas looked pretty much like any other early winter day, only a little more festive. Gladys put candles in the windows of the Glamour Nook, and he'd put out the big sign with the life-size picture of Santa Claus holding an automobile battery — *If your car isn't ready to start, ask Santa for a Reddy-Start* — but most just put up a tree and a few ornaments and let it go at that.

Not so with the Stacys. The grocery sparkled with red-and-green tinsel garlands, strings of colored lights illuminated the checkout counter and the lunch meat case, and bells of silver paper dangled from the ceiling next to the flypaper. Their house was equally overdone.

On Christmas Eve the entire town liked to drive by to see the spectacle before attending the pageant at the First Evangelical Baptist Church; it gave them something to talk about while waiting for the piano music to change to "O Come, O Come, Emmanuel," which was the cue to get quiet. Eden Hill's own Christmas parade.

"Virgil T. Osgood Jr., it's time to go!" The boy was stubborn, a trait he'd inherited from his father.

Vee finally sauntered down the steps, dragging an old Welgo shopping bag and looking despondent. Virgil checked his watch. "We've only got twenty minutes before you need to be there. Let's move."

There were several vehicles in line in front of the Stacys' home, all familiar. Arlie and Lula Mae rode in their truck in the very front, with Welby and Alma following a couple of cars back. The show was as flashy as expected. Santa and his sleigh flew toward the chimney, held in place with thin wire fastened to nearby trees. Rudolph's nose glowed red as a cherry, and the reindeer danced and swayed with every gust of wind. Dozens of brightly colored bulbs blinked on and off, while "O Holy Night" played through a small loudspeaker on the porch.

"What do you think of that, Vee?" Virgil turned to the back seat, where Vee looked glumly out the window on the other side.

"Neat. Can we go now?" Vee, it seemed, was unimpressed. Apparently something else he inherited from his father.

Welby and Alma were settled in their usual spot near the aisle when the Osgoods entered, Alma dressed in a red suit with her Christmas hat, and Welby in a crisp white shirt and a fashionable knit tie. In addition to her purse, Alma held a small leatherette case. Welby motioned to the Osgoods to join them.

"Alma brought her Brownie to get some snapshots of Vee." Welby grinned. "He's going to do a great job tonight!"

Mavine beamed. "Vee's really looking forward to it."

Virgil truly hoped his wife was right. But it seemed to him that Vee was most certainly *not* looking forward to it. He was dreading it, with fear and trembling. Their son would be playing Wise Man #2 this year and would have to carry a little filigreed jewelry box atop Mavine's white embroidered couch pillow. His costume consisted of Virgil's old flannel robe and a crown made out of shirt cardboard and gold wrapping paper. All these things had been stuffed into the paper bag along with a pair of squeaky brown flip-flops from Welgo. Vee would also have to sing "We Three Kings," with the right words like in the hymnal, not the ones Mavine had caught him and Frank Prewitt singing about smoking on a loaded cigar. Besides, old Toler was keeping a sharp eye on the boys from his music stand near the choir loft.

In a way, Vee was lucky. Virgil had seen the script Vee had brought home. Frank had been tapped to play Joseph opposite his younger sister Darlene's Mary, and so would have to be the one holding Baby Jesus, played by Darlene's Betsy Wetsy doll wrapped in swaddling clothes.

Reverend Caudill had arrived in time to pray with the children, whom he found ready and waiting in the vestibule. Surprisingly, they were all there.

And not surprisingly, he could hear them arguing by the time he took his seat at the side of the platform. He surveyed his congregation and sighed, content to see nearly his entire church family gathered together this holy night. And as he looked toward the entryway, where the costumed cast had convened, a bit of movement to one side caught his eye. A young couple, almost concealed by the shadow of the balcony, slipped in and found seats in the back row. He recognized neither of them. Visitors? But he had little time to ponder this, as the music began and all eyes were drawn to a slight commotion in the doorway to the vestibule.

"Stop poking me, Vee."

"I'm not poking you, Frank. That's your cue."

Toler was waving his hands in time with the music. They were up to the part about the Virgin when Frank, as Joseph, finally came through the door with Darlene in tow. She had missed her cue as well — probably flirting with Vee like she did on Sunday mornings. Fortunately, she'd remembered the baby, wrapped in swaddling clothes. Reverend Caudill's eyes were drawn to the young woman he'd seen come in; she wore an angelic smile and placed a hand over her midsection as she watched the holy family climb the steps to where the iconic Christmas scene awaited.

Mavine's magazine rack served as an acceptable manger and was filled with Arlie's straw. Mrs. Crutcher was complaining loudly from the front row that in *her* Bible, Mary wasn't delivered of the child until *after* they reached the stable, and that Reverend Caudill should be more careful to avoid scriptural error. Joseph, clearly not concerned with such details, took the doll from its mother and placed it on his shoulder according to the script. The organist was well into "While Shepherds Watched Their Flocks," with the congregation following, when two adolescents wrapped in bathrobes joined the tableau.

"Whatcha got there, Frank?" Eddie, Shepherd #2, had observed the obvious.

"Shaddup," Frank grumbled above the music.

"Looks like a baby doll, Frank." Richard, Shepherd #1, was covering his mouth, equally sympathetic. The organist was slowing down even more for the final stanza, while Toler, in the choir loft, was watching the commotion and glaring.

"Shaddup. You didn't have to hold a sheep!"

"Shhhhh, you're going to get us in trouble." Darlene glared at both boys.

Reverend Caudill scanned the congregation again, particularly noting the parents among them. Arlie and Lula Mae were about two-thirds back on his left, directly in front of Eddie's parents. Welby, Alma, and the Osgoods were in the front to his right. Everyone — so far — seemed pleased with the progress of the pageant. Except Toler and Madeline Crutcher, of course, who were never pleased with anything. And the young man who sat squirming under the balcony. The woman — his wife? — leaned her head onto his shoulder, but he shifted in his seat and divided his attention between his wristwatch and the church exit.

By now, two shepherds, one adoptive father, and one choir director were all grimacing, with the young virgin mother trying to restore order. As the last line of the carol echoed through the sanctuary, Frank looked straight at Eddie and said loudly, "Hold the baby."

Before Reverend Caudill or anyone else could intervene, Frank slapped the bundle on Eddie's shoulder and squeezed.

"Aw, man!"

Eddie froze for a moment, then fingered the damp splotch on his chest and shoved the doll into Richard's arms, who handed it back to Frank, who, having run out of shepherds, gave it to a startled Darlene. Someone was heard to mumble, "I'll get you," under his breath.

"Shhhhh! Be quiet!" Darlene began to cry.

Reverend Caudill, who had up to now enjoyed a stellar day, began to lose a bit of his smile. Fortunately, the lights were dim where he was sitting, so hopefully no one would notice. He could be grateful for *that.* And for the Goody's headache powder he kept in his office for afterward.

Just then, somebody plugged in the drop cord that powered the light bulb in the tin star hanging over the baptistery. Apparently this was the cue for the organist to launch into "We Three Kings." Toler, always more a follower than a leader, frowned some more and began waving his arms to the music. Wise Man #1 was by now halfway down the aisle with his bottle of green Kool-Aid, and Vee stood in the doorway, silhouetted by the light from the vestibule.

Mrs. Crutcher was right on cue with her biblical insights. "The magi found the babe in a *house,* not a *stable.* Why isn't there a house?"

Vee, undeterred by the theological contro-
versy, made his own entrance, a small jewel
box balanced precariously on Mavine's pillow.

At that moment Alma turned, pointed the
Brownie camera, and tripped the shutter.
The flashbulb went off with a spectacular
poof, the organist lost her place, and Toler
abandoned what was left of his composure.
Mrs. Crutcher shrieked and threw her bulletin in the air. Vee walked into the side of a
pew and then tripped on the dangling sash
of his bathrobe, launching the jewel box
down the aisle.

Reverend Caudill watched helplessly from
the platform as Vee dusted himself off and
limped to the side of the manger. Wise Man
#3, Toler's grandson, was nowhere to be
seen. He could be heard, however, sobbing
in the vestibule when the music finally and
mercifully ended. His grandfather, whimper-
ing, motioned to the organist, who began
"Joy to the World" in a surprisingly upbeat
tempo. Someone was sent to unplug the tin
star but pulled out the wrong cord instead,
knocking out the lights to Toler's music
stand as the last chord sounded.

Someone turned up the lights, and the
pastor rose for the closing prayer. Maybe he
wouldn't need the medicine after all. The

pageant had gone *much* better than last year.

But when he looked up after the closing prayer, he was surprised and a bit disappointed. The back pew, where the young couple had sat, was empty.

8

"Vee, you did a wonderful job tonight!" Mavine put her arms around their son, who turned his red face away. The day had been a long one, and Welby and Alma had joined the Osgoods for their traditional Christmas Eve dinner and tree decorating.

"You certainly did." Alma passed the bowl of green popcorn back to Mavine, who was spearing a puffy red kernel with a large needle. "I can't wait to see the snapshots!"

"Thank you, Aunt Alma."

Mavine knew her son well. He was being polite and trying hard to look pleased, but it was obvious his leg hurt from walking into the pew, and the taste of humiliation was no doubt still burning his mouth. "How about some music? Maybe there'll be Christmas carols on the radio."

"Yes, thank you. May I have some more hot chocolate, please?"

"Just one more cup, Vee." Alma poured

steaming cocoa from the pan into a mug and dropped in a couple of marshmallows. "It's nearing your bedtime."

"Alma's right, Vee. It's almost eleven o'clock." Mavine finished her garland with one last white kernel and tied a knot in the string. "Before you go to bed, why don't you put this on the tree?"

"Okay." He gathered up the multicolored strand and pulled a chair alongside the tall fir, where Virgil and Welby had just finished their handiwork with the ornaments. Alma and Welby had celebrated Christmas Eve and Christmas Day with the Osgoods for as many years as she could remember, even well before Mavine married into the family.

"Start at the top and work your way down," offered Welby, a grin brightening his broad face. Vee nodded and climbed onto the chair, stretching to reach the far branches. The glass balls danced as the tree shook, reflecting the colored lights and the glint of the tinsel. He stepped back to the floor and did nothing but stare at the tree for a long time. Bedtime it surely was.

"Good night, Vee!" Welby waved as Vee began slowly climbing the stairs. He stopped for a moment on the landing, taking a last look at the beautiful tree and at his family.

"See you in the morning, Vee." Mavine

wiped her hands on her chocolate-stained apron. "Merry Christmas!"

If Vee had looked very closely, he'd have seen the joy in his mother's eyes. She'd been talking to him, but looking at her husband.

And Virgil noticed. The man noticed.

"Where's the best spot to put this thing together?" Virgil's brow furrowed as he examined the top of the box he was carrying.

Welby pointed. "I guess the floor is as good a place as any."

The box was made of heavy cardboard and clanked as Virgil set it down. The top featured a picture of a colorful and thriving business and proclaimed in bold letters, *Superior Service Station.* In much smaller letters it also admitted, *An unassembled toy.*

"Looks like it could be a long night."

Mavine entered the living room carrying two steaming mugs. "More cocoa?" Long night notwithstanding, Virgil smiled; he and Welby would be well cared for.

"Thanks." Welby opened the box, pouring what appeared to be hundreds of tiny tires, oilcans, and other unidentified pieces onto the rug. The instruction booklet was buried at the bottom, along with the decals shown in the illustration. He held it at arm's length, then pulled his reading glasses from his shirt pocket and parked them at the tip of his nose.

"How's it look?" Virgil dropped a marshmallow into his mug and took out his own bifocals.

Welby's eyes twinkled. "No worse than an automatic transmission. Better fetch your screwdriver."

Mavine switched off the radio, as WNTC had played the national anthem and signed off at midnight after wishing everyone a very merry Christmas. Only faint winter static and some faraway mumbles could be heard. Vee's toy service station was assembled and placed under the tree, along with pretty packages and a basket of oranges and apples. Welby and Alma had wished them a good night and left until the next morning. Christmas Eve had become Christmas Day.

Virgil poured himself a glass of milk and sat across the table from his wife. "We had a splendid pageant this year. Vee did himself proud."

"Yes, he did indeed. He reminded me so much of you, in your bathrobe. You even have the same walk. Except for falling down, of course."

Virgil smiled — a tired grin. "Wasn't his

fault, Mavine. I've fallen on my face a few times myself."

"But you always get up, Virgil. That's one of the things I love about you."

"Well, so far nothing's knocked me down for good. But another service station? Nobody's done that to me before. It looks like those Zipco owners have moved into their trailer. Can the station be far behind?"

"I'm concerned too, Virgil, but let's not worry about it. Least not today." She reached out and took his hands. "It's Christmas Day already."

Virgil looked into her eyes and gently squeezed her hands. What had he done to deserve the gifts he'd been given, the ones right here under the same roof as him? Whatever it was, he wasn't about to argue.

"Merry Christmas, Mavine."

9

The little red teapot was whistling noisily, so Reverend Caudill turned off the burner. The screech immediately died down to a gentle wheeze while he prepared his teacup: one tea bag, one spoonful of sugar, and a splash of milk. Grover always said it looked like dishwater, but Reverend Caudill would only smile. He liked it that way.

The toaster clanked and popped up two slices of Roman Meal, medium dark. With a bit of marmalade and a dollop of butter, it would make a fine breakfast.

Right on schedule, the telephone rang.

"Hello, Madeline. Merry Christmas!"

"I still can't believe what I saw and heard on Christmas Eve! Scriptural error! You can't let something like that go. And your sermons lately! Soft, I tell you! You must convict the sinners of their sin."

"Actually, Madeline, convicting sinners isn't *my* job." He laid the telephone down on the counter and retrieved his toast.

"Then just what is your job?"

"Preaching the gospel and serving the Lord." He stirred the milky liquid, savoring the pungent aroma. "Thank you for calling, Madeline. Merry Christmas."

The old woman was still talking as he hung up the telephone. He'd risen early to get a good start on the day, and he was not about to let Madeline Crutcher spoil his mood.

He'd taken Christmas Day off, except for dinner with the Stacys. Grover and Anna Belle had made him a regular part of their celebration for many years. It was something he always enjoyed, as his only living family was a nephew at Bible college. The teapot, short and stout like in the children's song, had been their gift to him.

They'd had a lovely evening, and he'd had the chance to ask a few questions. Yes, the couple seated in the rear on Christmas Eve was almost certainly the Alexanders. JoAnn had been in the store a time or two, it seemed, and Anna Belle's description matched the woman Reverend Caudill had seen.

And he'd seen the trailer next door. Pink as a Pepto-Bismol bottle, gaudy, and hard to miss. He had new neighbors.

Well. Later today, it would be time for a visit.

The weather had turned markedly cooler, with a brisk and biting wind out of the north. Reverend Caudill, bundled in his overcoat and hat, was surprised by the sound of his tapping on the trailer's door. He'd been gentle and discreet, but instead of the solid wooden sound he'd expected, it sounded more like a child banging on a pie pan. The wreath on the door shifted slightly at his knock.

A young woman in ill-fitting pedal pushers answered. "Yes? Reverend — Caudill?"

"That's right. I don't believe we've actually met."

"No, I don't think we have. I'm JoAnn Alexander." She offered her hand. "Do come in, Reverend."

He took her hand gently and politely. "I don't want to impose — is your husband here?"

"Sorry, but Neil — Cornelius — has gone into Quincy to see about something to do with the station." She glanced at her watch. "I expect him back anytime now."

"Thank you." Visiting a woman alone was always awkward, and something he tried to avoid. But with Cornelius on his way home,

95

he'd make an exception.

"I'm sorry, but the only seat we have is at the dinette."

"Oh, that will be fine." He took his seat and looked around. The furnishings, to put it mildly, were sparse. The living room featured a small dinette with two chairs, a small chest of drawers with a missing knob, and several unopened boxes. "I saw you at our pageant on Christmas Eve. I'm so happy you came."

"I'm glad too, Reverend. And I'm so sorry that we had to leave early. I'm expecting, you see, and sometimes —" she drew a breath — "a woman becomes uncomfortable."

"I see. No apology necessary. I hope you and Cornelius enjoyed the evening." At the words *and Cornelius,* he saw a fleeting change in her expression. Dismay? Pain? Anxiety? "Hopefully you can return for worship on Sunday morning. We'd make you most welcome."

"I'd love to." She looked to the window. "And I would like for Neil to come as well. But . . ."

So. Cornelius might have been the less comfortable of the two in the back row. A different direction, maybe? "Where do you and Cornelius hail from? Anna Belle at the grocery said she thought you might be from near here."

JoAnn nodded and indicated a couple of nearby towns. "When we got married in September, we knew we'd need to move. So, here we are."

Reverend Caudill could add as well as preach, and a quick calculation told him what he needed to know. Probably a good thing they'd not been there for his series on marriage. But he was now here to offer grace. "And we're so glad you found your way to Eden Hill. Were you part of a church in your hometown?"

"I was. Good people, but . . ." She seemed to search for words again. "They didn't seem to like Neil very much. And I'm not sure he liked them either. We didn't have a church wedding."

Footsteps sounded on the little metal stairway, followed by the squeak of the door hinge. Reverend Caudill stood as the young man he had seen on Christmas Eve stood in the small doorway.

"Reverend Caudill? What a surprise."

"Delighted to make your acquaintance. I was telling JoAnn how good it was to see you at our time together on Christmas Eve."

Cornelius smiled and shook the pastor's hand. "JoAnn enjoyed it very much."

The conversation shifted to general pleasantries. Cornelius seemed more at ease talking about his new Zipco station, while JoAnn became quieter. After a couple of minutes, Reverend Caudill picked up his hat. "I must be going, but might I offer a prayer for you folks?"

Both said yes almost simultaneously. JoAnn appeared relieved, and Cornelius managed a polite smile.

The reverend prayed aloud for the couple, but in his own heart, he offered an unspoken parallel line of supplication, knowing today's would be the first of many visits. What they both needed was God's grace. And Reverend Caudill would do whatever it took to make sure that grace was what they heard and saw from the First Evangelical Baptist Church.

Mavine hated washdays. Even with the help of her shiny new Maytag, it meant a long day. This morning's snow made matters worse. Instead of drying the laundry outside, she would have to use the indoor clothesline. It sagged in the middle, so she would have to hang her dresses on the ends. And somehow, a porch decked with dangling underthings was just inappropriate in a way the line in the yard wasn't. On top of it all, there were seemingly endless loads of ironing.

She sighed and turned to the domestic task at hand. Virgil would be home for lunch soon, and she'd need to have something ready for him to eat. Or, like Vee, he could fend for himself at his noon meal. Mavine looked at the basket of dirty clothes, and out the window at the snow that was still coming down. With a twist of the taps she turned on the water, measured some Oxydol in a tin cup, and started tossing soiled things from the wicker basket into the Maytag. Lunch would just have to wait. The laundry certainly wasn't going to wash itself.

As the last of the basket's contents disappeared into the sudsy water, her nose began to tingle from a pungent odor. An acrid, smoky scent. Had she left the iron plugged in after pressing her clean things? Mavine raced up the stairs in a panic.

The scent was strong as she rounded the landing. When she reached the upstairs hallway, the source was clear. Wisps of gray smoke were curling from beneath Vee Junior's bedroom door. Mavine flew into the room in a panic.

"Virgil T. Osgood Jr.! What are you doing!"

The cigar was fat, brown, and smelly. Vee

was startled, wide-eyed, and in serious trouble. Mavine promptly snatched the abomination from the boy's mouth and, holding the disgusting thing at arm's length, marched it to the bathroom and dropped it into the toilet. It sizzled as she pushed the handle, hoping it wouldn't clog the plumbing.

She took a deep breath and strode back into Vee's room, where she discovered him on his bed, shoulders crumpled, cowed and contrite. A cigar! How could he do such a thing? With effort, she tried to remain patient and calm.

"Vee, you know better than this. I'll decide later on your punishment, but I can tell you this. Your snow day that you were so happy about is going to be a reading day. Frank and Eddie will be riding their sleds without you today."

"Aw, Mom."

"And just wait until your father gets home."

Mavine descended the stairs one slow, deliberate step at a time. Doing laundry could sour even her best mood. It could also set her mind to wandering in places it shouldn't go. About what was, and what might have been. Maybe it was just the Clorox. And now she had this discipline matter to contend with.

Mavine paused and scanned her bookshelf, looking for the punishment to fit the crime. She considered reading the classics a positive discipline for Vee. Virgil, on the other hand, usually considered a trip behind the henhouse more appropriate when needed.

She'd always hoped to become a teacher. An English teacher. Reading and literature had been her best subjects in school. Straight A's in both. Mrs. Randall had introduced her to the classics, and she'd been smitten from the first day. Mrs. Tandy, the librarian at the little four-room high school, would bring her books from the public library in Quincy. And when the bookmobile came once a month, the appearance of the little white panel truck was the highlight of the week. Some of the other students had teased her, called her "teacher's pet." But she didn't mind.

She wanted to go to the teachers college. She wanted to be the next Mrs. Randall.

And then she fell in love, and the war came. Marriage. A son.

A son who couldn't care less about the classics, and apparently preferred stogies to fine literature. Mavine returned to the kitchen and sank into the chair with her head in her hands.

Virgil's morning had been busy. By the time he broke for lunch, he'd already used his wrecker to pull Arlie's truck from the ditch and Mrs. Crutcher's Buick out of the creek, spent an hour trying to find brake shoes for Grover's Plymouth so he and Anna Belle could drive south for their vacation, and listened to Sam Wright spout off something about surviving an avalanche in the Himalayas.

Mavine was seated at the kitchen table when he arrived, but the only aromas in the room were soap powder and bleach. The dinette and the stove were clean and bare, with no evidence of cooking or food preparation in sight. And no sign at all of Vee.

"Hello, Mavine. Are we just having sandwiches today?" The washing machine was chugging and sloshing away, so she'd also been working this morning.

"I suppose so. There's bread in the breadbox, and Dixie loaf in the refrigerator." Her voice seemed strained and tired.

He tossed his coat onto the back of his recliner. "You feeling okay, Mavine?"

"Yes, I'm fine. I'm just not hungry right now."

Opening the refrigerator, he grabbed the

milk bottle and a small Tupperware that contained an old package of lunch meat. It popped when he opened it — not a good sign. A quick sniff, a grimace, and he reached for the peanut butter in the pantry.

Virgil sat down across from Mavine, and then remembered his milk still sitting on the counter. He arose and walked back across the room. "Are you sure I can't get you something? There's some leftover soup . . ." His voice trailed off, as he found Mavine not listening. She sat at the dinette and looked out the window.

He retrieved the forgotten milk, spread the peanut butter generously onto a slice of bread, and thought for a minute. Once again, he couldn't think of anything he'd done recently to deserve the cold shoulder, and this year he'd even remembered her birthday gift — early, for a change. Even though it was still over a month away, he had already bought her a nice pair of gloves from Willett's Dry Goods.

Had Mavine come home with yet another *Pageant* magazine? The old one was back on his desk — somewhere. Why couldn't the Glamour Nook subscribe to something like the *Saturday Evening Post*? Norman Rockwell would never get him in trouble with his wife like Betty LaMour did.

103

"Sorry you're not hungry, Mavine. Are you unhappy with me about something?"

"No, not at all, but I *am* unhappy with Vee. He's been a real challenge this morning." With that, Mavine returned to the back porch. Sounds of running water suggested rinsing of some kind, and soon the machine resumed its low rumble. She returned to the table, taking a couple slices of bread on the way past the counter.

"What did Vee do now?"

"I caught him smoking this morning."

"Smoking? Smoking what?"

"A cigar — a big fat one. I suspect he got it through the mail — from an ad in one of those horrible comic books he reads. The men all have blue hair, the women have way too much bosom, and they all use bad grammar. You've seen the mail-order advertisements in the back. Where do you think he got that disgusting thing he took to church last Sunday?"

"Mavine, he's ten years old. He spent his own allowance, and he also got a genuine miniature spy camera and a book about throwing his voice. And he told me it only cost four dollars for everything. Postpaid."

"That's not the point. It's what he did with it."

Virgil tried hard not to smile at the memory. Somehow Vee had placed the whoopee cushion in Toler's chair during the opening hymn. When the song leader sat down after the final notes of the amen, the entire congregation heard the expected result. Toler turned red as a beet, Reverend Caudill gave him a look that would freeze steam, and almost everyone else just tried to keep from laughing. Vee couldn't, so Mavine had hauled him out by the ear. His penance had been to read *The Scarlet Letter*.

"Mavine, boys do stuff like that. I think you get a little carried away sometimes."

"What do you mean, 'carried away'?" Mavine's voice was rising. "Vee needs to behave in church and pay attention to the Sunday sermons. And he needs to know the facts of life."

"He doesn't need to know all of that at his age. Vee asked me what adultery was, and I didn't know quite what to tell him. He thinks it just means being a grown-up, and can't figure out why it's such a sin. Couldn't you just have him read the Hardy Boys or cowboys and Indians or something?"

Mavine stood and returned to her shelf of classic books. "Virgil, I know you don't see the value in classic literature, but it's good for Vee. If I left it up to you, he'd be reading

Zane Grey. Or worse, a Louis L'Amour. But all right then, here's James Fenimore Cooper. So you get your Indians, anyway."

Virgil followed her into the living room and frowned at her choice of reading material. "Mavine, just what are you so unhappy about?"

"Virgil, he was being disobedient and obstinate. Probably sulking up in his room."

Obstinate? Something bad, apparently. "All right, Mavine, so Vee was smoking. He knows better and probably ought to have some kind of punishment for it, but that's no reason for —"

"Virgil, I have such high hopes for our son. He's a smart boy and is making such good grades in school. I want him to go to the university — I've always loved the idea of a university education. To be successful in life. That's why I give him good books to read; I want him to have the same love for literature that I have. To make his world bigger."

"And you think making him read on a snow day is going to help? I have high hopes for him too. The hardest thing for him right now would be to think about his friends having fun out on their sleds while he's stuck in here reading."

She looked to one side, not a good sign.

"Virgil, I kept my schoolbooks after graduation instead of selling them, even though my family could have used the money. They were about the only thing that kept me going with the war on and all. You were stationed at Fort Benning, so you never knew how much they meant to me. Vee's learning to love them too, even if he doesn't realize it yet."

"Vee loves other things right now," said Virgil, "like being a good, healthy kid. I don't see what you're getting at."

"I want Vee to make something of himself, Virgil. Something he'll be proud of. I don't want him to end up like you."

Virgil might as well have been smacked in the face with Mavine's steam iron. He said nothing for several seconds, trying to sort out the words he had just heard. Mavine clapped a hand over her mouth, then dropped the book on the table with a heavy thud, turned away, and buried her face in both hands. She seemed to be trying to say something, but no words were coming out.

For his part, he bit his own tongue, not sure he could trust the words he might say in return. He loved their son too. Didn't she understand that? Somehow, in one sentence, she'd reduced him to a nobody. Anger and confusion welled up inside him, and his thoughts were fuzzy and whirling. Was Mavine angry, hurt, disappointed, or confused? All of these? He couldn't tell, but he knew any response he might make right now would be one he'd likely regret.

Virgil stood, nearly knocking over his chair, only to find himself surprisingly unsteady on his feet. He leaned on the table for balance and took a breath, trying to quench the fires inside and pull his thoughts together into something that made sense. "So, Mavine. Is there something wrong with who I am? I may not have much schooling, and I haven't read all those classy books of yours, but I think I've done pretty well." His voice was rising in both pitch and volume, so he paused, looking for words that wouldn't make matters worse.

"I work hard to put this food on your table, keep you in clothes and buy you the washing machine to put them in. And I've tried my best to be a good husband for the last fourteen years. Is that not enough?"

"Virgil, I didn't mean . . ."

Suddenly, an unexpected sound broke the silence. Both looked at the stairway landing, where Vee had stepped on a squeaky board while eavesdropping. The boy's eyes were wide with fear and confusion, and he turned and ran back up to the second floor.

Virgil felt steadier now, and motioned toward the steps. "And I'd be more than happy to see Vee grow up just like me."

He started for the front door but turned to pick up his forgotten jacket. "I'm going back to work. And tell Vee I said no more cigars!"

Virgil closed the door harder than he should have, shaking the front room and rattling the windows. Hopefully Ticky would be waiting for him with her tail wagging. Right now, he could use a friend.

Mavine sat at the table, absently running a finger along the edge of *The Last of the Mohicans,* waiting for the rinse to end. It did, but she didn't move. Wringing out clothes was not what she wanted to do just then. This was the last load, the one with the sheets and pillow slips in it. It could wait.

Why in the world had she said such a thing to Virgil? She loved him dearly, didn't she? She certainly thought so. Running a service station was a fine thing for Virgil — he never even made it to high school, let alone college. He'd had even less opportunity than she had. Was she wrong to want more for Vee than a life like this? Certainly she was wrong to blame Virgil for it.

On the other hand, her husband made a good honest living. He was right — she and their son had never wanted for anything. Her own mother and father had struggled through the Depression, selling eggs, eating crackers and poke salad. Memories of patched dresses and hand-me-downs, darned socks and slivers of soap wrapped in pieces of burlap from a flour sack were still deeply etched in her mind. Her husband had been through it too, as his father worked hard to keep his own repair shop afloat. Virgil had to drop out of school to help, and then was drafted and served his country.

Mavine shoved the novel across the table, just like she'd done with the *Pageant* a couple of months earlier. Her hands, chapped by laundry soap and dishwater, told a story. Her story. With all her reading, all her dreams, what had she accomplished in life? Was it fair to blame Virgil for her dissatisfaction? Sure, he didn't act like the men in those magazine articles that Gladys had given her. And the recent sermon series by Reverend Caudill had made her feel . . . what? Afraid? It could be the toy service station Vee had received for Christmas, which seemed as though it might limit his potential. Or maybe it was just her.

Mavine sighed. She forced herself up from the dinette, tossed out the paper napkins, and dusted the bread crumbs into the trash. Laundry was waiting and couldn't be put off any longer, even with an argument as an excuse.

The wringer started with a mechanical groan when she flipped the switch. Vee's bedspread was the first to come out of the tub. The fringes were clean again, and the Oxydol had done its job well on the smudge just above Gene Autry's lasso. Through the mighty rollers it ground, water pouring back into the tub from both sides. "Cowboys!" Mavine grumbled to herself as she pitched it over the clothesline on the porch.

Next came a pair of Virgil's work pants. Mavine rubbed the stiff khaki fabric between her fingers and paused. The man who wore these wasn't perfect, but she did love him. And more than that, she realized, he loved and cared for her in every way he knew how. Reaching for the trouser stretcher, she smelled something odd. Burning. Quickly, she turned the wringer off, thinking that perhaps the motor wasn't powerful enough for a full bedspread going through crossways. No, it wasn't coming from the machine. Perhaps . . .

"That Vee," she growled under her breath,

"has done it now. Another — cigar!" She spat the word. "It's *A Tale of Two Cities* for him now, and maybe *War and Peace* too." Mavine ran upstairs, bent on full retribution. She stopped in the doorway and opened her mouth to issue Great Words of Wrath. Nothing came out.

There was no cigar, nor any other vice for that matter. Vee was engrossed in his toy service station, and making engine noises — pretty good ones, too — and it seemed that in spite of her rampage, he still hadn't heard her. One of Virgil's old work caps sat on his head, turned at just the right angle.

The oval rug was spread across the bare mattress, toy cars lined up on the pattern as on a racetrack. The service station that Santa had given him at Christmas fit well in the center of the bed; even the ramp to the upstairs parking deck lined up nicely with the design on the rug. Vee reached into the garage door and pulled out two cars and a pickup truck; the wrecker was retrieved from the top of his bookshelf. The plastic gasoline pumps were set up in front of his imaginary driveway.

Vee pushed the pickup up the ramp and began filling the cars with gasoline and running them around the track, making all the appropriate sound effects. The book jacket from his recent Hawthorne reading had been turned inside out and made into a fine billboard, lettered in pencil. He'd propped it against the front wall, right between the big doors marked *Engine Service* and *Tune-Ups.*

As the Ford in Vee's hand moved to the left, he looked up with a start. His eyes were red and puffy, and she could see streaks down his cheeks.

"Oh hi, Mom. Sorry, I didn't hear you coming." He looked down sheepishly. "Have you and Dad picked out a new book for me yet?"

Mavine smiled and felt a tear or two of her own. Vee had turned back around to put the little cars away, but before he did, she caught a glimpse of him about fifteen inches taller and fifteen years older. The cap was a good fit. The boy was a good fit too. Suddenly, she wanted more than anything else to have Vee Junior grow up to be just like Virgil Senior.

"Oh, Vee," she said, giving him a teary kiss, "I just came up to tell you that I love you, and that maybe I've been a bit too hard on you today."

Vee was visibly embarrassed. "Aw, Mom . . ." He turned his head aside. "It's . . . it's okay. Sorry about the cigar."

"Why don't you have a grilled cheese sandwich and go out and ride your sled? I know the other boys are out — I saw them through the kitchen window, probably heading for the old logging road."

"Okay . . . thanks!"

"Just be back before your father gets home. And wear your mittens!"

Vee was already halfway down the steps. Mavine looked at the elaborate toy, which Vee had left on the bed. The makeshift sign caught her attention again, so she picked it up. *Osgood's Superior Service,* she read.

"Vee," she said, knowing full well that he was out of earshot, "you're going to grow up just like your father. And maybe that's the best thing."

As she walked back into the hallway, she became aware once again of the smoky odor she'd forgotten. On an impulse, she dashed into her bedroom. The iron, left on all morning, had burned a brown mark right into her new pinstripe blouse. *Oh well,* she thought, *it's just been that kind of day.*

"I just don't get it." Virgil related the lunch conversation to Welby, who had had more experience in such things, and the older man just shook his head.

"Doesn't make sense to me either. You've

114

always been a man of good character. I suspect she'll get over it." Fortunately, they were both so busy mounting snow tires that afternoon — "A bit late," Welby had said — that Virgil didn't think any more about it until the long walk up the hill at closing time.

"Well, Ticky, what do you think we'll find?" Ticky, to all appearances, agreed with Welby and just wagged her tail.

What he found was his favorite spaghetti and meatball dinner, candles on the table, and his slippers waiting for him at the door. Mavine threw her arms around him and shouted, "Welcome home!" Virgil felt his face flush and started to say something — then thought better of it. Whatever was happening, he wasn't about to argue.

The spaghetti was delicious, and later on that night, after Vee was sound asleep, things got even better.

10

Reverend Caudill was tired, and he hadn't even finished his breakfast. His phone had rung, as usual, at six this morning. At least he could now answer on the extension he'd had installed in his bedroom, without having to get up and walk to the kitchen. Mrs. Crutcher's telephone call was as reliable as the little Westclox on his nightstand, and didn't need to be wound up every night.

This time, it had been something more about being too gentle in his sermons, and why couldn't he be more like Reverend Lewis Pritchett, whom she listened to on WNTC on Sunday afternoons? And couldn't he please wear something besides that hideous tie in the pulpit? He'd thanked her for her concerns and gently wished her a pleasant day.

Too soft? Well. He'd once liked the evangelist's style and delivery as much as she did. When the man had a good lather going, he could bring the Beast of Revelation right into your living room, with the lake of fire thrown in for good measure. Trouble was, after Reverend Pritchett's last revival in Eden Hill, Reverend Caudill had spent several months patching up the damage he left behind. The man might be a dynamic revival preacher, but a pastor Pritchett wasn't.

Sure, there were several decisions made at those meetings several years back. Four baptisms, including two adults: a good report to his district supervisor. But one couple in the congregation had threatened to leave, claiming the evangelist's edge was just too sharp. He'd had to smooth out some ruffled feathers and bandage up some hurt feelings. And move the church forward.

But he *was* a pastor. And as a pastor, he was responsible for his flock and for their spiritual nurture, wasn't he?

Reverend Caudill reached for the sugar bowl and spooned a generous portion into his oatmeal. The snow was still falling, and he needed more than a cup of tea to give him the strength to shovel the sidewalk and put the chains on his ten-year-old car.

And the tie with the Lord's Prayer printed on it? Well. It had been a birthday gift from his late wife, the first year they were married. Mrs. Crutcher would just have to put up with it.

Cornelius Alexander gathered up the breakfast dishes from the postage stamp–size table and placed them in the sink. JoAnn was having trouble bending now, so it was the least he could do. The well pump started as soon as he turned on the tap. Hot water, one of their few luxuries, began churning up suds in the tiny sink.

"Neil, when are we going to get a telephone? We've lived here for over a month now."

"Soon. Very soon. It was supposed to happen today, but the installer might not be able to get here with the roads being what they are. I haven't forgotten about it, JoAnn. I need to make some telephone calls myself."

"Then I suppose you'll need to go spend the day in Quincy. Again."

Her sarcasm was not lost on him. Hormones, maybe? "I'll need to put the chains on the car and wait until they plow the road. Even then, I'm not sure there's much that can be done today."

"So, another day with no phone." JoAnn Alexander sat in a worn easy chair in the living room. Cornelius had acquired the

cushioned seat — JoAnn called it an "upholstered monstrosity" — from a thrift store in
Lexington for five dollars, and while not
comfortable, it was at least serviceable. The
green in the worn plaid fabric clashed with
the blond paneling, but then again, nothing
else matched either. Someday soon, he assured her, a brand-new couch with real
leather would take its place.

He'd made a lot of promises in their two
years together, and he intended to keep
every one, right back to the first day he ever
saw her. They'd met at a fraternity party
when she was only nineteen. He was twenty-
one, had striking good looks, a ducktail
haircut, and a green Ford Victoria, and he
was an Alexander. What else could a girl
need?

A lot more, it seemed. College hadn't
worked out, but business school meant he
could still follow in the footsteps of his
father and grandfather and become head of
Alexander Motors someday, just like he'd
promised. A dream house, the good life.
Vacations to the beach every summer and a
wardrobe that Liz Taylor would envy. Whatever JoAnn wanted, he intended to give her.

And a houseful of children. They had a
good start on that, at least — a promise
kept. JoAnn had dropped out of nursing

school when she discovered she was pregnant. And when her father found out she was "with child," as he put it, a wedding was hastily arranged: a short courthouse exchange. The whole thing had taken less than ten minutes in front of the justice. Her mother was more sympathetic, offering to let her come home if things didn't work out.

They certainly hadn't worked out the way either one of them had wanted — at least, not yet. In the last year, she'd gone from being a single coed with a promising future to an expectant mother sitting in a trailer in a town that didn't even have a stoplight. And he'd gone from an impoverished student to a business owner. In debt, yes, but with a prosperous future on the horizon. He was sure of it.

But JoAnn wanted it all. Right now. And they'd argued again last night.

He couldn't blame her. The Zipco Super Service wasn't coming together nearly as quickly as he'd hoped, which meant no income. Sure, they were able to draw on a line of credit with Zipco, but everything was behind schedule. And now a winter storm and freezing temperatures. At least they had heat from the little propane furnace.

And a television. The set had come from the same place he'd found the chair, and for only another five dollars. A genuine seventeen-inch Silvertone. It was eleven years old and the little rabbit ears would only get channel three, but it did make a snowy and wobbly picture.

Now if she wanted to watch *Queen for a Day,* at least she could.

With the dishes dried and put away, Cornelius sat at the dinette and shuffled through some scattered papers, trying to decide which phone calls had to be made first. He jotted a list of figures and added up the numbers. The sums were bad. Then he added them again, to the same discouraging result. "JoAnn, we're going to need to take out another loan."

She sighed. "How much more are we going to have to borrow? That line of credit, or whatever you call it, has got to run out sometime."

"It's not a problem. Once Alexander's Zipco Super Service opens, we'll be making lots of money. We'll be able to pay back the loans in no time. Our grand opening will be spectacular, with clowns and giveaways. It'll be the biggest thing Eden Hill has ever seen. Customers will be flocking to our gas pumps, and buying things from inside as well."

"Neil, all you've got now is a trailer on a

cleared lot. I've got a refrigerator but no groceries, a living room but no couch, and a baby coming but no nursery. And," she added, "no telephone to call Mother."

It stung, but she was right. As of this moment, the business was nothing more than a flattened space with little flags, a stack of building materials covered with a tarp and six inches of snow, and a dream in his head. How could something that seemed so right have gone so wrong?

"Trust me, JoAnn."

"I wish I could right now, Neil. I really wish I could."

11

With Virgil fed and happily off to work, Mavine wanted nothing more than to go back to bed. The week had been taxing — she'd taken all afternoon yesterday to prepare meat loaf for dinner and had stayed up to read a bit of Longfellow — so she'd gotten to bed well after her usual bedtime. A short night, after a very trying day. She was tired, pure and simple.

But a morning nap was out of the question. Another snowfall had blown in overnight, but the sun was out now, making it extraordinarily bright outside. The light would certainly keep her awake.

Also, Alma was coming over for lunch today, so she needed to get the kitchen presentable. Virgil's empty breakfast plate went into the sink, along with the last of her bottle of Lux Liquid dishwashing detergent. Something was still bothering her, and she couldn't quite put her finger on it. Virgil hadn't said anything more about Monday's unpleasant luncheon conversation and seemed happy enough since, so . . .

"Mom?"

Mavine was caught quite by surprise. Vee was off school again today, but he was up before noon. Still in his pajamas, though.

"I'm hungry."

Which was not a surprise. At his young age, Vee already had twice the appetite of his father, and even after a big meat loaf dinner and coconut cream pie, the monster in his stomach was apparently growling and demanding to be satisfied.

"Alma will be here soon, and she's bringing our lunch. You don't need anything to eat before then."

"But I'm hungry *now*!"

Mavine sighed. "There are cornflakes in the pantry." She was cooked out, and besides it was high time the boy learned to fix his own breakfast.

"Where's the milk?" Vee had found the box and an empty bowl, and had managed to pour at least some of the flakes into the dish.

She opened the door of the ancient Kelvinator, retrieved the milk bottle, and slammed it onto the table in front of her son. "There." It would be up to him to pour it onto his breakfast and add his own sugar. If he wanted a spoon to eat it with, he'd have to get that too.

Mavine stopped. Why was she being so hard on him today? After all, he was only ten, and there were no cigars in sight this morning. And he was used to having his breakfast made for him. Virgil was also accustomed to having his breakfast, lunch, and dinner made and ready. But if her two men were spoiled, it was because she did the spoiling.

"I'm sorry, Vee. I'm just really tired today."

"It's okay, Mom. What time is Aunt Alma coming?"

"Anytime now." WNTC's eleven o'clock news had begun on the radio. "After lunch we're going to Gladys's to get our hair done. It's Friday, remember?"

Vee finished his cornflakes almost quicker than he'd poured them. Good thing, too. No sooner had Mavine sent the boy upstairs to get dressed and cleared the table than there was a knock on the front door. Alma held a basket with various small containers and several mysterious items wrapped in tinfoil.

"I brought pot roast and potatoes." She removed a covered dish and held it aloft. "Made it this morning. I thought you and

125

Vee might like something besides soup for lunch today."

Mavine followed her into the kitchen. "Thanks, Alma. Vee loves pot roast."

"Hi, Aunt Alma!" Vee had found some blue jeans and a shirt, and had managed to get them onto his body.

"Hello, Vee!" Alma smiled, and Mavine relaxed. "I'll get this, Mavine." Alma found a casserole dish and emptied the roast into it, spacing out the carrots and the potatoes to the sides. The foil shapes enclosed home-made rolls that went onto a cookie sheet for warming. She lit the stove and popped the meal into the oven to reheat.

"Thank you, Alma." Mavine was especially relieved; most of her dishes were still soaking in the sink.

Once the food was warmed through, Mavine removed the pan of rolls as Alma was filling glasses of water. "Vee, would you get the roast? And use pot holders."

Vee Junior dutifully, though awkwardly and begrudgingly, took the dish from the oven and carried it to the table, sloshing some of the beef drippings as he set it down. Mavine was about to light into him for soiling her best tablecloth when Alma intervened with a damp dishrag.

"Thank you for your help, Vee." Alma

smiled at him. "Don't you worry yourself. No harm done. This will come out in the wash."

"Yes, indeed," Mavine said as she withdrew several items from the cabinet drawer. "Thank you for your help. Put these around, please."

Vee grinned, then took the forks and knives from her and scattered them around the table. Mavine smiled; she could teach him the idea of place settings another time.

The door opened, and Welby and Virgil entered to join them for lunch, as promised. They all took their places and said grace, then began the meal. Conversation was pleasant, and Virgil seemed very much himself, although Mavine found herself quiet and with little to say.

Alma passed the food to Virgil, who filled his plate. "Welby tells me the new Zipco place is coming along across the street. Are you concerned at all?"

He wiped his mouth with a napkin, hiding his expression, but his eyes widened. "Yes, I am, Alma. Mr. Alexander is building one of those full-service places like the Shell station in Quincy. Moving kind of slow, though."

"Those things take time, I guess." Alma set the dish on the counter. With five at the small kitchen table, things had become a bit crowded. "And Vee, how are you doing? Are you enjoying your day off from school?"

"Okay, I guess. I've been reading," Vee said after swallowing the last bite of his third helping. Enormous quantities of beef and potatoes proved his cornflakes hadn't hurt his appetite a bit. "Mom, can I go outside and ride my sled now?"

"Yes, but be careful. And wear your heavy coat and mittens!" Her admonition was lost; Vee was already gone.

"Vee's been reading the classics," Mavine offered as their son closed the door, her spirits lifting from the thought. "Someday, maybe it will help him get into a really good college. Maybe even get a scholarship."

Virgil looked startled; he hadn't been able to get his napkin to his face quickly enough. Had she said something hurtful again, without really meaning to?

"Ladies, thanks for inviting us for lunch," said Welby, as he ate the last bite of the tender beef. "This has been delightful!"

Mavine brightened. "You're welcome, Welby. We're always happy to cook for our men."

Virgil agreed, having regained his composure. "Wonderful! Mavine, just think, if you'd become a teacher like you talked

128

about, Welby and I could only have a tasty lunch like this on snow days."

Mavine froze, like she'd been hit by Virgil's tire tool. All morning, she'd thought they'd both been able to come to peace with the discussion earlier in the week. Here Virgil was bringing it back up again. In front of Welby and Alma. Was he retaliating for whatever she'd said to offend him? It hurt, but she was too tired to argue. Did he have any idea what he had just said? Had she been reduced in his mind to simply the cook for a meal she hadn't even made?

She stared — no, glared — at her husband. Yes, he knew, at least now, that he'd said something thoughtless and insensitive. He looked like a farmer who'd just made a bad misstep in a cow pasture.

"May I drive you to Gladys's?" said Welby, nodding toward Alma. "Virgil and I need to get back to work, but I can take you over first."

Alma, who'd placed the leftovers in the refrigerator, answered for both, and without consulting Mavine. "You know, it's such a beautiful afternoon, I think we'll just walk over and enjoy the bright sun. The snowplows have been through this morning and the roads are clear."

"Well, we'll be at Osgood's if you need

us." At that, Welby nodded and eased Virgil out the door on both feet before he could plant one in his mouth again.

Sunny and bright or not, it was still cold. Mavine fetched her heaviest coat and scarf from the hall closet, noting that Vee's mittens were still in the basket. She tied the scarf under her chin, tucking the ends inside her coat.

While her back was turned, a friendly arm circled her shoulders. "What's the matter, Mavine? You haven't been yourself during lunch, or all month, for that matter."

"I'm just tired, Alma. Vee's more of a challenge these days, now that he's in the fifth grade and has to catch the early bus. He has more homework, and Virgil has to get up early and work so hard, and I have to —"

Alma turned Mavine toward her and looked straight into her eyes. "This has nothing to do with Vee. What's really the matter? Is something going on between you and Virgil?"

"Oh, Alma, we're both fine, and Vee is fine. It's just that I'm coming up on my fortieth birthday, and I wonder sometimes if I made the right choices in life. Marrying Virgil, becoming a mother, not trying harder

130

to become a teacher. And wanting Vee Junior to have more opportunities than what Virgil has had. Nobody's fault, of course."

"What brought all this on?"

Immediately the *Pageant* article came to mind, and Mavine chastised herself. After all these months, shouldn't she have put all that foolishness behind her? But if it stuck with her this long, maybe it wasn't foolish after all. "I read an article a couple of months back about men neglecting their marriage as they get — more mature. I showed it to Virgil, but I suspect he barely looked at it. Probably thought it was silly. I still love him, and I suppose he still loves me, but sometimes he just takes me for granted. Like today. And sometimes I wish he saw what I need without me having to tell him." Was she wrong to want that?

"Has Virgil ever done anything to make you doubt that he loves you?"

"No, but he seemed very surprised when I showed him the article. It was by a famous marriage counselor and had a questionnaire to go with it, and I took the test while I was waiting under the dryer. When I answered the questions, the score at the bottom told me that I could expect more of my husband."

"Mavine, Virgil's one of the finest men I

know. You know reading has always been difficult for him. He was probably just confused and didn't understand."

"But I want him to tell me he loves me. And recognize what I gave up to marry him. I need to hear him say it."

Alma took her own coat from the hall closet. "Honey, men don't always know how to say what they feel. He's showing you love the only way he knows how."

"But the article —"

"Mavine." Alma turned to face the younger woman. "Virgil loves you more than you can imagine. Don't waste a single minute doubting that. And he's concerned about the new service station going in. Give him some grace and the respect he deserves. Just love him through it. After all, a good man is far more valuable than a successful man, any day of the week. And one more thing, Mavine."

She stopped to look her older friend in the eyes. In those eyes was great wisdom. "Yes?"

"Never give up on your dreams. Or your dreams for Vee Junior. The good Lord may yet have something in mind for both of you."

The Glamour Nook was not crowded. Lula Mae Prewitt had brought her daughter,

Darlene, for her yearly trim, and Anna Belle Stacy, freshly coiffed and stiffly sprayed, had stayed to chat. Mavine looked around the room, particularly at the framed beauty school certificate hanging on the wall. One of her oldest friends, Gladys Blanford had run her beauty shop from the front of the little yellow house ever since she and Tom married, and before that she did hair out of her ex-husband George's home when they lived across the road next to Welby and Alma. Mavine had always felt it led to their divorce, that George got tired of walking through the house in his boxer shorts to get a beer only to find some woman under the dryer in the hallway. Gladys would only say they were happier apart than they were together. That fact never quite showed in her face, but then again, few things did behind two coats of foundation.

Actually, Gladys always said that George had been the reason she was a beauty operator in the first place. And she told the story often. His job at the power plant had him away for long hours and left her looking for something to do. She'd taken a job in Quincy for a few weeks, but the long drive and the work at the five-and-dime didn't suit her. She'd found a sixteen-week correspondence course from Mr. Timothy's

School of Hair Styling in Hollywood and signed up. Soon thereafter, she'd ordered the advanced course, which taught her how to do coloring and permanents, and came with tinfoil, rollers, and, when she graduated, an elegant embossed diploma.

Gladys opened the Glamour Nook, and most of the women of Eden Hill had become her customers. She was open on Fridays, and sold Avon and Tupperware the rest of the week, but on slow days she would look over her latest lessons. Mr. Timothy had just opened a school of cosmetology, she'd said, and as a *preferred customer,* Gladys was eligible for his introductory offer. Soon she would offer manicures and pedicures along with the usual gossip. Mavine couldn't wait — her nails were a wreck.

Not surprisingly, Eden Hill's newest residents were the topic of conversation.

"I hear she's in the . . . family way, and due real soon," Gladys was saying to Lula Mae while unbraiding Darlene's pigtails. "Anna Belle, you and Grover might want to stock up on diapers and pins."

"It's no surprise at all." Lula Mae hovered over the beauty chair, approving the beautician's handiwork. "You know how the kids are these days, listening to Elvis and all that electric guitar music. Reverend Caudill says it makes you lose all your virtues. I won't let Frank listen to the radio anymore."

Gladys fumbled and nearly dropped the scissors onto the floor. "My husband, Tom, says her husband, Cornelius — I think that's his name — seems like a decent fellow. Met him at the courthouse when he came by to fill out his tax registration. Supposed to start building soon, he says." She removed the smock from Darlene and brushed the clippings from the girl's neck.

"Well, I suppose the deputy sheriff ought to know. Thanks for fitting us in, Gladys. I never could cut her pigtails straight. Afternoon, Mavine. You too, Alma." Lula Mae handed Gladys a couple of bills from her purse, then pulled her coat over her shoulders. "See you all next time!"

Gladys brushed off the chair by the shampoo bowl, readying the space for two of her most loyal customers.

Before long, both women were styled and curled. Mavine was still sitting under the dryer, and Gladys had teased her friend's silver hair into a flattering style. Mavine had picked up the latest *Pageant* and was reading it when the dryer shut off.

"Mavine, let's get you brushed out and ready to go." Gladys helped her climb into the chair. "Doesn't Alma look beautiful?"

Mavine returned Alma's smile. "Indeed, she does." Soon Mavine was finished, and smiling into the mirror herself. "You've done a wonderful job on both of us."

"Thank you. I'll see you both in two weeks. Mavine, you can take the new *Pageant* with you if you'd like."

"No, thank you," said Alma, taking the magazine from Mavine's hands, tossing it onto the table, and ushering the younger woman to the door.

"Mavine, you certainly don't need another of those magazines." Alma fitted her scarf carefully around her fresh hairdo. "I suppose I'll walk on home from here. Thank you for the lunch invitation."

Mavine demurred. "It was your pot roast, Alma. I should be thanking you."

"Oh, it's my pleasure. And just send the dish home with Welby anytime next week."

"I'll do that. Good-bye, Alma, and thanks for your advice."

Alma smiled and started for her own little cottage just across the street. Yes, her older friend's counsel was good and trustworthy. She'd known Alma nearly as long as Virgil had known Welby, and she had deep appreciation for the woman's friendship. A friendship that went far beyond sharing lunch on a cold Friday in January.

The roast? Virgil and Vee would likely eat the leftovers for Saturday's lunch. Between the two, the pan would likely be licked clean and would only need a quick dunk in the sink with a splash of Lux Liquid to get it sparkling.

Dishwashing detergent? Oh dear. She was completely out, having used the last of it this morning. Fortunately, Stacy's Grocery was right on her way home, and she could quickly stop in and still return in time to have the kitchen straightened up before Virgil returned. Her funds were low, but she had a dollar bill left — enough for a squeeze bottle of the bright-pink dish soap.

Anna Belle was minding the counter when Mavine arrived, her hairdo still glued together from a fresh coat of Aqua Net. Not surprisingly, the store was quiet. Grover, clad in his usual greasy apron, was helping the only other customer retrieve an item from a top shelf at one side. She couldn't see the woman clearly, nor did she recognize the voice.

The Lux was right on the shelf where she expected, near the Duz and the Oxydol. She also grabbed a loaf of butter-top bread — Virgil's favorite — and a pound of packaged ground beef from the meat cooler. The total was well over a dollar, but with the change in her coin purse she could just make it. Tucking the bottle of detergent in her elbow, she walked around to the cash register. Grover spoke and waved as he went back behind the meat counter; she could only nod without dropping something.

A young woman stood at the register, chatting with Anna Belle. Her hair was tied back in a simple ponytail. There were several items on the counter, including a tin of Spam, a jar of Tang, and some cans of beans.

"That's two dollars and eighty-eight cents." Anna Belle pulled back the handle on the register, ringing the bell and allowing the drawer to spring open.

The shopper rummaged in her worn handbag. "I'm . . . so sorry. I'm a bit short. I'll put the pinto beans back."

"Oh, don't worry about it." Anna Belle slid the can into a paper bag along with the other purchases. "I think Grover put the peanut butter on sale this week, so you've got just enough."

"Thank you so much, Mrs. Stacy. We really appreciate it."

Anna Belle handed her customer a few coins and the paper bag. "No problem at all. It's been a delight to see you today. Oh, have you met Mavine Osgood?"

The woman turned and faced Mavine.

138

Young. Pregnant. Exactly as Gladys had described her.

There was an awkward pause. The younger woman looked up and down before offering, "It's a pleasure to meet you, Mrs. Osgood. I'm . . . JoAnn. JoAnn Alexander."

Mavine felt a wash of emotion and a surprising chill. The armload of groceries needed both hands, so she merely nodded as she placed her purchases on the counter.

"Good to meet you . . . too." She tried to smile. Tried very hard.

Anna Belle took the items from Mavine's hands and lined them up. "JoAnn's husband, Cornelius, will be running the new Zipco station."

"So I hear." Mavine looked for any sign of pleasure in JoAnn and found none. "When do you . . . expect to open?"

"Soon, Cornelius says." JoAnn slung her own purse onto her shoulder, tucked the grocery bag under her opposite arm, and moved awkwardly toward the door. "Very soon . . . he says."

Mavine wasn't sure, but thought she saw a lump rise in JoAnn's throat.

"I'll get that for you, Mrs. Alexander." Anna Belle had already stepped from behind the counter and opened the door.

"Thank you, Mrs. Stacy. And please thank

Mr. Stacy for us as well." JoAnn hesitated for a moment. "A pleasure to meet you, Mrs. Osgood."

Mavine, her hands finally free, gave a feeble wave.

The air that blew in was as cold as Grover's meat freezer. Along with her attitude, she realized. So this was the competition. The woman seemed harmless enough, sad even. Beans and Spam? Yet Virgil had seemed worried about the Zipco station. And he probably was right. . . .

"Mavine?" Anna Belle was behind the counter again, and had already checked and bagged her groceries. "One dollar and seventy-six cents. You okay, Mavine?"

"Yes, I'm fine." She handed over the dollar bill and squeezed the little coin purse for the balance. Nickels and pennies fell onto the counter, with one rolling off onto the floor.

"Sorry. I'm . . ."

"I'll get it, Mavine." Anna Belle scooped the coins into her hand, giving back a dime and a penny in change. "Why don't you go get some rest before Virgil gets home. You look like you've had a long, hard day."

"I think I will, Anna Belle." Yet another hard day.

12

Cornelius was enjoying his breakfast, a fine morning meal of his usual fried Spam and soft-scrambled brown eggs. JoAnn had learned to make good coffee, and his glass of Tang, while not quite orange juice, was tasty. She usually drank canned apple juice and ate bacon instead of the saltier canned meat that he preferred.

"Neil," she said, "I'm so relieved the telephone is finally in. Just in case . . ." She spread her fingers on her expanding middle. "Just in case something were to happen."

"Like what? The doctor says you're doing just fine."

"Well, I always worry."

JoAnn worried really well. She worried about the baby; she worried about their new service station; she worried their trailer would roll down the hillside into the creek. Someday, they'd build their dream house right here: a modern brick split-level with a front porch. But for now, be it ever so humble, this was home for Cornelius and JoAnn.

"Everything will be all right, JoAnn."

"Promise?"

"Trust me."

Cornelius was gratified to sit behind a real desk instead of their rickety dinette, even if the massive pile of papers in front of him still left him frustrated and unclear where to begin. He'd spent a full day back in early December arranging for a plumber, a septic tank specialist, an electrician, and the telephone company to take care of the details. These things were needed for both the mobile home and the business, of course, but no, it couldn't be all done at once, they said. It seemed that the electrician had to arrange for a pole to be moved, the plumber and the septic man both had to dig ditches, and everybody expected to be paid on the spot. The building and the gasoline pumps couldn't be built until everything else was in place, and a station with no building and no gasoline for sale was just a lot of bills, invoices, and bank notices. Which was precisely what he'd been looking at as the New Year dawned.

But now, at the end of January, and with

another advance from the friendly Zipco people, he had a building, lights, hot water, and restrooms. And telephones. The gasoline pumps and their underground tanks would still need to wait until a thaw, as the ground was now solidly frozen. He'd waited this long; what were a few more weeks? As long as he was open before the baby came, they'd be fine.

Today was his day to hire a mechanic, and a friend from high school was his prime candidate. Last he'd heard, the man had gotten married and moved to Quincy. Cornelius was reaching for the phone when it rang.

"Neil, it's JoAnn. The toilet is leaking again and you need to fix it. Now. When an expectant mother has to go she has to go. Now."

"Why don't you come here and use the restroom at the station?"

JoAnn sighed. "Neil." Her words were rapid and clipped. "Can we at least have a working toilet in our own home?"

"I'll fix it. Yes, now." Couldn't at least one thing go right? He tossed the phone book on the desk, knocking several items to the floor. Why did he get the impression his reception at the pink trailer would be as cold as the draft that blew under his door?

143

■ ■ ■ ■

Three hours, a shower, and a change of clothes later, the bathroom in their mobile home was patched but functional. He picked up the phone again and gave the operator the number for his old friend Wrenchy. Several rings later, Wrenchy's wife, Janet, answered. No, Paul — Cornelius had never known his given name — wasn't there right now, but he was hoping to be out of prison on good behavior soon. Could Cornelius maybe call back in a few weeks? He wished them good fortune and hung up the phone.

It was now early afternoon, and he was hungry and tired. He'd lost the entire morning, and still had no mechanic, no parking lot, but only a pile of bills several inches thick on a used gray metal desk that no longer seemed quite the luxury it did just a few hours ago. At least the place had a roof, and he had heat from the bottled gas stove in the corner. Whatever. He might as well go home and check on JoAnn and have some lunch.

He jumped at the knock. It wouldn't be JoAnn — she would call first. "Come in!"

The door opened slowly to a tall, slender woman clutching a purse. Behind her, and somewhat shorter and less imposing, stood a stocky and balding man holding a brown grocery sack with a slight stain on the bottom. The apron he wore was blowing about in the chilly January air, and looked as if it may have been white at one point but hadn't been washed in weeks. The woman was first to speak.

"Hello! You must be Mr. Alexander?"

Cornelius hesitated for a moment, and then remembered Customer Relations 101 from business school — and page thirty-four of the Zipco handbook. "That's right, Cornelius Alexander. The Third. My wife calls me Neil, but you may call me Cornelius. Please come in." He stood and reached for her offered hand, wondering how they had learned his name.

"I'm Anna Belle Stacy, and this is my husband, Grover. I — we — run Stacy's Grocery up on the corner. We've met your wife, JoAnn, but we'd like to welcome you to Eden Hill as well, Mr. Alexander."

"Thank you." Grover and Anna Belle, wasn't it? The woman was pleasant enough, smartly attired in a light-blue tailored suit. Her husband, who had yet to speak, was at least smiling.

Anna Belle continued, "We have a little gift for you and JoAnn to help you feel at home. If there's anything we can do to make this time easier for you, just let us know."

Grover held out the bag, still smiling. "I hope you like venison biscuits. We have more back at the store."

Cornelius managed another smile, thanked them kindly, and took the greasy bag from Grover's outstretched hand.

"We'll be going along now," said Anna Belle, "but do come see us at the store sometime. JoAnn told us about your upcoming new arrival. Congratulations to you both!"

"Thank you." Cornelius nodded and waved, but they were already gone. He looked at the bag of venison biscuits and whatever else it was and placed one hand beneath it to catch a drip before it landed on his trousers. The liquid looked like motor oil. Maybe this Grover fellow was selling this stuff wholesale to that rinky-dink service station across the street . . .

Across the street! He set the bag on a shop towel, wiped his hands on another, grabbed his coat and hat, and hurried out.

"Name's Welby, Mr. Alexander, just Welby. I saw Grover and Anna Belle over at your place. I hope they made you feel welcome here in Eden Hill."

"Please just call me Cornelius, Welby. And the Stacys were very warm indeed," he offered. "In fact, in a roundabout way, they suggested I come over. I noticed you had just finished with a customer and thought I might have a chat with you."

"Me? How can I be of help to you, Mr. Alexan . . . Cornelius?"

"You're the mechanic here?"

"That's right. Have been for years."

"Then I'd like to make you an offer."

"An offer?" Welby wiped his hands on a rag. "And what would that be?"

"I'd like you to come and work for me at the new Zipco Super Service. You'd be working for a nationally recognized brand, with the possibility of advancement. I'll offer a week's paid vacation and a competitive salary — and we provide Zipco uniforms complete with a hat."

Welby smiled. "Why would I leave Virgil? I'm very happy here, and I can take off and go fishing on a nice day if I want to. I can even take Vee Junior with me."

"I'll pay you 25 percent more than what Mr. Osgood is paying you. I need a good mechanic like you."

Welby grinned. "Well, I'm not sure you know how much that is, but Virgil has always taken good care of me, just like his father before him. I'm sorry to disappoint you, Mr. Alexander, but I'll just stay with Virgil."

"Will you think about it?"

"Already did. You seem like a fine man, Mr. Alexander, but Virgil and Mavine and Vee Junior are like family to Alma and me. I hope you'll have family like that someday. Is there something else I can help you with?"

Cornelius hadn't expected *this,* and it took him several seconds to manage a courteous smile. "Well, thanks anyway." As an afterthought, he added, "Would you by chance have a half-inch bolt to fit a toilet flange?"

"No, we're fresh out. Sorry. You might check at the tractor shop on the other side of town. They carry a line of hardware. Farm equipment, you know."

Virgil cleaned a spot on the front window of Osgood's with a shop towel. The dirt wouldn't give up willingly, so he used the same spray bottle he used on windshields. Several pulls of the trigger later, and the grime relaxed its grip and came off on the cloth. No customer was at the pump, but Welby was having a long and extended conversation with someone. The glass still wasn't as transparent as he'd like, but he could make out some details.

Welby was speaking to a younger man; seemed to have a ducktail haircut. After the conversation, the man walked across the road to the Zipco station and opened the front door.

Cornelius Alexander. Why had he been talking to Welby? Was he spying? Trying to find a crack or two in Osgood's armor?

He'd heard of such things. As soon as the old feed store lot was sold last fall, Virgil called his Army buddy Mac, who ran a service station up in a city a couple of hours away. He'd run into him at a convention several years back, and Mac had been through a rough stretch. Three different stations in as many years, all of which had failed. "Competition nearly put me under," he'd said. "Don't let the other guy even get near you."

But then again Mac was also on his third marriage. One for each station, it seemed. But was there any wisdom in his words?

And more frightening still, was there a connection between a bankrupt business and a marriage on the rocks? No, he couldn't let it happen. He just couldn't.

Welby came back in through the side door, closing it quickly behind him. He was grinning, as usual, and whistling a catchy tune. Virgil was waiting, and not smiling.

"Was that who I think it was?"

The mechanic walked toward the Warm Morning stove in the corner of the garage and rubbed his hands together over the front. "Cornelius Alexander, if that's who you mean. Nice fellow."

"What was he doing over here? Sneaking around?"

"He had a question, and I gave him an answer. That's all. And, no, he wasn't sneaking anywhere."

Virgil hesitated. "Welby, I'm concerned about the competition the Zipco will bring, and the last thing I need is to have him poking around Osgood's."

"And I'm concerned about you, Virgil." He poured two cups of coffee from the big percolator and handed one to Virgil. "You've always been good-natured and easygoing. Not much ever got you excited or worried. But lately you seem to be obsessed by this Zipco thing. You're unraveling like a bad fan belt."

"But I have to be worried. My friend Mac says . . ."

"I'm not worried about what Mac or anybody else says. You're letting yourself get worked up over somebody else's experience, somebody else's reaction. Relax, Virgil. You're better than that."

Welby's words were deceptively calm but had the ring of truth. Deep truth. The trouble was, he wasn't ready to hear it. Not yet, anyway.

But he trusted his friend and mechanic. Welby had been through more than he had in life, and knew him better than anyone except Mavine. If Welby said he was going overboard with this competition thing, he was probably right. But still . . .

"Welby, I just need to know that you're with me in this. That you're on my team."

Welby smiled, with a little bit of a wink. "I'm with you more than you know."

After two greasy biscuits and a quick telephone call to JoAnn, Cornelius locked the door of the Zipco and walked the two blocks across town.

Ray's Farm Equipment Sales and Service consisted of little more than a wooden barn and a cluttered, weed-filled lot scattered with tractors, hay balers, and various other agricultural machines. Ray's advertised, *We service all brands,* and the varieties littering the yard seemed to prove it. He should have thought of this before — not much difference between a car and a tractor. They both had tires, an engine, and needed mechanics.

Nobody was at the counter, but he could hear voices coming from a room in the back. The door was ajar, so he walked in to find several young men gathered, all dressed in work shirts. A game of pool was in full swing on a large, rickety table.

He watched for a few seconds and approached the nearest chap. "Who's your best man?" he asked. The fellow pointed to a lanky player who, with cue in hand, was about to place the number four ball in the side pocket. "That's Charlie . . . He's the best one here."

Cornelius introduced himself to the player, a likable fellow about his own age. "Charlie," he said, "I'm prepared to make you an exciting offer to get in on the ground floor of something big. Let's chat over a friendly game. A bet of, say, five dollars?"

Two hours later, Cornelius returned to his makeshift office a very happy Zipco owner. He was five dollars poorer but had found his half-inch bolt and had hired his new mechanic. He hadn't bothered to say the Zipco station was behind schedule; it didn't seem necessary. Charlie would be starting in three weeks — well before the grand opening. And he'd gotten him for much less than what he thought he'd have to pay.

■ ■ ■ ■

Across the street at Osgood's, Virgil was positioning a jack under the rear of Madeline Crutcher's Buick when Arlie's farmhand poked his head in the doorway. "Is Welby here?"

"What can I do for you, Charlie?" Welby said as he walked out from the storeroom with a brake cylinder.

Charlie took his hat off and scratched at his head. "Well, turns out I need to learn something about engines."

Virgil placed the wheel in the corner. "Arlie got you working on his tractors now?"

"It's not Mr. Prewitt. He works me hard, but he's been good to me. Strangest thing, I stopped in at Ray's for a couple rounds of eight ball with the boys, and some guy comes in, asks who's best, loses five bucks to me, and then offers me a job fixing cars. Don't quite get it, but I'm not about to argue."

Virgil felt the blood rise to his face, and he started to say a few choice words when Welby cut him off with a chuckle. "Sure, Charlie. I'll get you started with the basics."

Sunday morning had turned to midday, the

153

organist had finally finished her postlude, and Reverend Caudill stood at the back of the sanctuary to greet his congregation and offer his personal benediction. The crowd was smaller than usual; the bitter cold had no doubt kept some of his parishioners at home. Unfortunately, Madeline Crutcher was not one of them.

Grover Stacy took the pastor's hand in both of his, his whole face animated and beaming. "I don't know what's gotten into you, Reverend, but you've been in fine form lately. There are probably some who expect to be shouted at, but I'm getting a lot more out of your sermons. Really forward thinking. I've got some things to chew on over the next few days." He pumped the handshake one last time, then slipped out, as Anna Belle was pulling him by the sleeve. Reverend Caudill was delighted, but perplexed. He'd never heard such effusions from anyone, let alone Grover.

But the warm glow didn't last, as a familiar and irate voice rose from the nearly empty sanctuary. The reverend turned to see Madeline Crutcher shuffling toward him, eyes wide and piercing. She'd apparently waited in her usual seat until the church had emptied so she could lash out with as much force and vigor as her age and stature could muster. Instinctively, he took a step back-ward.

The old woman lit into him while she was still on the move. "Some people may enjoy this little fireside talk you call preaching, but I say it's coddling. Nothing but pablum, I tell you! We need the power of the gospel, Pastor, not some namby-pamby drivel. You'll be hearing from me tomorrow."

Without waiting for a response — not even expecting one, surely — the woman strode out the door and down the steps toward her Buick. Midway to the car she turned. "And don't think others don't feel the same way I do."

Well. Reverend Caudill's shoulders slumped a bit as he moved to turn off the lights and noticed that Virgil Osgood was still in the sanctuary, picking up stray bul-letins and a few peppermint wrappers from the pews.

Virgil scratched at the back of his neck as he approached, then looked out toward the receding Buick even as he addressed the pastor. "I don't quite know what pablum is, but I seem to recall someplace in the Bible — don't remember where exactly — when an earthquake was quiet and God's whisper came through loud and clear. Me, I like this new style. Makes the Bible seem more personal and meaningful, not so long ago and far away. Mavine feels the same way, and so does Vee. So whatever you're doing, keep it up." He dropped the church's leavings into the wastebasket by the rear doors and stepped through them.

And Eugene Caudill gave thanks to God for simple encouragements — a warm gift on a cold day. And for the challenges? Well. Harder, but he'd certainly try.

13

Mavine arrived right on time for her appointment at the Glamour Nook on Friday afternoon and was surprised to find the Closed sign still hanging in the window. The door was unlocked, so she peeked inside. Nobody was there. "Gladys?"

"Mavine?" The voice came from back in the kitchen. "I'll be right there. Sorry, I canceled my earlier appointments and forgot you and Alma were coming this afternoon."

"I can come back later . . ."

"No, no, I'm just . . . getting some things together. Come on in and have a seat. I've added some more magazines to the table."

"I'll be right here when you're ready. No hurry."

Mavine hung her coat on the hook next to the Nook's growing display. For years, Gladys had decorated her salon with various interesting items from around the world. After the holidays, she'd taken down the candles and the little German figurines, replacing them with her usual bulletin board covered with exotic postcards. Mavine paused to admire the colorful one from Mexico and the shiny new souvenir folder from the Seattle World's Fair before choosing a magazine and climbing into the swivel chair by the shampoo bowl.

"I'll be out in a minute." Shuffling sounds were heard, along with drawers opening and closing.

Curious, she thought. Gladys had always been ready and waiting when she arrived, eager in her pink cotton uniform and matching smock with the little happy scissors sewn next to her name. This afternoon Gladys seemed to be busy about something she didn't want Mavine to see. Suddenly it occurred to her: Of course! Her birthday was coming, and Gladys had something special planned!

Mavine was surprised when Gladys appeared a couple of minutes later, still in her housecoat. "I'm sorry — I'm not really myself today. You want your usual hairdo?"

"Uh . . . sure." Maybe this wasn't a birthday surprise after all. Hoping her disappointment didn't show, she climbed into the chair. "But can you tease it up a little more on top?"

"I'll see what I can do."

Gladys made ready, pulling pink bottles from a shelf next to the sink and placing various scissors and combs into a plastic tray. She fumbled for something, dropped it with a clatter, and groaned.

Mavine looked up, and for the first time saw her friend's face. Her eyes were red and puffy, and Avon was smeared down her cheeks. Her hands were shaking. No, certainly not a celebration.

"Are you all right, Gladys? We can do this another time."

"I'm fine, it's . . . I've not had a good day, that's all."

Something was definitely wrong. Maybe she and Tom had had a fight. Whatever it was, Gladys probably wouldn't tell. Her fingers seemed to relax as they worked her scalp, and Gladys seemed noticeably calmer now.

"How's Virgil doing?"

Mavine relaxed as well. "Just fine, Gladys. He's looking forward to spring, just like everybody else in town. He and Welby are already talking about going to the lake. How's Tom?"

"Couldn't be better. He's working security at the basketball game in Quincy tonight."

Gladys's hands seemed steadier, which was a relief since they now held a pair of scissors. "He'll also be adding some additional hours this spring as part-time game warden."

"That sounds wonderful, Gladys." Well, it didn't seem like a problem with Tom. Maybe just a bad time. She wondered if the beautician had ever tried Cardui elixir, which had always helped her during those dates she circled on the calendar each month. Soon they were finished, hairpins and curlers were inserted without incident, and she was ready for the dryer.

With a knock on the door, Alma arrived, right on schedule. Greetings were exchanged, and Alma took her place in Gladys's beauty chair. Mavine moved to the dryer, tipped the hood down, and set the timer. An article on Natalie Wood from an April *Photoplay* had captured her attention, and with luck she'd have time to finish it while her hairdo set.

The dryer shut off just as Mavine finished the magazine piece — she was quite surprised to read that Natalie and Robert Wagner had divorced. She'd gotten rather absorbed in the scandalous romantic details and slowly became aware of the conversation in the room.

Without the rushing noise from the dryer, she could hear Alma talking gently and Gladys sobbing. They had moved to two of the waiting room chairs, and Alma was holding the beautician's hand.

Mavine lifted the hood of the dryer chair and joined the two women. She sat and grasped Gladys's other hand. Gladys clasped Mavine's hand tightly.

"There, there. Why don't you just tell us about it?" Alma was digging in her purse and produced a small package wrapped in cellophane. "It's okay, Gladys, whatever it is. It's just us. We're your friends."

"It's hard for me, and you may think it's silly." She took several of the offered tissues and drew a deep breath.

"I always thought of her as my Depression baby," Gladys began. "I never did feel as guilty as Mama wanted me to, since I did it for my family in the first place. Right before the war began, I was working at the soda fountain at the old Rexall drugstore in Quincy. You remember, Mavine?"

She nodded, but clearly Gladys was about to reveal something she'd never known. The beautician clutched her hand even tighter.

"Papa had died the year before, and then Mama lost her job at the switchboard. Everybody was saying the Depression was

161

over, but that sure wasn't true for our family. We were dirt poor. My father had a hard time finding work. The grocery he started was barely making it, and the family had to run it after he passed. Mama was never happy again after that."

Mavine wasn't sure what to do next and felt bad. Gladys was clearly hurting, and she'd been blind to her pain. Had been too involved in a silly magazine article to even notice. So she did something she hadn't expected. She prayed. She didn't even know what to say, so she just reached out in her own mind and wordlessly asked the Almighty to come close.

Gladys continued. "I was pretty naive back then. One afternoon a young man I'd never seen before came into the soda fountain, and he took a shine to me. He said he was on his way home to Louisiana from a college up north somewhere and had stopped in for a chocolate malted. He promised me five dollars and a ride in his Ford roadster, so I agreed. We drove to a place in the country where there was a barn and straw, and he gave me the money on the way back. I took it home and gave it to Mama to pay the rent. It was a long time before I understood why Mama was so angry and called me such awful names.

Before long I began to show, and Mama sent me to Florida to live with my aunt Ellie. Nobody around here ever knew."

Mavine's head was whirling in amazement. Poor woman! Gladys had kept such a secret all these years, even from her closest friends.

"Several months later, the war was on, and she was born — a seven-and-a-half-pound girl with blue eyes and a full head of beautiful curly blonde hair. Healthy and strong. Mama signed the adoption papers, and I came back to Eden Hill to finish school. I never saw the baby or her father again. Never even knew his name."

Alma stroked Gladys's shoulder and asked gently, "So what brought all of this up today? Did Tom say something?"

"No. I've never told Tom about it. And he's gone until late tonight."

"So what happened?"

Gladys couldn't answer. Finally, with trembling hands she reached in the pocket of her robe and pulled out an envelope. "This came in the morning mail. I guess I always knew this day would come."

Alma looked it over and showed it to Mavine. "Well, what does this have to do with you being all in a dither?"

"Look at the postmark. It's from Florida.

I understand they open the adoption records after a child reaches legal age. She was born twenty-one years ago last week."

"So you're afraid to open the envelope? Afraid it's from your daughter?"

"Yes." Gladys eagerly accepted a few more Kleenex that Alma found in her purse. She dabbed at her eyes. "I'm afraid she'll hate me, I'm afraid I won't be able to love her after what I've done, and I'm afraid Tom will leave me when he finds out. That's what George did when I told him. Said he didn't want no 'used woman.' " She spat the words and started sobbing again.

Mavine fought back tears and finally quit trying. All three women were crying. All these years she'd been a friend to Gladys, and she never knew the pain her friend had gone through, the suffering. But now she did, and it explained so many things. And her heart broke for her.

Gladys cried quietly for a couple more minutes before becoming calmer, Alma and Mavine stroking her arm and shoulder.

Alma squeezed her hand. "Honey, did I ever tell you about Danny?"

"No. Who's . . . Danny?"

"Danny was our son. Welby and I wanted a child, but it just never quite happened. The doctors didn't seem to know why, so we kept . . . trying. Finally, I conceived, and I was the happiest woman in the world. Welby was still working for Mr. H. C. Osgood then, and we felt we had a wonderful family life ahead of us. We'd picked names: Julia Marie for a girl and Daniel Welby for a boy."

"When Danny was born, we knew right away something was wrong. He was all blue and quiet, and the nurses ran down the hallway with him. The doctors started giving me oxygen and a blood transfusion. I don't remember too much right after that except the doctors had to do something to me, to save my life, that meant I could never have children again. Danny lived about two hours — something about his lungs wasn't right.

"He was a beautiful baby. We buried him with a little stuffed bear — a gift from Mr. Osgood. How I loved — and still love — that child! And Welby did too — it just broke his heart. Danny would have been twenty-nine this year. I often wonder what he'd be doing if he'd lived."

Gladys began sobbing again.

"Oh, honey, I'm not trying to make you cry even more."

"You still love Danny that much?"

"Oh yes. I'm not trying to be morbid or

anything like that. I'm saying that, knowing how much I still love my departed Danny, I know you love your living daughter whose name you don't even know, even if you gave her up twenty-one years ago. And I'll bet she loves you too — and so will Tom."

"But what will Tom think of me?"

"Now don't you worry about that. Tom loves you even more than you know. I'm a pretty good judge of such things. And I think he might just like to have a stepdaughter."

Mavine sat quietly, her mind and emotions whirling. She'd heard words like this before, from the same woman who was comforting and ministering to her friend. She was overcome with love for her friend Gladys, who'd lived for over twenty years with a scandalous secret, and respect for Tom, who would no doubt love Gladys just the same.

And somehow, love for her own husband. Gladys's dreams had been dashed even more than her own.

The room was silent for several minutes. The only sound was the wind around the storm windows. Finally, Gladys raised her head and dabbed away the last of the tears. "Alma, how can I thank you?"

Alma merely smiled in return. "Open the letter."

Gladys slowly opened the envelope, her hands still shaking and Mavine now stroking her shoulder. Several items fell out, including a note:

Dear Gladys,

Having a wonderful time, wish you were here (ha ha). While we were in Panama City, we went by Aunt Ellie's old house. They tore it down to build this hotel! Here are a couple of postcards for your collection — didn't want them to get beat up in the mail. Love to all. See you soon.

> Your brother and sister-in-law,
> Grover and Anna Belle

Gladys's eyes were the size of saucers. Her mouth hung open for what seemed a full minute before she started laughing. Once she started, she couldn't stop. They were all roaring with laughter. Glorious, blessed laughter.

Gladys gave Alma's arm a playful slap. "You knew who that letter was from all along!"

"Honey, not that it matters, but I'd recognize Anna Belle's handwriting anywhere.

I'm surprised you didn't. You know she'd never let your brother write a note all by himself!"

The three hugged and laughed until they were out of breath. Finally, Gladys spoke. "I guess I'd better see if I can put some curls on that wise head of yours, Alma."

"Honey, it's too late for that today. You just finish up with Mavine, and I'll come by sometime next week. You say you're by yourself for dinner?"

"Yes, Tom won't be home until after eleven."

"Why don't you come over and have dinner with Welby and me? I've got pork tenderloin and homemade chess pie. Welby always says it's the best he's ever tasted."

"I really can't . . . Yes, I think I can. I'd love to."

Mavine walked home in twilight, her coat doing little to dispel the chilly air. Her head was still spinning. The visit to the Glamour Nook had taken longer than she'd planned, so dinner would be late. No matter — there were leftovers in the refrigerator. She'd learned so much this afternoon.

Alma had been a wonderful friend to her and to many over the years, and had showed what true friendship meant. And Gladys?

The woman had been through more than anyone knew. How could a person not hurt for a woman who'd lived such hardships?

The sun was going down when she returned to the house on the hill. Vee would be home from school, and Virgil would soon be closing Osgood's for the day and returning himself. If she could be anything in the world, she now realized, she wanted to be a woman like Alma. Wise and compassionate. Not complaining about her situation, but content. Focused on others, not herself.

And filled with grace.

Cornelius had spent the entire day in Quincy writing checks, arguing with contractors, and trying his best not to lose his temper in the process. Another challenge, and then another. Permits. Licenses. Red tape and regulations. How hard was it to get a business going? All he wanted to do was walk in the door of their pink trailer home and into the welcoming arms of his loving wife. He climbed the metal steps with anticipation and yanked the door open.

Reverend Eugene Caudill, Bible in lap and hat in hand, was seated at the dinette.

"Good evening, Cornelius. I was afraid I'd miss seeing you tonight, but JoAnn said you'd be home any minute."

The last thing he wanted this evening was another visit from the pastor. "Good evening, Reverend." Cornelius hoped he sounded more enthusiastic than he felt.

He forced a smile. His wife seemed determined to get him together with Reverend Caudill and the First Evangelical Baptist Church. They'd attended a couple of times, at JoAnn's insistence. If it made her happy, then he'd go along, but it did make him uneasy.

"So, how have you been? It's been so good to see you both in church."

"She's enjoyed it very much. Though we're still finding out where we belong in Eden Hill."

The minister made no move to leave. "JoAnn was telling me how hard you've been working, and that you've been making good progress toward opening."

"I suppose so." The easy chair was empty, so he took it. "It's been an uphill climb, though."

JoAnn chimed in. "Reverend Caudill stopped by to ask you for something."

Cornelius paused. His father had always said preachers were trying to get their hands into your pockets. "Pastor, I'm afraid we're in no position to —"

"Oh no, not money." The pastor rose to

his feet. "It's a favor, actually."

"A favor? What sort of favor?"

The older man grinned disarmingly. "We have a few things at the church that need doing. Chores and repairs. One Saturday a year we all get together and get them done. Will you put it on your calendar?"

Cornelius hesitated. His first response was to decline. He was tired, and anything that smacked of manual labor was just too much to ask right now. But then he looked at JoAnn. She was smiling and looked to be at peace. And heaven knew he'd let her down enough already.

"Yes." His grin was less strained this time. "I'd be happy to."

"Excellent!" Reverend Caudill beamed and named the date. "Thank you. I must be going now."

"You're welcome, Reverend." JoAnn nodded, her delight evident.

The pastor turned as he opened the door. "And Cornelius?" His eyes twinkled. "Church is *exactly* where you belong."

14

"Okay, Welby, I need your advice." Virgil took off his cap to scratch his head, vaguely noticing that his hairline was farther back than it used to be. "You and Alma have been married for what, over thirty years?"

"Thirty-two in August."

"I've been trying to compliment Mavine lately, and I'm still in the doghouse. Even when I try to do the right thing, it never seems to fix the problem. It only makes it worse."

"You're thinking like a repairman, Virgil." Welby had returned to a disassembled carburetor on his workbench. "Logically."

"What are you getting at?"

Welby peered toward the rafters a moment before continuing. "It's like this: we find out what's wrong with cars, and we make it right. If they're low on gasoline, we fill them up. If the brakes squeak, we put in new parts. If the oil's dirty, we change it. Find the problem and fix it." He held up a broken spring. "Right?"

"Well, yes. My father, H. C., and the Army both taught me that. What are you getting at?"

"It took me a long time to learn this, Virgil, but women aren't like cars and trucks. Men aren't either, for that matter. They don't always tell us where they're hurting or why. Sometimes I think they don't know themselves."

Welby selected a shiny new spring from a small metal parts box, and twisted it into place. "But I've found one thing that always seems to work, at least with Alma."

"What's that?"

"Leave that kind of thinking here at Osgood's. When you go back up the hill to your house, you're there to be a husband and father, not a service station operator. Try to find out what she wants most from you. Ask her outright, if you need to. It sounded to me like she feels she's not getting enough attention and appreciation from you."

Virgil let those ideas sink in a bit. "And what about when we disagree?"

"Well, part of loving Mavine is wanting the same things she wants. Take Vee, for instance. I'll bet if you encourage Vee in his studies, it'll mean as much to Mavine as if you did it just for her. Maybe he's meant to go to college."

The words were painful, but as soon as he heard them, Virgil knew they were also the truth. "So, how do I fix it?"

Welby chuckled. "Start by not trying to 'fix it.' People aren't meant to be fixed; people are meant to be loved, Alma always says. Show her you love her, Virgil. Do something really nice for her."

"Like what?" Virgil poured a full mug of coffee, finishing off what was in the percolator.

Welby had disappeared under the hood of a large Chrysler. "Does she have any special occasion coming up, like a birthday or anniversary?"

Something clicked. "Her birthday is a week from today. But I've already gotten her a gift."

"Maybe the best gift is to spend some extra time with her. Just with her. Remember that magazine article you showed me a few months back? It was pretty silly, I'll agree, but sometimes you find wisdom in the midst of foolishness."

The magazine. It was somewhere on his desk, having been back and forth from his coat pocket for the last couple of months.

"Yes, I believe you can."

"Then there you are. Okay, let's see if this thing will run. Start it up, Virgil."

He slid into the wide seat and turned the key. The engine started smoothly and settled into an easy idle.

"Purring like a kitten." He closed the hood with a gentle shove. "I'll bet Mavine will be just as happy as this Chrysler."

He had to agree. But, he noted, the Chrysler *did* come with a service manual.

Wives didn't.

The *Pageant* was where he remembered it, only turned upside down under a box of wiper blades. The paper clip still marked the page, and he stumbled through the article again. If he ignored the big words and just looked at Mavine's answers to Betty LaMour's questions, he began to see a pattern. Welby was right, of course. He'd not been a good husband. Not because he didn't have good intentions, but simply because he didn't know how. And he still didn't. But he *was* going to do something out of the ordinary for her birthday.

One of the questions had something to do with an "intimate romantic dinner." He smiled. Well, if that's what Mavine wanted, then he would do just that.

His telephone directory was buried under the same heap as the magazine. Leafing through the yellow pages, he found what he was looking for. The restaurant answered the phone on the first ring. "I'd like to take my wife to dinner next Friday night. An 'intimate romantic dinner.' "

Reverend Caudill rolled another page out of the Underwood and laid it facedown on top of the stack. All morning long he'd sat in front of his typewriter, pecking at the keys and listening to the melting snow drip into a bucket by the window. Yes, it was Friday, but these were the final touches on his Sunday message, not the beginning. And this time he knew where the sermon was coming from and where it was going. For the first time in years, he was excited.

It had been a good week — mostly. Madeline Crutcher had made her usual series of early morning phone calls, including one on Wednesday morning to let him know that she wouldn't be at prayer meeting that night because of the weather, and again at the crack of dawn Thursday to apologize for not being there. He'd dug his car out of the snow by Tuesday so he could make his pastoral calls: Arlie had needed a visit after Frank had gotten into some kind of trouble at school, and one of his deacons was in the hospital in Quincy. The patient was going to be fine, but Reverend Caudill's own nerves were shot from driving on the slippery road.

And last night it snowed again, and this morning his Chrysler wouldn't start. Just kept cranking until it let out one last groan and would budge no more. Welby and Virgil pushed it into Osgood's, promising to have it back by the end of the day. Not a bad metaphor for his life over the last couple of years. His inner battery, his source of energy, had gone flat. But his whole outlook had been different of late. More pastoral encouragements, more counseling breakthroughs.

He looked over at Louise's sweet face, once again wishing she were with him — sitting across the room or puttering in the kitchen. But he noticed, instead of a tear on his cheek, there was a smile on his lips. And Louise's smile in the picture looked a little brighter too. Why this had all happened he didn't fully understand, but he was grateful.

Perhaps it was his visits to the pink trailer next door. JoAnn had grown up in the church, he'd learned, and seemed to have some level of faith, but Cornelius was tougher to get a handle on. The man had been cordial enough but was wary and suspicious. What little interest he had in the church seemed more social than spiritual, almost like a business partnership. He was willing to attend with JoAnn, but he was doing so to please her.

Well. God had brought Cornelius next door to him, almost like an assignment.

He'd stopped in on the Alexanders several times, usually in the evening when he could catch them both at home. Nicodemus had come to Jesus at night, so why couldn't Reverend Caudill take Jesus to them the same way?

Or perhaps it was his Sunday afternoon conversations with Grover and Anna Belle. They often invited him for dinner after services, and he usually accepted. The couple had been his biggest supporters when Louise died and had said then that they'd always be there for him. Took him under their wings, built him up. Neither was a theologian or a pastoral counselor, but he knew exactly what the love of God looked like. A tall, take-charge grocery clerk dressed to the nines and a shy and hesitant meat cutter in a soiled apron.

His growling stomach informed him that lunchtime had arrived, and his taste buds reminded him that he was not going to have another bowl of condensed tomato soup. Time for a trip to Stacy's Grocery.

The grocery was relatively quiet when Reverend Caudill arrived, and he soon remembered why. Grover and Anna Belle were on vacation, and not due back until tomorrow. Every year they spent a week in Florida with family. They'd miss at least one Sunday at church, so he'd have to find someone to do nursery duty. If the church had any children in the nursery, which right now they didn't.

Brenda, the young woman who helped out when the Stacys were gone, had the store all to herself.

"Hello, Reverend. What might I do for you today?"

"I know Grover isn't here, but might I trouble you for a bologna sandwich? Brown bread, if you have any."

"Yes, sir. We don't have fresh meat while Mr. Stacy is gone, but we do have cold cuts." She sliced a chunk of the loaf with a large knife. "Anything on that?"

"No, thank you." As much as he liked his mustard and horseradish, he'd wait for another time to indulge. "What do I owe you, Brenda?"

"No charge, Reverend." She presented

him the sandwich, cut in two on a paper plate with a pickle and a handful of chips. She motioned him to a seat. "Mr. Stacy's instructions, sir."

"Well, thank you. I'm just a bit surprised."

"He does it for my father too."

"Your father. Is he a pastor?"

"Yes, sir. He's the preacher at the Pentecostal Holiness church. Brother Taggart. We meet at the old hardware store across from Willett's Dry Goods."

Of course. He'd just not put it all together. Their church was best known for loud evening meetings that ran long, often with electric guitars and drums. Some said the place was often lit up well after midnight, with maybe twenty-five people there, sometimes dancing and shouting. It was also known for having both white and Negro participants, which Madeline Crutcher often pointed out.

To him the worship style seemed improper and outrageous. But whites and Negroes together? Well. That sounded like what the church ought to be.

And Brenda, her skin the color of his creamed tea, was gracious and endearing.

"How's your father doing?" It was small talk, and he knew it.

No one else was in the store, so she came

over toward his table, keeping a respectful distance. "To tell you the truth, Reverend, he's very discouraged. It's been a really hard year for him. He works full-time as a janitor at the elementary school in Quincy since the church can't pay him anything. Mr. Stacy lets me help out here sometimes. Momma died several years ago, and I'm raising two little sisters."

"Does he have anybody to encourage him, give him a boost?" The man was cleaning toilets during the week so he could preach on weekends? The thought boggled his mind.

"Mr. Stacy sits with him at lunch sometimes when the grocery isn't busy, but that's about it. Mr. Stacy is a very nice man, but he just doesn't understand. Can't understand."

Reverend Caudill finished his sandwich, both troubled and challenged. Another widower, a minister of the gospel, discouraged just as he had been? Less than a block away, and he'd done nothing to even meet the man, let alone offer . . .

"Brenda, have him call me." Not finding a business card in his shirt pocket, he scribbled his telephone number on a small piece torn from the paper plate. "I think I *do* understand, and I'd like to meet with him sometime."

Mavine was thrilled. Really and truly excited. Not only had Virgil remembered her
birthday this year, he was taking her to dinner! An intimate romantic dinner, he'd said!
All week long, she'd wondered about what
to wear and how she'd look. Mavine had
chores to finish during the day, but Gladys
had managed to fit her in for a later appointment, so her hair would still be freshly
done for the evening.

But it was her new outfit that made her
heart sing. She'd taken Virgil's suit to Willett's Dry Goods to have it sent out for
cleaning, and had seen the dress on the very
end of the women's wear rack. Unlike the
usual gaudy prints and muted ginghams
Mr. Willett usually carried, this one was a
brilliant blue with a rose print, touches of
velvet trim, and a lace collar. And it was on
sale, and in her size! Almost. Mr. Willett
had agreed to take it out a bit in the places
where she needed it. She'd saved some of
her egg money, and Virgil agreed to let her
put the balance on their account.

Gladys seemed happy when Mavine arrived. It was near closing time, and Gladys
was finishing up with her last appointment.

"Right with you, Mavine, and happy

birthday!" Gladys alternated between combs and brushes, spray and something out of a tube, and her customer sported a sparkling new 'do that swirled forward at the bottom, ending at a point near her chin. "How's that look?"

The woman seemed pleased with her style, wrapped her head in a scarf, and departed. Gladys cleared off her trays and brushed off the chair.

"Come on up, Mavine. Let's see what we can do for your birthday date tonight." The beautician was humming a tune as she collected her scissors and combs. Mavine hadn't seen her friend in over a week and was quite startled by her joyous demeanor.

Mavine hung up her coat and climbed into the beauty chair as Gladys whistled something catchy and pleasant. Then Gladys did something quite unexpected. She spun Mavine toward her, leaned on the arms of the chair, and looked her right in the eyes.

"I told him," she said.

"Told who what?"

"Tom. I told him everything I told you and Alma last week. About my Depression baby."

"And?"

"Alma was right, of course. Tom gave me a great big hug and kiss and told me he loves me. And you know what else?"

Gladys had spun Mavine back around and tipped her head into the shampoo bowl. "Tom said he already knew; my ex-husband George told him. Said he'd never brought it up because all that was in the past and didn't matter to him."

"That's wonderful! Sounds just like the forgiveness and grace Reverend Caudill's been talking about at church." She felt her hair being combed, rolled, and twisted as they continued to chat. "You and Tom really ought to come on Sunday, Gladys."

"Used to a long time ago, Mavine. Never felt quite welcome there, like everyone was looking at me." Gladys led her to the dryer chair. "Besides, isn't church for good people? Like you and Virgil?"

"It's for everybody, Gladys."

Gladys sighed. "That's just what Alma and Welby said." She placed the dryer hood over Mavine's head and resumed her whistling.

It seemed like only a couple of minutes when the timer on the dryer clicked and Gladys stood by her, still humming. "Time for your comb-out, Mavine."

The last part of her styling took only a minute or so, with Gladys pulling out bobby pins and tossing them into a basket. "Sit still for a minute, Mavine. I've got something for you."

Something for her?

Gladys fetched a small box and opened it, revealing an assortment of cosmetics. She laughed, her eyes twinkling. "Avon calling!"

Before she could say anything, Gladys had dipped a small brush into something in the box and was dusting it onto Mavine's face. Lipstick and a couple of other items followed, and then a final flourish with the brush.

"Ta-da!" Gladys gave her customer's chair a spin facing the mirror.

Mavine couldn't believe her eyes. The woman in the mirror looked utterly transformed.

"Oh my, Gladys. I can't believe this! You've done an incredible job." While she'd used a tiny bit of makeup in the past, she wasn't sure if someone forty years old should look quite this good.

"Virgil doesn't know what he's in for tonight." Gladys laughed. "Okay, Mavine, off you go to your date. Just watch the lipstick when you get dressed."

She reached for her purse. "What do I owe you, Gladys?"

"Not a thing, Mavine. It's your birthday, remember? And besides, you and Alma have given me so much more than you know."

Mavine hung Virgil's suit and dress shirt on the hanger on the porch, as he was coming back early to change clothes. She dressed upstairs in their bedroom. Vee had gone to spend the evening with Welby and Alma, who promised to bring him back after Virgil and Mavine's special night out.

The dress was a tight fit, even after Mr. Willett's alterations, but she could make do with it. She'd covered her mouth with a tissue when she put it on, so as not to get any of her fresh makeup on it, and looked in the mirror. Virgil would be more than pleased. Her purse wasn't a close match, but it went fine with the dress and the shoes, so she went downstairs to meet her husband. His expression was everything she'd hoped for.

"Mavine, you look absolutely beautiful!" His tie was crooked, and he shifted awkwardly in his suit, but he was ready for their dinner date.

"You look pretty good yourself." She smiled, and her heart beat a bit faster. Yes, this was going to be a special birthday.

They drove into Quincy, turning left at the main intersection. Another left turn, then a right, and they pulled into a parking space.

"Here we are, Mavine."

"Here we are? Virgil, are you sure this is the right place?"

"Yes, it is. I called ahead and made reservations."

Mavine looked around. The place advertised *Dine in or carry out* with a large neon sign, and as she stepped out a young girl passed her, carrying a tray to a waiting auto. A cartoonish figure in checked overalls stood in front of the door, holding high a sandwich on a tray, and a jukebox somewhere was playing something with a beat.

Virgil held the door for her as they entered. She walked inside in a daze. The place was filled with young patrons eating with their fingers and slurping milkshakes.

"We've been expecting you, Mr. and Mrs. Osgood." A young man, twenty-five or so, led them down rows of booths into an empty area at the back. Dimly lit and almost hidden, a table with two chairs was tucked in a small alcove. "Here you are."

The waiter held the chair for Mavine and seated her gently into place. Virgil plopped into the seat across from her. They were each given menus with colorful pictures of the offerings for the evening.

She looked at the menu in some disbelief, and then at Virgil with astonishment. How could she tell her friends about her birthday, which turned out to be celebrated . . . here?

When the waiter returned, Virgil ordered the same meal for each of them. Something called a Big Boy platter: a double-decker cheeseburger with fries and a milkshake. The house specialty, the young man had said. Mavine kept her hands in her lap, her gaze fixed on the mustard stain beside the pepper shaker.

After the waiter had gone, she lifted her eyes toward Virgil, with a tear working its way out in sadness, disappointment . . . anger, maybe. She wasn't sure.

And then something amazing happened.

"Happy birthday, Mavine." Virgil had somehow pulled two candles and holders from a pocket in his suit, and lit them with a match. "I hope this is intimate and romantic enough. I'm sorry if I don't know exactly what that means, but I hope this is something you'll enjoy. Welby said this was his favorite restaurant in Quincy."

In the candlelight she looked at her husband. There was something tender and innocent about his face. "It's lovely," she said. No, it wasn't white tablecloths and seven courses, but it was her birthday with her husband, who cared enough about her to take her to dinner.

Later, Virgil gave her a little wrapped box with a pair of gloves inside. And the waiter brought a modest cake with a small number of candles — nowhere near forty. Before they left, Virgil put a dime in the jukebox and played "Crazy" twice in a row. And he held her hands, just like they used to do when they were first married.

Patsy Cline wasn't a string quartet, but for Mavine Osgood, a double cheeseburger and fries might just as well have been truffles and caviar.

15

Cornelius shook his head and drummed his fingers on the only clear spot on his messy desk. He'd agreed to something called "Work Day" at the First Evangelical Baptist Church, and while it felt right, he was trying to figure out why. And where had he seen something like this before? The Zipco manual was somewhere under the Goodyear catalog and the overdue electric bill. Tossing the papers aside, he found the thick notebook and began flipping through it. Yes, there it was in black-and-white, right in chapter four: "Community Relations."

"The successful Zipco owner will involve himself in his community. Join a civic club, support youth activities, sponsor a Little League team, and become involved in a local church or synagogue." Yes, he'd made the right decision. And the church was certainly local — right next door, in fact. They were neighbors. Hopefully JoAnn would be pleased with him for this. And he certainly hadn't given her much to celebrate lately.

Reverend Caudill had been persistent; he'd give him that. The pastor had paid several visits to the station, checking on progress, which remained at a standstill. He'd also come by their mobile home a couple of times and had encouraged them to visit on Sundays. But in spite of the pastor's invitation, he remained wary. His father held a poor opinion of preachers, a viewpoint Cornelius had no doubt inherited. Only in it for the bucks, he'd said.

This particular reverend certainly didn't seem that way. A bit stuffy in his black suit, but friendly and agreeable. A good neighbor. Disarming. And he'd never mentioned money. Not even once.

But he had talked about *service*. Work Day was tomorrow, and a number of the men of Eden Hill would be coming, he'd said during his visit earlier today. "And bring a paintbrush," he'd added in parting, peering over the top of his bifocals.

Virgil usually looked forward to Fridays, and this one was promising indeed. Three cups of Mavine's black coffee had cleared any lingering cobwebs, and the double helping of scrambled eggs and bacon from her iron skillet would hold him until at least noon. Vee was actually out the door on time — and remembered to close it behind him — and a fresh pair of khaki work trousers hung taut on their stretcher. All was right with the world.

Until Mavine sat down across the table from him.

"Virgil?"

He gulped and looked around. "Yes?"

"The chicken coop. Will you please paint it? I got the eggs this morning, and I was ashamed of what it looked like. You promised to fix it up last fall, but you said it got too cold. Well, spring is here."

He drew a long-overdue breath, grateful that his most recent failure involved only paint and a brush, not romantic flair. And he *had* promised. Winter had been cold, hard, and seemingly endless, but the snow had been gone for over two weeks now, and crocuses were beginning to poke up by the back porch. Buds had finally appeared on the trees, and patches of green were popping up in the brown yard. Mavine was right. But ashamed of a chicken coop?

"Okay, Mavine, I'll do it next weekend if the weather holds."

"Can you please do it tomorrow? Vee can help."

"Tomorrow is church Work Day, and I promised Reverend Caudill I'd be there."

Which he had. Every third Saturday in April was Work Day at the First Evangelical Baptist Church, when Reverend Caudill would round up every man he could find, pass out paint, hammers, and buckets, and see to it that whatever needed fixing was repaired. Grover would bring a radio and tune in *The Saturday Morning Gospel Barn* on WNTC, and while the minister preferred hymns to twang, he wouldn't complain as long as the work got done. Since the women stayed home, the men usually didn't argue either.

Unfortunately for Virgil, this was not an acceptable excuse for Mavine. "As long as you have a paintbrush in your hand, you can put a coat on the henhouse after Work Day is over. I've already talked to Reverend Caudill. He said you'll be finished right after lunch, and that you'll have some help."

Paintbrush? "I'd planned to try for some white bass at the lake with Welby. Spring run, you know." He went for sympathy and found none. Mavine's upturned eyebrow assured him that when he got home tomorrow afternoon, the outbuilding would be waiting, and so would she.

"Tomorrow."

"But Welby —"

"Welby will be digging up Alma's flower beds tomorrow afternoon. I've already spoken with her too."

"Okay, Mavine. I'll paint the henhouse." He sighed. It was a disappointment, but he took some comfort in knowing Welby was having the exact same conversation at that moment with Alma. With that, he put on his cap and headed down the hill.

Welby was already hard at work, as usual, and not alone. Arlie was at the station too, which was less usual — Virgil expected him to be plowing his cornfield for spring planting, or more likely, fishing. Reverend Caudill was also there, no doubt hoping to recruit more workers for the next day. All three men were examining the back of Arlie's truck, which had been in a fight with something and lost. The rear bumper was bent outward at a sharp angle.

"Frank hung it on a stump chasin' that old brown sow of mine. Shoulda whupped him good," Arlie was saying, "not for tearin' up the truck but for runnin' the hog. He knows better than that."

"Patience, Arlie." The pastor stood to one side to avoid an oily puddle. "Have you tried talking to the boy about his poor behavior?"

"I'll talk to him about it with a belt behind the barn! That fool kid . . ."

Welby, under the truck with his feet sticking out, interrupted. "Arlie, your bumper was already bent, so don't blame it on Frank. You're going to need a new one. It doesn't look like anything else is hurt, so I can bend that bracket back in shape with a torch and a pipe wrench." He rolled his mechanic's creeper out from under the truck.

"So I can count on each of you fine gentlemen tomorrow morning?" the pastor asked, looking at each one in turn. "We have just the sort of work to be done that you do so well."

"What's that, Reverend, bending metal? Arlie's sure good at that, now." Grover had wandered in unnoticed, munching on something wrapped in a paper napkin.

"Hey, fellows, it *is* my truck, and I'm gonna have to pay for it." Arlie was red in the face, but his language was surprisingly restrained. Apparently Reverend Caudill's presence kept the color out of Arlie's speech.

"Just kidding, Arlie." Grover wiped his mouth with the remainder of the napkin. "Stop by the store for some venison sausage when you're done. Anna Belle baked some biscuits to go with it. On the house!"

Reverend Caudill, who was not about to allow his question to be dodged successfully, repeated it as a statement. "So. I will expect all of you good men to be at the church at nine o'clock. Sharp. And Virgil?"

"Yes?" Virgil had been standing by the arc welder, watching the proceedings and slurping his coffee.

"Bring a paintbrush. A big one. I've already talked to Mavine."

"Best I can tell," said Welby, munching on a pepper loaf sandwich, "the women just have it in for us."

"How's that?" asked Virgil, reaching for the jar of mustard. The two had walked over to Stacy's Grocery for lunch and were relishing thick-sliced lunch meat with all the trimmings.

"None of them will be at Work Day. Alma said it's because we do repair work much better than the women, and besides, they've just had their hair done and don't want to get it all messed up."

"Are they going to mop floors with their hair?" Grover pulled up a third chair as everyone laughed. "I think they just don't want us showing them up. You boys want some of that venison sausage? Anna Belle has some left over."

Welby assumed a nauseated look and waved his hands, while Virgil said simply, "No, thanks. Mavine piled on the bacon this morning, so I barely have room for lunch. By the way, where is Anna Belle?"

"Oh, she's off to the beauty shop like the rest of them this afternoon. Got a lot to talk about when they all get together."

Welby, who was beginning to show some color coming back into his face, seemed eager for the change of subject. "Probably talking about us, just like we talk about them on Thursday nights. Must have something to do with hair, I think."

"You may be right," Virgil brushed crumbs off his shirt. "Well, I've been given my marching orders for tomorrow. Painting something. What will you two be doing?"

"Reverend Caudill wants me to see about the motor on the furnace blower," said Welby. "He said it squeaks at him during the sermon and it gets too cold if he turns it off. How about you, Grover?"

"Well, for some reason he thinks I'm just the one to clean out the gutters. Said he saw me on the roof putting up Anna Belle's decorations last Christmas, so he knows I have a ladder. What he doesn't know is that I was hanging on to it for dear life. We're also going to bring over some cold cuts at lunchtime. Have to eat, you know."

"You reckon Arlie'll come this year?" Virgil asked.

They all looked at each other. "Hard to say." Grover peered out the window. "You know how he gets sometimes."

Reverend Caudill was the first to arrive for Work Day, and he headed straight for the sanctuary to turn up the thermostat by the baptistery. The ogre in the basement was a terrifying thing — an old coal furnace that had recently been converted to fuel oil. Fortunately, the pilot light was burning, so it came on as soon as he adjusted the dial. Good — the less time spent belowground the better. More than once, his Sunday sermon had been inspired by an unpleasant trip to the cellar. Few in the congregation knew the reverend's heated homily last year about the three Hebrew children in the fiery furnace had been brought on by a balky and terrifying pilot light. Well. Inspiration is wherever you find it.

Welby walked in carrying a large box, followed by Virgil, whose hands were also full. "Welby, why don't you go on down to the furnace room and see what you can do about the blower. I'll just stay up here. It's scary down there."

"That'll be fine," answered Welby. "I brought some tools and an oilcan."

Reverend Caudill smiled. "Excellent." Welby would surely tame the screaming beast.

As the mechanic whistled his way down the steps, Virgil stepped up, waving a paintbrush.

Reverend Caudill grinned. "You, my friend, will work on the baptistery. This time I got the right kind of paint."

"Is Arlie here yet?"

The minister hesitated. "Arlie probably won't be coming. I think he's attending to some other things today."

"Probably fishing." Virgil shook his head. "I'd hoped to go myself, but Mavine has asked me to do some work around the house this afternoon. She mention it to you?"

"She may have brought it up. But first, the baptistery."

Virgil groaned under his breath. Painting was to him what a trip to the furnace room apparently was to the reverend: as near to hell as he ever wanted to get.

The preacher pointed him to the tank behind the pulpit, which had thoughtfully been emptied for the occasion. "Last year Arlie painted it for us — used something he got from the farm supply store. It all came off the first time we filled it up."

Virgil remembered. For several weeks, the baptistery looked like it was filled with Ty-D-Bol. Today the tank was quite bare and empty, except for a round gallon can and some old newspapers. He read the label on the side of the container:

Waterproof Marine Enamel
Seafoam Aqua
Ideal for:
Swimming Pools
Outboard Motors
Boat Docks
Birdbaths
Shower Stalls
Stock Tanks

Not one word about baptisteries. He looked at the blotch on the lid, tilting it so the light was falling on the sample. The stuff was blue-green, the same color as Mavine's blueberry-and-lime salad mold from last Sunday's dinner. He hadn't dared ask what was in *that*. The cover came off with the twist of a screwdriver, and he began to stir it with the little wooden paddle. Welby was downstairs whistling "Colonel Bogey March," which echoed through the duct-work, and Reverend Caudill was in a spirited conversation with Grover and someone else outside the door.

And indeed the radio was the subject of the discussion. Remarkably, Grover had remembered to bring it, and the preacher was explaining the rules. "Remember, Grover, this is a house of worship. I want only clean and wholesome music played in here. No rock and roll. No rhythm and blues. I don't want to hear anything by the Beverly Brothers or whatever they call themselves. And definitely no Elvis."

"Absolutely, Reverend, we'll leave it on WNTC all morning. Their gospel show is on until noon. Good music. None of that devil music you preach against. And besides, they have the daily devotional minute every morning after the farm news."

"That will be fine, then. Off to work you go, gentlemen. I'll get you started outside, and then be in my office catching up on a few things."

Grover came into the sanctuary, where Virgil was preparing for his task. "I'll bring you guys the radio to listen to in here, since there aren't any outlets outside where I'll be working. Just turn it up loud enough for us to hear."

You *guys*?

"Thanks, Grover." Virgil turned the device on to let it warm up. "Just look at this stuff." He showed Grover the can of paint.

Grover read it over and whistled. "Ugly, ain't it! Well, if it's good enough for a ten-horsepower Evinrude, it ought to be able to stand one of Reverend Caudill's dunkings! Anyway, I'll be outside if you have any problem with the radio. Sometimes it quits playing and you have to slap the top of it."

Grover disappeared outside, and Virgil set himself to the task at hand. The Statesmen Quartet was now singing "Mansion Over the Hilltop" on the radio, with a bass vocalist who rattled the window with every word. The music was pretty good, he had to admit. Maybe this wouldn't be too bad after all.

Better start in the back, below the painting of the Jordan River. He'd just dipped the brush into the paint when, as Grover predicted, the radio quit. Just quit. One electronic crash, and the tenor soloist and his ridiculously high note vanished into an annoying buzz.

Humph. The brush was dripping, so he laid it carefully across the top of the can. What was it that Grover said? Smack the top of the set? As he began turning to do just that, he heard a dull thud, followed by the final note of the number.

If he'd still held his paintbrush, he'd have dropped it. A young man with a ducktail haircut knelt with his fist on top of the radio and a brush of his own in the other hand. And he seemed as surprised as Virgil.

"Reverend," Grover whined, "it ain't right for me to be up here getting the good Lord's view of things. Man was meant to stay on the ground. I'm supposed to be on the inside looking out."

"Sorry you feel that way." Reverend Caudill wasn't going to let him out of his job that easily. "Unfortunately, the same good Lord has seen fit to use us as his instruments to clean out the gutters. Welby, make sure he doesn't slip." Welby, apparently finished with his furnace job, had been appointed guardian of the ladder.

"Yeah, Welby, hang on to that thing. I'm on the other end of it." Grover stretched out his free arm and dragged his hand through the gutter. Old leaves, dirt, and pieces of shingles all came out in one sloppy glob, which he flung to one side. "This is about the nastiest job there is. How'd I get talked into this?"

Reverend Caudill grinned. He'd talked to Anna Belle first, so Grover had little choice in the matter.

"You're doing fine up there, Grover," said Welby, dodging whatever Grover was throwing down. "What time did you say lunch is coming?"

"Whenever Anna Belle gets here, and there's no telling when that will be." Grover paused for a moment and gazed out toward the road.

Virgil was face-to-face with Cornelius Alexander. Now what? He'd met the Zipco owner and his wife briefly on Easter Sunday, when Reverend Caudill introduced them. Enthusiastically, as if he expected them to be great friends. The encounter had been awkward enough with the preacher standing there, but now he was on his own and was expected to be civil and gracious. The two sized each other up like boxers poised for the opening bell and waiting to see who would be the first to blink.

Cornelius spoke first. "Virgil Osgood, I believe."

"Cornelius Alexander. And what are you doing here?"

"Reverend Caudill asked . . ." His voice trailed off. They stared at each other, and then at the baptistery. The Dixie Melody Boys were singing now, and the piano player was off on a spirited riff.

"Well," Virgil said, finally. "Let's get this over with." The baptistery wasn't going to paint itself.

The two began brushing on Seafoam Aqua, a difficult task since there was no thinner to be found. The paint was thick, so it was more like icing a cake from the inside out. At least it seemed to stick. The baptistery was small, less than six feet from end to end. Grover had often said that if Reverend Caudill were ever to baptize anyone taller than that, he'd have to do it one end at a time.

"This isn't working." Virgil's voice was louder than it should have been. With both at work in the baptistery, they were painting each other more than the walls of the tank. After a couple of minutes, Virgil laid his paintbrush to one side. "Cornelius, this baptistery just isn't big enough for the two of us."

The younger man stood, laid his own brush aside, and said loudly, "I couldn't agree more."

And with that, Cornelius Alexander walked down the aisle and out the front door.

■ ■ ■ ■

The radio continued on its good behavior, with the Jordanaires belting out "The Church in the Wildwood." Virgil noticed his foot tapping away. Thankfully, Elvis wasn't singing along on this one.

He added the final stroke to the baptistery and stepped back to admire his handiwork. Not bad, in spite of a blotch or two made when Cornelius hit his arm. Why in the world did Reverend Caudill put them both in there together?

Welby came by, whistling. "Well, Virgil, how's the painting coming along?"

"I think I'm finished." Virgil had parked himself in a pulpit chair, stretching his stiff knees. "Where's Grover?"

"Taking a break. Said heights make him dizzy, and he's still tired from a long week at work."

"What about the furnace?"

"Nothing wrong with it, as far as I can tell. I found a couple of mousetraps to take care of the squeaking. As soon as Anna Belle gets here I'll put some cheese on them."

Virgil raised his eyebrows, trying to decide if Welby was pulling his leg again. He wasn't. "You mean to tell me all this time . . ."

"Yep!"

"That's the best one I've heard in a long time," said Virgil. "Well, there it is, Seafoam Aqua. Whatever that is. I need to clean out this brush, but we don't have any thinner. Otherwise Mavine'll skin me when I get home. Any ideas?"

Welby thought for a minute, his eyes twinkling. "How about painting the chicken coop the same color? Yeah, I talked to Mavine."

Reverend Caudill had climbed up to the darkened balcony so he could look in on his little experiment. Tension had risen between Virgil and Cornelius lately, and while the new Zipco station still hadn't opened, the rumor mill was going strong. What, he thought, might happen if he used a little pastoral influence to put them together on Work Day? In the same room with a common task? Arlie had once told him if you wanted two cats, you had to introduce them a little at a time, or they'd fight like, well, cats. Might a little careful, controlled introduction be a good thing?

They were at least having the beginnings of a conversation. Good. He thought maybe the gospel music was smoothing over some rough edges and encouraging them to get along.

But then it all blew up, with Virgil grumbling and Cornelius storming out the door.

Well. He'd chalk up this experiment as a failure. He'd apologize to Virgil after the painting was done; he'd not want to interrupt him in the middle. And Cornelius. He'd make yet another visit to the hideous pink trailer.

Careful not to be seen, he tiptoed down the stairs and outside just in time to see Anna Belle Stacy driving their Plymouth up to where the men were working. Welby, ever the gentleman, let go of the ladder to open Anna Belle's door just as her husband was stretching to reach the end of the gutter. A shout from Grover and a huge crash followed in quick succession. The result left the ladder on the ground, Anna Belle scared out of her wits, and Grover holding on to the gutter with his feet dangling. The nails holding the gutter were no match for Grover's bulk, and one by one they popped out as the sheet metal peeled away from the ends of the rafters. The spectacle ended with a muffled grunt from Grover as he hung on all the way to the ground.

Virgil also came running outside to find Grover and the ladder both on the ground.

The gutter was strewn along the foundation. A heated discussion of the cause of the incident was also well under way.

Welby and Virgil helped Grover to his feet. He seemed unhurt but would need some cleaning up. Anna Belle was at his side, mopping dead leaves and such off his head. She was also giving him a hard time for getting his clothes dirty.

At any rate, the gutter was now sparkling clean; although, lying on the ground, it didn't really matter much. Welby looked it over. "Good job, Grover. It needed replacing anyway! And bending metal is also one of your greatest talents."

The disheveled grocer looked up. "Reverend, I told you I wasn't the one for this job. I'm not a roofer."

Reverend Caudill was quite relieved to find Grover unhurt, and made a mental note to hire a professional next time. "You did your best, Grover, and we're sure glad you're all right. Maybe it's time for lunch after all."

Reverend Caudill watched as Grover carried the cooler from the trunk of the car to the fellowship hall and set it on one of the tables. He laid several items out in front of him, while Reverend Caudill blessed the food and gave thanks.

With dexterity, Grover carved off a slice of bologna from a large roll. It peeled away perfectly — a uniform quarter-inch thick. Onto a slice of bread it went, precisely centered. A square of cheddar fell smoothly away from the cheese block with another deft movement of the blade. Two more cuts, and a circle of tomato landed on the sandwich. He then traded the sharp knife for the flat one. Into the mayonnaise it went, a single motion, and onto another slice of bread. A twist of his hands, and the lettuce was in place. With surgical precision, Grover trimmed the crust away, put the sandwich on a paper plate, and handed it to Virgil. The entire process had taken just over fifteen seconds.

The group stood in silence. Even Anna Belle had nothing critical to say. As in the hands of a sculptor, the bread and meat became art through Grover's work. Soon everyone had a perfect sandwich, including Reverend Caudill, who had broken the sacred silence by offering thanks again and requesting horseradish instead of mayonnaise.

Virgil spoke up. "By golly, this is just about the best sandwich I think I have ever eaten!" Welby mumbled in agreement — his mouth was full.

Anna Belle, who had remained silent up to now, said, "Grover, you've outdone yourself this time."

Everyone was enjoying a sandwich, including Grover, who had finally found time to make one for himself. Reverend Caudill noted that Virgil was sitting with Welby, and Cornelius was nowhere to be seen. Well. Some things just take time, with both cats and people.

"Grover," he said finally, "I think next year we'll just put you in charge of lunch. You do a better job than anyone else. Thanks so much!"

"Good idea. It'll let me do something I'm good at." Grover beamed. When Welby asked for seconds, he prepared another sandwich with the same ease he'd made the first.

Reverend Caudill smiled. A couple of wins and a couple of losses, so not a bad day. He made two mental notes. One was to finish his sermon before next year's Work Day began.

The other was to keep his Pepto-Bismol close at hand anytime he had horseradish for lunch.

16

Cornelius sighed and considered his cluttered desk. The bills tucked under the telephone were past due, several promissory notes with Zipco would be due next week, and their baby was due any minute. Bluegrass Vending was coming sometime before lunch to put in the coin-operated machines, which was a good thing, and the Zipco representative was coming in the afternoon, which wasn't. The spring thaw had finally softened the ground so that the backhoe man could dig holes for the underground tanks, so Cornelius was beginning to believe he might actually be able to open by the end of the month. But the man would have to be paid. Beforehand, and in cash.

Because the baby was so near, he'd had to keep the Chevy's fuel tank topped off for a run to the county hospital in Quincy. And because his own pumps still weren't in, he had to fill up across the street at Osgood's

— which was hard. Not that it wasn't his own gasoline, but that Welby always squirted and wiped his windshield and wanted to check his oil. His *competitor,* for crying out loud. And three times in the last week!

Actually, he also had much to be grateful for. Or so JoAnn had said. The white metal panels on the front of the building were polished and gleaming, and the engine hoist and the tire-changing equipment for the garage had been delivered and installed. The heat was still on thanks to another loan from the friendly folks at Zipco, and the toilet in their trailer was working much better with a tight bolt and the new septic tank. Charlie turned out to have some mechanical ability and said he actually looked forward to getting greasy. JoAnn's last checkup had been very encouraging, and even suggested that the new arrival might be a boy, as they both wanted.

Grateful. JoAnn had become enamored of the First Evangelical Baptist Church and Reverend Caudill's sermons. But why did anybody need religion, anyway? Back when he was seven years old, his mother had taken him to a tent revival with someone named Lewis Pritchett, and the man had terrified him.

But Reverend Caudill did seem different.

Like he actually cared about him and JoAnn and wasn't pointing fingers and looking for a handout. Sure, the man had placed him and Virgil Osgood together on Work Day, which was more than he could handle. Almost as though the pastor expected the two to become friends. He'd simply had to walk out.

Yes, Reverend Caudill had stopped by that night and apologized. A genuine and heartfelt apology.

But whose fault was it? Maybe he did need religion after all. The pastor had said that *religion* wasn't a word he liked to use; he preferred to talk about *faith.* Cornelius had said he'd think about it.

So with all the things going on in his life, he was doing just that.

A honk of a horn announced the arrival of the truck from the vending machine company, a bit earlier than he expected. A quick look at the sky and the reason was obvious: a dark cloud was approaching, with jagged lightning and low rumbles of thunder. He helped the man get the large crates off the back and wrestle them into place. The cigarette and candy machines would go in the front under the sign marked *Convenience Center,* and the Tom's snack rack and the soda case would go inside near the counter so the drinks wouldn't freeze in cold weather. The task didn't take as long as he expected, and he had yet another invoice to place under the telephone.

After the truck drove away with a promise of inventory to be delivered within a week, he plugged in the cigarette machine and the candy dispenser. The lighted panels on the machines in front shone brightly and gave Cornelius a sense of satisfaction. Soon he would be open for business, and the glowing signs and the illuminated pictures conveyed a sense of progress. The vending man even gave him a sign saying, *Come on in, it's Kool inside,* in case he ever put in air-conditioning.

He leaned back in his chair and cleared a spot on the desk to prop his feet. The soda case was chilling nicely, its motor making an agreeable rumble that accented the clatter of the rain that had just begun. He took the Zipco operations manual from the shelf behind him and flipped to the chapter titled "Planning Your Grand Opening." Looking a bit farther, he found his legal pad and began scrawling a to-do list:

1. Install banners and flags to attract attention

2. Call local florist for flowers for the ladies
3. Order "Grand Opening" sign
4. Schedule an appearance by Zippy the Clown

He was about to add "5. Place an ad in the local paper," when the telephone jangled. Couldn't be JoAnn; she would be right in the middle of *As the World Turns.*

"Zipco Super Service. How might I be of assistance?"

"Neil? It's time."

Mrs. Madeline Crutcher had driven to Quincy to fill up her Buick, which she did once every six months. Because the large engine required premium gasoline, which Virgil didn't carry, she would make the trip to the Standard Oil station in town. Just as she left Eden Hill, a couple in a Chevrolet passed at high speed, nearly sending them both into a ditch. She mumbled something about kids and driver's licenses, forgetting her own had expired in '55.

The twenty-mile round trip had taken her about three hours, partly because she never shifted past second gear and partly because of the stormy weather, but mostly because she'd stopped at the A&P supermarket to pick up several tins of Tube Rose snuff and the latest *Newsweek* magazine.

As soon as the Buick crossed the bridge back into Eden Hill, the storm reached its peak. Ever the careful driver, the woman steered toward the nearest pullout, which happened to be the Zipco station parking area. All the lights were out, except for two brightly lit panels beneath the sign marked *Convenience Center.*

Between swishes of the windshield wipers, two gleaming vending machines came into view. One had on its lighted panel *Hungry?* and an oversize illustration of a Hershey's chocolate bar, but it was the other that immediately caught her attention. It carried no words that she could make out, but the life-size Marlboro Man was staring directly at her through the streaks of rain running down the glass. The cigarette dangling from his lip suggested Moral Failure of vast proportion, as did his black hat and sneer.

The steady clacking of the wipers alternately blurred the image and brought it into focus, each time mocking and taunting her with his seductive eyes. Madeline Crutcher knew she had to see Reverend Caudill as soon as the weather cleared and make sure this foul new tool of the devil would be eradicated from Eden Hill.

Frank Prewitt was spending the afternoon with Vee Junior because Lula Mae was taking Darlene to the chiropractor in Quincy at three o'clock. Darlene had complained of a stomachache, and Lula Mae had commandeered Arlie's truck for the afternoon to do it. This in turn left Arlie in a mood sourer than usual, as he had a hog he wanted to deliver and thought Darlene was faking to get out of her arithmetic test.

The school bus had dropped them off at Osgood's just as the heavy rain began to fall. Neither boy had an umbrella, so the driver was kind enough to pull into the lot by the pump, though he had to wave off Welby, who had come out with his window cleaner and rag in spite of the storm. The two boys dashed through the front door, dodging puddles and holding their schoolbooks over their heads.

Virgil was busy in the front room, filling the Nabs rack from a brown carton that had been delivered earlier in the day. "Afternoon, boys! Glad you're home and out of the storm."

Vee was grateful to be in from the weather, which had gotten worse. He'd hoped to read

218

comic books with Frank in his room but did not relish the idea of the trip up the hill in the downpour and the mud, nor was he too keen on the thunder and lightning.

"Why don't you boys do your homework in my office? Mavine will know you're here and not at the house. And Frank, your mother called and said she'd be by to pick you up when she and Darlene get back."

Vee was happy with the arrangement, as it meant he'd stay dry, and besides, he always enjoyed puttering around in his father's messy office. Frank readily agreed, as he hoped he'd get a peek at The Calendar.

Vee had told Frank about The Calendar. Every December the Safe-T-Made tire company would send their dealers a wall calendar for the coming year. The promotional gift always featured the Safe-T-Maid, usually wearing a two-piece bathing suit at a beach. This year's calendar was no different except for the clear plastic covering the picture, and the skimpier-than-usual outfit the model was wearing. Virgil hung it on the wall behind his desk, vaguely noting that her bathing suit was badly tailored, and promptly forgot about it. The month still said *January,* as he'd never bothered to change it.

It was Vee who discovered the reason for

the poor fit of her scant clothing: it was printed on the clear cellophane sheet, which was fastened only at the top and could be lifted by a small tab at the bottom. Frank went straight to the calendar, ignoring all the debris on Virgil's desk.

"Hoo-wee!" Frank's eyes grew wide and his jaw dropped. "She's amazing! Will you just look at —"

"Shhhhh! Keep your voice down! If Dad catches us back here looking at his calendar, he'll take it down and whip us both."

"What's the big deal? Nothing different here from the women in my old man's magazines."

Such was the fascination with the enticing image that neither boy noticed the footsteps in the doorway behind them. They were startled by the gasping, piercing shriek of a shocked woman's voice.

"Frank!" Lula Mae's outburst was almost a gurgle. Her eyes grew to the size of silver dollars, and her face turned ashen in disbelief. "What? How? Get over here this minute — both of you!"

They did not argue, as she was breathing fire. "Frank! Come with me. Vee! Get to your house. Now!"

"Yes, ma'am." Vee started to say something, thought better of it, and shot out the back door and up the hill in the pouring rain, leaving his schoolbooks behind. Frank started past Lula Mae, but was grabbed by the ear and marched toward the front door, where Virgil stood wondering what the commotion was about.

"Virgil Osgood, how could you even *have* such a thing? I'm going to go tell the preacher about that calendar!" Lula Mae shot him a look of utter disgust and hauled Frank to the waiting truck, where she shoved him in next to Darlene, who had watched the spectacle from her seat and wondered what her brother had done now. Lula Mae was still moving her mouth and making angry sounds when she started the truck, which belched black exhaust and roared away.

Virgil pondered all these things and surmised that he was once again in some kind of trouble. And once again, he had no idea why.

Reverend Caudill was having a difficult afternoon. The stormy weather had made his knees hurt, the roof over his office was leaking even more with the gutter gone, and the work on his next sermon series was proceeding slower than he'd hoped. He was about to close his books and go home when he heard a roar and a screech outside his study window. Looking out through the blinds, he recognized a pickup truck, a familiar black Buick, and two women walking hurriedly toward the church door. Now he had a headache, too. Why today?

Lula Mae Prewitt and Madeline Crutcher burst into his office without knocking, both waving their arms and talking excitedly. They were red in the face and looked as though they'd just seen a ghost — maybe two.

"Ladies! What is the — ? One at a time, please!"

The pastor's admonition was ignored. The women were shouting and gesturing wildly, at Reverend Caudill, at each other, and at parties known only to them. Mrs. Crutcher almost knocked over the desk lamp, saved at the last second by Reverend Caudill's lucky catch.

"Ladies, please!"

His plea vanished into the cacophony of high-pitched and agitated voices. He was able to catch a few words when one woman or the other paused for breath. Young Mr. Alexander's name came up, as did Virgil's, and a few scattered and confusing details. Finally, both women seemed to run out of wind simultaneously. "I knew you'd want to know!" was Lula Mae's parting shot, as Mrs. Crutcher slammed the door, knocking askew his picture of Jesus at the Last Supper.

As near as he could make out, it had something to do with a naked cowboy on a calendar smoking a cigarette. Or was he wearing a plastic bathing suit? Reverend Caudill reached into the desk drawer for his Goody's headache powder.

"She's beautiful. And so are you." Cornelius looked at his wife and daughter snuggled together in their bed in the maternity ward. Constance Suzanne Alexander had come into the world at 6:40 in the evening at King's Daughters hospital, weighing seven pounds, two ounces.

JoAnn smiled back. "She has your eyes. Just look at her."

He gazed at his daughter's eyes, slowly closing to sleep, and something came over him he'd not experienced before. Thankfulness, maybe?

"The doctor says you're both doing fine and should be able to go home right on schedule. I wish I could stay with you the whole time."

"I wish you could too, Neil." She smiled again, the most peaceful expression he'd seen from her in months. "Let's call her Suzy."

It was his turn to smile. "Welcome to the world, Suzy girl. I'll be the best father to you that I can be." He turned to JoAnn, who was also falling asleep. It had been a long day.

"And the best husband. I promise."

When proud papa Cornelius returned that evening, he found two notes on the door of the Zipco station. The first was from the Zipco representative, who had arrived to find nobody around, and was staying in room seven at the Sleepy Head Tourist Court in Quincy. The second was from Reverend Caudill, who requested a return phone call as soon as possible.

The telephone was both friend and enemy to Reverend Caudill. Often it solved problems, but just as often it created more.

His first call was to the Prewitt home. Frank answered.

"Reverend Caudill here. Want to tell me what happened?"

Between sobs, Frank told the story from beginning to end. "And Dad gave me a whipping out by the barn and wants to talk about something to do with birds and bees."

At least the calendar part made sense now.

"And what else?"

"I dunno. Mom called Mrs. Osgood. So Vee's probably in trouble now too."

"Have you learned your lesson, Frank?"

"Yes, sir."

Reverend Caudill doubted it, but moved on to the next call.

"Vee? Reverend Caudill. What happened?"

His account agreed closely with Frank's. "And Mom's making me read *Moby-Dick*."

"A good book, Vee. Lesson learned?"

"Yes, sir."

"What about your father?"

"Mom said he's in trouble when he gets home."

Well. He hung up the phone. The calendar part was all sorted out. And he'd seen the cowboy on the vending machine at the Zipco. It made sense now. Sort of.

The phone rang.

"Reverend Caudill? Cornelius Alexander here . . ."

The younger man was talking so excitedly, it was all the pastor could do to make out words. "A girl? How exciting. A wonderful blessing from the Lord."

"Yes. We're going to call her Suzy. She and JoAnn are coming home the day after to-morrow."

"I'm sure you all will be resting this

225

weekend, but might we expect you in church the following week?"

After a pause, Cornelius said, "I think you might."

Mavine sat on the edge of the couch, staring, wondering how she measured up to the pinup girls Virgil had been ogling. Her eyes started to moisten a bit, but she'd allow no tears this time. Just anger.

A fine man, Alma had called him. Maybe so, but a man with wandering eyes, it seemed. Where else might they have been roving? He'd better have a good answer.

Five o'clock. On schedule, the front door opened. She stood to her full height. "Virgil." A deep breath.

But before she could say another word, Virgil sheepishly held up a hand. "Mavine, I threw that calendar in the trash, where it belongs. I wouldn't have even kept it if I'd known . . . After Lula Mae pitched a fit, I went in and . . . I didn't know about the clear plastic thing. It's not like —"

"Virgil." Mavine cut him off. The man had enough sense this time to keep quiet while she took a deep breath. "I just need to know that —" despite all her resolve, she fought to keep the tears at bay — "that you're faithful to me. That all those things you told me on my birthday are true."

"I'd never even look at anyone else, and that's the honest truth."

"Promise?"

He nodded. "If you only knew. I don't think of anybody else the way I think about you." Virgil stammered a bit as a splotch of red rose up from his collar.

Her anger waning, Mavine couldn't help but smile at this blushing, stuttering man — still true to her. "One more promise?"

"Yes?"

"Carry a different line of tires."

He relaxed. "I can do that, Mavine."

"And —" she nodded toward the stairway — "you'll want to have a long talk with our son. He needs to know the facts of life after all."

17

Reverend Caudill put down his *Pulpit Digest* and reached for his cup of tea. Here he was on a Thursday night with his sermon unwritten. Mrs. Grinnell's mother had been put in the hospital on Monday, and Tuesday was his day to visit the shut-ins. On Wednesday a late cold snap froze a pipe at the church because the furnace was acting up again. Welby came over to relight the burner, but the reverend had spent most of the day finding a plumber to get the baptistery working in time for prayer meeting — just in case. His latest sermon series had finished the week before, and a topical message would make for a welcome change next Sunday. He called it "Faith in Life" in the bulletin, which seemed vague enough for just about anything. Usually, running late on preparations meant a check through his old Bible college notes for something fresh and inspiring. This time, though, a search of the old binders and file folders came up as empty as his baptistery.

Well. Since it *was* Thursday night, he decided to visit Welby.

"Hello, Reverend!" Welby was in his usual good spirits. "Come on in and take your coat off. You're up next after Grover."

"Thank you, Welby." Reverend Caudill nodded to Grover, who was having his neck shaved, and then to Arlie and Virgil, both freshly shorn. "Seems you have a good crowd tonight."

"A fine group indeed." Sam Wright strode in, assaying the others. "We even have spiritual guidance tonight." Grover rolled his eyes — the only safe move he could make while in Welby's barber chair.

"Actually, I was hoping you might help me. I'm working on my Sunday sermon, and I thought you folks might be of assistance. I need some good ideas for topics."

"You could talk about family values again." Grover could speak safely now, as Welby had set aside his razor and was dusting his neck with a small brush. "I hear Mavine wasn't too happy about your tire company calendar."

Virgil reddened. "Where did you hear

about that?"

"Vee and Frank came by the store after school today." The grocer was back to merely rolling his eyes, as Welby had picked up his scissors and was working on his sideburns.

"Guys," Virgil pronounced, "there will be no more Safe-T-Made tires — or calendars — at Osgood's. If I'd known what was under that plastic, I'd have switched to Fisk a long time ago. Their calendars have a little boy in his pajamas."

Reverend Caudill smiled. Clearly his telephone conversations had borne fruit. "Gentlemen, I've already preached about family values twice in the past year. I'm looking for something more timely."

It was Arlie's turn. "How about dancin'? The last time you did that one, I didn't ever want to do the polka again!"

"Arlie, when did you ever go dancing?" Welby shook talcum powder into his left hand and slapped it onto Grover's neck.

"Never did, only thought about it. After that sermon, I didn't even think about it."

Sam Wright spoke up. "Perhaps a biblical discussion of the present political and social situation would be most appropriate. There's a lot going on these days."

Reverend Caudill felt an odd chill. Current events were definitely *not* his specialty. There was a lot he hadn't learned in Bible college, but he'd learned when to preach and when to meddle. This sounded like meddling. Fortunately, he didn't have to reply.

Grover, who had been powdered and given a splash of tonic, took a seat atop a case of transmission fluid and rolled his eyes again. "Sam, what do you know about all that?"

"Only what I read in the papers. You know, Will Rogers said that to me one time. . . ."

"So, how should I approach it?" Reverend Caudill had taken his seat in Welby's chair, and he would soon be limited to eye-rolling himself. "I'm writing my sermon about how faith should affect our everyday lives."

Sam was quick to reply. "It should compel us to live like Jesus and love everybody — especially the poor and helpless. He sought out blind men, tax collectors, and Roman soldiers, and gave them sight and invited them to dinner and healed their households. When people were hungry, he had compassion on them and multiplied the loaves and fishes. When he saw the crippled man, he told him to take up his pallet and walk. He freed people from their demons and gave the living water to the thirsty."

Throughout the room, jaws dropped and eyes stopped rolling. Welby even stopped clipping.

Reverend Caudill, who was used to seeing Sam's name on the prayer list, was flabbergasted. "Sam, where did you learn so much about the Bible?"

"Traveled with Billy Sunday for a time. Used to fly him around in my airplane once in a while."

Grover looked at Arlie who looked at Virgil. "So Billy Sunday taught you the Bible?"

"No, I learned it *while traveling* with Billy. Our plane ran low on fuel down in Mississippi one time, and we had to land on a road next to a cotton field. We were miles from the nearest town and were trying to decide what to do next, when this big fellow drove up. Told us we were both going to the bad place in a handbasket for trying to fly when the Lord intended for men to stay on the ground. Drove right off. Then another fellow came by — seems he was delivering Bible tracts to some church over in Meridian. Said he'd stop back by if he had time. Finally, some colored men who were picking cotton came over. They'd never heard of Billy, but helped us get the plane turned around and siphoned enough gas out of their pickup truck to get us to Hattiesburg, which was where Billy was holding his meetings. Wouldn't take any money, either."

"What an amazing story." Reverend Caudill was moved. "I had no idea you had spent time with Billy Sunday."

"Yep. Also used to fly Will Rogers around before he hooked up with Wiley Post. I remember the time he was showing his rope tricks to the Inuit in the Northwest Territories . . ."

Welby soon finished with Reverend Caudill and placed Sam in the chair. Sam blabbered almost nonstop, relating not only his adventures with Will Rogers but also his adventures with Teddy Roosevelt, Andrew Jackson, and Napoleon. Welby smiled and nodded at all the right places.

After Sam received his own talcum and tonic, he tipped Welby and headed for the door. "Preach it well, Reverend."

"I'll do that, Sam." The pastor managed a slight wave. Billy Sunday? Well. Sam might be a bubble or two off center, but he'd spoken truth whether he'd meant to or not.

The Good Samaritan it was, then.

Reverend Caudill was having a remarkable Sunday. If the semiannual business meeting at the First Evangelical Baptist Church was going to measure up to the morning sermon, it would have to be something spectacular. He was in rare exegetical form, and with all due humility, his sermon on the Good Samaritan was powerful and mesmerizing. The truth was, his corns hurt and he couldn't find a comfortable stance, so he settled for leaning on the pulpit and shuffling his feet back and forth. Every now and then an important point received particular emphasis when his left big toe barked up against the leather of his wing tips.

He did have some concerns about the day. Ever since the church voted to sell the old feed store lot during the fall business session, people had been talking about what might happen at the spring meeting. Usually the time would be spent with Anna Belle reading the minutes, Anna Belle taking some more minutes if anyone else had anything to say, someone — usually Anna Belle — making a motion to approve the minutes, and Reverend Caudill looking at his watch to see how many minutes were left until he could move to adjourn. Welby would usually second his motion, and then be called upon to close in prayer. This served double duty as the blessing for the potluck dinner, which always followed the business session. With luck, the food would still be warm when everyone filed down the stairs into the basement.

The first indication of trouble was Mrs. Madeline Crutcher, who was sitting in the center of the front row rather than at the side. The second was the *Life* magazine sticking out of the enormous shopping bag that served as her purse. The third bad omen was the way she fidgeted and glared at him during his sermon, like an anxious cat about to pounce. He'd seldom preached on the Good Samaritan, since he'd always felt Jesus was a bit hard on the clergyman in the story. Still, his three points were all nicely in a row, and the poem at the end drove the point home.

So he avoided Mrs. Crutcher's pointed gaze, knowing his song leader would stare her right back into the hardwood pew when he led the closing hymn. Grover had once said that old Toler could crack the statue in the courthouse yard with a single look.

He ended his sermon and sat down, grateful to be off his sore feet. Toler led the congregation in "Joyful, Joyful, We Adore Thee" in his usual lethargic style, but without noticeable distraction from the elderly woman, who had by now retrieved the illustrated weekly from within the depths of the bag and had opened it to a page filled with black-and-white photos. Whatever her agenda, she was loaded for bear. His stomach began to hurt and add to the pain of his throbbing toe, and his appetite for fried chicken and beaten biscuits started to evaporate. As the last amen sounded and Toler stopped waving his arms, Reverend Caudill delivered the benediction and the business meeting began.

"The business session of the First Evangelical Baptist Church is now called to order." He was listing slightly to his right, mainly to take the weight off his sore foot but also to avoid Mrs. Crutcher's piercing gaze, now visible over the top of her thick spectacles. "Mrs. Stacy, would you please read us the minutes of the fall meeting?"

"The meeting convened following the morning worship —" Anna Belle had the floor, and played it like an actress would use a stage — "and was presided over by the Reverend Eugene Caudill, who had just concluded his sermon on tithing and stewardship and reasons why we should put more money in the offering plate." He grimaced; that had not been one of his better Sundays. Anna Belle continued, "When the floor was opened for new business, it was brought to our attention by Reverend Caudill that certain repairs were needed on the parsonage and the church facility proper."

Anna Belle had it mostly right as she continued, noting for the record that the proposal to sell the lot next door had been moved, seconded, and approved by vote of the church body, and so on. He looked at his watch. The second hand was moving much too slowly for his satisfaction.

"Motion seconded by Mr. Letcher that the church engage the services of Henson Commercial Properties in Quincy . . ." Anna Belle, who had written the sentence much too long and should have known better, paused for breath. At this point, Madeline Crutcher rose to her feet.

"We have before us today a matter of far greater importance!" She waved the rolled magazine in the air.

"Mrs. Crutcher, you are *out of order*!" Part of him enjoyed this aspect of moderating a meeting. The statement reminded him of stopped-up plumbing, which in turn made him think of Madeline Crutcher. It gave him a certain satisfaction. "Kindly allow Mrs. Stacy to continue."

"Don't you shush me, young man!" She took a step forward, causing him to move back awkwardly.

And she would not be silenced. Anna

Belle, clearly taken by surprise, muttered something, folded her notes, and waved in the elderly woman's direction. "I yield the floor to Mrs. Crutcher."

She not only took the floor; she went straight to the pulpit, climbing the two steps with surprising ease and determination. He considered an attempt to stop her but sat down in the nearest pulpit chair instead. Whatever it was she had to say, let her get it out of her system and be done with it.

Mrs. Crutcher, who was never done with anything, cleared her throat and held up the *Life* magazine for all to see. "People of the First Evangelical Baptist Church, are you going to let this happen here?" The congregation craned their necks to make out the headline. "It says," she began, " 'Negro Activists Arrested in Birmingham.' What did this colored boy do? He tried to go into a white Baptist church, that's what! Sooner or later some of the colored people from over on the other side of the creek will decide they want to come here. We can't let that happen! We must pass a resolution to keep something like this from happening here in *my* church." She held up the magazine again, picturing a young dark-skinned man seated in a church pew, surrounded by scowling white worshippers.

"Just this week, I saw a colored man walk right in the front door of this church. I couldn't believe what I saw, so I watched for a long time. Sure enough, he came back out an hour later. He was practicing for something, I tell you."

Whatever he'd been expecting, this wasn't it. A headache had begun to drown out both the churning of his stomach and the throbbing at the end of his foot. Judging by the silence in the room, no one else had expected this, either. He'd tried to avoid current events, and they fell into his lap.

"Mrs. Crutcher, this is most inappropriate," he squeaked. Two deacons rose from their seats, looked at each other, and began to move toward the front of the church. She was not dissuaded, but screeched, "Do I hear a motion regarding this situation?"

Reverend Caudill had lost control of his meeting, and was in danger of losing his breakfast, too. He prayed for help and Pepto-Bismol, and from the very back of the church help arrived.

A figure on the left side stood up slowly and deliberately, but with determination on his face. "I've never made a motion in a meeting before, and I'm not sure how to do it," said Virgil T. Osgood, "but I'm going to make one now. I make the motion that if any colored person comes to this church, they will be welcomed with a smile and ushered to *your* seat, Mrs. Crutcher."

Welby jumped to his feet, almost losing his balance. "I second this motion!" He grinned at Virgil.

Reverend Caudill, who chose to ignore the fact that everyone standing was out of order, didn't know whether to be thankful or to pray some more, so he did both. He also made a mental note to buy a full tank of gasoline from Virgil on Monday. Maybe two or three.

Regaining at least part of his composure, he motioned to Anna Belle, who had dropped her pencil on the floor and had sent Grover looking for it. "The floor is open to discussion. And just *what* do you say to that, Mrs. Crutcher?" He'd regained the upper hand, headache or not, and wasn't about to lose it this time. The deacons took another step forward. Sometimes the Lord provided strength just when a person needed it.

Mrs. Crutcher glared at Reverend Caudill, the deacons, and then at Virgil. Whatever she had expected, this didn't seem to be it. The men in the outside aisles had stopped to look again at each other, and decided to just let her go until she ran out of breath and magazines. "Virgil, what would you do if a colored man tried to buy gasoline at that place you call a service station? Just what would you do?"

Virgil leaned forward. "I'd be honored, Mrs. Crutcher. Mr. Johnson buys gasoline when he goes to town, and I'm proud to say he is a friend of mine. Mr. Warren's widow gets eggs from Mavine, and gives us tulip bulbs and tomatoes. You knew my father, Mr. H. C. Osgood — knew him well. One thing my father taught me was to treat everyone with courtesy and respect, whether white or colored."

"Grover, what if one of them came to your store?"

"He'd sell him groceries, just like he does you." Anna Belle had answered, but then Grover himself stood. His voice was shaky, but his posture was solid. "And if he wanted one, I'd fix him a bologna sandwich — a thick one. With lettuce and extra mayonnaise on it."

Mrs. Crutcher's eyes blazed, which caused the deacons to back off a step. "I'm surprised at you — all of you." Her voice began to waver. All eyes in the congregation were now on Virgil, who had left his seat and begun walking up the center aisle. He stopped square in front of the pulpit, looked directly at its angry occupant.

He cleared his throat. "Mrs. Crutcher," he said slowly and precisely, "have you forgotten who you are and where you came from?"

The church was silent, except for the slight croak that came from Reverend Caudill. Whatever Mrs. Crutcher wanted to say, she swallowed. Her veins tightened up and the red drained from her face.

After a long pause, she picked up her *Life* magazine and slapped it solidly on the podium, bringing everyone back to reality. "I'm not finished with you, Virgil T. Osgood." She looked back at Reverend Caudill. "Or you either, for that matter. And just *who* was that colored man I saw?"

Reverend Caudill rose to his feet. Something within him welled up and couldn't stay inside. "That man," he said, solidly and firmly, "was Brother Jeremiah Taggart, the pastor of the Pentecostal Holiness church."

He stared at the woman, who was suddenly speechless, and then spoke slowly and deliberately. "And I invited him."

And with that, she walked down the steps, past Virgil and the deacons, and out the front door.

Reverend Caudill somehow managed to adjourn the meeting, and get to his office for a Goody's, a Dr. Scholl's corn plaster, and a shot of Pepto-Bismol, all the time regretting that he was a teetotaler. The congregation — excepting Mrs. Crutcher — had gone straight down the front steps to the fellowship hall in the basement for fried chicken and country ham, biscuits, and apple pie. For most, the potluck dinner was the only reason for staying for the business meeting, but today the entertainment had come before the meal.

"Virgil, that was a brave thing to say. I don't know exactly what you meant by it, but it was still mighty courageous." Grover had pulled Virgil aside while Mavine helped Vee find a drumstick among the thighs and wings.

Virgil reddened and looked down. "You just have to stand up for what you believe in. Mr. H. C. Osgood always taught me to do the right thing."

"Your father taught you well." Welby had taken his place in line on the opposite side of the food table, and was heaping black-eyed peas onto a plate already filled with chicken and dumplings. "Alma has a table picked out for us over by the door. Will you join us?"

"We'd be happy to." Virgil set his own

overflowing plate down where Mavine had already placed a large cup of strong black coffee from the forty-cup urn. "Welby, thanks for helping me out."

"Glad to do it." And with that, both men began eating with enthusiasm, not noticing that the room was quieter than usual and that all eyes were on them. They did notice, however, that Reverend Caudill had taken a seat at the adjacent table, and he had nothing but a small bowl of Jell-O.

The meal passed with only small talk, except for Anna Belle, who came by to ask Mavine how to spell *spectacle* and *bizarre.* Mavine was more than happy to write them out for her on the back of the meeting minutes, but seemed more concerned that her onion-and-pickle loaf had met with little interest. In the meantime, Welby had spotted Anna Belle's apple pie among the desserts and brought two slices back, handing one to Virgil. "Now —" he winked — "are you going to tell me what you know that I don't? What was all that 'who you are' business about?"

"Welby, you know that little settlement up the creek where Mr. Johnson and Brother Taggart live?"

He nodded. "Sure. Colored Mills. I used to fish for smallmouth bass up there."

"You're almost right. The name of the place is really Collard's Mill. A man by the name of Colonel William Collard came in sometime after the War of 1812. Bought some property along the creek and built a flour mill. He came from Carolina somewhere and brought slaves with him to run the place. The big house and the mill are gone now, but several of the little houses are still there. Mr. Johnson lives in one of them. Brother Taggart and his children live in another.

"The colonel had a no-account son by the name of Jack William, who took to some of the slave women. There was a slave girl born about 1840, who was light-colored and had blue eyes. They named her Pearlie, because she was the color of Mrs. Collard's necklace. Nobody could ever prove it, of course, but everybody knew she was Jack William's daughter. They kept her around the house, where she learned how to cook and wash, and by the time she was sixteen and Mrs. Collard had died, she was pretty much running the household. Jack William had long since taken off to California to look for gold and Indian girls.

"Anyway, Colonel Collard always looked on Pearlie as his granddaughter, and disowned Jack William. When she turned eighteen, the colonel granted her freedom, but she stayed around to take care of the man, as he was getting along in years. After he died, she took up with a white mill hand by the name of Thomas Osgood."

Welby's brows rose. "An ancestor of yours?"

Virgil nodded. "It was a common-law marriage, but they managed five children along the way. Pearlie inherited the place, and she and Thomas tried to keep it going with the rest of the freed slaves, but it never worked out. The railway came through Quincy a few years later, and the mill went out of business. They tried to make a boardinghouse out of it, but that didn't work out either, and late one night some people came and burned the place down. Said it wasn't right for whites and coloreds to live under the same roof. They beat Thomas up something terrible, and he died. Pearlie died soon after that — of grief, they said.

"Of the five children, two lived to tell the story. One of them was my great-grandfather Robert Osgood — H. C.'s grandfather. Dad always taught me that it was important to remember who you are and where you came from. So you see, Welby, my great-great-grandmother was half-colored, and kin to many of the colored people who live in Collard's Mill today."

Welby sat in silence. "You know, Mr. Osgood never told me that story. I knew he grew up in Eden Hill, but I had no idea of that part of his history. But what does this all have to do with Mrs. Crutcher?"

Virgil pushed aside the empty pie plate. "I said that Pearlie had two children that lived. The other was a girl, Sophie, who married a man named Joseph Wright. Joseph Wright was Madeline Crutcher's father."

Welby narrowed his gaze. "So her grandmother was half-colored Pearlie?"

"That's right, and she knows it well. We're all related — the Osgoods, the Crutchers, the Wrights, the Johnsons, the Taggarts, and probably most of Eden Hill. We're all the same, Welby. Neighbors. Just like in Reverend Caudill's sermon this morning. And sometimes we're even kin. We just need to learn to act like it."

18

After six long and discouraging months, the Zipco was finally ready to open. Cornelius had picked up some packages yesterday at the bus station in Quincy, ones he'd been expecting. To his delight, the uniforms looked much better than he had anticipated. The polished brass buttons featured the Zipco logo, and the patent-leather bands shone on the peaked hats. Another box had *Zippy the Clown* written on the side, and he set it aside near the motor oil display until Zippy arrived. Later that afternoon, the florist had delivered four dozen red roses individually wrapped in waxy paper, which Cornelius had stored inside the indoor drink cooler to keep them fresh. Their grand opening was going to be everything he'd hoped for.

The weather was his only disappointment. It had looked like rain the night before and JoAnn had heard a rumble of thunder while nursing Suzy during the night, so he was glad for the umbrellas he'd bought yesterday at the five-and-dime. All his vending machines were lit and stocked, the streamers and pinwheels were in place, and the newly painted sign that proclaimed *Grand Opening Today!* had replaced the *Coming Soon* placard on the plywood frame out front.

The underground tanks were installed and filled for both regular and premium, the snack rack was loaded with bags of chips and crackers, and Charlie was ready to tackle oil changes and tire rotations. The pavement and parking area still smelled of new asphalt, and the driveway bell dinged nicely when Cornelius stepped on it with the heel of his freshly shined shoe. Perfect.

The illuminated Zipco sign was the coup de grâce. It rotated several times each minute with a slight whir, proclaiming its inviting message like a lighthouse beacon. The fluorescent tubes lit the trademark lightning bolt with confidence and authority, and the changeable sign just below proclaimed the price of regular gasoline at 27.9 per gallon, with premium at 29.9. Virgil's station across the street, he also observed with smug delight, was still dark at almost six o'clock. When the sun finally began to lighten the overcast sky, Virgil's unlighted board and single pump would still read 29.9 cents per gallon — regular only.

"Well, here goes, Charlie!" At exactly six o'clock Cornelius flipped a switch, which powered the neon sign in the window that proclaimed *Open.* The display buzzed and flickered to life as a sleepy JoAnn, carrying an even sleepier Suzy, walked to his side.

"Neil, there's . . . no one here."

"Oh, they'll be along soon enough. 'Give the customer what he desires . . .' "

"Neil, for that Zipco book to be any good you need to first *have* a customer." Without another word, JoAnn trudged back to the mobile home.

Cornelius was in trouble and he knew it. He'd known it all along, but he finally had to admit it. His debt to Zipco would take years to pay, and his wife was unhappy with him as well. Suzy was probably disappointed with him too. The eastern sky was now glowing, and he could hear a tractor starting somewhere on the other side of town. He was about to say something to Charlie when he noticed a pair of headlights coming down the street. Were they slowing down?

"Charlie! It's a customer! Stand at attention! Remember chapter five!"

Charlie did as he was told — he, too, had read the Zipco manual. Both stood arrow straight in their best West Point military form when Welby's '56 Chevy pulled up to the regular pump. The bell sounded an agreeable welcome as the tires rolled over the hose.

"Good morning, Mr. Alexander — and a fine morning it is indeed. Might you be good enough to fill it up with regular?"

"Absolutely, sir!" Charlie was following his directions to the exact letter, as Cornelius, puzzled, adjusted his hat and walked to the driver's window.

"Good morning, sir! And what brings you *here* this fine day?" His voice held a trace of cynicism, which he couldn't conceal. Including their first awkward meeting, he'd run into Welby several times over the last few months, but he didn't know exactly what to make of this. According to the manual, a competitor was to be treated with suspicion, especially one who had declined a job offer. Was he spying on them? The book admonished him to be wary of darting eyes and sideways glances. Welby showed no signs of either.

"I just wanted to congratulate you on your grand opening!"

"Begging your pardon, sir, but where do I

put in the gasoline?" Charlie, red-faced, held the filler nozzle but could find no obvious place for the spout to go. He looked like a dog in search of a hydrant.

Welby smiled. "I'll show you — it's kind of odd on these." And with that, Welby climbed out of the car and limped to the rear. "It's right here. See?" Welby pushed the concealed button that caused the taillight to pop out of the way, revealing the elusive opening. There was no ridicule in his voice, only help and gentle assistance. "Some of these Chevrolets are a bit tricky!"

"Thank you, sir!" Charlie inserted the nozzle and squeezed, and the numbers on the pump began to whirl.

"Well, thank you, Welby!" Cornelius, while still wary, was indeed grateful for Welby's advice. Truth was, *he* didn't know where the gasoline filler was on a '56 Chevy. He also had no idea why this man would come by on his way to work at his competitor's station, but was still happy to have a customer. Any customer.

"That'll be $2.25, sir." Charlie had finished dispensing the fuel, closed the cap, and pushed the taillight back into place with a solid click. At a nod and a whisper from Cornelius, Charlie took the two bills and the quarter from Welby and tipped his hat.

"Thank you, sir. We appreciate your business!"

Cornelius spoke next. "Might I give you a rose for the little lady in your life? It's our special gift to you for our grand opening." He had four dozen roses in the drink cooler, and at this rate might still have forty-seven at the end of the day.

"How kind of you, Mr. Alexander!" Welby clutched the stem carefully as he climbed back in the car. "Alma loves roses. Thank you so much — and again, good luck!" He started the car and drove directly across the street to Virgil's and began to open up.

Several others came by in the next hour. Grover, with some more greasy biscuits from Anna Belle, stopped in and departed with a rose and a Nehi orange drink. Mr. Willett ventured over to see what was going on and to see if the Zipco carried floor mats for his Nash Metropolitan.

By eight o'clock, Cornelius was becoming discouraged, as he hadn't had a customer in almost an hour. He was also becoming a bit concerned about Zippy, who had yet to appear. "Charlie, why don't you go ahead and open his box and have it ready when he arrives?"

"Yes, sir." Charlie pulled a penknife from the pocket of his uniform and sliced through the tape. "Uh, Mr. Alexander?"

Both Cornelius and Charlie looked in the package in disbelief. Inside was a clown costume, a Zippy hat, a bright-red rubber nose, a bag of balloons, and mimeographed instructions.

Thanks to an executive decision, Charlie became Zippy the Clown for the day. Cornelius thought his assistant would fit the costume better than himself, and besides, he had to greet customers as the Zipco's proprietor. By late morning Charlie had figured out how to blow up the balloons with the air hose and twist them into shapes something like those shown in the directions. Most looked more like toilet seats with tails than the swan and the horse in the picture, and he had to be careful around the thorny roses, but he seemed to be having a good time anyway.

By noon, a few more people had stopped by. Sam Wright drove in on his Farmall, almost hitting the pump island, but he did buy some gasoline. He left with a rose for his Bertha. Mrs. Crutcher bought a quarter's worth of premium for her Buick. She turned down the rose but drove away with a green balloon that looked like an overgrown slug.

Realizing that it was past noon, Cornelius left Zippy to mind the shop and walked up to the trailer for lunch.

"Hello?" There was no reply, but he did hear sounds from the bedroom. JoAnn was crying. Again.

"What's wrong, JoAnn?"

"You know very well what's wrong! Why did you ever think we could just come into this little town, open a service station, and make a living at it? You believed all that stuff the Zipco people said about profit, and becoming wealthy, and living the good life. Look around you. Does this look like the good life?"

Cornelius had to admit it didn't. Their mobile home looked nothing like the brick split-level shown on the back of Zipco's promotional literature, and so far there was no sign of the line of cars waiting for service on the front-cover illustration. And though the truth had always been in the back of his mind, for the first time it was front and center. JoAnn was right. Zipco's pitch had been high and inside, and he'd swung for the fence.

"JoAnn, I promise you that we'll make it here. As soon as people learn who we are and that we're open, they'll come. You'll see."

"Do you really believe that?"

He hesitated. "Yes, I do! And I'll do everything I promised for you and Suzy!"

Suzy had awakened and immediately announced her hunger. "I need to give Suzy her bottle. There's bread in the breadbox and leftover Spam in the refrigerator." She gestured toward the kitchen. "I'll get something later."

By now he'd lost his appetite and made only a single sandwich, not even bothering with mustard. If he got hungry that afternoon, there were always Anna Belle's biscuits and a Royal Crown Cola from the drink cooler.

By the end of the day, Cornelius felt better. Lula Mae Prewitt had stopped by to put some gasoline in Arlie's truck and to make sure there were no inappropriate calendars on the Zipco wall. Anna Belle had stopped in to say hello and see if he needed any more biscuits, which he didn't, and left with two long-stemmed flowers. A photographer from the *Quincy Reporter* drove all the way from town to take pictures of the new business and of Zippy, who gave him a red balloon and a rose for his wife. Several others had driven through just to wish him well, which was an encouragement. Zippy had given away all his inflatable novelties, and he'd passed out most of the flowers. Charlie was more than happy to get out of the Zippy costume, and Cornelius was ready to take off the itchy hat and loosen his bow tie.

"Well, Charlie, what did you think of our grand opening?"

"It was a fine day, Mr. Alexander. See you tomorrow."

A fine day? At least somebody thought so. As Charlie walked up the street, Cornelius folded the plywood grand opening sign and moved it inside the garage door. The Open sign was still lit, so he turned it off and also pulled the switch that controlled the rotating Zipco emblem. It went dark and slowly wound to a stop.

He emptied the coins from the vending machines, added them to the register, and counted the cash in the till. Counting the two candy bars and pack of cigarettes Charlie had purchased, the day's revenue amounted to just over fourteen dollars.

It'll get better. As he started to lock the door, inspiration struck. Inside the drink case he counted twelve red roses, still individually wrapped. He gathered them together, pleased at his artistic arrangement, and walked back home to where JoAnn and Suzy were waiting.

19

Virgil slurped his fifth cup of coffee and watched the goings-on at the Zipco. The Open sign had just been turned off, as had the big rotating lightning bolt. "What do you think, Welby?"

Welby took a sip from his first cup. "It was an impressive first day; I'll allow him that. Big light-up sign. Fancy uniform. Charlie was pretty funny in that clown suit and red nose. I didn't see a lot of business, though."

"Did you see his prices?"

"Yep. A couple of pennies cheaper. Not to worry."

"So what do you think I need to do?"

"Go home and have a good dinner with your family."

Virgil had to admit it; all the action at the Zipco yesterday had shaken him up a bit. While the festivities were unfolding across the street, he'd been planning his own response to the competitive challenge. It was a modest reply: cleaning the garage floor, a new sign for the pumps, and Mavine's suggestion from several months back — a fresh coat of paint for the building. All of these needed to be done anyway, Zipco or no Zipco.

His wife's reaction had been on a smaller scale and involved his wardrobe. Four pairs of new khaki trousers had dried overnight on metal stretchers, hanging like flags from the makeshift clothesline on the back porch. She handed a pair to him and was taking the last three down while the morning coffee was coming to a boil.

"Mavine, what did you do to these pants? They feel like plywood." Virgil didn't ordinarily dress on the back porch, but she'd confiscated all of his work clothes the night before and promised a fresh outfit.

"I asked Grover to get me some heavy-duty starch. Alma is doing the same for Welby. If it isn't enough . . ."

"They're fine, Mavine. I'll get used to them."

"I also put your name on your new shirt!"

He looked down. Sure enough, she'd embroidered *Virgil* in cursive letters in white thread just above the pocket. The *g* was a bit crooked, but otherwise it looked good. His shirt, he realized, was as crispy as his trousers.

"You'll want your feet to look nice too." She handed him a clean pair of argyle socks, his shoes, a tin of black Kiwi, and a scrap from her ragbag. Clearly, the polish was to be his task.

Grumbling, he got dressed, grateful she hadn't put starch in anything else. "I'm still concerned that this grand opening thing is going to be a problem. He's making quite a splash. I saw several cars over there yesterday that I recognized."

"Well, it's modern, very tidy looking, and advertises 'clean restrooms.' And I hear he was quite charming to the ladies."

"But we're more than flowers and clowns, Mavine. People know us. We've been here for a long time, and we've done things right. That ought to count for something. We've never been very busy, but we've never gone without dinner either."

The words sounded familiar, as he recalled an earlier conversation. If he were going to be the kind of husband and father that Mavine could respect, he'd have to think of something. If an occasion needed rising to, well, he'd rise.

"Or breakfast." She poured steaming

black coffee into his mug. "But you've never had any competition either."

Vee joined them in the kitchen but seemed oblivious to what was going on.

"Mavine, I've talked a lot to Welby, who doesn't seem to be bothered at all. Says he hopes Cornelius does well with his station, that everyone deserves a chance. After all, he has a wife and a baby daughter. Zipco had a few customers yesterday. So did we. We have a thing or two planned, but what else do we need to do?"

Soon the biscuits came out of the oven, and fresh scrambled eggs appeared on his and Vee's plates. He gulped the food down with gusto, thanked Mavine, and wiped his face with the rag.

"Virgil! That was for your shoes!"

"Mavine, I've got work to do." He stood, dropping the tin of Kiwi into his pocket and filling his coffee mug with the last of the brew in the percolator. "I'll clean up my shoes if I get something on them. I promise." He winked and followed Vee out the front door, leaving it to swing in the fresh morning breeze.

Virgil walked down the path, his new trousers crackling the entire way. He was not prepared for what he saw next. The Zipco Super Service was in full operation, even at seven o'clock in the morning, with new prices posted on the sign. Zipco premium down a penny, with the lower grade also one cent cheaper across the street. No clowns could be seen, but Cornelius was out front dressed in his snappy uniform, cleaning the windshield of Arlie's truck. The two were chatting away like old friends while Charlie pumped his gasoline. With a smile.

Virgil avoided spilling his coffee, but barely.

Welby had exchanged his own starched work shirt for his white barber's jacket and was holding his Thursday night tonsorial court. Virgil had decided to visit to get a trim and observe the proceedings. The usual suspects were all there: Sam Wright sat in the chair, Grover was parked awkwardly in an old dinette seat, and Reverend Caudill was waiting his turn under the clippers. Not surprisingly, the new Zipco station was the topic of the lively conversation.

"Quite a show over at the new place, Virgil. What do you suppose he'll do for an encore?" Grover slouched down in the plastic cushion and crossed his arms.

"Well, I don't know." Virgil, finding no remaining chair, chose to stand and lean against the doorframe. "Kind of hard to beat all the stuff he had on Monday. He's cut his prices too."

Grover crossed his feet to match the rest of his body. "We have a saying in the grocery business: 'You can't sell below cost and then make up for it on volume!' "

Virgil straightened. "What volume? Sam, you're the only one here that I've seen buying anything over there."

Sam jerked, nearly costing him a bald spot. "Well, he had what I needed. Gave me a rose for Bertha too." He settled back down, such that Welby could shave his neck without worry.

Grover spun his chair around and straddled it. "Sam, what do you put in that Farmall anyway?"

"Moonshine. Throw in some octane booster, and she'll run all day!" Sam, his haircut half-finished, climbed out, paid Welby two silver dollars, and headed out the door and into the night. The tractor rumbled to life, its growl rattling the back door.

"He might be right, you know. Arlie can run that old John Deere on coal oil if he has to." Virgil took the seat vacated by Reverend Caudill, who had now placed himself in Welby's able hands.

The pastor settled into the chair. "Speaking of Arlie, has anybody seen him? He's usually here on Thursday nights."

Welby pumped the handle to adjust the seat to a comfortable level and reached for his scissors. "Last I saw him was across the street. He's bought gasoline for his truck at the Zipco the past few mornings. I suppose it gives him an early start on the day."

The room fell silent. "Virgil, I thought Arlie was a good friend, one of your best customers." Reverend Caudill leaned forward and risked a shaggy sideburn.

"He was — is. No reason he can't buy from the Zipco place. No reason at all." Virgil stood, knocking over his chair. "It's a free country, isn't it?" His voice was more than needed for the small room. Forgetting his haircut, he stomped red-faced out the door, not bothering to push it closed.

Reverend Caudill sat in his office on Friday morning, pondering the events of the previous night. He'd put his foot in his mouth and angered Virgil, and that called for an apology. Clearly, Virgil's friendship with Arlie was strained by the events of the week, and by the farmer's absence at the gathering with Welby. Still, there was more to it than this. He would go by Osgood's later to see Virgil and to make amends, and he'd planned to pay a pastoral call at the Prewitt farm today anyway. All was not well in Eden Hill, and the grapes had soured on his watch. He would see it put right.

He'd meddled once, and he planned to meddle again.

It seemed he had a sermon to write. This Sunday, his planned message on Jesus and the Pharisees would just have to be postponed.

Cornelius spent most of Friday morning on the phone with the Zipco people, who were becoming less friendly with each conversation. The visit with the Zipco representative last month had been very awkward. His line of credit had dwindled, his newly opened station had "not met expectations" for the first week, and several bills lay on his desk demanding payment. The Zipco management had finally agreed to an additional loan, with several conditions. The rotating sign would run twenty-four hours a day, thus making maximum use of its promotional potential. Another painted sign would be posted reading, *We Service Foreign and Domestic Cars.* He would also make several additional changes, beginning on Monday. Cornelius jotted a few notes on the back of his electric bill envelope.

To make matters worse, Arlie, one of his few customers the day before, had tried to hire Charlie back away from him. The farmer had come by every day this week. He'd had to give Charlie a raise to keep him, further straining the station's finances.

JoAnn was not happy with him either, so breakfast had been decidedly unpleasant. Her mother's prenuptial advice came up several times in their conversation, as well as his irresponsibility in providing and caring for his family. He'd had cereal instead of eggs, as the refrigerator was empty. If they'd owned a couch, he'd have slept on it.

Chapter four in the Zipco manual was about becoming involved in the community. For the last several months he'd been so focused on getting the Zipco off the ground that he'd practically ignored its recommendations. And after walking out on the church Work Day, he was even more ashamed to show his face there. Some people in town he'd come to recognize, but he knew little else about them. Virgil and Welby he knew — at least by name — and he'd made the acquaintance of Grover Stacy over at the grocery.

JoAnn had gotten to know Anna Belle, who seemed to have taken a special interest in her. Often Anna Belle would bring something from Stacy's Grocery, and had even offered to come sit with Suzy so they could have a night out. Reverend Caudill had come by several times, but his church was right next door with the parsonage behind, and wasn't visiting part of a preacher's job? The Methodist minister had also stopped in with some brochures and an invitation to visit. To be expected.

In all this and more, he'd failed. Miserably. His credit, marriage, and patience had been stretched to their limits. Nobody at Zipco or the Bluegrass College of Business had ever talked about failure. Business would certainly pick up during the summer, with people driving more, but in the meantime . . .

His funk was interrupted by a loud ding. A large black Buick had pulled into the pump area, and an elderly woman was talking to Charlie. The conversation, which could be heard at some distance, included a fill-up with premium gasoline, a full oil change, and a new set of tires. Mrs. Crutcher also wanted a chassis lube; said she was off to see her lawyer and didn't want to go with a squeaky car.

He gave a sigh of relief. The maintenance on the Buick would bring in more revenue than they had seen all week, and "the appearance of a busy shop will invite additional business." Page sixty-six in the Zipco manual was a favorite. Improving finances would certainly make JoAnn happy. Or at least happier.

It was a hard morning. Virgil hadn't slept well, probably due to a cup of leftover coffee before going to bed. Mavine had tossed and turned as well, and woke later than usual. Vee needed a lunch packed for a school field trip and almost missed his bus. Virgil finally made his own breakfast of cereal and bananas and got to work a half hour late.

He was always grateful for Welby's friendship and advice, and today he needed both. "Was I wrong last night?" Virgil sat carefully in a nearby chair, not yet used to his newly starched trousers.

Welby rolled his creeper out from under Grover's old Plymouth. "You lost your temper — can't say anyone blamed you. Reverend Caudill caught you by surprise and felt bad about it afterwards. Said to tell you he's sorry and meant no harm."

"And Arlie?"

"Came by earlier this morning to buy some Nabs on his way to the lake. Said he sat up with a sick hog last night. Seemed to be having a really hard time about something. Had his boat with him, so he'll probably be out there all day."

"So?"

"He's still your friend, if that's what's worrying you. Said he stopped at the Zipco to talk to Charlie about something and got gas while he was there. Virgil, you say you're worried, and I think you're really wondering what's best to do." Welby wiped his hands on a greasy towel. "The most important thing you can do right now is to help out Mr. Alexander."

"Help him out? Of what?"

"His situation. Look across the street. Mrs. Crutcher took her Buick in for tires, gasoline, and some chassis work. Probably the first real business he's had since he opened."

"How do you know that's what she's having done?" Virgil found a stool near the parts washer and parked on it.

"I sent her. She came here first."

"You did *what*?"

"Virgil, I came in to work early this morning, before the Zipco opened. I could hear Mr. Alexander and his wife arguing when he left their trailer to go to work. My hearing's not what it used to be, but I didn't have to know what the words were to know what's going on. He needs the business more than we do. It also gave Mrs. Crutcher a chance to do something good for a change."

Virgil started to say something, but Welby held up his hand. "I know you and Mavine have been mulling over how to respond to the Zipco station. Alma said she's talked with her, and Mavine thinks you need to do something about it. Yes?"

Virgil nodded.

"Remember Reverend Caudill's message on the Good Samaritan?"

"One of his better sermons."

"How did the Scripture passage start out?"

"Let's see, a man asked a question: 'And who is my neighbor?' "

"And then Jesus told a parable. How did it go?"

"A man went down to Jericho, if I remember correctly."

"Exactly right. And he fell among thieves. We both remember the rest of the story. Virgil, a man went down to Eden Hill and fell into some hard times. The way I see it, you have a choice."

"A choice?"

"That's right. You can either be the guy

who beats him up, or you can be the one who picks him up. I saw you take a stand for the right thing when Mrs. Crutcher went on her tirade, so I know you have it in you. Which one are you going to be?"

"But Mavine expects —"

"Mavine expects you to be the good neighbor. And a good neighbor is probably a good husband and father. Do the right thing and help Mr. Alexander. You'll not regret it."

Reverend Caudill was not in the mood for pastoral calls, but he had to meet with Arlie and apologize to Virgil. Clearly he'd spoken out of turn the night before. Knowing that Mavine would be at the Glamour Nook after lunch, he went by Osgood's to clear things up and to learn more. Welby was still tinkering with Grover's sedan, so they met in Virgil's office in the back. The calendar, Reverend Caudill was happy to see, had been replaced by a photo of Mavine and Vee Junior.

"Virgil, I guess I'm here to say I'm sorry about what I said last night."

"Don't worry about it, Reverend. I haven't been myself lately, either."

"Anything I can do to help?" The pastor found the old dinette chair, which Welby had returned to Virgil's office. This might take a while. "This new Zipco place is really bothering you, isn't it?"

Virgil looked off to his left and paused. "Yeah. Welby and I have been talking about it too. I think Mavine's more worried than me now. She's got me in starched pants and shiny shoes. Thinks we need to do something more so we won't lose business. Competition, she keeps calling it. Welby, on the other hand, thinks we ought to send some work his way. Says it's the right thing to do. I'm confused, I guess."

"Well, I do understand competition." The Methodist church up the street came to mind. "But Welby's right. You need to make Mr. Alexander your friend and not your enemy."

"And how do I do that?"

"It seems to me that you can start by walking across the street." Reverend Caudill rose from his seat. "Well, I must be going. By the way, are you and Mavine getting along okay?"

Virgil stiffened and didn't answer.

For the second time in less than twenty-four hours, Reverend Caudill savored the taste of shoe leather, and it was just as bitter as it had been the night before.

Reverend Caudill's telephone call to Arlie's farm resulted in a lengthy conversation with Lula Mae, who was most concerned about Frank's moral upbringing. After being assured that Virgil's raunchy calendar no longer posed a threat to Eden Hill's morality, she allowed that Arlie had gone to the lake fishing for the day. He wasn't hard to find. Reverend Caudill simply followed the tracks of the pickup truck, easily visible in the damp grass. Arlie himself had pushed his boat into the water and was unwrapping a plug of chewing tobacco as the pastor pulled up.

"Afternoon, Reverend. Something you need?"

"Actually, I wanted to talk with you."

"Well, get in the boat. I'm fishin'." Arlie was not a man of unnecessary words. "I've got plenty of minners and an extra pole, if you want to use it."

Well. Reverend Caudill had not been fishing since he was ten years old, but the memory was pleasant, and he *did* need to chat with Arlie. He climbed in after Arlie, being careful not to step on the cane pole in the bottom. The Jon boat sported an outboard motor, which started with a tug on the starter rope, and soon they were well away from the bank. The vessel sat low in the water on Arlie's end but was large enough that there was no danger of tipping over. As they approached a fallen tree, Arlie switched off the motor and dropped a small anchor over the side.

"Here we are." He handed the bamboo rod to Reverend Caudill. "It's already got a hook and line, and there's minners in the bucket."

He suddenly realized that he was dressed in his ministerial suit and tie — hardly appropriate clothing for angling. The bucket in the center was indeed filled with minnows and contained a dip net, and the pastor chose a small but chubby one for his initial bait. No sooner had he dropped the line in the water than the bobber disappeared, the water churned, and he pulled in a nice-size crappie.

"Nice one. There's another bucket there for the keepers." Arlie pointed to a galvanized washtub in the middle of the boat. "Limit's sixty."

Arlie was next to land a frisky fish. Into the tub it went, and soon there were fifteen swimming around, splashing water in all directions. Reverend Caudill was catching the finny creatures as fast as he could reload minnows, with Arlie doing the same. When one fisherman hooked a particularly large example, the other would use a landing net to ensure there was no escape for the hapless crappie.

"Arlie, what I really came for was to talk with you about your family. And your relationship to God. I've not seen you at church for a while; just wanted to see if everything was okay."

"Nothing I can't handle. And me and God are just fine."

"And your son, Frank?"

"Put your line in over by that old dead tree."

By four o'clock, Reverend Caudill had lost track of time and space. It wasn't exactly the pastoral visit he'd expected, but he was having a grand time, had gotten to know Arlie somewhat better, and had discussed the issues he'd come to talk about — sort of. Thirty of the crappie in the washtub were his, matching the number tossed in by his companion. Fish were flopping about the bottom of the boat as the tub overflowed, and his best suit was soaked up to his knees. No problem — he'd take it by Willett's Dry Goods to be sent for cleaning and wear his other suit on Sunday.

Sunday? For the past two hours he'd not thought about Sunday's sermon, nor Madeline Crutcher. Surprisingly, he did not feel guilty at all. Truth was, he needed a hobby, some pastime to help him relax.

Arlie pulled the rope again and the motor putted to life, belching nearly as much smoke as his truck. As the Jon boat approached the bank, Reverend Caudill became aware that a third vehicle had pulled up beside his car and Arlie's truck. It was black-and-white and sported a rotating red light on the top.

Deputy Blanford met them and helped pull the small craft out of the water. "Good afternoon, gentlemen! May I see your fishing licenses, please?"

Arlie dug into the pocket of his overalls, and among the duct tape and baling wire managed to produce his wallet. Inside he found the crumpled official certificate and presented it to the officer for approval.

The deputy nodded and handed it back. "Reverend?"

He was caught and knew it. He tried a diversion. "No license, Officer Blanford, but I'm here on the Lord's work, ministering to one of my parishioners. Surely you understand."

"I'm sure you are, Reverend, but I'm here

on the state's authority and I'm going to have to issue you a citation for fishing without a license. Sorry, but you'll also have to give up your fish."

Arlie spoke up. "Tom, how do you know which fish are his? They're all in the same bucket!"

The deputy scratched his head. "Now that's a good question." He paused for thought. "Okay, you can keep the fish, but I still have to give you a ticket." With that, he scribbled a few words on a pad, tore off the top sheet, and handed it to the minister. "Good afternoon, gentlemen." His task finished, the deputy and part-time game warden climbed into his patrol car and drove away.

Reverend Caudill stared at the citation for a long time, looking for a loophole.

Finding none, he folded the paper and put it in his suit pocket. It was going to cost him a ten spot for his afternoon's ministry. "Guess I'd better be on my way too."

"Not without your fish." Arlie found a flimsy but serviceable plastic bucket in the back of his truck and filled it with lake water and squirming crappie. "Roll 'em in flour and fry 'em up in bacon grease. Mighty good."

The pastor helped Arlie get the boat back

onto its trailer, cranking the winch while the farmer guided it into position. Arlie's washtub of fish went into the passenger seat next to the truck's owner, who climbed inside and rolled the window down. "Reverend?"

"Anything I can do for you, Arlie?"

"I suppose you can pray for me."

He started the truck, filling the pastor's face with blue smoke, and rumbled away.

Well. Reverend Caudill had a ten-dollar fine, a spiritual burden, and a bucket of fish. He had no idea how to clean and cook crappie, and they were ill-gotten besides. Dumping them back into the lake wasn't an option — Arlie had stuck his own neck out on his behalf. He poured out about half of the water, opened his trunk, and jammed the pail in place with his spare tire.

As he drove away, he was nursing his guilt. The deputy was right: he'd not rendered unto Caesar that which belonged to Caesar. There was no way he could keep his catch, or he'd feel even worse. As he crossed the bridge into town, an idea occurred to him. If he couldn't take the fish home, he'd just have to give them away. At the Zipco Super Service, he made a hard left.

"Afternoon, Reverend." Cornelius, snappy

and uniformed, met him as he braked to a stop. "What can I do for you today?"

"Actually, I've come to do something for you." Reverend Caudill had gotten out and opened the trunk. "Got a gift for you and your wife. Dinner." With that, he lifted out the white plastic container and set it on the blacktop.

Cornelius stared at the bucket, started to speak, then fell silent. "Why, thank you, Reverend. They'll make a fine dinner, indeed." He looked at the bucket of fish, then back at the clergyman, who thought he saw some deep pain along with the smile. Yes, this was the right thing to do.

"How do I fix them?" Cornelius's voice was breaking.

"Roll them in flour and fry them up in bacon grease. Mighty good, I'm told!"

Reverend Caudill found Sunday worship at the First Evangelical Baptist Church a glorious occasion. The weather was spectacular, Toler's direction of the choir was surprisingly energetic, and the sermon, "Casting Our Nets on the Other Side of the Boat," was followed with interest by most of the congregation, which pleased him greatly. Madeline Crutcher was noticeably absent from her front pew, and nobody snored. The crowd was larger than usual, including all the regular families and one less-familiar couple: the Alexanders sat in the rear under the balcony. Following the benediction, he quickly made his way to the door to greet parishioners. Even his corns were quiet this morning. The Osgoods shook his hand as they left, as did the Prewitts. The Alexanders were the last ones to the door, waiting quietly to one side while the others departed.

The reverend smiled. "So glad to see you fine folks this morning. Hope you've been blessed today."

"Happy to be here." Cornelius offered a firm handshake. "Thank you so much for the fish. They were quite tasty."

"Happy to oblige." He thought of the citation and swallowed a wince. "Where's your daughter this morning?"

JoAnn brightened. "Anna Belle took her to the nursery so we could attend the worship service. She said she'd meet us afterward. Oh, here she is!"

Anna Belle appeared at the doorway, carrying a contented little bundle. "Suzy's been great! We've had such a good time this morning — she even fell asleep on Grover's shoulder while he was rocking her." Her husband had come alongside, carrying a bulging pink diaper bag. "She's been changed and is all ready to go." She handed the cooing infant to JoAnn while Grover handed the bag to Cornelius.

"Well, it's been a fine Sunday. Might we look for you again next week?" The pastor was at his best with contented babies and happy visitors.

"We'll try to be here. Welby and Alma even invited us to Sunday school." The young family walked down the steps and headed for the Zipco station and their home behind, JoAnn carrying Suzy while Cornelius followed, leaning to one side from the heavy bag slung over his shoulder.

Reverend Caudill smiled. Fishers of men, indeed. It had cost him a trip to the courthouse and ten bucks for a fishing license, but it had been well worth it.

Cornelius and JoAnn stepped into their front door and put the now-sleeping Suzy into her makeshift baby bed made of empty soda crates and a large cardboard box. They'd get something better when they could afford it or when Suzy outgrew it, whichever came first. Cornelius hadn't been keen on attending church, but JoAnn wanted to go and thought they ought to show some appreciation to Reverend Caudill, who had been so kind on Friday afternoon.

Cornelius put the diaper bag on the floor next to Suzy's bed. It was much heavier than he remembered, and he wondered if Grover and Anna Belle had forgotten and left a soaked diaper behind. Gingerly feeling the bottom, his hand found something round and heavy.

"Well look at this!" he whispered. JoAnn leaned closer as he pulled several items from the bag: Enfamil, followed by small jars of pureed carrots, spinach, peas, and something called fruit dessert. There was also a note, written on the back of a Sunday school quarterly:

We were so glad to see you in church today. Grover went to the store while I was changing Suzy and brought these back for you. If she's too young for the food in the jars, she'll grow into it.
Blessings, Anna Belle and Grover Stacy

For the first time in many days, JoAnn laughed. Then she leaned over and planted a juicy kiss on her husband's cheek. "You know, Neil, I think God is trying to tell us something here."

Cornelius puzzled over her words. Was it

God, or just two kind people reaching out a helping hand, right where his family was hurting the most? Cornelius stared at the unexpected gift in front of him. Did God know their cupboard was empty? Why would he pay attention to the Alexanders, especially when Cornelius had paid him no mind for so long?

His life was empty, too, he had to admit. And falling apart, at that. He'd never thought of church in terms of buckets of crappie or jars of baby food, and if he wasn't careful, he might just give in to one of Reverend Caudill's invitations.

JoAnn had fallen asleep in the upholstered chair and was breathing softly. Her eyes were closed, but peace was written across her face.

20

Glorious worship services notwithstanding, Virgil's weekend had been decidedly unpleasant. Saturday had been spent mowing the yard and planting zinnias like Mavine wanted, instead of fishing at the lake like he wanted. She'd pushed hard to get the family to church on Sunday morning, rushing both him and Vee out the door, and was quite upset that Vee's shirttail wasn't tucked in all the way. Sunday dinner had been delicious but quiet, and she had little to say and his compliments went unacknowledged. Virgil was carrying his own dishes to the sink when the phone rang.

Mavine answered. The caller had gone on for a full minute after "Hello," before she spoke again. "He said what? And was telling this to Frank?" Mavine's color changed from ashen white to beet red and back again. "Yes, Lula Mae, I'll deal with this right away."

Mavine hung up the instrument with a slam and a resounding clang. "Virgil T. Osgood Jr.! Get in here!" Vee had started for the door with his baseball glove but came running. Fear shone in his eyes.

"Yes, ma'am?"

"I just spoke with Mrs. Prewitt about your behavior in Sunday school this morning. It seems you told Frank a joke."

"Uh . . ."

"A knock-knock joke. And when Frank said, 'Who's there?' you said, 'Sawyer,' and when he said, 'Sawyer who?' what did you say?"

Vee had assumed a color similar to Mavine's. "Uh . . ."

"What?"

He mumbled something and looked at his shoes.

Mavine's eyes grew as wide as Virgil's coffee mug, and the pitch of her voice climbed half an octave. "Go to your room while I decide what you'll be reading for your punishment."

"Awww, Mom. I wanna go play ball with the guys." He looked to his father and found no sympathy.

"Get up there right now or you'll be reading *War and Peace.*"

Vee stared at the thick tome on Mavine's

bookshelf. His eyes grew wide, and without hesitation or further argument he shot up the stairs, stomping defiantly on each step.

Virgil stifled a laugh. *"Saw your underwear"* seemed a harmless if silly joke, but clearly Mavine thought otherwise. Still, it didn't belong in Sunday school, especially if Lula Mae Prewitt was the teacher. He grimaced at the memory of the Calendar Fiasco, but this was a bit much, even for Lula Mae. Hoping to ease Vee's pain, he scanned a row of thinner books just above Tolstoy's classic. "Mavine, how about this one? The cover has a picture of a fish on it. *The Old Man and the Sea*?" With luck, Virgil expected, he could still get to the lake this afternoon.

Mavine snatched the book from Virgil's hand and skimmed the first few pages. "Well, it might be good for him." She grumbled up the stairs, punishment in hand. The conversation that ensued, as Virgil heard it, was lively but muted, ending in another "Oh, Mom!" from Vee.

Mavine's departure gave Virgil a moment to sit and think. He'd learned something over the past few months and needed to remember what it was. He hadn't understood that entire *Pageant* article, but he now knew that Mavine needed more attention from him, which he had tried to do. He was expected to at least ask the right questions and not defend himself.

"I don't know what's gotten into that boy!" Mavine descended the stairs with only slightly less noise and drama than Vee's ascent. "Trashy stories, acting up at church. The school principal even sent a note home on Friday."

Virgil sat up sharply in his chair. "What'd Vee do now?"

"Pulled Darlene Prewitt's pigtails in the lunchroom, that's what. If he hadn't been riding the school bus that afternoon, Mrs. Dawson would have made him stay after school and write sentences on the blackboard."

"He got sent to the principal's office?" Virgil scowled. "Did she say anything else?"

"Only that he seemed upset about something at home."

Virgil looked toward the stairway and scratched his head. "Well, it *has* been busy around here, with the new service station across the road. Maybe that's it. Vee doesn't miss much, you know."

"Frank Prewitt got sent to the principal along with him."

Virgil stopped scratching and looked straight at Mavine. "What did Frank do?"

"Fighting."

An unexpected twist. "About Vee pulling Darlene's pigtails?"

"No, Frank would probably find that funny." She paused. "Virgil?"

Here it comes. Virgil steeled himself for it this time. "Yes?"

"Lula Mae and Arlie are getting —" Mavine paused and swallowed a lump in her throat — "a divorce."

"A . . . what?" His friend? Arlie? "Where did you hear that?"

"Gladys was telling us at the Glamour Nook on Friday."

"Mavine, Gladys is a very nice lady and a good friend of yours, but you shouldn't believe everything she says."

"Virgil, she said Lula Mae told her herself. They've been talking to Reverend Caudill and some marriage counselor in Quincy. Lula Mae's tried to make it work, but says Arlie is angry all the time and won't let her do anything or go anywhere. She's worried about Frank and Darlene too. Frank's been in trouble at school, and Darlene's been sick off and on all spring." Mavine squinted away a tear. "And I'm worried myself."

Virgil, who had never been comfortable around emotions, was at a total loss. Not only had he not seen this coming; he wouldn't know how to prepare for it even if he had. Arlie could be a bit gruff and short with words and Lula Mae a bit overbearing, but he never thought they might consider ending their marriage. Except for Gladys, that kind of thing just didn't happen around here. Not in Eden Hill, it didn't.

"Virgil?" Her blinking no longer held back the flow.

He paused. "Yes?"

"You've seemed angry lately too. At Arlie, at Mr. Alexander, maybe even at Vee and me. Could that ever happen to us? Separating, I mean."

Virgil started to say something, then paused. He'd called her ideas foolishness once before, and that had not gone well. Clearly his wife was hurting — both for her friend, and in her own imagination — and there was nothing foolish or silly about *that*.

He remembered something from his conversation with Welby too. He knew who he was, where his values lay, and just how much he loved Mavine. And he'd picked up some courage. If he could stand up against Madeline Crutcher, he could certainly stand up for Mavine.

"I'm sorry if I've acted like I was unhappy with you or Vee. This new Zipco station across the road is turning out to be more trouble than I thought. We'll probably make less money, and that will be hard some-times."

She looked away. "You didn't answer my question."

Virgil stood up. "Mavine, I'll never want to be away from you. Ever! And I'll do whatever it takes to keep you. You're my wife and the mother of our son."

She brightened and reached in her purse for a Kleenex. Finding none, she grabbed the nearest dishrag. "Promise?" She wiped at her damp brow.

"Mavine, when I said, 'I do,' I meant it. And I meant all that other stuff too."

"But you forgot our anniversary. Again. Everyone at the Glamour Nook wanted to know what you had given me."

"Our . . . what?" He sat back down.

"It was Thursday. I really thought you'd remember this year."

It was all making sense now. "I'm so sorry, Mavine. I'll make it up to you." He started to say something about stress and business and Zipco, but thought better of it. He was already in enough trouble.

This was one of those situations where anything he might say would be wrong. Everything he'd said and done that he thought showed deep affection, she'd seen as shallow. And all the things he was trying to do to keep their little business afloat weren't enough. On one hand, Welby and the Bible seemed to be saying that Cornelius was his neighbor, and he needed to be, well, neighborly. On the other hand, Mavine wanted more effort on his part.

It was going to be hard to keep God and his wife both happy.

The next few minutes passed awkwardly, with Mavine saying nothing and clunking around in the kitchen, and Virgil flipping through the new *Popular Mechanics.* Saying nothing was better than offering anything when he had failed, so he decided to just wait until she became talkative again. And Arlie's marriage falling apart? That explained a lot. Virgil decided he didn't like magazines, so he tossed it in the basket by the couch.

After about ten minutes, Mavine had put all the pots and pans away and cleaned the basket in the coffeepot in preparation for the next morning. She wandered past the table, patted Virgil on the shoulder, and said, "I love you anyway," and went outside to check on her zinnias.

By evening, the family had come to a truce. Mavine had agreed to allow Vee to watch *Wild Kingdom* on television — but only because the host was named *Marlin*

Perkins and she thought it would be educational. Virgil had planted some flower seeds where Mavine wanted them, touched up a couple of places on the chicken coop he'd missed the first time around, and still got to spend an hour at the lake. He caught one pitiful bluegill and lost two of his best lures. Having had all the fun he could stand, he went to bed at nine thirty — well before Mavine retired. Since he too was worried about Arlie and Lula Mae, he tossed and turned until almost ten before falling into a fitful sleep.

Virgil, at Mavine's suggestion, set his alarm clock for five thirty on Monday, climbed into his rigid trousers and shirt, gulped down his coffee, and headed out his front door thirty minutes later. There was no work to do at six o'clock, but she'd claimed, "You'll look so much more successful." If it would make her happy, it would be worth it.

Ticky and her three puppies followed along, running in circles. He patted her head, grateful for the company and companionship. Across the street the Zipco sign was illuminated and turning, a glowing beacon in the morning twilight. Sometime over the weekend, the price signs had been updated, reducing the cost of gasoline another penny per gallon for both grades. Mr. Alexander was chatting with a customer. Charlie was filling the woman's tank with deeply discounted fuel while two more cars waited in line.

21

Madeline Crutcher's death came as a surprise to everyone, and apparently to Mrs.
Crutcher as well. She had neglected to
report the upcoming event to Reverend
Caudill, who'd noted her absence on Sunday morning with some satisfaction, consid-
ering it part of the general blessing of the
day. But after two days without a single
complaint or early morning telephone call,
he asked Deputy Blanford to check on her.
Reverend Caudill had tried to call her
house, but she rarely answered the telephone, so twenty rings meant nothing one
way or the other. Even when she did answer,
he usually wished she hadn't.

Tom had found her dead as could be, still
sitting at the kitchen table. "Reverend," he'd
said, "she was in her robe and bedroom slippers. The slippers had bunny rabbits on
them, just like a little kid might wear. There
was a bottle of ketchup on the table, but

her cat had finished whatever had been on the plate. That's a hard way to go." Tom had found something to feed the cat, he'd said, and then called the funeral home.

At least it had been quick and painless. Natural causes, according to the coroner. Arrangements were to be handled by a mortuary in Quincy, but the visitation would be held at the old Crutcher Funeral Home in Eden Hill. It had been closed ever since her husband, Tom Crutcher, had died several years before. Their son, Del, didn't want it, not with his job in town at the hardware store, though he'd kept the building and would occasionally open it up for local clientele. "Mama wanted it that way, Reverend," Del had said when they met. "She told me not to sell it because she might need it someday. Looks like she finally did."

Del had helped him write the obituary for the *Quincy Reporter:*

MRS. MADELINE W. CRUTCHER

May 18, at home. b. Aug. 9, 1880 in Eden Hill, widow of Oscar Thomas (Tom) Crutcher. Survivors include two daughters, Mrs. Virginia Cousins of Winchester and Mrs. Carolina Wilson of Pasadena, California; one son, Mr. Delbert Crutcher of Quincy; a sister, Mrs. Alene Burton of Lawrenceburg; four grand-children; and several nephews. She was a member of the First Evangelical Baptist Church of Eden Hill, Daughters of Confederate Defenders, and a former member of the Quincy County Library Association. Visitation will be Wednesday evening at the former Crutcher Funeral Home on Front Street in Eden Hill. Services will be held noon Thursday at the First Evangelical Baptist Church, Rev. Eugene Caudill officiating. Interment will follow in the Eden Hill cemetery.

Del had come out to get the place cleaned up and meet with the minister, and they both went to Stacy's Grocery for lunch. "I'm sorry to hear about your mother," said Grover, as he cut off a slab of bologna from the big roll in the meat case. "You want mayonnaise and lettuce on that?"

"Thanks about Mother, but no thanks on

the mayo. It was just one of those things."

"Has everyone in the family been notified?" Grover placed the sandwich carefully on a paper plate, arranging chips and a pickle on the side.

"Everyone I can reach. Mother never talked much about her family, except for her sister, Alene, but I have telephone numbers for my sisters. Her only friends were in the Daughters of Confederate Defenders. A strange group of women."

Reverend Caudill raised an eyebrow.

"They put on all kinds of airs claiming to be of pure white blood, or something. Never made sense to me. Thanks, Grover!"

By this time, Grover had come around the counter carrying two sandwiches. "Outlived most of her friends, I'd guess. Most of the folks from church will be there, though. They always come out for a funeral, and will cook up something if they know where to send it. You and your wife need anything?"

"No, thanks, we're fine. I do need some sixty-watt lightbulbs, though. A couple of the torchieres are burned out."

"Just got some in," Grover reached into a large box behind the cold-cut case. "Sam, we'll get back to the game in a minute."

Sam Wright, who had been playing pinochle with Grover at the table before Del and the minister arrived, grumbled. Not only had he given up his table to a paying customer, but he also had to abandon the best hand he'd had in months.

"Do I have to go?" asked Virgil, as Mavine finished ironing his white shirt. "You know how fidgety I get." At issue were the suit and tie as well as the visitation.

"Yes. And I expect you to look nice and well-groomed."

"She was a grumpy old woman. I didn't think much of her."

"Nobody did. But you used to service her car and eat her green beans at church potluck dinners. And you're friends with Del. Besides, I've already made a casserole and you know I can't go by myself."

"A casserole? Who are you going to give it to?"

"I'll find somebody."

Virgil groaned but hoped she couldn't hear. He still remembered the seafood Jell-O ring Mavine had brought to the church potluck last spring. Grover didn't have any canned salmon, so Mavine settled for some of Virgil's crappie from the freezer. Somehow, it just wasn't the same.

"Here — put this on." The shirt was crisp,

having had a dash of Grover's heavy-duty starch.

Virgil knew when he was beaten. None of his usual excuses had worked, including the itchy suit and wrinkled shirt, the latter of which Mavine had more than rectified. Mavine's sense of correctness and respect for the dead was not about to be questioned. But she was right, of course. The truth was, he simply didn't care for funerals, or anything else the least bit morbid. The idea of spending time around a lot of people and being introduced to new folks didn't sit well at all. He shrugged in resignation and buttoned up the shirt all the way to the top.

"Mom, do I have to?" Vee Junior had just come downstairs wearing the mandated tie. He was scratching at both his shoulder and his back.

"The answer is yes to both of you. Honestly, I don't know what has gotten into you two. Gentlemen, this is called 'courtesy.' " Vee started to reply, but a glare from Virgil cut him off. Mavine made hand motions indicating that the casserole was to go in the trunk of the car. Right now, and without further argument.

The trip was made in silence, except for Vee complaining about the late supper. Several cars were parked by the funeral home when they pulled up.

"Good to see some lights on." Mavine was trying to make conversation. "It has looked pretty dreary for the last couple of years."

"It's a funeral home, Mavine. It's supposed to look dreary." Virgil had no intent of being talkative, cheerful, or otherwise lively, particularly in front of a mortuary. He was relieved to see Reverend Caudill standing at the door, greeting the bereaved as they wandered in.

"Evening, Reverend. So sorry to hear about Mrs. Crutcher," mumbled Virgil, trying to look more comfortable than he actually was. It wasn't only the location that made him feel funny; Virgil just wasn't the kind to wear a suit and tie. He'd have felt the same way at a party.

"Evening. Glad you and Mavine could come, Virgil. So sad, so sad. I should have realized something was wrong when she wasn't at services on Sunday."

Virgil was quite relieved when the pastor motioned him inside and to a corner. The Crutcher Funeral Home was the same old place he remembered: frumpy and run-down. The new lightbulbs and fresh dusting couldn't hide the neglect that had taken its toll over the years. Madeline Crutcher was on display in a side room lined with heavy curtains. Mavine took Virgil by one arm and Vee by the other, easing them both inside, over their protests. "Couldn't I just wait in the lobby?" Vee pleaded.

"Absolutely not! You'll both show some respect for the dead!" It was a whisper, as if Mrs. Crutcher might wake up if someone actually spoke, but it was a whisper that would cut steel. Both did as they were told.

Several floral arrangements were on display by the coffin. Del and his wife, Elizabeth, were seated nearby, chatting with Welby and Alma. Welby looked even more uncomfortable in his suit than Virgil, but seemed more at ease around people.

"Such a shame," Welby was saying. "Very sad. I wish more people were here."

Alma shook her head in agreement. She too had brought a casserole, which she was holding in her lap: something brownish-green with onion crisps on top. She offered it to Del, who shook his head.

Virgil spotted Deputy Blanford and extended his hand. At least he could wear his uniform instead of a suit. "So sorry, Tom. I heard you were the one who found her."

"Part of the job, Virgil," said the officer, who was also squirming. "Been over to the lake lately?"

For the first time since he arrived, Virgil relaxed. Misery loves company, and he'd just found a kindred spirit. If he was lucky, he could talk fishing with the men until it was time to go home.

Mavine was quite willing to let Virgil talk with the other men, whether it was about fishing, cars, or sports. This was awkward for him, she knew. As long as the husbands kept out of the way, the women could do the important things. Like exchanging covered dishes and warm condolences.

"I swear," said Gladys, "getting Tom to a visitation or a funeral is like pulling half his teeth. In fact, I think he'd rather have that done. What's that, Mavine?"

"A casserole. It's a new recipe I found on the back of a cornstarch box."

"Looks interesting. What's in it?"

"Cauliflower, rutabagas, eggplant, tomatoes, and zucchini — plus, of course, the cornstarch to thicken it up. The box said it won first prize at a county fair somewhere in Arkansas last year."

"What's the white stuff on the top?" Gladys asked.

"Coconut and whipped cream. The box said you could serve it as dessert, too."

Gladys nodded and smiled.

The Prewitts had just come in, carrying soup pots and pans covered with aluminum foil. Arlie and Frank made a beeline to the gathered men; Lula Mae and Darlene had gone straight toward Mavine and Alma. "Such a shame, such a shame," Lula Mae muttered, taking a sturdy chair offered by Alma. "She was such a shining light in the church."

"Sad, indeed." The irony was not lost on Mavine, who remembered the equally sad news about Lula Mae and Arlie. "You're both dressed so nicely tonight."

"Thanks, Mavine. Arlie sold one of his hogs, so I was able to buy a ten-yard bolt of fabric from Willett's. He ordered this in especially for me; I really liked the daisies. So Darlene and I both have new dresses."

"Ten yards worth?" The fabric was covered in daisies. Big daisies.

"Last year I could get by with seven, but Darlene's grown and my patterns work better with an extra yard. And then there's the curtains in the kitchen."

"Is Vee here tonight, Mrs. Osgood?" asked Darlene, with stars in her eyes.

"Yes. He's with the men, I think." They'd be grown soon enough, but for now she thought the whole thing cute.

■ ■ ■ ■

Several others had come in toward the end of the visitation, including Grover and Anna Belle, and surprisingly, Brother Taggart. Reverend Caudill had relinquished his spot at the door and was moving throughout the room, talking with each of the mourners. He chatted at some length with Virgil, desperately searching for something good to say about the deceased at the funeral the next day. "All I can think of is that she always paid cash," Virgil had said.

Fortunately, Welby and Alma shared a couple of anecdotes about Mrs. Crutcher once bringing cookies to vacation Bible school, and the time she'd given the church some fans from the funeral home. "A shame," Welby said. "And such a good woman too."

Alma chimed in with a compliment of her own. "She always had such a generous spirit."

A good woman? A generous spirit?

But what about those things he'd learned from Del over lunch at Stacy's Grocery? Daughters of Confederate Defenders? Surely a darker stain than he'd imagined. That *did* explain some things.

Well. Reverend Caudill swallowed a reply and wrote these down in a small notebook, where he'd already scribbled a few notes. Not much to go on. He'd already chosen his message from the ministers' manual: "Funeral Message for Person(s) Unknown to the Clergyman." Wishful thinking, perhaps.

Soon Grover and Anna Belle took their leave, apologizing to Del for leaving so early. The Prewitts slipped out, followed by the Osgoods. Welby and Alma stayed until almost nine o'clock talking with Del and Elizabeth. "Once again, I'm so sorry, Del," Alma said as she put on her scarf. "Call us if we can do anything."

"Thanks, Alma," Reverend Caudill answered. "We'll let you know. Thank you for coming, Welby. Del, I think we're ready for you and the family to have your time alone with your mother before they close the casket. I'll get the lights in the back, and then have prayer before we leave."

Reverend Caudill closed the door behind them and went to the back room to turn out some lights. As he returned to the parlor to close the casket and lock the front door, he came upon a scene that stunned him to silence.

Brother Taggart stood in front of the coffin beside Del and his wife, his hat held respectfully in his hands. They were speaking softly.

Reverend Caudill cleared his throat. "Begging your pardon, Brother Taggart, but this time right now is only for the family."

Nobody moved or spoke, but Del held up his hand.

Brother Taggart stepped forward. "Reverend Caudill, there's something you need to know." The man paused. "Madeline Crutcher was my mother."

Reverend Caudill grabbed at a flower stand to steady himself. "Your . . . what?"

"My father told me it was her idea, but she always claimed he'd forced her, and she hated Negroes because of it. I think she hated herself. My father and his wife raised me as one of their own. Del's always known, I think, but I promised Mrs. Crutcher I'd never tell anyone so long as she was alive.

"So now, my new friend, you know her secret. And mine."

Reverend Caudill led in prayer, including prayer for himself. And all those gathered around the casket. It may not have been too connected or coherent, but it was sincere. Yes, even in a little village where everyone knew everyone else, there were still unknowns.

But at least one secret, and the one who had forced it into hiding, had been set free this week.

The funeral and burial were uneventful, and Reverend Caudill was grateful. Virgil and Grover both closed shop during the service, and a good portion of the congregation turned out for the event. Carolina and Virginia were both there, Carolina having flown in by jet the evening before. Several of Del's friends attended as well.

Del's half brother, Jeremiah Taggart, was not there. He'd called earlier to say he wouldn't be attending, didn't want to be a distraction.

It was a good funeral, if such a thing can be said. Reverend Caudill wouldn't have admitted as much aloud, but he thought he'd done a masterful job of delivering a message that painted a glorious picture of the Promised Land but avoided any mention of the deceased.

22

Virgil's breakfast coffee was not sitting happily in his stomach, but was arguing with Mavine's fried bacon and losing badly. Two tablespoons of Maalox had only made it worse. The early hour didn't help either, and this morning Ticky and the pups were nowhere to be seen. He'd have to go it alone.

Mrs. Crutcher's funeral had caused him to close the station down for most of a day, and he was behind in his work. Both he and Welby had been obliged to attend, and Reverend Caudill asked if the church could use his parking lot because the pastor expected quite a few people to show up. Cornelius had kept the Zipco station open during the memorial service, which Virgil thought was in poor taste, and had filled the fuel tanks of several attendees as well as the hearse driver. Virgil had several repair jobs to be done today, and hopefully some gasoline customers would come by as well.

Welby was once again working on Grover's Plymouth. The car had been dropped off two days before, but Grover had said there was no hurry because he could walk if he needed to, and he wasn't planning on going anywhere anyway. The hood was open, and Welby's trouble light was hanging from the prop rod.

"Morning, Virgil!" Welby had placed a box of spark plugs, a distributor cap, and several electrical items on a mat on the fender. "You're early again today. You okay?"

"I suppose. What's the price of gasoline at the Zipco today?"

"The same as yesterday, but he's giving away a free coffee cup with a fill-up. Has a sign out with a picture of one on it. They look cheap, like they're imported from somewhere — even have a lightning bolt on the side. Where's your own mug, by the way?"

"I quit at a single cup this morning. Mavine says I need to cut down because it's making me nervous."

"Makes sense." Welby had disappeared under the hood to tweak something.

"On the other hand, she says I'm not nervous enough."

"The Zipco thing is getting to her? Well,

Alma can never make up her mind either."

Virgil reached for his coffee and then realized it wasn't there. "Welby, what do you think we ought to do now?"

"We ought to finish this tune-up and give Grover back his car. Would you hand me my plug socket and torque wrench?"

Virgil passed the tools to Welby's outstretched hand. "No, what else do we need to do about the Zipco station? Mavine has been talking about it all weekend."

"I thought we had all this settled."

"I did too. Like we talked about, the Bible says I need to be a good neighbor. But I need to be a good husband too. I'm trying hard, Welby, but I'm just not sure I can be both at the same time."

"So what's she saying?"

"That I need to be more . . . aggressive. I think that was the word she used."

Welby twisted the ratchet. "Did she have any specific ideas?"

"To begin with, she says our place needs paint. Honestly, I've had the same notion myself lately. Vee gets out of school soon, and maybe he can do some of the work. A fresh coat on the walls couldn't hurt. Besides, she thinks it will be good for his character."

Welby grinned and laid a corroded spark

plug on the radiator. "So far, I'd agree with her. Did she say anything else?"

"Yeah, she wants us to put in a nice ladies' bathroom with a commode and sink and running water. Says that would bring in more women as customers."

"Alma always wants our bathroom to look nice. Even put a little fuzzy cover on the lid. One of those things that women like." He adjusted his light, directing it into the engine compartment. "What else?"

"She kept talking about a uniform. Said we ought to look more professional, whatever that means."

"Professional?"

"That's what she said. Cornelius Alexander wears a company uniform, with a fancy hat and everything. Gets them through Zipco, I suppose. I guess we could buy something like that through Petroleum Supply, but then we'd have to have them fitted and probably dry-cleaned. She and Alma already have us in starched pants and shirts. Something else to itch." Virgil's memory of the suit and the visitation were still fresh in his mind.

"She read in *Photoplay* or some magazine about how women are impressed by a man in a uniform. Says it gives women confidence. Maybe that's why several women who used to come here have started buying gasoline at Zipco."

"Virgil, we never had very many ladies come by anyway. Around here, men do most of the driving, and their wives just ride along. Mrs. Crutcher always drove herself around, and Gladys does sometimes, and that's about it. Would you hand me a small screwdriver?"

"That's changing, Welby." Virgil found the tool in the box and handed it over. "A lot of things are changing, and I don't know what to do about it."

Welby snapped the distributor cap in place and carefully backed out from under the Plymouth's hood. "I still wouldn't worry, Virgil. Fix the place up if you want to, but changes are going to happen regardless of what you do. These things have a way of working themselves out."

He cleaned the screwdriver, wiping it on the ever-present shop rag. "On the other hand, it's a good idea to do whatever Mavine wants."

Virgil spent most of the morning on the telephone after locating the instrument under a pile of catalogs and junk mail. Del Crutcher was back at work at the hardware store in Quincy, and was happy to supply good quality paint in whatever shades Virgil needed, and yes, he always kept the basic colors in stock. He also had a selection of brushes and thinner. Besides, Del wanted to talk to Virgil about selling his mother's Buick. "It has all new tires and a recent tune-up," he said.

Another call, and the plumbing estimate was scheduled. And most importantly, Virgil made an appointment tomorrow with his banker. Somehow, all of these improvements would have to be paid for.

"I have your lunch almost ready." Mavine had the iron skillet hot and the hamburgers frying when Virgil arrived. The aroma of burnt grease and toasted bread had greeted him at the door, along with an unfamiliar scent he couldn't quite place.

"Thanks." He took off his work shoes at her request, placing them on the mat by the front door. "Del is coming this afternoon to give us an estimate on the paint, and the plumber should be here about the same time. Looks like we'll be able to fix the place up before the Fourth of July."

"That's wonderful news!" Mavine plopped the blackened patty of meat on an equally abused bun, globbed on a teaspoon of mustard, and centered it on a plate. A pickle and a heap of potato chips finished off her presentation. "I told Vee he'd get to help with the painting. For some reason, he didn't seem to be too excited about it. I was hoping that reading Twain would inspire him."

Virgil started to say something, thought better of it, and poured himself a glass of milk instead. "Mavine, he's still in school because of the snow makeup days. I'm figuring Welby and I will be doing most of the work. We can close the garage for a day or two if we have to, and only sell gasoline. Grover has a ladder I can borrow, and we have a couple of brushes left over from the church Work Day. The building just isn't that big."

"All the same, I don't want Vee up on that ladder. Remember what happened to Grover at church? He scared Anna Belle nearly half to death!" She'd joined Virgil at the table with her own sandwich.

"I won't let anything happen to Vee. He can paint the floor, if that's what you want. He can't fall off the floor."

"Well, we can worry about that later. Today, you have plenty to do. Tomorrow, you'll want to go over to see Mr. Willett to have your uniform altered."

"Uniform?"

"Yes. It's in a box by the door. He'll need to measure you and make some changes so it'll fit properly. It'll need cleaning, too."

"Mavine . . ."

"It'll wait. Right now, we're enjoying our lunch."

He knew better than to argue, at least this time. He relaxed as best he could and took a bite of his meal. "Mavine," he said, "just what is in this hamburger?"

"Pineapple! The recipe was right on the side of the can. It said, 'You can have the taste of Hawaii right in your own home!' "

Virgil finished his hamburger — with effort — and ate the potato chips, even though they were now mushy from swimming in fruit juice.

Cornelius smiled. Not only had business picked up, but Charlie was staying busy mounting tires and doing oil changes. For the first time since opening, he was able to make a full weekly payment against his balance with Zipco and still have some money left over for food. Writing the check gave him a certain satisfaction, tempered only by the bills still coming in for Suzy's delivery. He'd even bought them a couch — from a thrift store in Lexington.

He'd taken a late lunch so he could watch

315

Suzy while JoAnn went to Willett's Dry Goods to buy a new dress. "Get whatever you like! We've done really well over the last two weeks, and I want you to have something just for you!"

"I could alter my maternity clothes, but there is only so much I can do." Her eyes twinkled. "Besides, they might be needed again someday!"

Cornelius shone as well. "It would be nice for Suzy to have a little brother." He handed JoAnn the car keys and had Suzy wave bye-bye as JoAnn went out the door.

Business wasn't the only thing that had improved. For the first time in a long time, JoAnn seemed happy and at peace with herself, and with him. She hadn't mentioned her mother's opinion of him for some time now, and they were having fewer arguments. His increasing success had been part of it, she'd said. But she also said that her growing faith had played a stronger role.

Reverend Caudill's visits had been welcome, if a bit awkward, and Grover and Anna Belle had been very kind and generous. He was beginning to like Eden Hill, and even the church.

The pastor had said there was much more to church than sermons and music and nice people, and that made Cornelius think a bit deeper. But while Cornelius liked the preacher, Reverend Caudill had lately been bringing up topics that made Cornelius uncomfortable: faith in Jesus, grace for people who'd fallen short of God's expectations. Was he trying to imply Cornelius wasn't good enough? That somehow his efforts weren't enough?

Cornelius had to admit things hadn't been looking too good before, and when everything seemed like it was crashing down, he was almost inclined to believe the pastor's line. But with some hard work and a bit of good luck, things were looking up now.

He had been gently rocking Suzy, who had just finished her bottle and was falling asleep with a full tummy. As he gazed into her closing eyes, it was as though his own eyes were opened. This precious child was in his care, dependent on him and JoAnn for everything. She would need a loving father. There were good people in this world, and Cornelius Alexander III was determined to be one of them.

As he laid the baby into her makeshift bassinet, he was startled to feel dampness. But not from Suzy; the moisture was on his own cheek. It had been a long time since he'd experienced enough happiness to cry.

■ ■ ■ ■

JoAnn returned at about two o'clock with a white blouse, a pair of pedal pushers, and a disappointed sigh. "They're the only things Mr. Willett had in my size. He has just one small rack of ladies' clothes, mostly prints and dresses like my mother would wear. Plenty of fabric — seems most women around here make their own. Interesting fellow, though. Said he'd be happy to order in anything I'd like, to save us a trip into town. Was Suzy good while I was gone?"

"Yes, she was good. She was very, very good."

Del pulled up about quarter after two, driving the Buick owned by the late Mrs. Crutcher and apologizing for not being on time. After looking everything over, he sat down with Virgil at the messy desk.

"Here it is, Virgil. Six gallons of paint should be enough for the walls, and an extra gallon should do the doors and the trim."

"What about the garage floor?" This was beginning to sound expensive.

"Two more gallons, but you'll need to scrub it down with special cleaner so the paint will stick. I've got some figures for you, including some scrapers, brushes, and a couple of gallons of thinner."

Virgil looked at the final tally and gulped. Not as bad as he'd feared, but they'd need to scrape off any loose paint first, so it would take extra time. A deal was struck; it would be delivered the next day.

Before leaving, Del asked Virgil and Welby to take a look at the Buick. "We'll auction the house and furnishings next month, but I'd rather sell the car separately. What do you think it's worth?"

"Well, I know it's in good condition." Welby was already under the front on a creeper. "Looks fine under here. I'd say it has a lot of miles left in it for someone who wants a big car."

"Upholstery is like new, and only 28,000 miles?" Virgil had climbed in behind the steering wheel. "You should get top dollar either way. I'm thinking a thousand would be about right."

"Good. Will you sell it for me? I'll give you a 10 percent commission."

He hadn't expected this, so it took him a minute to answer. "Okay, Del, it's a deal." He'd sold several cars over the years, parking them at the side of the station. Virgil wasn't sure how much 10 percent of one thousand dollars was, but he figured it would be enough to pay for the paint, and maybe to pay Vee, too.

"Excellent! I'll make a sign to put in the window, and bring it out when I deliver the paint."

"I'll be here," Virgil said, closing the door and handing Del the keys. "I'm a bit surprised that you could get an auction scheduled so soon. It wasn't like you knew your mother's death was coming."

"Well, she didn't really have as much as you might think. My wife and I spent last weekend boxing up clothes for the church's rummage sale, and there really wasn't much in the way of furniture. Several rooms were completely empty. Putting it off further didn't make any sense, and the auctioneer had an open day."

"I would have thought you might want to keep the house." Welby had rolled out into daylight. "Maybe move back to Eden Hill."

Del shook his head. "Turns out my sisters and I may not be the only heirs. According to her attorney, she'd recently updated her will, and he's working out the details. My family's happy living in town now, and the lawyer says it's best to do it this way." He looked at his watch. "Sorry, but I ought to get back to the store. I'll see you both in a day or two."

The three exchanged pleasantries, and Del climbed in and drove away, scattering gravel, just as a panel truck marked *Joseph Dillermann Plumbing* pulled in. The driver was a likable fellow who introduced himself and retrieved a clipboard from the cluttered dashboard. Virgil explained the need.

"Where's your septic tank?"

"Don't have one down here. Just for the house." Virgil pointed up the hill.

Joe scratched on the clipboard. "Gonna need one. I put one in last fall for the place across the street. Gonna need to hire a backhoe, too. Where's the room?"

"Room?"

More scratches. "Water?"

"There's a sink in the garage and another in the back room."

Scratches and a frown. "Well, let's have a look around and see what we can do."

Virgil and Joe walked around the building and the property, while Welby watched the pumps and finished Grover's tune-up. After several trips, a lot of measuring, and a meeting in Virgil's office, another deal was made. Virgil would have to give up his office, but the cost was less than adding a room, and he could stay closer to his budget. He never used the office much anyway, and he could have the telephone moved to the front counter by the snack rack. The old Volkswagen that served as Ticky's doghouse would have to be moved to make way for the septic tank, but he could find another place for her and the pups. The back of the station needed cleaning up anyway. He'd call someone to take the old VW and Arlie's old Army surplus truck away when he went to town to see his banker tomorrow. Maybe he could make this work after all.

Grover came by at closing time to pick up the Plymouth, bringing a bag of Anna Belle's venison biscuits to share. "That's the last of them! No more until November, when hopefully we'll get another deer. Who was the guy in the truck?"

"Plumber. We're putting in a bathroom so we can attract women as customers. Mavine's idea."

"Probably a good idea. Every time we go on vacation, Anna Belle always wants to see the service station's restroom before we fill up, just to satisfy her that the place is classy. One of those things about women we'll never understand, I guess."

"We're also doing a bit of fixing up. Paint, cleaning the floor. Maybe even a new sign. Wondered maybe if we could borrow your ladder?"

"Sure. But be careful on that thing. By

the way, have you seen Arlie lately?"

Virgil and Welby looked at each other and shook their heads.

"He used to come into the store and play pinochle with Sam Wright and the old guys on slow days, but I haven't seen him in a while. Hope he's doing all right."

"He's been fishing a lot lately." Welby handed Grover the keys. "You might find him over at the lake."

"Well, I may just look over there." Grover climbed in the Plymouth, causing notice-able sag on the driver's side, and started the engine. "Runs great. Thanks, both of you. The ladder's behind the store; borrow it whenever you like."

"Thanks for your business, and for the biscuits!" Virgil had already dug deep into the sack. Mavine's exotic lunch had left a taste in his mouth for something normal.

Cornelius watched the scene across the street with curious interest. Del and the old Buick he recognized immediately, and Del and Virgil were walking around the building together. Their voices were too faint for him to make out what they were saying, but the proceedings involved measuring tapes, outstretched arms, and much pointing to the walls and the trim. Clearly, Virgil was up to something.

They had met on several occasions, including at church, and while their encounters had become more cordial, he remained skeptical. Virgil had been distrustful of him, and not without reason. For that matter, he hadn't trusted Virgil either. The Zipco manual contained an entire chapter on dealing with competition but he'd dismissed it out of hand, preferring to focus on the sections on marketing and business development. He was trying to get involved in the community, as chapter four suggested, but while he'd become friends with Grover and Anna Belle, he had never walked across the street to visit Virgil. Nor, he recalled, had Virgil come by the Zipco either. Welby had been his very first customer, so maybe that was where he should start.

He was preparing to do just that, when he looked back across the street. Del and the Buick were gone, but another vehicle had taken his place. The plumber and his panel truck were also familiar — it was the same man who had worked on the Zipco station. Once again, the tradesman and Virgil were circling the building, pointing and measuring. This time the plumber was scribbling on a notepad and shaking his head, and after a bit they went inside Osgood's.

Something big was going on. Welby had chatted with Del, but now he was wandering back and forth between the pumps and working on something in the garage while Joe and Virgil discussed whatever they were about to do. Several things came to mind: a major redo of the station? No, there wasn't much there to redo. Adding on? The building was made of concrete block, so an addition would require knocking out a wall, which didn't seem likely.

The third possibility made him shudder. What if Virgil had bought a franchise, maybe even with Gulf or Texaco or some really major company? Zipco's shiny metal edifice looked pretty good compared to concrete with peeling paint, but what if Virgil was preparing to build anew, maybe even with . . . brick? The Sinclair dinosaur on a tall pole, spinning its long tail in circles as the sign rotated? Too frightening to think about.

Maybe he'd been too aggressive, and had awakened the sleeping giant across the road.

23

Reverend Caudill was having a Saturday lunch with Brother Taggart and Bob Jenkins, the Methodist minister from up the street. They were telling stories, laughing, and sharing tips. Grover, as promised, had carved signature sandwiches for each of the three and moved the pinochle games to the front porch. And also as promised, they had the place to themselves once the doors closed.

"I'm so glad we got together. Thank you both for doing this. I feel a bit selfish, like I need it more than you. It is like asking you to minister to me."

Bob — it's what he wanted to be called — nodded. "My pleasure, Eugene. It's good to finally meet you."

"I'm delighted to be here." Brother Taggart dabbed at his mouth with a napkin. "And I'm happy to minister to either of you.

So what can we pray about for one another?"

Reverend Caudill was caught by surprise. Pray for one another? He'd just preached on that topic the week before. And he was willing, but others being willing to pray for him? He hadn't expected that.

"I've had a rough spell in my ministry, but I think I'm on the way back. I've got some changes in my flock, and I feel like changes are on the way for me, too."

Bob replied, "I'm still going through that rough spell. I guess every minister hits a rocky time and wants to quit. I fear my faith is sagging too."

Brother Taggart watched with understanding as both men were speaking. "I understand both of your challenges. When my wife died, I spent several years being angry at God. I was angry at my congregation as well. We're small, but somehow God used them to speak to me. To get me through it. And God said, 'My grace is sufficient,' just like he told Paul."

Everything the man said made sense. And like Bob, Reverend Caudill had known how it felt to want to quit. "So, Brother Taggart, what would you like us to pray for?"

"Gentlemen, you know we rent space at the old hardware store across from Willett's.

The lease is up for renewal, and we're concerned the monthly rate may go beyond what we can pay."

A rent hike? The First Evangelical Baptist Church might have a leaky roof, but they were never in danger of eviction. Both he and Bob placed their hands on Brother Taggart's shoulders and prayed for him, for his church, and for Eden Hill.

It had turned cold and stormy overnight and was raining hard when Virgil came to work on Tuesday, carrying the large box Mavine had left next to the door. He'd wrapped it in an old dry-cleaning bag in a heroic attempt to keep it from becoming soaked. These precautions did nothing for his head, and the old baseball cap did equally little.

His new early schedule meant that he left the house before Vee Junior, who would catch the school bus in front of the service station at six thirty. Breakfast also came earlier, and everyone was counting the days until school would finally be out for the summer. When he left, Mavine had been struggling to get Vee into a shiny yellow raincoat, which fit neither the boy's stature nor his personality. Virgil was glad to have missed the tussle.

Welby had just unlocked the door when he arrived and was carrying something inside. "The wind kept blowing the price sign over, so I'm bringing it inside until it lets up." He held the door open for Virgil with his free hand.

"Good idea, Welby. Unless the Zipco has lowered its price again, I'm not going to change mine." He peeked out the front window. "Looks like he's open for business and already has a couple of customers. Price is the same, though."

"Well, I don't expect him to change it again. He's got to be selling at cost as it is, then has to pay for the coffee cup if they get a fill-up." Welby had hung up his coat by the tire rack. "You can't make money that way."

"And we can't make any money if he takes away all our business. Sorry, Welby, but I've decided that Mavine is right. We have to move forward, to change too. To 'compete,' as she calls it." Virgil had found his usual stool and was wringing the water out of his pants onto the concrete floor.

The door opened again. Vee had come in where it was dry and warm until the bus came, looking neither pleased nor awake. He stared at the floor. "I'm going to have to paint *that*? With a brush?"

"Yes. It won't take as long as you think, and you'll have the rest of the summer left. Besides, I'm paying you ten dollars."

"Ten . . ." Vee paused. Gainful employment was clearly a fresh concept. He was contemplating this opportunity as the flashing lights of the bus appeared in the window. "Gotta go," he said, and dashed out the door, almost forgetting his lunch.

"So you're going through with it." Welby was arranging his tools by size.

"Yes." Virgil sighed. "We're doing it. Del thought he would be by about one o'clock this afternoon with the paint. I bought the gray enamel for the floor and the special cleaner, too. Vee can do that, but we'll need to do the rest. It'll have to dry out, though."

"Everything needs to dry out, including you. What's in the box?"

"My uniform. Mavine says I need to take it over to Mr. Willett's to get it fitted up for me."

"Uniform? Well, I suppose he can do whatever needs to be done. May need to go see him myself if Alma keeps making that pot roast." Welby patted his own expanding waistline. "By the way, Mr. Willett stopped by yesterday while you and the plumber were walking around in the back. Said Mrs. Alexander had come by his store to buy some new clothes."

"Well, glad she's getting out some. New baby, you know. When Vee was born, Mavine didn't leave the house for at least three months, except for church, of course. What about Cornelius? I've seen him at church every now and again."

Welby sat in his own barber chair — a favorite perch. "They've come to our Sunday school class a couple of times. Nice enough folks. Anna Belle and Grover have watched their baby during services and have gotten to know them a bit. They come in Stacy's Grocery sometimes."

"Welby, I keep thinking we ought to pay him a visit, but Mavine is wary. She says I shouldn't trust him."

The mechanic shook his head. "He's just trying to make a living, Virgil. Same as all of us. We still have enough customers to keep us both busy, and you've never missed a paycheck. You should get to know each other. Make friends with him. After all, you're neighbors, and now you go to church together."

"But what if he *is* trying to close us down?"

"That shouldn't stop you from doing right by him. What was it you said at the church business meeting? 'Have you forgotten who you are?' Mr. Osgood taught you right and wrong, and how to treat other people. So did the gospel. In spite of Mavine's worries, you need to do what's right. She'll respect you all the more for it."

Virgil had not been in Willett's Dry Goods in several months. He'd had no need to, really. Mavine usually bought his clothes through the Montgomery Ward catalog, though she visited Willett's frequently, usually to buy fabric or notions, and occasionally something from the ready-to-wear rack along the wall.

Willett's looked exactly the same as always. Packages of sewing patterns and bolts of cloth lay scattered on tables. A couple of rotating displays featured buttons and rickrack, and a small hi-fi set in the corner was playing something classical and soothing. Mr. Henry Willett, usually less pleasant, was nowhere to be seen, so Virgil rang the little bell on the counter.

"Hang on, I'll get there." The voice came from somewhere in the back of the shop, and was accompanied by sounds of a chair being scooted and general irritation.

The proprietor appeared, wearing his usual tape measure around his neck. "Mavine said you were coming."

"Good afternoon, Mr. Willett. I need to get this altered, or let out, or whatever you call it." He took the box from under his arm and set it on the counter.

"Let's see." Instead of opening the box, Mr. Willett wrapped the measuring tape around Virgil's waist, *hm-hmm*ed, and wrote something on a scrap of paper. "Thirty-eight inches. Hope we have enough fabric to work with." He then measured Virgil's chest, sleeve length, and embarrassingly, his inseam, followed by more pencil scratchings. "Now let's look in here." He opened the box and *hmm*ed again, holding aloft a pair of trousers. "I can do it, but just barely."

"It's Mavine's idea."

"Of course." Mr. Willett held aloft a second item from the box, a jacket, judging it more by eye than by measure. "Try this on."

Virgil did as he was told, feeling awkward. He'd endured the same indignities once before at Welgo when he and Mavine went to get his Sunday suit. The uniform was tight, but at least it wasn't wool.

"I can have it ready next week."

"That's fine." For all it mattered to Virgil, Mr. Willett could take all month.

"I'll bring it over. Besides, I need you to take another look at my car. I'm thinking of selling it."

"That'll also be fine. Come by whenever you can."

Wednesday and Thursday remained rainy and cold, more like April than early June. Vee's last day of fifth grade was supposed to include a picnic, and Mavine sent him with a banana, a cheese sandwich, and a bag of potato chips. She'd been packing apples until she found out that he was trading them and his milk money on Fridays for Darlene Prewitt's MoonPies. Vee *did* sometimes eat bananas, so he might get at least something healthy for lunch. As it turned out, the picnic would be in the school gym because of the bad weather, on tarps put down to keep the basketball court from being ruined.

Osgood's would be busy. Welby was working on his own car today, and a new customer was coming over in the afternoon for a set of tires — Fisks this time. This morning, he also needed to clear out his office so the plumber could transform it into the ladies' room.

He sent Vee off to catch his bus and came in the side door. "Morning, Welby."

"Good morning, boss. Still raining?"

"A drizzle. WNTC says it's supposed to clear up later. What's the cost of gas at the

Zipco this morning?"

"Same as yesterday. I don't think he's changed anything this week. He's had a customer already, though. One of the boys from the tractor shop."

Another customer lost. "So, we've got our changes all planned. I'm hoping it will dry out so the backhoe man can dig for the septic tank next week. Del should be bringing more paint this afternoon. It still won't leave us much time before Mavine wants us to have what she calls a 'grand reopening.' "

"Sounds good!" Welby could always be counted on for affirmation.

Virgil sighed and rubbed his stiff neck. "I'll need you to watch the pumps out front. I'll be in the back clearing out the office."

Virgil's desk was a legendary mess. He didn't do much of his work there, largely because he could never find anything, but mainly because Welby usually helped him with his sums when he was trying to pay bills, and he typically placed his orders for gasoline and supplies when the representative stopped in every other week. The room served as his phone booth and catchall, and little else.

Nevertheless, it had to be cleaned out, which meant that he'd have to sift through the piles of papers and catalogs to see what needed to be kept. The telephone was on top for a change, and was holding down several old newspapers, along with an old JC Whitney catalog. Below that lay a yellowed issue of *Grit* from 1957 and one of Vee's long-forgotten school papers with an A in the upper left-hand corner. He was ready to shovel everything into the trash when he uncovered something unexpected: the *Pageant,* its shiny paper clip still marking the troublesome article.

Virgil looked at the magazine again, then at the framed photo of his family that had replaced the Safe-T-Maid calendar, and finally at the little mirror in the corner. Was Mavine right about a grand reopening? Or was Welby right, and he ought to help Cornelius succeed? He'd talked those questions over right in this very building, on more than one occasion. Jesus said, "Love your neighbor." Virgil also seemed to recall something about serving Jesus being the most important thing of all. Did that mean he had to love Cornelius Alexander as much as he loved Mavine? The thought made his head spin.

Virgil flipped open the *Pageant* again. He certainly hadn't done any of those terrible things that Betty LaMour said men do, but had he truly lived up to all the things he'd vowed to Mavine: to love, honor, and cherish her?

And what about Vee, who looked to his father for advice and an example of good living? And what about Mavine herself? She'd been so worried about Arlie and Lula Mae separating, which he'd brushed aside, but was she also really worried that something like that might happen to them? What kind of example was *he* setting for his own family?

No, those questions hadn't gone away. If anything, they were more troubling than ever.

He'd been ten years old when the previous preacher had given his invitation, and he'd professed his faith and been baptized, in the same baptistery he'd lost his temper in just a few weeks before. "Jesus is Lord," he'd said all those years ago, and meant every word. Still did.

But sometimes doing what Jesus commanded didn't seem so simple. Wasn't following Jesus supposed to make you a good husband? Reverend Caudill had said something to that effect in his sermons. But Welby was saying he needed to be more like the Good Samaritan. One or the other he could manage, but both?

He pulled a chair inside the door and sat

337

with his head in his hands for a long time. He'd always provided for Mavine and Vee, and had tried his best to live a good life. Sure, he'd made his share of mistakes, but his family had always come first for him, as it was with his father. He wanted to honor Mavine in every way, and to be what she wanted him to be, but Welby was right too. Cornelius was a neighbor, and neighbors were to be treated kindly and, well, neighborly. The Golden Rule. Yes, the Bible and Mr. H. C. Osgood had both taught him the right thing.

Vaguely he became aware of a spot on the leg of his khakis. It was neither rain nor coffee nor antifreeze, but an unexpected tear that had fallen. He *would* do right by Mavine, and right by Cornelius. And he would do right by Virgil T. Osgood, both junior and senior. There was a way, and he would find it.

The driveway bell sounded, announcing the arrival of a customer. Welby's tools clattered into their trays, and he could hear the man's uneven footfalls heading out into the rain. Good. Welby was taking care of business and wouldn't see him like this. No matter — he pulled up the old oil drum that served as his trash can and got to work. After all, the room wasn't going to empty itself.

Mavine placed supper on the table and sat down, grateful that everyone seemed in a pleasant mood. Surprisingly pleasant. Vee Junior had eaten nothing for lunch but potato chips because he'd traded his cheese sandwich *and* his banana for a *Little Lulu* comic book. As this lacked both literary and nutritional merit, he was more than ready for spaghetti and meatballs if not for *Oliver Twist,* which was Mavine's latest disciplinary assignment.

Mavine considered asking Virgil about Osgood's — the painting, the uniform, the restroom, all the things she'd suggested. But seeing her husband's contented, placid expression, she smiled gently. Maybe, for tonight, those matters should rest. Mealtime discussion instead included the washout of Vee's picnic, finding homes for Ticky's pups, and one mildly contentious topic: Virgil's need for a haircut.

"It's way too long in the back. Not professional. Why don't you go see Welby tonight? And take Vee with you. It's summertime and I'll not have you both going around with sweaty hair on your necks."

"Aw, Mom." Vee hadn't yet learned when not to argue.

"Vee, go with your father. And no back talk, or you'll be reading *David Copperfield*."

Welby's barbershop was nearly full when Virgil and Vee arrived, with only a couple of empty seats left in the make-shift waiting room. Grover was in the midst of his usual political debate with Sam Wright, whose Farmall was parked awkwardly beside the station. Sam appeared to be losing, as he squirmed in Welby's barber chair and lent his support to Calvin Coolidge in the upcoming presidential race.

"Sam, he's been dead for thirty years."

Sam was not dissuaded by trivialities. "He can do a better job dead than any of these candidates could do alive."

"Gentlemen, the presidential election is over a year away. Can't we find something else to talk about?" Welby was not only trying to get Sam to hold still and not lose an ear; he was asserting his own neutrality.

Sam fired a parting shot. "I still think he ought to run." He paid his two dollars, both silver, and waved to Grover, who was next in line, before bidding good night.

Just as Grover was issuing one final comment to Sam, a tall figure appeared at the open door, cutting Grover off midsentence.

"Mr. Willett? How good to see you tonight! What brings you here?"

"Haircut. Don't you cut hair on Thursday nights?" As Mr. Willett had never been seen there before, this was a reasonable question.

"Indeed we do." Welby adjusted the chair for his next client. "It'll be a bit of a wait, though. Several fellows ahead of you."

"That's fine." He glanced around, finding the empty seat Grover left behind. "No hurry."

"Nobody's in any hurry here." Grover was relishing his political victory. "Don't you usually get your hair cut in Quincy?"

"Yes." And with that said, he picked up an abandoned *Field & Stream* magazine and would say no more about it.

Grover's haircut took all of two minutes, as Welby had only a fringe and a few unruly top strands to work with. The grocer had soon finished, paid, and was standing in a corner rubbing his shiny head, freshened with Wildroot tonic. Virgil's cut took only slightly longer, as did Vee's crew cut and butch wax. Both decided to stay along with Grover and watch the rest of the evening's proceedings. Welby thanked them both, pocketed three dollars, and beckoned to the latest arrival.

"Well, Mr. Willett, you're next. Come on up." He retrieved his scissors from the jar of alcohol where they had been placed. "How would you like it cut?"

Mr. Willett climbed awkwardly into the seat, with Welby lowering the pedestal as far as it would go. "Clean and neat. Not too short, but not too long either. Something sensual and alluring, maybe?"

The room suddenly became quiet. Every set of eyes stared, and someone coughed. Virgil recognized the words — they were both in the article by Dr. LaMour — but Mavine had blushed when she explained to him what they meant, and they were embarrassing to him, too. They certainly weren't something Mr. Willett had found in *Field & Stream.* He was very glad Reverend Caudill was not here this evening, and wished that Vee wasn't either. Welby was turning a bit red, and Grover's jaw had fallen to his second shirt button.

"Let's see what we can do." Welby hesitated for only a second and then draped a large cloth over Mr. Willett, being careful not to disturb the tape measure still hanging around his neck. Given Mr. Willett's hairline and bald spot, Cary Grant or even Jimmy Stewart was out of the question. He began trimming the back and bringing out the fullness on the sides with his comb. The barber, or perhaps the mechanic, would rise to the challenge.

Mr. Willett sat still and smiling in the chair as scissors snapped and clippers buzzed, bits of pepper and an occasional trace of salt falling onto the white cloth. Welby, who disliked silence even more than politics, spoke first. "Well, Mr. Willett, how is business at the dry goods store?"

The man in the chair beamed. "It's been quite good lately. I have a new line of ladies' sportswear and even some bathing suits coming in. Lula Mae Prewitt has been by recently, and bought some fabric and notions. I have a new customer too: Mrs. Alexander."

"Glad to hear she's getting out some. New baby, you know." Welby grinned at Virgil, who looked at Grover, who looked at the *Field & Stream* magazine left behind by Mr. Willett.

The conversation continued, with even Virgil and Grover pitching in, and Mr. Willett saying little. Welby produced a hand mirror so his customer could examine the completed handiwork.

"It'll do." He twisted his head from side to side to examine the back through the large mirror on the wall. "What do I owe you?"

"Nothing at all! The first one's always

free." Welby brushed his client clean with a small whisk. The haircut wasn't quite James Bond, but it wasn't Maynard G. Krebs, either.

"Thank you, Welby. And Virgil, I'll have your uniform ready next week." Mr. Willett checked his image in the mirror, smiled, and started toward the exit.

"And thank you, Mr. Willett." Virgil had heard more words from the man in the past five minutes than he'd heard from him in the last ten years. Some people just weren't predictable.

Grover, whose chin had regained its normal position, seemed dumbfounded. "Uniform? Virgil, are you going to start wearing a uniform like this young fellow across the — ?"

For the second time in one evening, Grover's words were cut short by a new arrival. Cornelius Alexander stood in the doorway. Vee studied his tennis shoes, while Welby beamed with delight. "Welcome to my barbershop, Mr. Alexander. You're next in line!"

If Mr. Willett's attendance had been unexpected, Cornelius's appearance was inconceivable to both Grover and Virgil, who looked to each other for an explanation. Vee continued examining his lowtops.

Welby's reaction was characteristic, that is to say inviting and casual, as if this happened every day. He ushered his new customer into his chair, made him comfortable, and pumped the chair to an appropriate level.

"What'll it be, Mr. Alexander?"

"I generally wear it in a ducktail, with the front long enough to pull over behind my ear on the left." He scanned the small room. Virgil and Grover were by now looking at each other, while Vee had found a comic book and had buried his freshly burred head in its colorful pages.

"I'll do my best, Mr. Alexander. I think you know Virgil and Grover." Both managed a courteous gesture.

Grover rose with some effort and offered a hand. "Very good to see you again, Mr. Alexander. Good to see you at church, too. Anna Belle and I have enjoyed watching your daughter in the nursery."

At the mention of Suzy, Cornelius warmed. "JoAnn and I so appreciate that, and thank you for all that you've done for us. Especially the baby formula."

Grover reddened. "Happy to help out. Thanks for your business at the grocery."

Virgil was fidgety and uncomfortable, as the evening had taken a very different direction than he'd expected. He finally stood and nodded. "Welcome to Osgood's, Mr. Alexander."

Welby was trimming Cornelius's sideburns low on his cheeks but was looking at Virgil. "I'm so glad you came over tonight, Mr. Alexander. I don't think you've been in here before."

"Only as far as the gasoline pumps, I think. I don't recall ever coming inside."

Welby smiled, still looking primarily at Virgil. "You know, Virgil's daddy, Mr. H. C. Osgood, taught us both a lot about life, and one thing he always taught is that it's often more important to forget things than to remember them."

Virgil looked at Welby, the clock, Grover, and his own shoes, and found no help from anywhere. Welby had not been on his soapbox at all this evening, and he was claiming it now. "I think that's what President Kennedy was talking about this week, when he said that time will change our relationships with our neighbors. We learn things about people that we didn't know before." He paused for breath, and to find a comb.

"Welby, I didn't think you cared for politics? And you know about the president's speeches?" Grover, who had been about to leave, sat back down.

"I'm not talking about politics, Grover. I'm talking about peace. Mr. Kennedy said it makes life worth living, and he was right. Jesus said, 'My peace I give unto you.' And *he* was right."

Virgil's head was spinning. First, Mr. Willett had gotten a "sensual" haircut. Then, Mr. Alexander had arrived. And now Welby was quoting both presidential speeches and Scripture — in the same breath. His world no longer made sense.

Welby found the mirror, which Cornelius used to examine his haircut, particularly the back.

"Very fine, Welby. What do I owe you?"

"Not a thing, Mr. Alexander. Like I told Mr. Willett, first one's always free. I hope you'll come again." Welby smiled. "It's all about being a good neighbor. Isn't that right, Virgil?"

Virgil grabbed Vee by the arm and walked out without a word. He didn't want to say something in front of his son that he might regret later.

24

Virgil hadn't slept well. He was unhappy with Cornelius, confused by Mavine, and downright angry with Welby. After much pondering, the events last night at Welby's barbering session left him still puzzled, upset, and confused. He and Mavine were trying to save their little garage and service station, and Welby was doing his best to undo all of their hard work. Welcoming the competition!

Mavine was surprised as well. "Virgil, I don't know what he was thinking. You mean he was happy to see Mr. Alexander, and didn't even charge him for his haircut?"

"First one's free. That's what he's always said, but he was smiling when he said it. I don't understand either."

Mavine poured a single mug of coffee. "Well, I'll probably see Alma at the beauty shop today. I'll ask her if Welby has been acting strangely lately."

Virgil drank his coffee almost in one chug, savoring the last drop. "Welby and I are going to have a long talk." He set the cup down harder than necessary and strode out the door.

As he walked down the hill, Ticky and her pups by his side, he began to cool. The scent of honeysuckle along the fence no doubt helped, as did Ticky's playfulness. He wanted to believe Mavine, but he also trusted Welby. Or used to. Just what was going on?

By the time he reached the door of the garage, he didn't know whether to be mad, sad, perplexed, or all three. He closed the door with a satisfying bang and turned to the barber chair, where Welby sat smiling.

"Welby, what was going on last night? Was that some kind of a joke, or are *you* trying to put us in the poorhouse? What was Cornelius Alexander doing in our back room?"

"Getting a haircut. A good one, at that! And no, I'm not trying to put us under."

"But you just let him walk in!"

"No, I actually invited him."

"You *what*! He saw everything we have here. Mavine says that if he knows what we are doing, it gives him an advantage over us! He saw our stockroom, and my old office — the room that's going to become the women's restroom — even the garage floor!"

"Calm down, Virgil. I suspect Mr. Alexander knows what an old metal desk and a case of oilcans looks like. Probably has a few of his own. The garage looks like just about every other repair shop in this country. He's probably seen a tire or two before too."

"But Mavine says he could put us out of business!" Virgil found the swivel chair and fell into it.

"I don't think he will. But you could do that to *him.*"

"What's that supposed to mean?"

Welby leaned forward, still smiling and steady of voice. "Virgil, listen to me. You've run Osgood's since before Vee was born. Our customers have been steady and loyal. You'll never get rich, but you'll probably not go hungry, either. But Mr. Alexander is just now getting started in business — and in life. He and his wife have a baby, and babies need to be fed. He needs his place to succeed. Enough people pass through Eden Hill to keep us both going."

"But Mavine —"

"You and Mavine were young once, too. When Vee came along, you had a hard time of it. I remember you eating nothing but oatmeal for two weeks while you were trying to build this place. And you were luckier than some soldiers coming home from the war. You had both hands and both feet, and you'd learned a good skill. And you've got Mavine and Vee Junior."

"You and Alma were a big help, Welby." His anger was slowly leaking away like air from a bad tire.

"I worked for your father, and he taught me a lot about helping other people. I suspect he taught you the same thing."

Virgil nodded and began to relax. "You helped Mom and all our family while Dad was in the sanatorium. And I've never forgotten that."

"Well, do something good for Mr. Alexander. Help him get started."

Virgil sat up. "Like what?"

"Keep taking care of your customers, and don't worry about his." He chuckled. "Don't fight so hard. And don't worry so much."

"I'm trying, Welby."

Mavine was celebrating the renovation of Osgood's with a cut and a perm, so she made her appointment with Gladys an hour earlier than usual to give Gladys plenty of time. She left a note on the kitchen table telling Virgil and Vee that there was bologna in the refrigerator, bread in the breadbox, and plates in the cabinet. Not being there to fix lunch always made her feel guilty, but she half expected them to go to Stacy's Grocery anyway. Grover would no doubt make them exactly the same thing. She'd finished her Metrecal diet drink, its awful taste washed out by a glass of buttermilk.

When she arrived, Gladys was standing in the doorway waving to an older woman and a younger girl — her earlier customers. Mavine recognized the girl as Darlene Prewitt by her pigtails, while the woman — she had to be Lula Mae! Her usually frazzled hair was now cut in a very flattering style, teased in all the right places and with a fresh perm. Mavine barely recognized her.

"Goodness, Lula Mae, don't you look — wonderful — today!" Heading into a divorce and being this happy about it?

"Why, thank you, Mavine! You look very fine yourself. Isn't it amazing what a new hairstyle can do for a woman? Thanks again, Gladys! Come along, Darlene, we've got fabric to buy and sewing to do."

"Good-bye! See you next week!" Gladys sent them on their way, while Mavine watched, dumbfounded. What was going on? A return visit to the Glamour Nook in a week? The Lula Mae she knew only came to the Glamour Nook three or four times a year, and did a Toni home permanent on herself the rest of the time. She watched as the truck filled the air with black smoke and rumbled down the street.

Then it dawned on her. Perhaps Lula Mae had a boyfriend, and this was why her marriage to Arlie was falling apart. And at her age! She absolutely ought to be ashamed.

"Mavine?" Gladys had stooped over to look at her eyes, just to be sure that she was listening. "You ready?"

"Oh yes, I'm ready. Those two seem very happy today — and she looks wonderful."

Gladys laughed. "Yes, she looks ten years younger and twenty pounds lighter." She led Mavine up the two steps and into the door. "Make yourself at home in the chair, and we'll get you looking just as fine. A trim and a permanent wave today, is it?"

"What? Oh yes. Virgil has a big day coming up soon, and I want to look my best for him. By the way, where's Alma?"

"Alma won't be here for another hour. You came early today for your perm, remember? Is everything all right?"

"Oh, Gladys, I'm just so worried about Lula Mae and Arlie with the divorce. And now here she is so happy and getting all fixed up. And even bringing Darlene along to — celebrate — with her. It just isn't right."

"Divorce? Oh, Mavine, you haven't heard the latest. She and Arlie have worked it out. She got all dolled up and had her hair fixed just for him."

Mavine blinked and stammered. "You mean . . ."

"Yep. They've come to an agreement. They both had to give up some things, but it sounds like it was worth it."

"So, what did Arlie have to give up?"

"Chewing tobacco. He needed to get rid of that anyway. Nasty habit."

"What about Lula Mae?"

Gladys laughed again. "No more kitchen curtains with big yellow daisies on them. And, Mavine?" The beautician was practically dancing. "I want you to meet someone."

Meet someone?

"Dorothy? Would you come out here for a minute?"

A tall and strikingly beautiful young woman appeared at the door, sharply dressed.

"Mavine." Gladys paused a moment, then regained her composure. "I want you to meet my daughter. Dorothy, this is Mavine. One of my dearest friends since grade school."

Dorothy hurried to the chair, giving Mavine a big hug. "So you're Mavine. Gladys has told me how much your friendship has meant to her."

"My delight, Dorothy." Mavine's heart was swirling with emotions. Gladys had finally, after all these years, met her daughter. And it was good, very good.

After Dorothy had retreated to the back of Gladys's house, the stylist returned to her task: Mavine's cut and curl. "She came up on Tuesday, right after her college graduation. Be here all summer, at least. Isn't she beautiful?"

"Why didn't you tell me she was coming?"

"To be honest —" Gladys took a deep breath and let it out slowly — "I was worried it wouldn't go well. So I didn't tell any of you. I only told Tom a couple weeks ago. Dorothy went out of her way to track me down, and said she wanted to meet me. I wrote her back and invited her for a visit, but I was anxious, thought it might be very awkward. I wasn't much of a mother to her, you'll have to admit."

Mavine took her friend's hand. "She wanted to meet you, Gladys. That says a lot about her feelings."

"But I gave her away. I was worried she'd

see me as just the one who abandoned her as a baby."

"Gladys, you didn't just give her up. You loved her enough to find a family who could raise her and care for her. And now I can see how much she loves you, and how much you care for her. Can't you see that too?"

Gladys sniffed and nodded.

"You know, Reverend Caudill preached on love last Sunday. Said that love pushes fear out of the way. Can you believe that?"

"But this is so much more than I deserve."

"Gladys, it's not about that. It's about what the good Lord is kind enough to give us. And he's chosen to give you this gift: something very precious." Mavine both spoke and heard the words; they were in her voice but not her own. She too had been given Virgil and Vee, wonderful gifts by any measure.

"I've got a lot of catching up to do. She's such a wonderful young lady. Tom has become quite fond of her, and so have I."

"And so lovely. You know she has your eyes?"

"Sure does." Gladys bent over to whisper in Mavine's ear. "And I'll tell you a secret. She's quite taken with Henry Willett. They are going out tomorrow night."

Oh my. Gladys's long-lost daughter, dating Mr. Willett? And Arlie and Lula Mae getting back together? Almost too much to take in.

Mavine roared with laughter and giggles, suddenly realizing how silly her concerns had been. While the weight of the world hadn't been completely lifted, at least a couple of pounds were gone. As for the ten years younger, that was up to Gladys.

Vee Junior was not looking forward to painting the floor of the garage, but he turned out to be fairly good at it. Welby and Virgil had moved everything out front except for the tire rack, which was bolted down, and the workbench, which was too heavy to lift. Welby's barber chair was also bolted to the concrete, but he was hoping to put down some linoleum in the back room anyway, so it really didn't matter. They had all scrubbed the floor with some of Del's special cleaner, so the battleship gray paint would stick well.

The paint on the floor would need to dry for at least forty-eight hours before it could be driven on, so they put Vee to work on Friday. Del had said that the paint should be ready by Monday, but not to leave a car on it too long. This was not a problem, as the only car in the shop was the late Mrs. Crutcher's Buick, which was displayed for sale outside. By Tuesday, however, the automobile would have to be moved so that the plumber could get his backhoe in to dig for the septic tank.

All in good time, thought Virgil. The work had started later than expected, partly because the rain had been relentless for the last several days, drenching everyone's spirits as well as the soggy ground, but mostly because his excavator wanted money up front. His trip to the bank had provided a line of credit sufficient for the improvements, along with an offer of a shiny automatic toaster for Mavine if he opened a new savings account. Business was always slow in the summer, so it was excellent timing. Vee was itching to play baseball with his friends, but he'd have plenty of time for that after the work was done.

The Zipco station was never far from his mind, he had to admit. Cornelius had gained several customers over the past week alone, including several farmers from the area. He had a sign advertising a special sale on tires for pickup trucks — 10 percent off and free mounting — which must have contributed to his increased business. The price of gasoline hadn't changed since sometime in May, which was a relief, but familiar cars were often filling their tanks there instead of at Osgood's. Some of their owners were even going inside and coming out with coffee mugs and road maps. Cornelius, dressed in his snappy uniform and fancy hat, smiled and waved, speaking with each customer as they did business.

Mr. Willett kept his promise and brought over Virgil's own uniform, which Mavine had stored in the upstairs closet until needed. As promised, it fit, but barely. Welby had said that the name on his work shirt was uniform enough, and Virgil had to agree. Welby could change eight quarts of oil in a white shirt and still keep it clean enough to wear to church on Sunday.

Mr. Willett had also asked about Mrs. Crutcher's car. He'd flinched a bit at the price Virgil quoted but had come back a second time to look it over. So far, he was the only potential buyer, but Virgil was in no hurry. He'd just be glad when this whole renovation thing was over and he could get back to fishing.

Everything else was going smoothly. The man from the junkyard had bought the VW for twenty dollars and even hauled it away. It meant Ticky wouldn't have a doghouse anymore, but since the pups were born she'd been sleeping under their front porch anyway. Arlie had taken to stopping in again and reclaimed his old Army surplus truck, even if the engine was shot and Virgil couldn't get the parts to fix it. He and Frank had pulled it home with the John Deere.

By late June, the ground had been cleared, the hole was dug and the pipes laid, and the new ladies' restroom was complete. Even Mavine and Alma were impressed. Osgood's smelled of fresh paint, its white outside walls contrasting against the red gutters and blue window trim. It even had a new screen door, with hinges that didn't squeak anymore and a handle with a latch. Mavine had planted marigolds and zinnias in a couple of old tires, placed them on each side of the garage door, and had used some leftover white paint to give them extra gloss. When the time came, Virgil would be ready.

Mavine seemed proud of him, but Welby just shook his head.

25

JoAnn Alexander had just put Suzy to bed for her nap when Cornelius returned after lunch. "So," she said, "did *anybody* come by today?"

"I'll say! I have a new customer, a real estate attorney from Quincy who had come to appraise the house where Madeline Crutcher lived. We filled his tank and sold him a radiator flush on Monday. A *Cadillac,* JoAnn! It's going to work, just like I told you it would!"

She stroked her daughter's fine hair, waiting for Suzy to close her eyes and fall asleep. "Really. What about this? It came in today's mail." She handed him an already-opened letter from the Zanesville International Petroleum Company, on very official stationery, and provided a summary of its contents. The gist was that if a certain payment were not made by the end of July, foreclosure proceedings would begin.

"Hang on to that lawyer — you may need him." She thrust the letter into his hand. "I didn't sign up for this, and neither did Suzy!" And with that, she kissed the baby on the forehead and went to her bedroom, crying.

Just when things seemed to be getting better. His relationship with his wife had been on the upswing, almost like it had been when they married. But what goes up . . .

Cornelius started to say something in defense but thought better of it and looked at the letter instead. It was signed "Regrettably yours" by the president and chief executive officer of Zipco in large scrawling script. He recognized the name immediately: the same man he'd defeated in a pool game a few months before.

Everything was ready for the Osgoods' big day. The floors were scrubbed and shining, the paint job looked cheerful and inviting, and the new toilet was installed in the restroom and working as it should. Mavine had placed little American flags in the planters to go with the zinnias and marigolds; red, white, and blue crepe paper was hung from the newly guttered eaves; and the garage floor was swept clean. Virgil's line of credit was also brushed bare, so new equipment had been out of the question. Welby had installed a new lightbulb in the globe on the gasoline pump and oiled the bearings on the shop fan so it wouldn't squeak. Even Ticky had gotten into the work, wagging her tail as Virgil finished the final touches to the screen door.

Mavine's remodeling suggestion had led to a beautiful ladies' room but had left Virgil without an office. He'd had the telephone moved to the front counter and had ordered a cash register to replace the tin box with the broken hasp. Even the Nabs rack had been updated, with the new "gourmet cheese" crackers replacing the rye crisps.

"We're ready," he said.

"We're ready," she said.

"Can I play baseball with Frank now?" Vee said.

The folding price sign was carried in, the tire display was rolled in, the lights were turned out, and the door was locked.

Tomorrow morning, Osgood's would be ready to go head-to-head with Zipco.

A crying woman is not something most men are prepared to handle, and Cornelius Alexander was no exception. With JoAnn in the bedroom sobbing, and Suzy off to dreamland, he was desperately trying to think. He

363

could make the required payment, but it might mean letting Charlie go, or at least cutting his wages or hours.

The Stacys had been very kind, as had Reverend Caudill, and he was beginning to like Eden Hill. He'd also made friends with several of the farmers in the area and would hate to start over somewhere else. But one more blow might just bankrupt him, and he'd still be left owing most of the note.

He read the letter again, and the truth began to sink in. He'd been had — taken for a fool. He couldn't deceive himself any longer.

And JoAnn's remark about the lawyer? Was that an encouragement to face up to Zipco or a divorce threat? Or both?

Failure was now a bitter possibility, one that he'd never prepared for. He could not let that happen. He couldn't.

So he did the only logical thing. He kissed Suzy on the forehead and cried himself.

The Fourth of July began with sunny skies and warm air. Birds were singing, interrupted occasionally by the chug of Arlie's John Deere and the occasional firecracker.

The Osgoods were excited about the grand reopening, which had been the focus of their lives for the last six weeks. Except for Vee, of course, who wanted to either sleep in or set off fireworks with Frank. He was needed at Osgood's, however, so Mavine had fixed their usual breakfast spread at six o'clock so the service station could open its doors at six thirty.

Virgil's uniform was pressed and ready. After the alterations and adjustments by Mr. Willett, Mavine had sent it to the dry cleaner, who had done a wonderful job getting it as sharp looking as possible.

At seven o'clock on the dot, the lights were turned on and the new and improved Osgood's was open for business. Mavine had baked sugar cookies for the occasion, and Vee had received strict instructions to stay away from the platter. The red, white, and blue sprinkles were her own special touch. Virgil looked them over for mysterious ingredients, but they appeared to be at least edible.

Across the top of the door she hung another sign at Vee's suggestion. It proclaimed *Osgood's Super Service* in bold black letters, a fitting addition to the rest of the decor.

Virgil himself was resplendent in his uniform. His private first class stripe had lost a bit of its zing over the years but was still prominently featured on his shoulder.

Mavine had polished his discharge pin to a glorious finish and fastened it prominently on the breast pocket. The dress hat, with its eagle medallion, still fit perfectly. Virgil hadn't worn it since '45, but Mavine had kept it in a box at the top of the wardrobe — just in case. The only part of his attire not government issue was his shoes, oil-resistant and freshly shined with Kiwi.

Mavine had also made a sign on the back of one of Vee's old school posters. It read *Remember WWII and the Veterans* in large red and blue script, and was clipped over the laughing Santa on the Reddy-Start sign and placed in the front.

Welby had already opened the doors and saluted as Virgil entered. "Ready for service . . . sir!" The mechanic's own khakis closely matched Virgil's uniform, as did his shoes, which were buffed to a shine.

Business was brisk as soon as the doors were open. Arlie filled his truck's tank and helped himself to Mavine's all-American cookies. "Frank's takin' care of the chores, and I'm going fishin'. The crappie are bitin' in spite of the heat."

Mavine, wearing the blue dress she'd worn to her birthday dinner, was the perfect hostess. "Arlie, fish get hungry, even in the summer. Have another cookie, and please say hello to Lula Mae for us. And Darlene, too."

Arlie grunted his assent, finished his cookie, and bought a package of Double-mint gum from the new display rack Virgil had installed just two days before. "Gotta chew on somethin' — just ain't fishin' otherwise."

As Arlie and his truck pulled out, his boat bouncing behind, Reverend Caudill came by. "Just stopping in for a visit. Looks like your grand event is going well."

Virgil agreed. "Most of this was Mavine's idea. Especially the flags and the sign about World War Two and the veterans." He beamed and stood at attention. "The uniform was her idea too, but I picked the paint for the outside."

Reverend Caudill smiled, wished them well, and tipped his own hat in leaving. Mavine offered another cookie and gestured toward the rear of the station. "We even have a fresh, clean restroom. Sorry — ladies only. Please tell the women of the church to come by."

Several other customers visited in quick succession. Several regulars, on their way to picnics and celebrations, filled their tanks. A couple of drivers had their oil changed. One woman slammed on her brakes and pulled straight up to the garage. "I saw the sign and the man's uniform and knew immediately what I had to do," she said. Welby fixed her up with four new whitewall tires. And to Mavine's delight, she visited the new ladies' room.

One customer stopped in twice: once to fill his tank and a second time to buy antifreeze. He saw Welby's barber chair and promised to come back next week for a haircut.

Patriotism ran deep in Eden Hill, and by early afternoon Virgil had served over thirty customers for fuel, three for oil changes, and several for snacks or cold drinks. Welby had installed two full sets of tires, fixed a flat, and scheduled two tune-ups. Mavine had returned to the kitchen to make more batches of cookies, and Vee Junior had wandered off with Frank to blow things up.

One other visitor had come by. Mr. Willett purchased the Buick for the full asking price in cash. He also complimented Virgil on the fine fit and look of his uniform, and took much of the credit.

Cornelius opened the Zipco on schedule after a night sleeping on the threadbare couch in their tiny living room, and couldn't believe what he saw at Osgood's. The steady stream of traffic mocked the lack of business at the Zipco. By noon he'd sold six dollars' worth of gasoline, all premium, a Royal Crown Cola from the cooler case, and two packs of cigarettes from the vending machine. After lunch by himself — JoAnn wouldn't come out of the bedroom — he lowered the cost of his gasoline by one cent per gallon to undersell Virgil. He didn't bother to check with Zipco first; that didn't seem to matter much anymore.

If he were going under, at least he'd do so in a blaze of glory.

Reverend Eugene Caudill was usually grateful for a holiday, especially one that fell during the middle of the week. A day to get at least one sermon ahead, to relax, or to stamp out any congregational fires. Today he found himself with an inferno.

He hadn't seen such a traffic jam since he'd been in Eden Hill. Even the grand opening at the Zipco station hadn't created that much of a hubbub. And Mavine dressed like an opera singer? What was that all about? And Virgil in his Army uniform, the sign, all the flags.

He'd stopped by to see Cornelius Alexander on his way home, a man who probably couldn't even remember the Korean conflict, let alone World War Two. An empty driveway, an empty garage. And the bags under his eyes. Clearly the man had been through a bad night. All was not well there, either.

And the drop in price at the Zipco. This looked like desperation. He'd worked at a service station to help put himself through Bible college, and he knew what gasoline ought to cost. Cornelius was losing money, no doubt about it. What was his task as pastor? The Osgoods, and now the Alexanders, were part of his flock. What's a shepherd supposed to do when his sheep are fighting each other?

Eden Hill was falling apart — again. He needed time to think, and he needed a headache powder. As he opened his desk drawer, he spotted his new — and expensive — fishing license tucked between some old sermon notes and a letter he needed to answer.

It was almost dark now, and somebody, probably Frank Prewitt, had fired a skyrocket that lit up the evening sky. With a sudden flash of inspiration and a glance at his watch, he picked up the phone to call a familiar number.

"Arlie? Eugene Caudill. I need to borrow your boat."

■ ■ ■ ■

Cornelius was back to sleeping in the bedroom, for which he was grateful, but JoAnn was still not talking much. Meals seemed especially quiet. She'd called her mother long-distance a couple of times, which he should have expected. He'd tried to call Zipco several times the day after Independence Day as required to report the adjustment in his prices, and got no answer. Reverend Caudill had called last night with an invitation, or rather an order, to accompany the pastor on a fishing trip on Sunday afternoon. He'd agreed: the station would be closed, and the diversion would do him good. Fishing it was, then.

Friday had shown some improvement in sales. The real estate lawyer had stopped in again, and the fellow who ran the tractor repair shop came in and bought several cans of brake fluid. Charlie was agreeable to scaling his hours back to three days a week, as long as he could work for Arlie the other two days.

The mailman had come about one o'clock, just as he was closing. He'd brought the monthly telephone bill, a postcard from Cornelius's friend Wrenchy, and another ominous-looking letter he'd had to sign for, this time from an attorney in Columbus, Ohio.

Cornelius opened the letter with resignation — the ax had certainly fallen. The way his week had gone, he could be on the street by Monday. He took a deep breath and began to read. As he read, he gasped. This was not at all what he'd expected. He had to read it a second time, sitting down and focusing on every word.

Dear Mr. Alexander:
This letter serves as official notification that an investigation of the Zanesville International Petroleum Company by the office of the Attorney General has resulted in multiple indictments of the principal(s) of the company. These indictments include multiple felony fraud charges, and lawsuits have been filed on behalf of franchisees. As all business operations have been halted, any monies owed are deferred for at least ninety days pending litigation and a full audit.

The letter concluded with more legalese, the name of a company that had agreed to supply gasoline to Zipco franchisees, and other information.

He stared at the letter in disbelief; this was better news than he ever could have hoped for. His ship may still be on the rocks, but he'd have at least ninety days to arrange the lifeboats. He tucked the page back in the envelope and ran to the trailer to tell JoAnn the news.

"JoAnn! Look at this! JoAnn?"

She wasn't there. She and Suzy were both gone. No note, nothing. Just gone.

26

Virgil had spent the morning checking out Mrs. Crutcher's Buick, now Mr. Willett's, getting it ready for the title transfer. Mr. Willett's Nash Metropolitan was now parked outside Virgil's garage where the Buick had been. Yes, he could fix the rusted-out muffler, and he would sell it for a reasonable commission, same as he'd done for Del and the Buick.

When the phone rang, it took Virgil a few seconds to find it at its new location on the front counter. Reverend Caudill's call was unexpected but welcome. Yes, Osgood's had a very successful event, and yes, he'd be happy to accompany Reverend Caudill on a fishing outing.

Welby had taken the day off, and Vee Junior was grounded and reading *The Complete Sherlock Holmes* after he and Frank had cherry bombed the henhouse, sending feathers flying, wood splintering, and Mavine's nerves fraying. "Those hens won't lay for at least a week, and you've ruined your father's paint job," she'd said, so she dropped the Big One. Only Virgil's intervention had diverted her from assigning *War and Peace.*

The gasoline trade had dropped off on Friday, as he expected. They'd had a good grand reopening, probably their biggest day ever. Best of all, Mavine hadn't made him wear his old Army uniform today, which turned out to be as itchy as his suit. Even with all of his wife's starch, his usual khakis were infinitely more comfortable, and he could wipe his hands on the legs without incurring Mavine's wrath.

He'd pulled the Nash into the garage and jacked up the front end when the phone rang again. The muffler for the Nash would be delivered next week instead of today because the driver had been a little too independent on Independence Day and didn't make it in for work. Virgil sighed; Welby and Alma were visiting family in Indiana and wouldn't be back until Tuesday night. No matter, he could operate the welder by himself, and Ticky would be there to keep him company.

In the meantime, he would flush out the Metropolitan's radiator and dream of crappie and bluegill.

Reverend Caudill was already seated at the little table at Stacy's Grocery when Brother Taggart and Bob arrived. Turning this into a weekly gathering had been his idea, and as long as Grover was agreeable he'd keep it up.

"Welcome, gentlemen! Please pull up a chair."

"Thanks." Bob was wearing denims and scuffed shoes. "We just had our Work Day, so I'm a bit scruffy."

"Thank you, Reverend." Brother Taggart slid into place with a smile.

Grover came out from behind the meat case to where the men were seated, offering his greetings. "Well, what'll it be, fellows? Bologna? Dixie loaf? I think Anna Belle got in some ham."

"You know, a ham sandwich sounds good." Bob grinned. "And might I have just a little mustard?"

"My specialty! And you, Brother Taggart?"

"I'll have the same."

"And you, Reverend? Your usual bologna? Thick sliced?"

"That sounds good." Reverend Caudill smiled; the grocer knew him well. While he'd answered Grover, he was watching

Brother Taggart. Something wasn't right, but he couldn't put his finger on it.

Bob — who was long-winded — led in prayer, and by the time they looked up, their sandwiches and potato chips were ready and waiting. Grover was standing respectfully by the table.

"Anna Belle made a big pot of iced tea, if you'd like some."

Everyone enthusiastically agreed. Lunch was mostly small talk, with Bob telling a joke about three preachers who met for dinner (the punch line landed on the Methodist), and the Pentecostal answering with one about a rabbi and a ham sandwich. Everyone enjoyed a good laugh.

Bob took a deep drink of his sweet tea. "The past week has sure been an encouragement for me. I've had two good counseling sessions with parishioners who were having spiritual problems, and I'm working on a new sermon series. The Lord knows just what I need and when I need it. What's happened with the hardware store, Brother Taggart?"

The preacher looked up from his ham sandwich, his countenance having fallen. There was no longer any funny story on his lips or humor in his eyes. "The owner has refused to renew our lease. There's a padlock on both doors. And a sign that says *Negroes Go Home.* There are only a couple dozen of us, both colored and white, but we have no place to go. Will you pray for us?"

Reverend Caudill hadn't seen this coming. Bob seemed surprised as well. Brother Taggart had shared the likelihood last week, but somehow the other pastors never dreamed it would come to this. A church without a place to gather? Reverend Caudill had no idea what to say. Now his friend was a pastor without a pasture, leading a flock without a fold.

He led the three in prayer as only a Baptist can do, calling to mind Moses and the Israelites wandering in the wilderness and Joshua leading them forty years later into the Promised Land. He prayed that somehow God's purpose would be seen in their struggle, and that they, like Noah, could come to rest on the mountaintop.

And he prayed for a miracle. " '. . . ask any thing in my name, I will do it.' Amen. Straight from the Gospel of John, gentlemen."

"Thank you, both of you. I need to get back to Collard's Mill and visit some folks so we can figure out what we're doing tomorrow. And do keep me and my little church in your thoughts and prayers."

Reverend Caudill stood to shake hands with both. "Anything I can do to help, I'm more than willing."

Reverend Caudill's old Underwood was clacking away as he typed the poem at the end of his message for Sunday. His luncheon gathering had left his belly full but his heart troubled. Padlocked out? On the weekend when everyone was celebrating freedom? It just wasn't right.

Brother Taggart and his tiny congregation could certainly use a good helping of grace.

27

Cornelius sat at their dinette, holding his head in his hands. He dearly loved his wife and daughter, and now they were gone. It was entirely his fault, thinking he could make a living with a service station in this town. His ego, again. The blame wasn't with Zipco or with the Bluegrass College of Business, or JoAnn, or her father, or anybody else; the problem was with him, and him alone.

So she'd finally gone home to Mother. The car was still there, so she must have had someone in her family pick her up — probably her brother. He'd opposed their marriage from the start, so that would make sense. He was also in law school, so the legal proceedings would probably be next.

He looked again at the latest letter, the only good news he had. A reprieve, but only a brief one. How could he carry on without JoAnn? She'd stood by him all this time, even when he was driving their boat right onto the rocks. She and Suzy deserved better.

JoAnn was right, he'd best be connecting with a lawyer. A good one. She'd likely be calling sometime this evening to let him know to expect the papers. Probably the same day the debt deferral would run out and he'd be hauled into court. Hit with a debt he could never repay and a life that would be miserable, at best.

But if she was right about faith in God carrying people through the hard times, then maybe there was hope. Reverend Caudill had been talking about grace a lot lately. Cornelius had been taken by the idea that it might actually be true. But was it for a failure like him? Maybe the pastor needed to be his next call.

Cornelius picked up the telephone and then put it back down. It was Saturday afternoon and not a time to bother the pastor. Probably working on a sermon. He'd let it go until tomorrow at least.

In the meantime, he'd pray. In his own stumbling, awkward way, he'd pray. If there were second chances to be had, he needed one.

Mavine had spent the morning catching up

from the rush. She'd hung her blue dress on a padded silk hanger by the front door, a reminder to take it to Willett's to have it dry-cleaned the next time she went out. This would probably be sometime next week, as the Glamour Nook had closed this week so Gladys and her daughter could visit Tom's family. She could just pull her hair back for a week, or throw on a scarf. The dress had served its purpose well. As best she could tell, Osgood's had far more business the past couple days than their competitor. Good.

In celebration, she was making a special lunch for Virgil and Vee: tuna-and-macaroni casserole. Actually, she didn't have any tuna, so she substituted some cut-up catfish that Arlie had given them. There wasn't any macaroni in the cupboard either, so she found an almost-forgotten box of spaghetti in the back of the cabinet and estimated the portions. The recipe called for cheddar cheese, which she was out of, but she did have butter left over from the cookies and some sour cream. Some onions and green peppers went in the dish for good measure, along with something called "salad topping" that came in a foil pouch. It had all gone in the oven at 400 degrees at eleven o'clock, so it should be ready when Virgil returned, which she expected to be at about noon.

At eleven thirty, there was a knock on the door. Virgil, early? Puzzled, she walked toward the entryway. Perhaps Virgil had his hands full. "Coming!" she said, and pulled on the handle.

The visitor did indeed have full hands. JoAnn Alexander stood on her porch, gingerly holding a very fussy baby in her arms. Her eyes were red and her cheeks were streaked.

"Mrs. Osgood? I'm JoAnn Alexander. We've met a couple of times. This is Suzy, and . . ." Her mouth kept moving but no more words came.

Something in Mavine melted. "Please come in, JoAnn. Sit down." She motioned toward the couch.

"Thank . . . you." She spoke her words between gasps and sobs. "Would you by any chance . . . be able to spare some milk? We have some formula left for Suzy, but we have nothing to mix it with."

"Of course!" Mavine didn't hesitate. Her refrigerator held plenty — two full quart bottles, in fact. "Let me see what else I can find."

As Mavine turned back from the refrigerator with milk and an apple, her heart broke wide open. "Honey, has it been this hard for you?" She poured the milk into a glass and handed it to JoAnn.

JoAnn drank over half the contents before answering. "We've not been able to buy food for nearly a week. Grover and Anna Belle have been very kind, but we — I — just can't ask for anything more. Neil — Cornelius — owes so much money to Zipco, I'm afraid we'll never be able to pay them, and we'll lose the station and everything we have."

Mavine was surprised to find herself on the couch, holding first JoAnn's hand, and then Suzy, who was now contentedly enjoying her bottle.

"I've talked to Mother before about going home, but she now says I should have never taken up with Neil, let alone gotten pregnant and married him. I didn't listen, and now here I am with a baby girl and a husband who's broke. I want Suzy to have a future — something more than what we have now."

The words sounded strangely familiar. Mavine patted JoAnn's shoulder while Suzy drank her fill. JoAnn's tears were falling across her hand, but Mavine's own were now streaming down her face. "Have you eaten today, child?"

She shook her head. "We don't have any

groceries. Neil was hoping to make some money yesterday — cash — so we could go to Stacy's and buy some bread and milk, but there just wasn't enough. I don't want to buy anything else on credit." She stroked Suzy's hair. "I . . . I'm so sorry, Mrs. Osgood. I've made you cry, and I didn't mean to do that. I shouldn't have come, and Neil will be unhappy with me. I need to get back now."

"Honey, you're staying for lunch, and that's all there is to it. I have a casserole in the oven that's about to burn. Please stay and let us give you a good meal." Mavine wiped a tear. The dish probably *was* ruined, but no matter. It was food, and what Suzy and JoAnn needed.

JoAnn placed Suzy, now asleep, in Virgil's La-Z-Boy, tipping it back so she wouldn't fall. Mavine showed her to the table, found her a comfortable chair, and took the warm pan from the oven. Her offering was overcooked and unrecognizable but not burned, and JoAnn savored it like it was caviar. She wiped tears and drank her milk, and even ate some of Mavine's leftover cookies from the grand reopening.

"I don't know how to thank you, Mrs. Osgood. I just don't know how to thank you."

"JoAnn, you just be a good wife to Cor-

385

nelius. And you're doing that. You love him; you care about Suzy. And you care about your own future. I am so sorry for your — misfortune. I'm just glad I could help."

"Thank you. Please don't tell Neil I was here. And could you not tell Mr. Osgood?"

"I won't." Mavine dug in her purse for her egg money from the past week. All of it. "Here. I want you to take this and go up to Stacy's for some bread and milk. Will you promise me you'll do that?"

JoAnn was hesitant, but relented, dropping the money in a pocket and picking up the sleeping child. "Thank you for all your help, Mrs. Osgood."

"Please call me Mavine," she gently corrected. "I'm so glad you came over, and I'm sure things will work out. Now, if you hurry, you'll miss running into Virgil coming home for lunch."

JoAnn thanked her again, embarrassing Mavine, then carefully made her way back down the hill with sleeping child in arms, smiling and with her appetite satisfied.

Mavine swallowed hard. *Help?* After she was the one trying to drive the poor man's business into the ground.

Mavine watched her until she passed Osgood's before letting the tears flow again. It was all her fault: the grand reopening, the rush to remodel their service station, the painting and fixing up. Even the dress and Virgil's Army uniform; that had all been her idea. And what it led to was this: a poor young mother bringing a hungry baby to her doorstep. She'd never felt more ashamed.

Mavine looked at the blue dress with the red roses. The garment somehow glared back at her, pointing an accusing finger right in her face, the very emblem of her sin. She could never wear it again. Sighing, she picked up the dress from its hanger and walked to the back porch, where she hung it on one of the hooks. It would make a good quilt someday.

Vee came down the stairs carrying his Arthur Conan Doyle to find his mother crying again.

Virgil was surprised to see JoAnn crossing the street in front of Osgood's, carrying what looked to be a heavy bundle and heading for the Alexanders' trailer. He'd been learning how to use his new cash register and could see her easily through the open garage door. Curious, but no reason for alarm. Looking at his watch, he decided he'd been at it long enough. If the parts weren't coming until Tuesday, then the

Nash would just have to wait.

There were chores to be done, and fishing with Reverend Caudill on Sunday. He placed the Closed sign in the window and locked the doors. Ticky wagged her tail and followed him back up to the house for lunch, her pups underfoot.

He was thinking again. The grand reopening had been such a success; maybe it needed to be an annual event. Probably wouldn't cost as much — he had some leftover paint for touch-ups, and he could do without a men's restroom. No premium gasoline, though, he was adamant about that.

He opened the door to an interesting aroma. "Hello, Mavine, I'm home. What's for lunch today?"

"A wonderful casserole! I thought we'd celebrate our good fortune."

He sat down to the table with Vee, who was looking dejectedly at the blob on his plate. Grace was said, and he took a bite. "Mavine, what exactly is this?"

She told him the full details.

He grimaced but tried to hide it. If this was food for celebration, he was glad he hadn't failed.

Cornelius looked around the trailer for

388

some tissues, found none, and settled for a roll of toilet paper. His stomach was beginning to growl, as he'd still not had lunch. With the thought that he'd better eat something, he opened the little refrigerator. It was as empty as his bank account.

His misery was interrupted by a knock at the door. Probably somebody unhappy that he'd closed early; another customer he'd lose. Wiping his face with the back of his sleeve, he made his way to the door and opened it.

JoAnn, with Suzy in her arms, was standing on the metal step.

"JoAnn!" Cornelius threw his arms around his wife and clutched her as tightly as he could with Suzy between them. "I thought you had left me!" Even if she was angry, she'd come back. She had returned to her miserable excuse for a husband.

Tears flowed freely from both as Suzy was laid gently in her makeshift bassinet. They embraced, and neither one would let go of the other.

Cornelius was the first to speak. "I have wonderful news, JoAnn!" He reached for the letter, dropped on the table. "It's going to be all right; everything's going to be all right!" He read the letter aloud, both so she could hear it and so he could believe it himself.

"That's fabulous!" She hugged his neck. "I have news too."

"What's that?"

"We're expecting again!"

"You're . . . we're . . ." Whatever Cornelius was thinking was lost, and he held his wife close. He forgot any concerns about JoAnn, Suzy, Zipco, attorneys or attorneys general, or anything else. They held each other for a long time, until Suzy woke up and began to coo.

Christmas in July? Who would have expected it?

28

Reverend Caudill had never been comfortable with the obligatory patriotic sermon on the Sunday after Independence Day, and this year he'd put in less effort than usual. Patriotism had done more harm than good the previous week, and he wasn't about to wave the flag too much this morning. He would have Toler lead the congregation in the usual "My Country, 'Tis of Thee" and "Faith of Our Fathers" and beg him to pick up the tempo a bit. A few words acknowledging the holiday would be sufficient. His sermon from the eighth chapter of John would deal with grace, of course, but he'd also toss in some material from Matthew about "love your enemies." Given the events of the last week, it seemed best.

The start of the morning service was still ten minutes away when Reverend Caudill entered the sanctuary. He was in a surprisingly good mood. His corns were unusually quiet today, and so far his breakfast was equally cooperative. As he laid his Bible and sermon notes on the pulpit shelf, he looked around. Cornelius and JoAnn were in the third row on the right, and both looked content. Good, they'd moved up from under the balcony. Virgil and Mavine were about halfway back on the left — their usual spot — with Virgil glancing over his shoulder. Also good. Arlie and Lula Mae should be along shortly, as soon as Sunday school was over. Grover and Anna Belle were nowhere to be seen, but were probably in the nursery watching Suzy.

He could now greet his parishioners and still have a couple of minutes before the prelude began.

As he started down the aisle, he became aware that Virgil was not the only one in the congregation looking toward the rear. Most of the people seated in the pews were doing the same, and the room had become unusually quiet. Reverend Caudill followed their gaze, which led to the back door. He stopped in his tracks.

Silhouetted in the door was Jeremiah Taggart, along with Willie and Mamie Johnson and the congregation of the Pentecostal Holiness church, smiling and wearing their Sunday best.

Reverend Caudill held his breath. He'd promised Brother Taggart he'd help in any way he could, but this wasn't exactly what he meant. How would his congregation react to the Negroes from the little settlement on the other side of the creek? One problem in the church had already demanded his attention; he didn't need two. He'd read in the papers about something called the civil rights movement, especially since Madeline Crutcher's outburst. Had the old woman come back from the grave to haunt him this morning?

He needn't have worried. Virgil, true to his statement in the business meeting months earlier, rose from his seat and, though patently nervous, greeted the new attendees warmly and seated them at the front. Brother Taggart he led to Madeline Crutcher's old pew, vacant since her untimely — or perhaps very timely — passing. It seemed to be fitting, somehow.

Reverend Caudill also noticed a couple he'd not seen in worship before but recognized immediately. They sat in the very back row under the balcony, the same place he'd first seen Cornelius and JoAnn. Tom and Gladys Blanford, after many years of invitation, had finally come. Henry Willett and a tall young woman sat with them.

He'd never been more proud to be the pastor of the First Evangelical Baptist Church.

The worship service went extraordinarily well. Reverend Caudill preached on grace with the same vigor he used to reserve for preaching on sin, and his sermon seemed to be well received. The Johnsons, in the front row, were affirming and even said "Amen" and "That's right" on a couple of his more significant points. Even Lula Mae, who'd taken to telephoning him on a regular basis, nodded several times.

He glanced at his watch during the final hymn: a rendition — rousing, for Toler — of "Rescue the Perishing." Three minutes to twelve. Time for dinner with Grover and Anna Belle, who had invited him for leftover barbecue, and then off to pick up Arlie's boat and be at the lake by two o'clock. He delivered the benediction from memory and greeted all attendees — especially Brother Taggart and the Johnsons. Grover and Anna Belle had made sure Suzy was happily returned to the Alexanders, so the pastor turned out the lights and joined them. It had been a busy morning and would be a big afternoon.

■ ■ ■ ■

The morning had been filled with surprises. Cornelius felt a little uncomfortable when the colored people arrived, but it didn't seem to bother anybody else too much, and after a while it seemed, if not familiar, at least appropriate. Reverend Caudill's sermon was gentle yet powerful, a combination that Cornelius found fascinating. The preacher stood at the pulpit, looking at each one in the room, barely glancing at the notes in front of him. He talked about freedom and release, which prompted Cornelius to keep going over that incredible letter, which he had nearly memorized. Only a few days ago, the darkness might just have swallowed him up, but now light was slowly breaking through the clouds.

Reverend Caudill was concluding. "Jesus wants you free. Free from all that is holding you back. We all come to him captive to our worry and need. And we walk away unshackled.

Through the sacrifice made by Jesus Christ, our debts to God are erased. Our account, our obligations, our sins are marked 'paid in full.' " He closed his Bible, and the crotchety song leader took his place at the podium. The closing hymn was painfully slow, but slow enough for the words to sink in. Cornelius found himself humming along, even joining in a few words on the chorus. JoAnn shot him a shocked smile, at which he just shrugged and gave her a sheepish grin.

As the diverse congregation filed out of the sanctuary, Grover and Anna Belle appeared with Suzy. She was making happy screeches, which turned some heads. Cornelius looked up from his daughter's face, ready to apologize for her, but instead of scowls, the faces were beaming, some even with misty eyes. Grover handed him the diaper bag, once again a bit heavier than usual. Another can of formula? Cornelius gripped the man's hand a bit tighter, all the thanks that either man needed to exchange.

They reached the door, where the pastor customarily stood. "Thanks for the message today, Reverend," Cornelius said. "Feels particularly timely right now."

Caudill's eyes grew a bit wider. "Oh? How so?"

"Well, I was reaching the point where I could never pay Zipco back. But I just got notice that my debts have been suspended. We're not out of the woods yet, but we're back on the path at least."

Reverend Caudill closed his eyes and sighed. "That is something to thank the Lord for. As I said in my message, he's big on canceling debts himself."

"Are we still planning to head out fishing this afternoon? Didn't know you could fish on Sunday, Reverend."

"It's all part of the Lord's work." There was a twinkle in the pastor's eye.

After the service, Virgil Osgood picked up a few stray bulletins and a forgotten pencil or two. He finished near the rear, where Jeremiah Taggart stood at the door beaming, the Johnsons beside him.

Virgil stepped into the center aisle and walked toward the waiting visitors.

The visiting pastor stretched out a hand, and Virgil received the man's strong grip. "Can't thank you enough," Brother Taggart said. "When we decided to come worship with Pastor Caudill, we didn't know how his people might react, but you up and greeted us right at the door. Just like the Good Book says: 'There is neither Jew nor Greek, there is neither bond nor free, there is neither male nor female: for ye are all one in Christ Jesus.' "

Virgil shuffled a bit and looked at the floor, then met the man's eyes. He looked directly at each of the Johnsons in turn as well. "You've been our neighbors all these years. Only right we should be neighborly."

The man clapped him on the shoulder. "Right you are, Mr. Osgood. Sometimes neighbors show up where you least expect them."

Though Virgil had been concerned about how Sunday worship might go after he seated Brother Taggart and his little flock, it had turned out just fine. Sunday dinner, on the other hand, was a less enjoyable affair, with Mavine extremely quiet and Vee being sent to his room for making ugly faces. Vee had complained all morning about having to read the massive book Mavine had assigned, although their son had been absorbed in it this morning when he was supposed to be getting ready for breakfast. Vee had whined far more yesterday about having to repair the henhouse, claiming that it was all Frank's fault and he didn't know that six cherry bombs together would do that kind of damage. Besides, he claimed, wielding a saw and hammer was not something he was good at, and why wasn't Frank here fixing the broken boards? Frank, it seemed, had received an educational trip behind the Prewitts' hog barn, courtesy of

Arlie, not for blowing up the Osgoods' chicken coop but for goofing off and not getting the hogs fed. Virgil wound up spending most of his Saturday repairing and repainting the thing, picking up feathers and eggshells.

Mavine had not been herself all weekend, like she was unhappy again, and Virgil couldn't come up with any obvious reason. She'd taken the dress down from the front doorframe and hung it by the laundry, but he'd learned not to ask about Mavine's clothes. Women could be funny about such things.

He was looking forward to fishing, as the day was a bit cooler and overcast, and several days of rain were expected the coming week. He usually fished with Welby, but he would enjoy spending some time with the pastor. He was also looking forward to an afternoon away. As much as he loved Mavine, sometimes he just needed to get out of the house.

Cornelius oiled up his spinning reel and dug through their tiny closet in the back of the trailer until he found the tackle box, right next to his old baseball glove and tennis racket. He opened the latch and glanced over the contents, including his license —

good through September. The fishing outfit brought back memories; it had been a birthday gift from JoAnn before they married. He'd only gotten to use it once, back when he was in business college. The future looked so promising then, and with luck, it was looking promising again. A wife, a daughter, and another child on the way? He'd gotten better than he deserved. Far better.

The lake was lovely. The water was up from the recent rains, but the limbs from the submerged trees were still showing. Reverend Caudill was already there with Arlie's truck and boat, wearing a pair of overalls that were a bit large on him, probably also borrowed from Arlie. The pastor was barefoot with his pants legs rolled up, launching the small craft into the lake. Cornelius had never seen the pastor without a suit and tie. Was that even legal?

"So glad you could make it, and so good to see you and JoAnn in church today."

"Thanks, Reverend. We're really enjoying it there."

The pastor beamed. "Good, good! Can you give me a hand with this?"

Whatever skills Reverend Caudill had, seamanship was not among them. Cornelius helped him get the boat off the trailer and into the water without tearing off the outboard motor, then laid his tackle box and fishing rod into the bottom. They tied the boat to the trailer to keep it from floating away and took a bucket of minnows from the back of the truck.

Reverend Caudill also had a landing net, a can of worms, and a bag of sandwiches. "Grover wanted us to have this," he said. "Oh, here's our other companion for the afternoon."

Virgil Osgood had driven up beside Arlie's truck, looking quite puzzled.

"Good afternoon, Virgil! Glad you could join us! Hope you and your family had a wonderful dinner!"

He rolled the window down. "Uh, is Arlie here?"

"Nope." The minister retrieved a couple of items from the truck. "But I borrowed his boat."

Suddenly reality struck Cornelius. He'd been had. Again. But unlike the rep from Zipco, the pastor seemed to have his best interests in mind.

"Well." Reverend Caudill put his socks and shoes back on. "Get in. We're going fishing."

Virgil retrieved his tackle from the back of his car, together with a coffee can of night crawlers, then took the seat at the rear of the boat. Cornelius sat in front, and Reverend Caudill parked himself in the middle.

Virgil started the outboard motor, and Reverend Caudill directed them to Cumber's Creek, the very spot where Arlie had told them to go. The dead tree was right where he said it was, and Virgil dropped the anchor over the side.

Neither Virgil nor Cornelius spoke much. On the other hand, Reverend Caudill was unusually talkative. "Arlie says that the crappie and white bass are down deep, and you'll do well with a minnow and a big sinker on your line. The bluegill are usually in the shallower water this time of day, while catfish like it on the bottom. Carp are likely to be most anywhere. If you're lucky, you might even hook a largemouth on one of the night crawlers Virgil brought."

The pastor was clearly in charge. At his direction, Virgil and Cornelius baited their hooks with the tiny fish and dropped them over the side. Reverend Caudill had a short pole with some kind of shiny thing on the end of his line, which he also placed in the lake.

"You know, when Jesus needed time to think, he got in a boat and went out on the lake. And it was hard for him sometimes.

The pressure and stress must have been incredible. But something about being out on the water did him good. Even when the seas were rough, he could calm them. It gave him peace. Virgil, I think you've got a bite."

Virgil's bobber was indeed bobbing, and he pulled back and reeled in a small but lively crappie.

"Good work, Virgil!" He took the fish and carefully inserted the stringer, fastening it to the oarlock and gently laying it in the water.

Cornelius's float had vanished from sight and the line was moving, so he hauled back on the rod, hooking the hapless crappie. It was pan-size.

"Well, there's a keeper to take home to JoAnn. Hold it up so we can see it."

Cornelius lifted the flapping fish into full view.

"Nice one." It was Virgil commenting this time.

"Jesus enjoyed hanging around fishermen." Reverend Caudill tinkered with his reel, pulling out some backlash.

The pastor had an agenda, and Cornelius was part of it. So was Virgil, by the look of the fellow at the other end of the boat. But he'd heard enough from the reverend in the middle to know the man deserved listening to.

"They were good folk. Ambitious, hard-working people. He picked some men from other walks of life as his disciples, as well. And they didn't always get along; they'd sometimes argue among themselves. Another one, Cornelius?"

He pulled back on the pole and lifted a small bluegill out of the murky water. "I suppose you're right."

"And they had some things in common, just like you. The same goal, to make good lives for yourselves and your families." He looked at the bluegill and motioned for Cornelius to toss it back in.

Virgil looked puzzled. "So what are you saying, Reverend? What's your point?"

"I invited you both here to fish, but also to try to keep you from destroying each other. You need to learn to be like the disciples when they were working together rather than trying to see who's the greatest. Watch your line there, Virgil."

Virgil was about to say something, but his rod was bending, and he pulled in another nice crappie.

"Good fish, Virgil." Cornelius gave the compliment this time. "But, Reverend, you said yourself that the disciples were hard-working folks. Don't I need to make a living for my family?"

"Yes, I did. There's nothing wrong with ambition, but sometimes it gets out of hand. And can we agree it has gotten out of hand?"

The Zipco owner looked at the pastor. "I'm just following the Zipco manual. I was always taught to do things by the book."

"That's fine, but there's a more important book to follow." He pointed at a New Testament in his shirt pocket. "Why don't you both try using this one instead? Do unto others . . ."

Virgil baited his empty hook, this time with a chubby night crawler. "And how am I supposed to make my living if I don't — compete?"

Cornelius let out a yell. Something had taken his bait and run with it, bending his rod nearly double.

Virgil reached for the landing net. "Tighten up the drag and play him! I'll be ready." Cornelius played the fish as it tried to go under the boat, finally bringing it to the surface flipping and fighting. Virgil slipped the net under the largemouth and brought him aboard.

"Hoo-wee, look at the size of that fish! Must go at least five pounds!" Cornelius freed the creature from the net and held it aloft.

Reverend Caudill chuckled. "Gentlemen, see what happens when you work together? Neither of you would have been able to land that fish alone. That's what I'm saying. Nobody needs to put anybody out of business. There's plenty to go around, like when Jesus fed the five thousand. Just do your job well, and stop trying to harm each other. That's not the way Jesus would do it. Virgil, has something got your night crawler?"

Virgil reared back and set the hook. After much thrashing and commotion, Cornelius was able to get the net underneath, and soon another largemouth was aboard.

"Thanks, Cornelius. It's a beauty."

Reverend Caudill watched the exchange as more fish were hauled into the boat. Soon the stringer was full, and he found a second, which was soon also filled. The day was everything he'd hoped it would be. He'd prayed hard for this afternoon, and he'd been rewarded. And the fish were biting like none of them had seen before; surely that was God's gift and with it his answer.

Soon Virgil and Cornelius were talking about their families, their hobbies, and how hard it was to remove the oil filter on a

Plymouth six-cylinder. Common goals, common interests. Virgil's brother had gone to school with Cornelius's uncle, the young man's grandfather had been a very good friend of Mr. H. C. Osgood, and they both liked Patsy Cline and had mourned her recent passing.

And the fish kept coming. When they were finished, they counted ten on two stringers, including the two large largemouth bass, and one that got away. Virgil said it would have gone ten pounds — easy.

They also agreed to end the price war and go back to sensible rates for gasoline: thirty-two cents a gallon for regular and, for Cornelius, thirty-four cents for premium. They would also get together for dinner sometime in the next several weeks, and would all be at the church cookout next Saturday.

Soon the bait and the afternoon were exhausted, and Virgil started the little Mercury motor to head back to the truck. "Reverend, it just occurred to me that you haven't caught a single fish all afternoon. What do you have on the end of that line anyhow?"

Reverend Caudill held the little spinner lure up for both to see. "Arlie gave it to me to use. Said fish couldn't resist it." He laughed. "Besides, I was here today to be a fisher of men, like Jesus said. Looks like I caught a boatload!"

29

Cornelius stepped into the trailer to a sleepy wife and wide-awake daughter, his catch on a stringer and a spring in his step. Both were thrilled as he related the events of the afternoon. A truce had been called: no, more like a treaty. He actually liked Virgil T. Osgood, and he had at least a chance of keeping his business.

Early that evening, he called Reverend Caudill, first of all to thank him for the fishing outing, and secondly to make an appointment for him and JoAnn to meet together in the pastor's office.

It was time.

They stayed up late reading: she the letters, over and over again, and he the Zipco manual. JoAnn smiled and carefully placed the two letters in their respective envelopes for safekeeping. He frowned and threw the Zipco manual in the corner. All three fell happily asleep, filled with hope for the coming days.

Virgil slept late on Monday morning, having been up until eleven o'clock cleaning fish and showing off his largemouth bass to Arlie, who suggested he have it mounted and hung on the wall in his living room. Mavine was none too keen on the idea, arguing instead for her paint-by-number of *The Old Mill,* which she'd finished in April and Virgil had never got around to framing. He promised to buy her a frame the next time he went to Del's hardware in town. The fish would just have to go on the wall at the service station.

Vee also slept in, claiming he stayed up reading *A Study in Scarlet,* which amazed both his parents. Vee had always enjoyed the Hardy Boys and Tom Swift, but his enthusiasm for Sherlock Holmes was especially gratifying to Mavine. Better that than the smuggled *Wonder Woman* comic he'd gotten from Frank on Sunday and hidden inside his shirt. She'd caught that one.

Mavine had breakfast by herself on Monday morning, the same bacon and eggs as usual, but with a guilty pleasure: a leftover slice of cake that she'd made the night before. It gave her time to think: a quiet house, an empty table.

Thoughts of JoAnn and Cornelius just wouldn't leave her alone. It had been hard to concentrate on Reverend Caudill's sermon yesterday, for her eyes were drawn to the young mother and her husband. Mavine had been teary all during church, but Virgil hadn't noticed. He'd only been concerned about his fishing outing with Reverend Caudill.

Virgil had told her last night about his trip to the lake and how well it had gone. He'd eaten his dinner with enthusiasm, devoured the dessert, and then wandered off to fillet his crappie. First thing today, he was going back to his old gasoline prices. Didn't seem quite right to her, but he'd said that the Zipco station was raising their rate as well, so she guessed that it would balance out.

But had he noticed her pain and concern? All he could talk about was that fish, that bass. Then again, maybe she was being selfish. Virgil had been under a lot of stress lately, and maybe she'd been the cause of much of it. If so, hopefully he'd forgive her.

Welby had definitely been right. She felt far better about helping JoAnn and little Suzy than about all the things she'd done to help Virgil be successful. Maybe she'd helped too much, pushed too hard.

Mavine found her mind wandering, and

411

her thoughts settled on the blue dress. She washed her hands, walked over to where the garment was hanging, and stroked the fabric with its smooth, velvety texture. She examined the lace collar, mentally measuring. Yes, it would do.

Reverend Caudill was planning to take the day off, but he'd taken some time off around the Fourth of July and his work was backing up, so he was in his office at the church. There just might be a baptism the following Sunday, so he had to make sure the freshly painted baptistery was filling properly. He was meeting with the candidates this afternoon at two o'clock, so he'd need to pick up his other suit at Willett's before then. Next Sunday's sermon would be a bit different, so it would take extra preparation time. He also had a letter to return, which couldn't wait any longer, and . . .

The phone rang.

The voice on the other end was an estate lawyer in Quincy. The reading of Madeline Crutcher's will would be at one o'clock on Wednesday, and Reverend Caudill needed to be there. *Very* important, he said.

The pastor sighed. He was hoping to keep Wednesday afternoon free for pastoral visits and to get ready for prayer meeting, but if indeed it was *very* important, he'd be there.

The attorney gave the address and directions, thanked the clergyman, and hung up.

Well. In addition to everything else, he'd have to referee the reading of the old woman's will. Some people never quite had the decency to go away. He reached into the desk drawer for his Goody's and saw a letter he'd avoided for much too long. He pulled it out and read it again, vowing he'd answer it by the end of the week. But first, the headache powder.

Breakfast was Spam and Tang, as usual, but JoAnn had been awakened early by Suzy and had made cinnamon toast: a special treat. It was a happy morning. Charlie opened the station on Mondays, so Cornelius could come in as late as he pleased.

"JoAnn, we're raising our prices. This gas war thing has gone on long enough. As soon as I get down there, I'm calling Zipco."

"No, you're calling this attorney." She pointed to the letter. "Neil, there isn't any more Zipco. We're on our own now."

He pondered this. "You're right. And it's about time! Let's do this our own way."

She smiled and reached out to hold his hands across the table. "Yes, and let's do it the *right* way!"

Virgil had breakfast on his own, with Mavine very quiet and doing laundry. "I'm off to work, Mavine. I don't expect much to be going on today, but Welby's off until Wednesday, so I need to be there."

"Fine."

"Are you okay, Mavine?" If he'd learned anything over the last few months, he'd learned that silence from Mavine was not to be ignored.

"Yes. I just feel like we've done a terrible thing to Cornelius and JoAnn, and we need to make it right."

"I suppose we both did. We were focused on doing right by ourselves, but probably didn't act too neighborly."

She sat across from him. "Virgil, I've pushed you into being something you're not. I've been selfish, wanting things that you simply couldn't give me. I feel badly for that, too."

Virgil reached out to take her hands. Not typical for him, but it seemed to be the right thing for his wife. "I'm sorry. I'm trying to be the best husband I can be, and the best father. Don't ever forget that, and please forgive me if I fail you."

Mavine rose from her chair, rounded the

table, and embraced him. "I forgive you, Virgil. And I'm proud of you."

Virgil received Mavine's hug; it was what they both needed. And as they separated, he took her hand and kissed her cheek before stepping through the screen door and ambling down the hill, Ticky right behind. The first order of business was to change the pump price and fix the signs. He was pleased to see that the Zipco station had already changed its prices. A few tweaks with a screwdriver, and it was done. Thirty-one point nine cents per gallon for regular. Same as across the street. He breathed a sigh of relief. At least that part of it was over.

He was also pleased to see that Cornelius had a customer — one he didn't recognize. At the same time, Arlie stopped in at Osgood's to fill his truck. It seemed Reverend Caudill had neglected to put gas in the tank when he returned it the day before. Virgil gave him five gallons for free as thanks to both Arlie and the pastor.

"What'd you decide to do with that big bass?"

"I put it in Grover's meat freezer until I can get it mounted. Probably put it right here behind the cash register. It'll be a good reminder."

"Reminder of what?"

"A good afternoon fishing with Cornelius and the preacher. Learned a lot yesterday. Turns out Cornelius is a really fine fellow. Thanks again for loaning us your truck and boat."

"Anytime. Anytime I'm not haulin' a hog around, at least. Well, have a fine day!"

"I'll try, Arlie."

And he did have a fine day. A number of customers came by in the morning, with several stopping in to chat. Del was in town to see to some final details on the sale of the Crutcher estate and to have lunch at Stacy's Grocery. Sam Wright drove up in his Farmall to buy gasoline and a can of brake fluid.

Sam stayed for a while, talking nonsense and drinking Virgil's coffee. "Well, got to go have lunch. Bertha's making beans and corn bread."

"Enjoy some for me." Virgil looked at his watch. It was indeed lunchtime, and he'd not gotten to the muffler on the Nash yet. The parts were supposed to be here Tuesday morning, the man said. He found the *Out to Lunch* sign and hung it on the front door. He noticed two cars lined up at the Zipco. Somehow, this pleased him.

■ ■ ■ ■

Cornelius had done something right but wasn't sure what. He'd had a steady stream of cars and pickups all morning long, including Mr. Willett and his Buick, several folks from the next town over on their way to the county fair, and Grover, who'd brought a bottle of milk for Suzy. Charlie was busy also, mounting a set of tires and minding the pumps.

He himself had spent the morning on the telephone with the attorney who was representing Zipco franchisees. The lawsuit was in progress, and an agreement was being reached even as they spoke. Zipco did not exist anymore, so he'd need to turn off the sign until he found another company. Yes, he could do whatever he wanted with the price of gasoline and with his station. No, he didn't have to wear the stupid uniform, which still said *Zipco* on the pocket and the hat. And most importantly, all monies due were deferred for ninety days while it got sorted out. And, by the way, the lawsuit promised a sizable settlement for all former Zipco franchisees including punitive damages, so there was a good chance much of his debt could be erased. Completely.

He was ecstatic. A debt erased! Wasn't that also the way Reverend Caudill put it on Sunday? Things were definitely looking up.

Mavine was still quiet at lunch, but at least pleasant. She'd spent the morning sewing, she said, and was almost finished.

"What are you making?"

"You know that old dress I wore on the Fourth of July? The blue one?"

"I thought it was new. Didn't you get that from Willett's for your birthday dinner?"

"Well, yes, but I just can't wear it anymore. I've cut it up to make a baby blanket for little Suzy. I know, it's blue and not pink, but it has some touches of lace and it'll be cute on her. It's a small thing, but it's something. I'm praying we haven't done anything to really hurt them."

"Mavine, he's got plenty of business today. And he was saying yesterday that there are some other things happening that will help his business. I think they'll be all right."

"I hope so, Virgil."

He reached out to hold her hands as he'd done at breakfast, and realized that it was just the two of them at the table. "By the way, where's Vee?"

"I ungrounded him for a couple of hours

to go do something with Frank. Probably a
bad idea."

30

Reverend Caudill hung his freshly cleaned suit on a hook in his office, opened a window, and turned on a fan. Summer had fully arrived in Eden Hill, and the heat and humidity with it. He'd also borrowed two chairs from one of the Sunday school rooms and had them arranged and waiting.

Right at two o'clock, there was a knock. He opened the door to Cornelius and JoAnn, with Suzy sound asleep in Cornelius's arms.

"Welcome, both of you. Actually, all three of you. Please have a seat."

"Thank you, Reverend." Cornelius adjusted himself in one of the chairs, while JoAnn smiled and took the other. Suzy, still sleeping, now lay peacefully in her mother's lap.

"So, you say it's time? To move forward?"

"Reverend, I've come to realize that I can't do it on my own. Never could." He stroked Suzy's hair. "I've made mistake after mistake and one bad decision after another. God's been there all along, of course, but I've never been willing to admit it. To let go."

JoAnn nodded. "And I've been so hard on him. I want to ask for forgiveness, too, both from Neil and from God. Welby's taught us the Bible in Sunday school, and we understand that Jesus died to cover our sins. And when you preached your sermon on 'paid in full,' well, we both understood. Finally."

The pastor leaned forward, his elbows on his desk. "Are you ready to affirm your faith in Christ and be baptized into him?"

The couple looked at each other, and Cornelius spoke. "Yes, we are. More than ready."

"And you do understand that the Christian life is not a guarantee of success, but a promise that the Lord will be with us through the good times and the bad?"

"We've talked about it, and we understand." Suzy had awakened, and JoAnn had taken her bottle from a bag. "We both now believe that Jesus is Lord."

"Wonderful! I'm so excited . . ." Suzy coughed, and Reverend Caudill sniffed the air. Something wasn't right. He could hear shouting outside the window, and the fan was pulling black smoke into the room.

Reverend Caudill bolted out of his seat and ran to the window, pulling the curtains back to see what was happening. At the sight, JoAnn screamed, and both men rushed out. The trailer next door was fully engulfed in flames, its pink aluminum exterior rapidly turning black. Windows were breaking from the heat, and the roof was sagging and buckling. It was all a blur.

Cornelius saw Virgil Osgood dash across the street carrying a fire extinguisher. He called to Charlie and handed him something, then rushed over to the side of the burning trailer. It dawned on Cornelius that while he was watching his home go up in flames, his neighbor had enough presence of mind to shut off the bottled gas and the electricity. And risked his life in the process.

He heard a rumbling noise and looked to see Charlie driving Virgil's wrecker straight at the trailer. Charlie rammed the disintegrating trailer and pushed it off the blocks away from the propane tanks. True to JoAnn's fears, it slid down the hill and into the creek.

Cornelius watched the unfolding scene in disbelief. Their home was a total loss, though the service station seemed undamaged. But even if the mobile home was destroyed, he still realized how lucky they were. If this had happened at night, when they were asleep, they could have all been killed. Thankfully nobody was hurt, and the bottled gas tanks hadn't exploded. At least he could be grateful for that.

Home, sweet home, was gone, and everything in it. The ashes of their mobile home had now combined with the remnants of the feed store, and the mess that was Cornelius's life. How could he have ever thought otherwise?

And he'd just decided to become a Christian. As Reverend Caudill had said, there were no guarantees. He was looking at the proof of that.

As Cornelius saw it, he had two choices. They could sleep on the floor of the garage tonight, or in his '53 Chevy.

Or he could leave Eden Hill, let JoAnn go home to live with her mother, and never return.

Mavine had returned to her laundry after Virgil went back to work. The Maytag was chugging away and her new dryer rumbling when Vee came tearing onto the back porch, shouting something about a fire. They both hurried to the front, where they could hear engines, excited voices, and crumpling metal. The view was limited by the maple trees in their front yard, but it wasn't coming from Osgood's. Whatever was happening was across the street, behind the Zipco station. Mavine turned off the washer, and they both went down the hill.

A large crowd had gathered. She could see Virgil and Charlie furiously working on the Alexanders' trailer. Cornelius was darting toward the burning mobile home, carrying a bucket of water. Reverend Caudill and a couple of other men, customers perhaps, were running a hose from the tap behind the garage and were spraying water on what was left, which wasn't much.

JoAnn stood at a distance, looking at the activity but not watching. Anna Belle had appeared and was holding Suzy and her bottle. Neither JoAnn nor her baby were crying. The woman was just staring numbly toward the smoldering mess in the creek, now mostly smoke and steam.

Never in her life had Mavine felt such compassion. She had a lovely house; JoAnn had so little — and now, nothing. There was only one thing she could do.

"JoAnn?" Mavine approached the young mother and spoke a few words in her ear, discreetly but loud enough to be heard over the hubbub.

JoAnn responded with tears, but also the beginning of a smile. She threw her arms around Mavine, buried her head in Mavine's shoulder, and seemed unable to let go.

Mavine turned to her son. "Vee? Remember how much you enjoy 'camping out' in our living room?"

Cornelius stood with an empty bucket, staring at a stinking pile of pink and black scrap that once was his home. Reverend Caudill, covered in soot and grime, had his arm around his shoulders and was saying comforting things into his ear. He saw JoAnn talking to Mavine, saw his wife embrace the older woman, and wondered what to do next.

One thing he knew for sure. He was tired of fighting.

Mavine's invitation to the Alexanders to stay in the upstairs bedroom was not something Virgil had expected, but it wasn't exactly a surprise either. He was also delighted, and glad she'd thought of it. She'd been unhappy with herself over her role in their grand reopening, that much he understood. At church on Sunday, she'd chatted with

JoAnn, almost as if they were old friends. And she'd positively fawned over little Suzy. Somehow, somewhere, she'd made a connection.

Everybody had pitched in. The Methodist church had a clothes closet, and Bob Jenkins found some things that would fit. Grover brought over a bag of groceries, which also included two cans of formula. "All we had left," he'd said. Willie Johnson came by with some home-grown tomatoes and a paper bag full of string beans. Reverend Caudill helped them get situated upstairs at the Osgoods' home, and someone had brought a little pink bassinet. Vee's bed would be small for the couple, but at least Suzy would have a comfortable place to sleep.

Virgil had closed Osgood's for the afternoon to help with the cleanup across the street. He and Cornelius had discovered a bond that went well beyond smallmouth bass and Patsy Cline. Now, more than anything else, he wanted to help the Alexanders. And love them.

Welby had been right all along. But then again, he usually was.

31

Virgil left early to get caught up at Osgood's, but Mavine was pleased to make a full breakfast for the Alexanders. The events of the last twenty-four hours had been difficult for everyone, but Cornelius and JoAnn said they and Suzy had slept well and were more than grateful for all the hospitality. Vee, who'd been happy to sleep in the living room, was more alert than usual given the early hour and was fascinated by Suzy, who again lay quietly in Virgil's La-Z-Boy.

"Thank you so much, Mavine." Cornelius took a sip of coffee. "We'll be spending most of the day in Quincy talking with our insurance agent and won't return to Eden Hill until later this afternoon. Charlie will handle everything at the station while we're gone. I hope that won't be an inconvenience for you."

"Not at all. If you can be back by six o'clock, we're having pork chops for dinner and would love to have you join us."

"It'd be a pleasure, Mavine. You've been such a blessing." JoAnn collected the sleeping Suzy and they left, well-fed and grateful.

Virgil returned to work after lunch with a solemn promise to Mavine to return by six for dinner. The Alexanders would be back by then, she said, and dinner would be done and coming out of the oven.

The auction of the old Crutcher place and funeral home was today, so traffic was the busiest he'd seen in quite some time. He'd had several customers in the morning, and several more customers came by in the afternoon. Two were coming home from the auction, and another was on his way back to Quincy from a couple of days' vacation. Welby would get home late this evening, he reminded himself. Hopefully he'd had a good visit with his family.

The parts man did not arrive until almost four thirty. "Bad traffic, there was an estate sale or something," he'd said. Luckily the replacement muffler was the correct part, and came with replacement mounting gaskets and clamps. Virgil checked the tags, signed for the items, and sat down in Welby's barber chair.

It had been a good day, a good weekend,

and a good week, though he'd like to have the Fourth of July back; the grand reopening had been a bit too much. Actually, the floor had needed painting for a long time, the gutters needed fixing anyway, and sooner or later he would have wanted a ladies' room in the station. Now to get that muffler fixed. The Nash needed to be on sale by tomorrow, and it couldn't if it growled like a bear.

He found a couple of wrenches and Welby's creeper, and slid under the car, already perched on the work jacks. He had to slide back out to get the work light so he could see what he was doing, but that was no big problem. It looked like a fairly easy fix; he wouldn't even have to use the welder. He'd be home in plenty of time for Mavine's pork chops and sweet potatoes.

He positioned himself under the front clamp and adjusted the light. The rust was heavy, and the wrench slipped off on the first try, skinning his knuckles. He fitted the end of the box wrench on the stubborn nut and tried again. Nothing moved, and the wrench slipped, banging his wrist against the frame. The third time is a charm, he thought. He positioned the tool again and gave it a mighty heave.

Everything moved, including the Nash.

The front jack stand tipped, buckled, and gave way, and the car fell to the garage floor.

Unfortunately, that fall was broken by Virgil, whose chest was under the oil pan. The creeper cracked and splintered, its wheels rolling out in four directions, leaving Virgil pinned.

And alone.

Mavine had allowed Vee to visit Frank again after breakfast, and he'd stayed for lunch at the Prewitt farm. He had returned sufficiently early to escape punishment, so the collected works of Washington Irving could stay on the shelf. To the best of Mavine's knowledge, nothing had exploded or been run over by Arlie's truck. It was starting to look like rain by late afternoon, so perhaps baseball had been less inviting. At any rate, he was home, and none the worse for his afternoon on parole.

Mavine had spent the afternoon working on the gift for Suzy. She'd set up the old Singer, hoping to catch up on a few other tasks as well, but the baby quilt had been her focus. It was something she wanted to do, a little token, perhaps, but might make up somewhat for all the grief she'd caused. She stopped only to peel the sweet potatoes and put the chops out to thaw, and then returned to her work.

It wasn't a quilt really, but it was a very nice light blanket that would keep Suzy warm in the fall. She'd outgrow it, of course, and she was probably too young to appreciate the material or the work; even the red roses would probably be lost on her. But she hoped it would mean something to JoAnn. Mavine found some material from an unused bedsheet to use for a liner, and fixed it so that the little embroidered flowers would be in front when it was folded. Pretty.

She and Virgil would start anew with Cornelius and JoAnn.

As Mavine clipped the excess thread from the last stitch, she looked at the clock. Time to get the potatoes boiling, get Vee cleaned up, and start Mr. Johnson's beans cooking. Virgil would be home in time for supper. He'd promised.

At six o'clock, the beans were steaming, the biscuits were cut and ready for the oven, and the main dish was cooling on the top of the stove. She'd thought about making an apple pie but was out of brown sugar. Besides, it would take too long, and she would need the oven for the biscuits.

JoAnn returned and related a disappointing day in Quincy. The insurance adjuster had been sympathetic, but the premium on their policy hadn't been paid in time, and as much as he wanted to help, there was nothing he could do. At least he'd been kind enough to take them to lunch. JoAnn offered to help with dinner, but Mavine sent her upstairs with Suzy. Cornelius had stopped at his own service station to check on Charlie and to tidy up.

By 6:15, there was still no sign of Virgil. Vee had washed his hands and curled up on the couch with his book. He'd turned the television on to see if there was anything of interest but quickly grew weary of both Huntley and Brinkley. The other station was also running the news, so he quickly gave up.

"Mom, do you want me to go get Dad?"

"Not yet. He was working on Mr. Willett's car this afternoon and should be here any minute."

Vee returned to *The Sign of the Four,* and Mavine pulled out her cutting board. If she wasn't going to bake a pie, the apples would make a nice salad.

By 6:30, Cornelius had arrived, but Virgil had not. Mavine frowned and put the chops back in the oven with the heat turned low. This wasn't like him. Sure, he'd been late before, but he'd always called to let her know.

As it neared 6:45, Mavine was hurt and angry. At least he could let them know he was delayed. He was spoiling everyone's supper. Virgil was usually a man of his word, but he'd really failed this time. She stomped to the telephone and called Osgood's, something she rarely did.

It rang nine times. No answer.

It was now seven o'clock and the beans were cold and Mavine was hot. Where could the man be? His car was in its usual spot — she could make it out through the trees. Maybe Welby had come back early and they'd gone somewhere, or perhaps Arlie had stopped in. He'd often said that fish bite well right around a good rain. And Virgil kept his tackle box in the back of the shop. And after all those good things he'd said at lunch. So she'd just have to go down there; that was all there was to it.

"Mom, do you need — ?"

"No, I'm going myself!"

She marched down the hill and flung open the door to the garage. "Virgil!" she yelled, expecting no answer.

She heard a small gurgle from under the Nash Metropolitan, which was sitting at a funny tilt. Then she saw a wheel from the creeper in the middle of the floor with a splinter of wood attached, and finally Virgil's legs, poking out from under the side.

"Virgil!"

And she did what she had to do.

When the ambulance driver arrived, Virgil was on the floor by the workbench, where Mavine had dragged him. The Nash pointed at a crazy angle toward the tire rack. Tools, equipment, and muffler parts were scattered across the floor. Mavine was cradling Virgil's head and talking quietly. He was whispering to her, saying something about being sorry he ruined their dinner.

Mavine's arms and back were strained, and when the ambulance attendants asked if she was all right, she admitted her knees and hips hurt as well. Vee and Cornelius had joined them; they'd heard Mavine scream and had run down to see what was happening.

After looking Virgil over, the attendants decided that he needed to go to the hospital and get checked out, so they eased him onto a stretcher and carried him outside. He was talking, but with difficulty, and had a nasty bruise on his chest, but his back and neck seemed to be uninjured. He held up a thumb before disappearing into the red-

and-white ambulance.

"Mavine, I'm so sorry this happened," he croaked. "I love you!"

Reverend Caudill answered the telephone on the first ring. He'd stopped into his office to place some buckets in case the rain didn't hold off, and wasn't expecting the call. On the other end of the line was an extremely excited man.

"Praise the Lord, he's given us the miracle. And before next Sunday, too." The Pentecostal preacher may as well have been speaking in tongues, as Reverend Caudill couldn't make out a word he was saying.

"Slow down, Brother Taggart. What was that again?"

"Only a miracle, Reverend Caudill. We made the winning bid on the old Crutcher Funeral Home and now have a place to meet. Glory to God! We don't rightly know how we'll come up with the payments each month, but I am trusting that God will provide. He always does."

"Glory to God, indeed. I'm so glad for you and your congregation."

As the man went on and on in his exhilaration, Reverend Caudill became aware of sounds coming in his window. Shouts, commotion, and a siren. Now what?

"Sorry, Brother Taggart. I'm very happy for you, but I've got an emergency. I'll call you back."

He hung up the phone as discreetly as he could and was out the door in a dash. The ambulance was hard to miss with the flashing lights.

"Mavine! What happened?" The ambulance's back door had closed, presumably with Virgil inside.

"Car fell on him. They're taking him to the hospital in Quincy. I'm riding in with him."

"Okay, I'll drive Vee to the hospital right behind them."

Cornelius spoke. "What can I do to help?"

She paused before closing the ambulance door. "You can help by enjoying dinner with JoAnn. And would you turn off the oven and put things in the refrigerator when you're finished?"

"We'll take care of it, Mrs. Osgood."

"Mavine. Please call me Mavine."

Mavine rode in the back with Virgil, who was awake and relatively calm.

"I'm so sorry, Mavine. I should have known better." His voice was weak; clearly he was in pain.

"Don't try to talk. I just want you to look

at me." She'd found a clean shop towel and was dabbing at the cuts on his chest. "On second thought, why don't you just close your eyes and relax?"

He smiled and held her hand.

Surprisingly, she found herself singing softly. One of the few songs she could remember, and his favorite. Patsy Cline would have been pleased to know that she was "crazy for loving" Virgil T. Osgood and that he'd never be off with "somebody new."

The trip to Quincy General Hospital was as calm as a high-speed ride on rural roads in a bouncing Oldsmobile ambulance could be. Virgil was wheeled into the emergency room to be examined, x-rayed, poked and prodded, and finally admitted. Mavine, Vee, and Reverend Caudill were waiting outside the door of room 142 when two orderlies wheeled Virgil into the room and placed him gingerly into the bed. The doctor in his white coat followed a couple of minutes later.

"Mrs. Osgood?"

"Yes?"

"Your husband has had a nasty accident, but it could have been much worse. He has a large contusion and a broken collarbone, but his back and neck are fine. We have him on a sedative and some pain medication, so he's pretty drowsy right now. He'll be fine, but we'll need to keep him here overnight for observation."

She sighed in relief. "Thank you so much, Doctor."

"Mrs. Osgood, I have to ask you. Just how did you get the car off of him?"

"I don't know. I just knew I had to lift it off."

The doctor smiled. "Adrenaline."

"What?"

"It's something your body produces when you need extra energy. I learned about it in medical school, but never seen it until now. When you're faced with a challenge beyond your abilities, you're given the strength to do what you need to do. You couldn't lift that car all by yourself, Mrs. Osgood. You had some help."

Reverend Caudill beamed. "I couldn't agree more!"

The pastor drove Mavine and Vee back home about ten o'clock. Vee promptly fell asleep in the backseat, so Mavine and the pastor spoke in hushed voices. It had been a hard day for everyone. Her emotions had been up, down, and all around. She told Reverend Caudill the story, or at least the ten-minute version of it.

"I hope I'm doing the right thing, Reverend. After JoAnn and Suzy came over last week, I knew I had to do something for them. After the fire, it became very clear. I realized that I had been doing a lot of things terribly wrong for the last few months. I just hope I haven't hurt our marriage or family — or theirs."

"Mavine, we all make mistakes in life, but God's grace covers it all. The main thing is to learn from them and go forward. Which I think you've done exceedingly well."

"But I've wronged JoAnn and Cornelius, and I've doubted whether I still have feelings for Virgil I once had, so I've wronged him, too. And tonight —" she began to cry — "I almost lost him. And I realized then just how much I love Virgil."

Reverend Caudill laughed. "Oh, Mavine. Do you understand that what you did tonight proved your love for Virgil more than anything else you could have done? You saved his life, Mavine. And the doctor was right. That strength came from somewhere beyond your power. Your love for Virgil is solid, no doubt about that."

Virgil awakened the next morning about nine o'clock after a good night's sleep. He found his left arm in a sling and something wrapped tightly around his chest, nothing on his face but a couple of bandages. The nurse came in to take the oxygen mask off and told him that the doctor had checked him at about six o'clock when he made rounds. The doctor had been very pleased with his progress and was willing to let him go home at eleven o'clock after one final check.

He was still sleepy — probably some medicine they had given him. There were several voices in the room, and he could make out Mavine and . . . Welby? It took several blinks until his eyes and thoughts cleared.

"Mavine?"

"Good morning, Virgil." She bent over and kissed his head. "I love you."

"And I love you too. Who's with you — Welby? Alma?"

"We're right here, Virgil!"

"But who's watching Osgood's? It's Tuesday — no, Wednesday — and we're supposed to be open. It's usually our busiest day . . ."

"Not to worry, Virgil," Welby chuckled. "Mr. Alexander is taking care of your customers for you. Charlie's handling things on his side of the street. It sounds like we missed a lot of excitement while we were gone."

Virgil tried to nod, but it hurt too much.

"He said it's the least he could do for you. And he sent you this." He handed Virgil a card, sealed in a small envelope.

Virgil took the reading glasses that Mavine had brought, propped them on his nose with some effort and pain, and opened the card. It still carried the Zipco logo, which Cornelius had scratched out and written over it *Alexander's.* Virgil read it aloud:

So sorry for your accident! Hope you get well soon. And thank you for letting us stay in Vee Junior's bedroom until we can replace the mobile home. Please let us know if there's anything we can do to help.

Your friends and neighbors,
Cornelius and JoAnn

Friends. He smiled and closed the card. "I guess everything works out, doesn't it?"

Welby nodded. "Just be glad it was the Nash instead of the Buick!"

Virgil started to laugh, but it hurt too much. "I'm glad, indeed."

There was a knock on the door, and a nurse appeared with a wheelchair and instructions from the doctor. "Take the rest of the week off. No heavy lifting. Take this pill twice a day, as needed for pain." She handed the prescription to Mavine. "And don't *ever* work alone under a jacked-up car!"

Virgil agreed, signed the release form, and was a free man. In more ways than one.

32

Reverend Caudill had come over to make a pastoral call and now sat enjoying a wonderful lunch, courtesy of Mavine, who had heated up the pork chops and green beans and made fresh biscuits to go with them. Virgil was still drowsy and sore, but was in good spirits and hoped to be in church on Sunday, and back to work — at least to pump gas with his right arm — by the next Monday.

Vee came rushing downstairs, excited and breathless. "Mom, look outside."

Mavine and Reverend Caudill followed Vee to the front windows and saw a van painted with a large NBC logo. What on earth was channel three doing in front of Osgood's?

The doorbell rang, and Vee jumped toward the front door. "Are we gonna be on TV?"

"Vee, *we're* certainly not," Mavine called, halting the boy in his tracks. "Reverend

Caudill, would you be willing to talk to the reporter? It hurts too much for Virgil to talk, and I'm terrified of being on TV."

Vee's shoulders slumped. Obviously the boy would have been more than willing to speak for the whole family. But Reverend Caudill agreed to be the spokesman. Besides, he would be able to tell the whole story. The real story.

He stepped outside with the reporter, a young man with immaculate hair and a large microphone. Another man carrying a large film camera followed, his eye glued to the viewfinder. The pastor straightened his tie.

"Can you tell us what happened when Mr. Osgood was pinned by the car?" the reporter asked, his microphone thrust into the pastor's face.

"Virgil T. Osgood is one of my parishioners, and I have to tell you he's a fine man. One of the best. He runs Osgood's —" he pointed — "a fine business and an asset to our community. He was working by himself when a car fell off the jacks, and his beloved wife, Mavine, found him in his predicament and did the impossible: lifted the car off Virgil's chest."

"Just like that?"

"Not exactly. She had the Lord's help."

"Thank you . . ."

"And there's more. There are other good neighbors in Eden Hill who pitched in to help out in his time of need. Like Cornelius Alexander —" he pointed to Alexander's — "who ran his business for him while he was in the hospital."

The reporter thanked him again, and the cameraman filmed both Osgood's and Alexander's, including the Nash that still sat askew in the service bay at Osgood's. They left with footage for the evening news, after Welby had cleaned their windows and checked their oil.

The reverend would have stayed longer, but he had to meet with the lawyer in town for the reading of Madeline Crutcher's will. The directions were clear; the meeting would take place in the attorney's office on Market Street.

He was the last to arrive: Del Crutcher and his wife were already there, as were Del's sister Virginia, another attorney representing Del's sister Carolina, and Jeremiah Taggart. Two people from the courthouse were also present to serve as witnesses. Pleasantries were exchanged all around.

The lawyer started right in. "Now that we're all here, we can begin." He held a short but impressive-looking document.

"Part the First. I, Madeline W. Crutcher, being of sound mind . . ."

Reverend Caudill suppressed a smile. He was open to debate about that.

". . . do hereby bequeath, and so order the disposition of my estate upon my demise —" the entire group leaned forward in rapt attention — "the whole of my properties to be sold at public auction."

They'd already done that. The anticipation was mounting. Reverend Caudill wondered why he was here. Might he have to make peace if things turned ugly? He'd done enough of that already in the past month.

The lawyer turned to the second page and looked up. "I will interject here that the proceeds from the auction and the liquidation of her financial assets resulted in an estate of two hundred sixteen thousand, one hundred forty-seven dollars and fifty-eight cents."

Even Del's eyes widened.

The reader continued, "Twenty-five percent of my estate I bequeath to my son, Delbert Crutcher." Del sat up straight in his chair, receiving a hug from his wife.

The lawyer continued, "Ten percent of the estate I bequeath to my daughter Virginia Crutcher Cousins."

Virginia smiled and began doing some figures on a notepad.

"Ten percent of the estate I bequeath to my daughter Carolina Crutcher Wilson."

The other attorney smiled and made some notes of his own.

He continued. "Five percent of my estate I leave to my illegitimate son, Jeremiah Ezekiel Taggart." The attorney paused and looked at the group over the top of his bifocals. "For the record, those were her exact words."

Brother Taggart looked stunned but threw his hands into the air and shouted, "Praise the Lord for his mercies! He has provided."

Reverend Caudill smiled. That ought to cover the old funeral home. He looked at his notes, where he'd been keeping a tally. This still left . . .

The designated reader took a drink from a glass of water. "The remainder of my estate I bequeath to the First Evangelical Baptist Church of Eden Hill, in honor of the Reverend Eugene Caudill, who has been an inspiration and ready help to me in my time of greatest need. So attested and executed this day, Friday the third of May, nineteen hundred sixty-three."

Well. Reverend Caudill couldn't speak, offer pastoral care, bless, or do much of anything else. He simply sat there, incredulous. Fifty percent of her estate, if he'd heard it right. And the amount? Something over one hundred thousand dollars? It would mean a new roof, replacement gutters, a well-behaved furnace, Sunday school rooms, missions. Those things and more. Even some help for his brothers and sisters in their purchase of the new Pentecostal Holiness church.

"Congratulations, Pastor!" Del was patting his shoulder and shaking his hand.

He looked around. Virginia and the other attorney had already gone, and Brother Taggart was rocking back and forth in his chair, continuing his praise to the Almighty.

The lawyer agreed to contact him for additional details regarding the transaction, and he as counsel and Del as executor would receive a nominal percentage, he'd said. It was still too much to fathom, but he was more than willing to try.

The drive back to Eden Hill was glorious. Even with the rain, the sky seemed brighter somehow, and some other things were much clearer as he returned to his office.

Madeline Crutcher, in death, had affirmed his ministry. What kind of woman was Madeline Crutcher? Even after all these years, he had to admit, to his own shame and regret, he didn't know. But her bequest was one final act of goodness that would pave the way for many good things in their community.

33

Mavine's Sunday morning breakfast was special. Not only was she feeding her own family these days; she was preparing for the Alexanders as well. And it was going to be a special day — for all of them. She'd set up a card table in the living room, and Reverend Caudill had brought a couple of chairs from his office for them to use.

They'd all left for Sunday school at 9:45. Virgil was unable to wear his sport coat with his arm in a sling, but otherwise he looked quite presentable. Vee had been given a stern admonition to behave in Mrs. Prewitt's Sunday school class. No jokes, and no comic books.

And the Alexanders looked quite sharp in their secondhand clothes. Grover was waiting for them at the door, ready to take Suzy to the nursery.

Mavine walked into worship with Virgil at her side, holding his free hand. He was still too sore to usher anybody anywhere, but Welby helped them to their usual seat.

She felt a tingling of excitement. Cornelius and JoAnn Alexander professing their faith and being baptized into the church, the body of Christ. Her friends and neighbors, about to become her sister and brother.

Toler's opening hymn, "Immortal, Invisible, God Only Wise," set the pattern for the morning. The man's tempos had become more upbeat of late, and it lifted her spirits and those of all in the church.

When Reverend Caudill came out in his waders, and the Alexanders in their white robes, it was all she could do to hold it together. And when they each went under the water three times, in the name of the Father, Son, and Holy Ghost, she wept tears of great joy. Almost as though she had been baptized again herself. She cried on Virgil's one good shoulder and hugged his one good arm.

And she felt within her a most unique thing. Forgiveness. Grace, far greater than any of them deserved.

It had been a glorious Sunday. Two baptisms. Something had happened to Mavine and Virgil too. He'd seen it in their eyes.

Truly glorious.

Reverend Caudill didn't often spend Sunday afternoon in his office, but after dinner with the Osgoods and the Alexanders, he'd retired to this familiar place.

He'd begun a sermon on "inner strength" while the doctor's words were still fresh in his mind. Funny how those things stuck, especially when facing difficult life decisions.

He sighed and turned away from the old Underwood. The message hadn't gotten far; the paper was still blank. No matter; it would need adjusting anyway. Opening the desk drawer, he brushed past the headache powder, which for once he didn't need, and located the envelope, which he did. An ordinary number ten business envelope, yet it held something that would change his life.

He extracted the letter from the dean of the Evangelical Baptist Bible College and read it for the umpteenth time. Would Reverend Eugene Caudill consider joining the college in the autumn quarter as professor of pastoral ministries?

It was the president's second letter. Reverend Caudill had put off the decision as long as possible, but he'd promised to pray about it and give the school an answer by next week. He had indeed prayed. Over and over.

And now it was time to reply.

He'd talked it over with Grover and Anna Belle, his closest friends and counselors, and they had told him to do whatever was best. The right thing. Until today, leaving Eden Hill was not the right thing. Eden Hill had needed him. But good things were now under way.

He could take no credit; he'd simply done his duty. The next pastor would serve a steady congregation with financial security. His sheep were more docile now, and relationships were healing and becoming stronger. He could leave with a clear conscience.

And with confidence in his ministry. That confidence had wavered but now was solid.

He placed two fresh sheets of paper in the old Underwood with a carbon between and began to type. "Dear Sirs, I am humbled and privileged to accept . . ."

After typing the envelope and sealing the letter, he began a second. "Dear Congregation . . ."

This one was harder to sign and seal. He'd keep the copy and give the sealed envelope to the church's board and read it to the congregation on Sunday. But he hesitated for only a moment; somewhere inside of him he found the strength. Maybe it was adrenaline, or just maybe it was divine leading. He sighed. He'd miss this place, and these people. But he knew it was right.

It had been a good sixteen years. And Eden Hill was in better shape than he'd found it. His work here was done. Virgil and Mavine would be just fine. Cornelius and JoAnn would do well; they'd find their strength too. Suzy would grow up in the church, where she'd be surrounded by love.

Well. He glanced at the portrait of him and Louise, shedding a small and unexpected tear this time. But it was for joy. He was finished here but would move on in his high calling. Eden Hill was in God's hands. And so was he.

DISCUSSION QUESTIONS

1. What are some of the major challenges Virgil faces throughout the novel? How do his responses differ in the various spheres of his life: home, church, work? Does he demonstrate consistent integrity throughout, or do these spheres bring out different aspects of his character? Do you respond consistently at home, church, work, etc.?

2. How would you describe Virgil and Mavine's relationship? What could improve their marriage?

3. As the story begins, Cornelius is driven to become a successful businessman. Why does he feel so much pressure to succeed? How does his motivation change? How do you define success?

4. Reverend Caudill feels responsible for

the well-being of the whole town. Should pastors take on this kind of responsibility? How far should pastors and ministers go to care for their flocks? Are there boundaries beyond which they should not meddle?

5. Madeline Crutcher is a self-appointed morality monitor. She feels the need to point out all that is wrong with her church and her society and try to effect changes. In what ways is this an admirable course of action? How can a person today be an agent of change without becoming pharisaical and judgmental?

6. What different parenting styles do you see portrayed in the novel among the Osgoods, the Alexanders, and the Prewitts? Which of your friends or acquaintances model excellent parenting?

7. Gladys eventually contacts and meets her long-lost daughter. How does this event change Mavine's perspective on herself? Was this a satisfying conclusion to Gladys's story? What challenges do she and her daughter face down the road?

8. In the early 1960s, race relations in the

US were rising to a fever pitch. Among the responses of Eden Hill residents, did any surprise you? What progress has our society made in this issue? What do we still have left to do to ensure that all people live with justice and equality?

9. When Virgil feels the pinch of competition, Welby's business advice to Virgil is counterintuitive: love your neighbor. From the very beginning, Welby believes there's enough business to go around. Why are people so prone to face off and fight for themselves? Are there times when it's necessary to choose competition over collaboration? When have you felt the urge to compete for position or resources? How well did you respond in that situation?

10. Cornelius and JoAnn married under less-than-ideal circumstances. What do you think about their commitment to each other? Was it right for them to marry in the first place? How do you see God's redemption at work in their story?

11. Were you surprised by Reverend Caudill's decision at the end of the novel? Why do you think he took the opportunity offered to him?

12. Based on what you know of the era, how was life different in the 1960s? Have people (or human nature) changed much over the past fifty years? Has the country changed? What advances have we made? Where have we faltered?

ACKNOWLEDGMENTS

As the son of an English teacher extraordinaire and a master storyteller, I suppose it was inevitable that I would tell stories in written form. It was my lot in life.

My mother, the late Mary Lee Higgs, drilled into me sentences and paragraphs, grammar and structure — and no small amount of grammar. Had she lived to see this novel's publication, I think she might have been pleased that I used adverbs correctly!

My father, Harold Higgs, relishes a good story, either in the hearing or the telling. His tales include red lanterns hanging on a box kite, biplanes flying under bridges, and exploding jugs of elderberry wine.

Many thanks to Julie Gwinn and my son, Matthew Higgs, who read the manuscript and offered many valuable suggestions. Grateful appreciation, too, to Blythe Daniel and Jessica Kirkland of the Blythe Daniel

Agency for their support and willingness to take a chance on an old gray-haired baby boomer. You've shown me that it is certainly possible to take on a new career when most of my peers are retiring!

At my age, most of my mentors have gone on to glory. I'm grateful for the lives of George Redding, who taught me the power of parable; and J. J. Owens, who taught me that the Bible is a living, breathing work that compels its readers to action.

Special thanks to my editor Caleb Sjogren, Jan Stob, Maggie Rowe, Maria Eriksen, Kristen Magnesen, and all the team at Tyndale House Publishers. *Eden Hill* is far stronger for your involvement in this project.

Most of all, thanks to my wife, Liz Curtis Higgs, who was willing to suspend her own successful journey as a fiction writer to encourage mine. Happy thirtieth anniversary, and all my love!

Soli Deo gloria,
Bill Higgs
Louisville, Kentucky, March 13, 2016

ABOUT THE AUTHOR

Bill Higgs holds a BA in religion and social work, an MDiv and a PhD in Old Testament languages. *Eden Hill* is his first novel.

Bill and his wife (Liz Curtis Higgs) reside in Kentucky.